COLLEEN SNYDER

Verdict at the River's Edge

Colleen K. Snyder

Dedication

To the pastors who taught me about freedom,
and the women who showed me what it looked like…

Thank you.

FRIDAY

As soon as Collin Walker's feet hit the bottom step of the bus, she heard it. The low, pounding, distinctive rumble of a river. A river somewhere nearby. She froze, overwhelmed by the panicked impulse to fight her way back upstream through the departing campers, dive under the backbench seat and not come out until the week ended. A thought kept circling through her head: *Dear God in heaven, there's a river.*

A hand on her shoulder interrupted her mental breakdown. A voice dripped sarcasm. "Hey, caseworker lady. You getting off this bus or what? They's some of us what wants to visit the facilities, you know? Been a long trip. Move it."

Life returned to Collin's feet, and she stepped off the bus, moving aside to let the remainder of the forty odd campers—and their vastly odder counselors—disembark.

Odder? Is that even a word? Collin shut down the internal tormentors before they could continue. *Sane. I will be sane for the remainder of this trip. And you all will keep your comments to yourself.*

It might be easier to believe without the cursed cackling in her head. Collin would deal with her demons later. She'd been dealing with them all her life. So what's another day? Collin leaned against the side of the bus to get her bearings and her breath. She wrapped her arms around her chest and began slow breathing to bring herself under the rigid control she learned over the years. In. Out. In. Out. In.

Rob Sider, her ward for the week, stepped in front of her. His eyes narrowed slightly in confusion. "Who you fightin' in there, huh?"

Collin jiggled her whole body to release the tension. "I'm working on a plan to beat your sorry anatomy in hoops."

Rob stepped back with half a grin. "No wonder you having a tough time of it."

Collin held a hand in front of his face. "Watch it, bro. You know the old saying, 'He who laughs last—'"

Rob interrupted "—didn't get the joke the first time. I ain't afraid of you or any plan you got." He crossed his arms over his chest.

Collin felt herself relaxing. She lay a hand on his shoulder. "What say you and me meet on the backcourt tonight about nine and see if this plan I got works?"

"Backcourt? What backcourt?"

Collin sighed. "Rob, if this place has more than one court, it has to have a backcourt. I'll meet you at nine on the backcourt, and we'll see if you're as good as your mouth on foreign soil."

Rob grinned evilly. "My mouth got nothing to do with it. Be my feet an' my hands do the talking. You ain't never beat me yet, and you ain't never gonna."

"Never's a long time, my friend."

Rob took two sliding steps back. "You'd be the one to know 'bout long times!" He took off running for the lodge.

Collin dropped her head, grinning all the while. Twenty-six made you old in Rob's world. Somedays, it felt old. She looked around the entrance to Camp Grace, forcing herself to suppress the ominous and omnipresent sound of the river. High in the mountains of West Virginia, planets away from the streets of Oakton, where she worked and lived and fought and died...

The sun lowered itself behind the towering trees, which sheltered the lodge. Even though the evening had barely begun, the valley would soon disappear in darkness. Vibrant green grass grew natural and wild in meadows and patches where the trees relented to allow sunshine. Flowering vines trailed up and around stumps, fence posts, and downspouts. Birds darted in and out of sight; fat crows cawed their superiority yet fled from kamikaze sparrows defending their territory. Paradise. At least for the week, if she could handle it.

For Rob, she would handle it. Collin cast off the shadows and moved slowly toward the entrance to the lodge. A "challenge camp," the flyer said, offering traditional and extreme sports to entice hardened and jaded youngsters ages ten to fourteen. Rob made the cut-off by four months. The camp presented as state-approved—but not sponsored—which meant the cost needed to be borne by the parents or the counselor.

Collin stopped at a "Welcome to Camp Grace" sign. She drew circles in the dirt with her foot as she looked at the map showing the "You Are Here" arrow.

The flyer stated financial aid or grants were available on request. But when Collin called the camp to request, the cost proved so ridiculously low she wondered if the camp could be real. She sent off the registration and fees to the address in West Virginia, only to have both returned. The registration approved; the fees waived.

Collin quit circling the dust and moved along the path. Quiet and careful inquiries to other attendees revealed they, too, were attending *gratis*. She determined then to find out all she could about this camp—who owned it and why they would be so interested in street kids. Paradise had its snakes, too.

Collin sharpened her focus and headed inside. She dodged a lone maintenance man unloading and carting the luggage. He may have smiled at her. He may have even spoken to her, but Collin didn't notice. Head down, eyes straight ahead. Focused. Something about this set-up read wrong, and she would be the one to find it. For Rob's sake.

I will not let anyone use these kids to fulfill some philanthropic need to make themselves look good. Not my kids. Collin marched through the lodge doors.

* * *

Collin followed an escort down the corridors to the female side of the building. She noted Rob's room number and the name of the counselor overseeing him.

The escort explained, "Only one child to a room unless they have requested otherwise." The escort smiled. "We know some of these children may be sleeping alone in a room for the first time."

Alone in a room? Some of these kids will be sleeping alone in a bed for the first time.

Collin envisioned a few sleepless nights for some of the younger campers. *They'll work it out.*

Luggage sat outside the doors, waiting to be carried into the rooms. Another guide brought two girls down the hall and presented them to her as her charges for the week, then left. Collin knew the girls well. Jill and Marites, both ten, roomed adjacent to Collin. They seemed the giggly, innocent type, not ones you would suspect of being in serious trouble. Certainly not on the verge of being placed in juvenile lockup. But Collin knew their jackets—and their counselors—well. Which explained why the girls were here and the counselors weren't.

A sign on the back of the door explained the basics. Collin read the salient features aloud. "Breakfast hours are seven to eight, no exceptions. Latecomers go hungry."

Jill tossed her head in disgust. "Can't make me go hungry. Gotta feed me, right? Anytime I want, right?"

Collin shook her head. "Nope. The card says healthy snacks of carrots, celery, apples, raisins, and assorted power foods are freely available at the health bar below the main concourse. Which means they have food available. If you like vegetables and fruit instead of pancakes and eggs."

Both girls gagged. Collin nodded. "I thought as much." She turned back to the sign. "It says lunch and dinner hours will depend on whatever the activity of the day is." She paused. "Which I'm sure they will explain later."

Jill and Marites looked at each other, then shrugged in unison. Collin mirrored their motion. "It goes on to say you should stow your gear and report back to the room just inside the doors where we came in at the head of the hall."

Fearing too many directives or instructions would be lost—or ignored— Collin said, "First things first: hand over the phones." Before the girls could deny the existence of said devices, Collin warned, "Having a phone will get you sent home at your parents' expense. I know you both have them. Give them up." Reluctantly the girls handed over the phones. Collin checked her roster to make sure the numbers matched. Once verified, Collin said, "Go store your stuff and wait for me here. I'll be right out."

The girls closed the door. Collin shut her door and listened for a moment. Yep, still there. Even with the windows closed and black-out drapes reaching below the jams, she could hear the rumble of the bane of her dreams. *It doesn't matter. Sound can't hurt you.*

Who says you have to go any closer than the lodge? No one. Get over it.

Coward.

Collin escorted the girls to the main hall and looked for Rob. She found him sitting by the window, staring up at the heavens. Rob did not stop staring but acknowledged Collin's presence by whispering, "I never seen anything this big before. Never been anywhere this big." Outside, pine trees soared to vast heights. Towering canyon walls marched away out of view to either side, their craggy peaks barely visible to human eyes.

Collin sat down beside him. "Now, you get an idea of what awesome means."

Rob turned and looked at her for a moment. "I guess so." He looked back out the window. "Can we go out there?"

"My guess is the next order of business will be introductions, a list of rules to remember, question and answer sessions, and maybe dinner. Then free time and finally bed."

Rob gave her a curious look. "You been to these camps before?"

"A few." She motioned toward the crowd gathering in the center of the room. "Let's join the circle and see if I'm right."

Rob reluctantly followed Collin to where campers and counselors congregated. They joined in time to hear a man speaking. "If everyone could close in enough to hear and be heard, I would appreciate it."

The speaker waited as the crowd moved in closer. "Good. Welcome to Camp Grace. I am Steve Parks, camp director. I won't bore you with our history; if you're interested, we have literature at the office. If you're not, we'll save a few trees. Our mission is simple and is directly for you campers."

Collin eyed the man. *This is where it gets real. What do they really want?*

Most of the youngsters raised their heads, curious. Rob kept his eyes fixed on the floor, feigning non-interest. The director continued, "Our goal is to teach you one thing: you can."

A girl spoke up. "Can what?" General murmurs echoed the

question.

"You can. Can do anything you set yourself to do."

An older boy snorted. "Yeah, right. Like I can jump like Michael Jordan."

Mr. Parks smiled. "Maybe. Have you tried?"

"Sure, man. I can't do it."

"Have you practiced the steps he takes? Have you exercised and worked out and jogged? Do you sweat like he does?"

The boy snorted again. "No."

"Then, you won't jump like he does." Mr. Parks looked around the room. "Doing isn't something magic. It's something you make happen using all the resources and talents and abilities you have."

Some heads nodded. Some dropped. Collin sensed they all listened, though.

Mr. Parks continued, "This week is to show you you can. We're going to give you opportunities to do and try things you've thought about, dreamed about, had nightmares about, or just wanted to see."

A nightmare or two flashed through Collin's mind. She shuddered. *Not now.*

"None of them will be simple. All will require thought, sweat, practice, and in some cases, teamwork. In the morning, we have a camp tour for anyone who can greet the daylight without a snarl. Snarlers can go in the afternoon." Laughs and catcalls followed, with elbows thrown for effect.

Mr. Parks glanced around the room at the campers. His eyes sparkled with what Collin took to be enjoyment. "You'll have the opportunity to sample some of our offerings this weekend, weather permitting. There is a partial list of activities on the board at the end of the hall to give you—I started to say 'fodder to chew on'"— the director chuckled—"but most of you would have no idea what I meant. So let's put it this way: it will give you something to think about."

He looked pointedly at the adults in the room. "A word to you, counselors." A grown-up head or two came to attention. "Show your kids you believe, too. Sign up with them. Show them it works."

As a means of closing, he said, "There are a few important people you will get to know. The first, we hope you never see: our camp physician, Dr. Wallace." A casual-looking gentleman in blue jeans, khaki shirt, knee-high cowboy boots, with sandy-blond shoulder-length hair pulled back in a ponytail, waved from his seat on the front desk.

Director Parks pointed to the side of the hall. "My assistant, Leeann Baker, will make any arrangements in case of emergencies either here or at home." An older woman, slightly overweight, wearing a red business dress, waved from her position against the wall. "Ted Johnson is our activities director."

Another wave from another strategically placed employee. Collin noted they seemed to be surrounding the group. Sizing up the kids? Watching group dynamics?

Mr. Parks continued, "Jeff Farrell staffs our maintenance crew." The director looked around then added, "And he appears to be missing." He looked at the activities director, who mouthed, "Generators." Mr. Parks nodded slightly.

The director finished with, "Our chief cook, Chef Michael, is downstairs preparing dinner. Enjoy your meal. Afterward, you may walk around outside or use the ball courts and recreation rooms. There is an indoor pool or you can sample the library. Relax and have fun. Enjoy your weekend, because come Monday, you're mine." He grinned evilly, rubbing his hands together. "Any questions?"

If there were, no one felt inclined to offer them. "You may consider yourselves dismissed."

The crowd moved off toward the dining hall. Collin caught Rob's sleeve. She warned, "Remember we've got an appointment tonight. Don't eat too much."

As they rounded the corner to the cafeteria, Rob sneered, "Caseworker lady, I could eat everything they got and still beat you."

The size of the buffet staggered them both. Rob did a double-take. Collin's mouth dropped. Grilled chicken. Beef tips. Fish. Pasta. Hamburgers. Fries. Pizza. Vegetables of every kind. Fruit. Gelatins. Pastries. Puddings.

Rob looked at Collin, his eyes wide. "Okay, I lied. Maybe not this time." He grabbed a tray and began loading it down. When his tray could hold no more, Rob headed off to a corner with some friends.

Collin filled a plate and looked for a place to sit. The cafeteria had plenty of room. Many of the tables remained unoccupied.

Maybe now would be a good time to start her investigation of the camp. Who here might tell her what she needed to know? Or—more important—what she wanted to know?

Collin saw a man sitting alone toward the back. A man by no means—well, maybe by some means—okay…some might call him handsome. Sandy brown—bordering on red—hair, late twenties, early thirties…honest features.

What does the expression mean, anyhow? How can a nose be dishonest? Eyes, now, those can tell a tale. Except his head is down. Good thing. He might catch you staring.

Sort of. A little.

The man wore the garb of a maintenance worker. Collin vaguely remembered passing someone in a uniform earlier this evening. The bus. He unloaded the bus. He'd spoken to her. *And you walked right past him.*

Collin's eyes widened at the memory. Her heart sank.

Maybe he won't remember. Maybe he won't remember you. Maybe…

The man had a book propped up in front of his tray, reading as he ate. Collin felt embarrassed at the thought of walking up and saying, "Hi. I'm the rude woman who ignored you earlier. Can I join you now?"

Shameless much? Maybe he doesn't want company. Maybe he doesn't want your company. Maybe…

Collin growled, *Shut up!* She straightened her back and walked purposefully across the room, only to slow to a stop again as she neared his table. Campers rushed past her, determined on emptying as much of the buffet as possible. Collin dodged and weaved while she tried to make up her mind. She couldn't walk up to a perfect stranger and force herself on him, could she? Could she?

The man looked at her and smiled. The eyes did, indeed, tell a story.

Collin rebuked the coward inside. *You bet I can.* She advanced to the table, smiled, and asked, "Mind if I sit down?"

The man waved gallantly, moving his books aside. "Of course not. It took you long enough to make up your mind, though."

So he'd been watching her? Did he remember the bus? Collin

8

demurred slightly at the challenge. "I promise I won't disturb you."

"Good. People tell me I'm disturbed enough as it is." He grinned.

Collin sat. She needed to take charge of this situation and fast. She extended her hand. "I'm Collin Walker."

The man reached out his hand but drew it back slightly. Collin noted his hands, though clean, bore the stains from oil, grease, and other lubricants of his trade. She reached out further and took his hand firmly. "Hi, I'm Collin Walker."

"Jeff Farrell." He pointed to the name on his shirt. "My reminder."

"I need something to remind me where I am, not who I am." *There are too many whos anyhow.*

Which we will not discuss now.

"Do you travel a lot?"

"More than I'd like but probably less than I should." She let Jeff chew on her statement while she bowed her head and gave thanks for her food.

When she looked up, the man wore a different look on his face, a look Collin couldn't read. Did she offend him? Better to find out now than later.

He smiled. "A woman who's not afraid to practice what she believes even in a crowd. You are a rare find."

Collin deflected the subject. She pointed to her plate. "I'm not sure what I've got here. What's good?"

"Everything Chef Michael fixes. He's a fantastic cook. Your kids will go home fat and happy—well, they will if we don't run the calories off them first."

Collin ducked her head. "We hope you do." She picked up one of the books sitting on the table. "What are you studying? Why are you studying? It's Friday night."

"Electrical wiring. So I can make sure we have power Saturday morning." He looked at her. "You know anything about electrical wiring?"

"I know enough to call an electrician when I have a problem."

Jeff stared at her as if floored. He closed his eyes, lowered his head in disbelief, and slammed the book shut. A grin appeared and he let out a satisfied, "Yes!" He nodded to Collin. "Thank you. Thank you very much."

Lastly, he looked skyward. "And thank You!" He grinned. "No, I'm not nuts. I've been fighting for two days trying to solve this problem, and it's not mine. I need to call an expert." He laughed. "I get so wrapped up trying to do things on my own." He stopped, straightened, and turned sober. "I'm sure you've never experienced anything like that. You wouldn't know."

Collin waggled her head. "Of course not. Never. Not even once." She looked at the ceiling. "You have lightning rods on your roof?"

"No. Do we need them?"

"If I don't quit lying, you will. What kind of problem are you having?" An orange missiled from one side of the room to the other. Collin stood, glared at the offending parties, and yelled, "Knock it off! You're not at school."

A chorus of voices called, "Sorry, Ms. Walker." She sat back down. "Your problem?"

Jeff looked surprised. "You actually want to know?"

"I actually want to know."

Jeff settled back in his chair. "Okay, it started Wednesday when we lost power to the horse barn. We thought a breaker might have gone out, but they all tested good. The power came back on while we tried the lines themselves, which proved a great shock to all of us."

Collin smiled at the joke and sampled her food. She tried the tuna casserole first. It smelled and tasted like what she remembered from home in Fort Newton.

The smell cracked open the door on a gaping black hole. Memories came flooding back, ones she thought she'd closed years ago. Collin stared into the depths, feeling the familiar death grip on her awareness. *"You're useless! You're stupid! You're a waste of time! No one loves you. The world is better off without you. Don't come back. Don't ever come back..."*

Collin sat paralyzed. Unable to think, unable to move, unable to shut down the memories, she stared into the abyss of her past.

A roar of laughter from across the cafeteria startled Collin back to life. She realized she'd blacked out when Jeff finished his story, "And why we used the elephants."

Busted. She tried to cover anyhow. "Fascinating. I thought you used kangaroos." She looked Jeff in the eyes as if nothing

10

happened.

He leaned forward and looked at her sideways. "Where did you go? I've never seen someone zone out so completely. I didn't mean to bore you, but you did ask."

She fumbled for an answer—or an explanation. "I'm sorry. It's not personal. Trust me." She smiled and shrugged. "It happens."

The man sat back in his chair. "Don't apologize. Teach me how to do it. I've got some professors I'd like to try it on. It would make their lectures a lot less boring. Or at least tolerable."

Collin gave him a half-smile. She followed his rabbit trail. "So you're in school? Where?"

He shrugged. "Grad school. Back in Oakton. Studying electrical engineering. But I think it's hopeless." He smiled. "And useless. All I need to know is to call the expert, right?"

"Right." She banished the shadows.

A raucous game of handball began across the way. Collin looked over to see if there were any other adults in the room. She saw Mr. Tremont accost the boys throwing the ball. Good. His turn to be monitor. Jeers rewarded his confiscation of the toy. Several of the diners headed out of the room, back to the top floor. Collin noted Rob wasn't with them.

Investigate the camp. Investigate the camp. "Are you from around here?"

"No. I commute from Oakton. I work the challenge camps and set up and tear down for the handicap sessions we offer in the late fall. I love to watch what this place can do for a kid."

"Camp Grace isn't just for kids?"

"We do about four challenge camps for the inner city crowd in the summer. Spring and fall, we're a regular for-hire camp. Winter, we're a ski resort."

"It must keep you busy."

"It does." He looked at her tray. "You stopped eating."

Collin's appetite vanished. She pushed her tray away. "I'm done."

Jeff frowned. "You can't be done. You never even started."

Collin ignored the comment, though his concern interested her. She changed the subject. "What do you do when you're not at camp and you're not in school? Isn't it tough on your family with you gone all the time?"

One corner of Jeff's smile lifted. "You mean like a wife-and-child-kind of family? Is that what you're asking?"

Collin shrugged. "Not exactly. But are you?"

"Am I what?"

"Married?"

"Would it make a difference?"

Collin said sharply—more sharply than she intended—"Yes."

"Good. It should. No, I'm not. No children, either. And I hope that makes a difference, too."

The man intrigued her. She couldn't read him at all except for his eyes. And she dare not look there too long, nor too deep. "It does." She challenged, "It means you at least have the decency to consider someone else before subjecting them to your harebrained lifestyle."

Jeff grinned. "*Touché*. It's not forever. One day I hope to work here full time. But now, economics play a big part in the decision. I have commitments in Oakton."

"Like what?"

"You are nosy, aren't you?"

"I'm a counselor. It's what we do. We ask questions. We make observations. We evaluate. We dig around, we…" Warning bells clanged in her head. Too much truth for this weekend. Collin sat up straighter and tried to smile.

Jeff rolled his eyes. "My turn to ask questions. I know you're a counselor. I know you're a very dedicated counselor because you're either using your vacation time to be here, or taking the week off without pay, which would mean you're a very wealthy counselor, and you wouldn't be in this line of work unless you really, really loved kids. In which case, you'd be the one bankrolling this trip."

Collin started to correct the man's impressions of her, but he continued without a breath. "Do you have any family? Meaning besides the obligatory mother, father, siblings, and yes, I'm asking specifically, are you married? I see no ring or ring shadow, but that doesn't mean what it used to. Married women don't wear rings, and unmarried women have them on every finger. How's a guy supposed to know the difference?"

Collin chuckled. "Did you have a question in there?"

"Several. One, are you married? Two, do you have a family?

Three, what do you do to enjoy yourself?"

"One, no. Two, no. Three…um…I am enjoying myself."

"You are?"

Someone must have announced closing. Campers jumped up and made a mad rush to empty the buffet line of as much food as they could carry. Collin nodded. "Yes, I am. It's been a while since I've conversed with someone older than seventeen. Not on this level anyhow."

Jeff looked around. "What, down in the basement?"

Collin tapped the table lightly. "Stop before you hurt yourself. You know what I mean."

Jeff spread his hands in acquiescence. "Okay."

Collin went back on the offensive. "When you're not in school, and you're not up here, what do you do for fun?"

"I'm a paramedic."

Collin grew solemn. "Oh, *this* is the fun stuff."

His eyes softened. "This is the fun stuff. It's not always intense, and I love what I do. But coming here gives me a break."

The maintenance worker stretched. "It also gives me a break from my dad. I manage some properties for him, and he's death on details."

Collin stomped the door to the black hole. *No memories. Not now.* "I see. How long—"

Rob sauntered up to the table with his "I be cool" act. But Collin read the excitement under the surface. At least him, she could still decipher. "Yes?"

"A bunch of us is gonna walk to the canyon floor to see the river. You want to come, caseworker lady?"

Collin waved him off. "No, Rob. You go. I'd slow you down, seeing as you're always telling me I'm 'old folk,' you know."

Jeff supported Rob. "It's beautiful. You ought to go."

Collin continued to refuse. "Maybe later."

Rob protested, "Aw, come on, caseworker lady. I promise, ain't none of us gonna fall in." The boy bounced on the toes of his shoes.

Jeff added, "The trail's well marked, and there's a turn out with benches. We keep it lit in the evenings. It's a great spot."

Collin studied the maintenance man. Why would he dismiss her so soon? Seen what he wanted, and she'd failed the test? What did she say this time?

Jeff stood. "I'll be here all week. I'd like it if we could talk again." He grinned. "Maybe you can explain about the kangaroos." He carried both his and Collin's tray to the counter and deposited them.

Somewhat encouraged, Collin nodded. "I hope so." She looked at Rob. "Okay, man. Do you know how to get there? More important, do you know how to get back?" Collin stood and pushed in her chair.

Rob laughed. "Lady, have I ever got lost?"

Collin glared. "Not the question. You've got me lost plenty of times telling me how to get someplace to pick you up or drop you off. I refuse to be a den mate with some grizzly because you can't remember the way home."

Rob chuckled. "Ain't no grizzlies in West Virginia."

"How do you know?"

"I learnt it in school."

Collin put a hand on her heart. "You learned it in school? You mean they taught you something you remembered? Will wonders never cease?"

Rob pulled her arm. "Yeah, yeah, I know. So maybe it wasn't all a waste of time. Maybe some stuff stuck. Let's go."

Collin waved at Jeff as Rob dragged her off. "I hope I see you around, Jeff."

As Rob pulled Collin out of earshot, she heard his assuring, "You will."

* * *

As ten kids—and one counselor—hiked ever downward toward the riverbank, Collin's fear grew. Even the jostling and jesting of the group couldn't keep the shadows at bay.

Finally, she reached her breaking—and braking—point. Collin stopped as they neared the lookout. They were still maybe fifty yards from where the river would be visible. Close enough to feel the throbbing pulse in her being, but not close enough to feel the spray in her face. On her face. Over her face...

Collin told Rob, "You guys go on. I'll wait here."

Rob looked at her, confused. "What? Why?"

14

"I got my reasons. You young guns forget what goes down easy goes back up exponentially harder. I'll rest up here and beat you all back up the hill. Go on."

She saw disappointment in his eyes. But he put on his tough-guy facade. "Suit yourself. We be back later."

Collin sighed as he turned and followed the crowd. She needed to come up with an explanation. One near enough to the truth so it wouldn't be a lie, but dull enough to keep anyone from asking questions. Collin sat back against a tree, set her mind on reviewing praise hymns she knew. It would occupy the time—and her brain—until the kids returned.

Half an hour later, a subdued group returned. Collin guessed the reason but decided to make them put it into words to help crystallize the experience. She asked, "How was it, Luke?"

The ten-year-old shook his head. "I never seen anything like it. Nothing. It's so...so..." He faltered.

Jeshua bailed him out. "So powerful. So big. Only running water I've ever seen comes out in the tub. I didn't know there could be something so..."

As the young teen ran out of words, twelve-year-old Awana picked up the torch. "Yeah, I know what you mean. I've seen rivers on those nature shows my folks make me watch." She grimaced. "But seeing it on a little screen doesn't give you any idea how..."

No one filled in the blank. No one could. Collin understood their feelings. "And this is only the first night. What else do you think they have out here?"

Silence met her, as ten teens and teen wannabes considered the possibilities ahead. Finally, someone—Collin couldn't be sure who—whispered, "Wow."

Suddenly someone else, equally anonymous, quipped, "Hey, I can say it backward! Wowww." He dragged the word out for emphasis.

Several someones slugged the jokester, who ran off, jeering at his jury. Swift pursuit followed and swiftly halted, as the steepness of the hill overcame even their youthful exuberance. A mid-range walk became the gait of choice and talking gave way to simply breathing.

As the group returned to the lodge, Rob pulled Collin aside.

"Caseworker lady, you mind not getting whooped in hoops tonight? It ain't gonna spoil your day or nothing, will it?"

"Why, Rob?"

"I don't know." Collin rarely saw Rob this subdued or contemplative. "I think I want to be alone for a while. Be alone and jus' think. Something 'bout the river jus' make me wanna think."

Collin nodded. "I understand." She let out a somewhat shaky breath. "Tomorrow night."

They came to the parting of the sexes: boys' rooms to the left, girls' rooms to the right, with a staffed entry hall between them. Collin stopped, turned, and faced Rob. "You okay, bro?"

He nodded. "Yeah. It's everything out there is so...so..." Collin waited for him to get his thought out. He apparently couldn't find the words any more than the other teens, so finished lamely, "...so big, I guess. I mean, city buildings is big, but man built them. I could build one of them. But the trees and the river, all of it...it's huge, and it got that way without me being here, without no man being here helping it or telling it what to do. Like we don't even matter or nothing."

Collin ached to hug the boy but knew better than to cross forbidden territory. "You matter, Rob. More than you know, you matter. Goodnight, bro. Get some sleep." *At least one of us should.*

"Night, caseworker lady."

The two parted company and went to their respective rooms. Collin checked on her two charges, who lay in the same bed. She set an eleven p.m. curfew on giggling and a midnight cut-off on talking. Probably a waste of time; the girls would be asleep within the hour anyhow.

Collin went back to her room. She debated whether to shower now or in the morning. The six a.m. alarm came early. But the thought of running water cascading over her head added more fuel to an already-glowing ember she meant to extinguish. Collin changed into her nightshirt, took her Bible from her backpack, and settled into bed. She muttered, "Numbers. Genealogies. If those can't put me to sleep, nothing can." She looked at the first page of the chapter. "I hope."

Outside the windows, the heartbeat of the river pulsed along.

SATURDAY MORNING

Collin welcomed the sunrise as relief from the never-ending night. She drifted in and out of fitful sleep, never allowing herself to fall deep enough to dream. She ached as she rose from the bed. Stretching alerted her to more places hurting. After the walk last night, today would be a thrill a minute. Oh, joy. She glanced at the clock. More good news. It read 7:30. She must have missed the alarm she'd set for six a.m. *By an hour and a half? How?*

You needed sleep.

You're lazy.

Collin knocked on the door of her charges' room. No answer. She popped her head in and saw the two girls still asleep: one in the bed and one on the floor. Collin went in and jiggled one camper carefully. "Come on, Jill. Rise and shine." She poked the girl in the bed. "Let's go, Marites. It's your first day at camp. Up and at 'em. Move 'em out."

A voice from the floor groaned, "I can't move!"

Collin smiled. "I know the feeling. But if you want breakfast, you've only got half an hour left to get it."

The sleeping bag on the mattress launched itself into the air. "Breakfast? Half an hour? No way, man!"

Collin nodded. "Find a way, man. I don't think these guys are joking about sending people away hungry. Unless you have a taste for apples and granola bars." Both girls began making gagging noises. "Exactly what I thought. You'll have to give up looking beautiful and settle for looking full. Now move it!"

She closed the door and retreated to her room. She knew she

would not make it to breakfast, either, but an apple and juice would be enough. *I want to eat light this morning. I want to make the morning tour and find out exactly where we've landed.*

Steve Parks, the camp director, said the tour started after breakfast. Which could be any time after eight. She should have checked last night for a more specific 'when.' She knew where: in front of the lodge.

Collin opened her window, drew in a deep breath, and immediately shivered. Though early in August, and sweltering back home, the air here felt crisp. Dress accordingly.

She washed in the sink, promising the world a full shower. Later. She chose her jeans rather than shorts and picked a short sleeve pullover with a zip-up sweatshirt. Collin ran the brush through her shoulder-length hair, pulled her hat on, stuffed her Bible in her backpack, and headed out the door.

She banged on Jill and Marites's door as she went by. "Ten minutes." Collin grinned at the resulting cries of anguish. Ah, lesson one compliments of Camp Grace.

No one stirred in the foyer as Collin arrived. She peeked outside, but no one moved there, either. Collin risked a trip to the health bar, picked up a banana, a bottle of juice, and a cup of coffee. She went out sipping her coffee, wondering when the tour would leave. Or left? She doubted it. Collin had yet to see more than three bodies moving about. Still, it paid to be early. She went out the front of the lodge and found an unoccupied bench. Collin ate the banana, chugged the juice, threw out the remains, and returned to her coffee. She pulled her Bible out of her backpack, pulled her hat down over her eyes, and began reading.

At 8:20, a tractor-tram combination pulled into the front parking area. Collin watched with mild interest while the driver circled the lot, straightened the rig out, and pulled to a stop. As the man stepped off the tractor, Collin recognized Jeff in "civilian" clothes. He didn't see her as he strode with purpose toward a shiny black jeep.

Suddenly Steve Parks burst out of the lodge. He yelled at the retreating maintenance man.

"Jeff! Jeff!"

Jeff stopped, turned, and walked back to meet the director. Collin tried concentrating on her reading but gave it up. She would hear the men's conversation, whether she wanted to or not.

Steve asked, "So, what have you got planned for today? Or specifically this morning?"

"I've got an appointment out at Shafter's pond. There's this big old bass with my name on it waiting for me."

"I see." Steve cocked his head and rocked back on his heels. "You know, Jeff, if it has your name on it, won't it be there tonight? Or Monday?"

Jeff closed one eye to look at Steve. "I don't like the sound of this. What do you need, Mr. Director?" The man stepped back and waited. Collin dropped her head so as not to watch the exchange.

"You know Gerald's out with laryngitis."

"Yeah, and Nash has the flu."

Steve hesitated. "Orlon called off this morning—said his wife's in labor."

Collin looked up to see Jeff throw his hands in the air in frustration. "It's false labor! After four kids, you'd think he'd know the difference." Collin snickered and bowed her head again.

"I hate to ask you, Jeff—"

"Then don't."

"—and I wouldn't if I thought there might be anyone else qualified."

"Send someone unqualified. It'll be a new experience for them. Cross-training, you know?"

Collin twisted around, putting her side toward the men. Less obvious to watch them.

"Jeff, would you take the tour this morning?"

"I've been on the tour. I don't need a tour."

"Please?"

Two campers in bathing suits and carrying towels walked through Collin's line of sight. Their chatter did nothing to interrupt the exchange between Steve Parks and Jeff. She waited until the swimmers passed to sneak another look at the men.

"Mr. Director, you don't understand. This bass is over seven pounds. Think of it. Seven pounds. It told me itself in a vision last night. It said, 'I'm over seven pounds, and I'm waiting for you. But you only get one chance tomorrow morning. Then, I'm history.'"

Steve's voice carried skepticism. "It said all that, did it?"

Collin peered out from under her hat to see Jeff nod solemnly.

"All of it. Every word. Except maybe the history part. I don't think fish understand the concept of history. Then again, this fish is old enough, it might know history."

Collin suppressed a giggle and looked at the ground. She began inscribing small circles in the dirt with her foot. The motion progressed to writing out names. *Erin. Rob. Collin. Jeff.* She erased the names, kicking the dust around the small bench.

The men's conversation continued. "I can't order you to go."

"Sure, you can." Jeff sounded as if he instructed Steve on some point of order. "You are the director, and I am the maintenance man. Your job is to tell me what to do. My job is to do it. If it comes right down to it, I'd much rather you told me than asked me. I wouldn't have to berate myself for being an idiot giving up this fish."

"You're sure about this?"

"I'm sure. Tell me, 'Jeff, you have to take this group.' I'll take it, no problem."

Collin gave up pretending she wasn't watching. Steve cocked his head to the side. "All I have to do is say, 'Jeff, you have to take this group' and that makes it better?"

"Absolutely."

Steve nodded. "Jeff, would you please take this group?"

Jeff groaned, bending over as if in pain. "Sure, boss. It'll give me the chance to get to know some of the faces better."

Steve slapped him on the shoulder. "Thanks, Jeff. I won't forget this."

"Neither will I. But I will forgive you." He grinned. "You want me to change into uniform?"

"Not necessary. I think we can tell you from the campers."

The two men separated. Steve went back to the lodge, and Jeff went back to the tractor.

Collin smiled slightly. Something different about the man. Something worth investigating. She put her Bible away and joined the small throng of brave and conscious souls who wandered out of the lodge.

Maybe a third of the campers gathered by the tram. Jill and Marites were not among them. Collin looked to see if Rob might wander in from the outlying areas, but no one appeared. *He never has been an early riser. I'll check on him when I get back.*

Collin took a seat in the back so she could keep the entire group in focus, as befitting the only counselor on the tram. *The day you can't handle thirteen kids by yourself is the day you turn in your badge.*

There's never too many. You can control all of them. If you want. You're lazy. Always asking for help. Looking for the easy way out…

Collin looked toward the front and saw Jeff's eyes in the mirror, studying her. He grinned. She smiled back with what she hoped looked like a polite, dignified, not too eager but not uninterested smile. All the while, feeling like a fool.

Stop acting like a lovesick thirteen-year-old. You're twenty-six. According to your birth record, anyhow.

Which one? The real one, or the revised one?

Collin grimaced at the inner demons. She needed to find something to distract them. Besides her inadequacies.

Jeff waited for the last two young people to get on board and started the motor on the tractor. He had a microphone, as his voice came out clearly over the tram speakers. "Good morning, and welcome to the first and only morning tour of Camp Grace for today. Your regularly scheduled guide is absent with an excuse about his wife having a baby. I prefer being here. Anyone with me?" Shouts of "Yes!" bounced off the lodge wall. Collin raised her hand to keep in the spirit.

"We'll cover approximately thirty miles on this trip, which is why it's not a walking tour. We tried to use the horses, but their union said they couldn't go more than ten miles in a day and no uphill climbs. We couldn't promise, so we use the tractor. This is a two-way radio system, so if you—meaning anyone back there—have a question go ahead and ask it. But one at a time, please. While our system's good enough to pick up all the voices, my hearing's not so good it can separate them. Got it?"

The kids nodded and generally complied with Jeff's request. "Okay, then." He slipped the tractor into gear, and the tram jolted into motion.

The group circled the lodge once, then headed down one of the many dirt trails crisscrossing Camp Grace. Collin watched the pine, oak, sugar maple, and black birch trees flow past her side of the tram. She thought she spotted at least one deer hidden in the undergrowth.

After fifteen minutes or so, the tram broke into a clearing. Jeff announced, "On your right is Highway 135, the only route through town, passing the only burger joint between here and the state line." Shouts and cheers and cries of "Let me out!" followed.

"On your left is our barn, home to our fleet of milk producers. They work day and night to provide you with fresh milk for your breakfast, lunch, and dinner consumption." A herd of cows lounged lazily over their hay mounds. "The ladies love it if you wave while we go by."

Collin watched closely to see who took the bait. Her heart smiled to see at least three of the younger campers secretively waving. As if on command, two cows lowed in return. Jeff commented, "They're saying thank you. Up ahead, we have our version of the 100-acre wood, complete with bears, rabbits, owls, and a very occasional lost piglet. But no tiggers or kangaroos." She could see only his eyes in the mirror, and they smiled.

One girl giggled and whispered to her seatmate, "He be talking 'bout Winnie the Pooh! How he be knowin' 'bout Pooh?" Her partner wrinkled her nose and giggled, too. Collin's heart ached; these kids were still babies. Inside the street-wise shells, they were babies.

Jeff continued his travelogue, pointing out features of the vast campgrounds. The path meandered through woods, past small streams, up and down gentle rises, until it reached its zenith an hour and a half later at a flat overlook. From there, the group could survey the entire county. Or the eastern half of it.

Jeff pulled the tractor to a stop at a picnic area. "Break time. Everyone out, stretch your legs and restore circulation to the feet. There are two coolers in the back of the tram underneath the woman with the mysterious smile."

Collin shook her head, embarrassed. His eyes danced. "Sorry, with the beautiful grin. Ask her politely to move and unload the coolers. There are drinks and snacks in there. It should be enough to keep anyone from dropping dead due to lack of nourishment, but probably not enough to spoil your lunch. We'll take about half an hour if you want."

Jeff removed the headphones and climbed down from the tractor. Collin didn't wait to be asked to move but vacated the premises on her own. She walked to where Jeff stood surrounded by kids asking him questions, asking to ride on the tractor, asking to drive the tractor, etcetera, etcetera. She waited until the din died down, and the crowd left to check the contents of the cooler.

Collin dipped her head to him. "Good morning."

Jeff cocked his head. "Morning. Why doesn't it surprise me to see you on this trip?"

"I'm an eager, get-a-jump-on-the-day kind of person, I guess. Why are you out this early?"

"It's my job."

"That's the only reason you're here?"

"It'll do for a start. What do you think so far?"

"It's huge, Jeff. I never realized the size of this camp." She looked out over the expanse. "You own all this?"

"Camp Grace owns all this, yes."

Collin laughed. "Of course. But who owns Camp Grace? I looked through the literature last night, and it never said."

Jeff glanced over toward a child climbing on the tractor. "Excuse me... off." He turned back to Collin. "It's a joint venture. God owns it and has a silent partner on the side. A very silent partner."

Collin cocked her head, curious. "Oh? How so?" She half-turned to keep one eye on the picnic area.

"He learned long ago to let God speak first. He says it makes things much easier."

Collin hmmed. "He must be an older man."

Jeff gave her a quizzical look. "Why?"

"You don't gain that kind of wisdom this early in life."

"I see your point. Well, he's not what I'd call old." Jeff turned to the tractor and banged on the hood.

Collin continued to quiz the maintenance man. "You know him?"

"We've talked."

Jeff's answers seemed a little guarded. It made Collin wonder about the relationship between the two. But caution kept her from pressing further. She looked around the countryside. "Tell me what I'm seeing. The camp I recognize. What's off to the left, there?"

Jeff looked where she pointed. "There's the town of Hillsboro, population 1,300, mostly related to one another." He continued describing the layout, moving in a clockwise direction. "The stand of trees marks the beginning of Shafter's pond, home to one of the biggest bass I've ever seen." He did not elaborate but sighed. Slightly. Collin swallowed a grin. "Depending on your eyesight, you might be able to make out Cotter's windmill. He put it up there so he could give people directions to his house. You know, 'Turn at the windmill. You can't miss it.' And you can't. Except at night or when the wind is blowing. Then you can hear it creaking for five miles."

While Jeff continued to describe the county, its occupants, and their quirks, Collin listened carefully. He seemed to know something about everywhere and everyone. None of it harsh. All in a good-natured spirit. She could tell he spent a good deal of time here to know it so well. As he finished his panoramic overview, she said, "You must love this place very much."

"I guess. I spent most every summer up here growing up. It got to feel like home, I suppose." He looked at her. "You have any place like that? Which feels like home?"

"No." It came out flat and hard. *Where did the anger come from?* Collin quickly covered with, "I mean, no, no place special. We didn't get out much as kids."

"You said, 'We.' It would seem to indicate there were more of you?"

Collin kept her tone cool. "I meant our family."

Jeff eyed her. "I understand." He turned to the picnic area where the kids lounged. "How do you think the tour is going so far? Are the kids staying with me, or am I boring them?"

"No, you're doing great. You don't talk down to them, and you don't talk over their heads. You seem to understand them at their level. You have to start where they are to bring them where you know they should be." She stopped, embarrassed. "Which you already know. It's what this camp is all about, isn't it? Stop me when I babble. I'm running on one cup of coffee this morning. My brain doesn't kick in 'til the third cup."

Jeff motioned toward the tractor. "I've got a thermos full of coffee if you want some. There are cups up there, too, if you need them. Kids may have to eat and drink healthy, but we adults don't have to suffer." He pointed with his chin. "It's under the seat."

Collin did a half-curtsey before him. "Bless you, kind sir. Bless you!" She stood. "Can I bring you a cup?"

Jeff nodded. "Put some coffee in it too, please. Black."

Collin grimaced but went and found the thermos. She poured for both of them and handed Jeff his cup. It felt good to be standing around, sipping coffee, watching the kids explore the "picnic" area. Some climbed trees—a first in their young lives. Some examined trees big enough to climb. Also a first. The birds, the squirrels, the chipmunks, the myriad of bugs all served to chip away at the hardened exterior the city formed around the hearts, minds, and souls of these kids.

As they played, it became evident none were too hard to be touched, or so old in street wisdom they couldn't still enjoy innocent fun. Collin couldn't keep the emotion from her voice. Her throat tightened. "This makes it worthwhile. Every penny they spend couldn't be enough to buy this."

Jeff looked at the kids. "Buy what?"

"That." Collin pointed out a tall, lanky girl of fourteen kneeling in the dirt with two other children looking at the bugs. "Molly. Talking to kids her age. She's down on her knees, actually touching dirt like a real kid. She's playing."

Jeff took a step forward to look closer. Collin cleared her throat. "Molly started walking the street three months ago. When she's dressed up, she looks every bit of twenty. Getting her to associate with kids of any age is a major miracle."

Jeff whispered prayerfully, "Dear God." He looked away. "I suppose it's stupid to ask, but where are her parents? Don't they care?"

Collin tossed her head in disgust. "Her mother is the one who sent her to the streets. Her father is gone, as usual, missing in action from the home front."

Jeff nodded as if he'd expected the answer. His voice tightened. "I see." Collin eyed him. *What bothers him? Her being here? Or her parents not caring?*

After several moments Collin cleared her throat. "We've got one week to teach her what life is like on the other side. I think they're all getting a good handle on the 'down and dirty' part."

The bug watching disintegrated into a dirt-throwing contest. Collin shouted, "All right, all right! Enough already! Brush it off, load it up, and let's move out!"

Jeff added, "We've still got maybe fifteen miles to go, a lot of territory to cover, and the river to explore."

Collin echoed his words. "And the river..." She trailed off, life draining from her. *The river? Today? Now?*

Her face must have revealed more than she thought. Jeff looked at her with deep concern. "Are you okay? What's wrong?"

The inner demons shrieked in terror. Every voice she'd ever heard cried out, panicked. Collin silenced them all and tried to smile at Jeff. "I'm fine." She saw disbelief in his eyes. "It's personal. I'll deal with it. Thank you."

He studied her for a long time. "Okay, if that's the way you want it. I'm up there if you need me." The man pointed to the tractor.

Need him? For what! We don't need no—

Collin nodded. "I know you are. And I appreciate it. This is old business. It pops up now and again. I'm fine. Really."

Jeff looked far from convinced. "Uh-huh." He walked back to the tractor and sat down. He waited until they repacked the coolers, the last child took a seat, and everyone settled before saying, "Ready to go back?" A chorus of noes and two yeses followed. "We'll take the long way home." He looked up in the mirror. His grin faded as his eyes met Collin's. Collin nodded curtly. *Deal with it. It's life.*

The remainder of the trip descended into a waking nightmare. As the roar of the river increased, reality receded into shadow, and only the sheer force of her will kept the darkness at bay. She sensed Jeff increase his banter, but to no effect. She sat pale and wan, fighting the memories threatening to overpower her.

Collin closed her eyes, clenched her teeth, and bit her lip so hard the blood trickled inside her mouth. But it felt good. It gave her a physical hold in reality to counteract the specters wanting to claim her.

She sensed the tram stop and heard Jeff instructing the campers, "Stay on the footpath. The slopes are covered with poison ivy and oak. If you don't know what it means, it's ugly red welts all over your body, which itch and burn like fire and prevent you from doing anything fun because you're so miserable. And they last at least a week, so you'll have come all this way to do nothing more than play in the weeds and watch everyone else have a good time. Stay on the footpath."

One camper snorted, "I ain't afraid of no plant."

Jules, one of the younger boys, waved his hands to ward off evil. "I is. I got poison one time. I's never so bad off in all my life. Couldn't eat, couldn't sleep, couldn't do nothin'. You couldn't pay me enough to go down there."

The doubter froze. "For real? You ain't jiving?"

"No jive, man. Driver ain't jiving, neither. It's some nasty stuff. Stay away from me if you go down there."

The kids moved off, still discussing the hazards of contact. The roar of the river's power pulsed through Collin, singing to her resistance was futile, and how she should give in to the siren song of the past. With thunderous tones, it commanded her presence and her obedience.

The spell of the river's demands broke as a calm, quiet voice spoke. "I've seen fear before, and, woman, it's all over you." A warm hand touched her shoulder. Jeff sat down on the bench beside her. "The river, right?"

She could only nod. Collin opened her eyes, expecting to see ridicule in his face. She saw only compassion. He asked, "Bad experience?" Again she nodded. "We'll leave."

Collin worked to still the tremor in her voice. "No." Jeff looked puzzled. "I don't want the kids to miss out on anything because I can't handle my past. I'll be fine." She saw the disbelief in his eyes.

Collin took a slow breath, let out another. "I'm fine." She forced the muscles in her shoulders to relax. "See? I wasn't ready. I am now." She put confidence into her voice. Collin touched Jeff's hand. "Thanks. I'm fine." The narrowing of his eyes said he didn't buy it. "I only needed a moment to pull it together. Now it's done, and I'm fine." She held her head high.

Jeff pulled a tissue from his pocket, reached up and wiped the blood from her lip. He studied her a minute, nodded silently, and stood. He squeezed her shoulder, turned, and walked off to follow the campers.

Collin let out a long sigh, wrapped her arms around her knees, and dropped her head on her arms. *Lord, why now? Why here, in front of him?*

Collin continued to force herself to breathe. Years of training bounced into action. *The river is not my enemy. We drink water. We bathe in water. We use water to feed our plants and our animals. Water is our friend.*

The river cannot hurt you as long as you stay away from it. You don't touch it, and it can't touch you. You're safe, you're dry, you're away from the river. Suck it up.

Coward.

Collin whispered defiantly, "Wrong." She pulled her head up, uncurled her body, and stretched. She scrubbed her hands across her face, forcing blood and color back to her cheeks. The panic attack ran its course as usual. She survived. As usual. The campers would see her under control and in charge. As usual.

Collin climbed from the tram and debated going after the group. No, she might be pushing things too far. Better to explore around here. She found a warm rock to perch on and worked on her "lizard in the sunshine" impression. The sun felt soothing, and the remaining tensions melted away. By the time the tour group returned, she managed even to give them an honest smile. "Everyone have a good time?"

One youngster yelled back, "Yeah, but Reeshard nearly fell in."

The boy in question, a lanky fourteen-year-old, snapped back, "No, I didn't. Rory pushed me!"

Rory shoved him good-naturedly. "I ain't never touched you. You trip over your own big feet. You feet bigger 'n Michael Jordan's."

Reeshard shoved back but with less play and more malice. "No way."

Collin slid off the rock, sensing the need for intervention. The boys stood taller and heavier than Collin, but nothing as minor as size ever stopped her.

She stepped between the boys. "Anyone know what size MJ wears?" Several suggestions were offered from ten to fifteen to eighteen to the absurd. Collin looked at Reeshard and asked, "What size do you wear?" Out of the corner of her eye, she noted Jeff returning with the last of the campers. Nice to have back up, but this she could handle alone.

Reeshard retorted, "Thirteen."

Collin nodded. "Thirteen. I know for a fact MJ wears a fifteen.

So, Rory, you owe the man an apology."

Rory, who probably hadn't been looking for a fight to begin with, extended his hand. "Hey man, no big deal. I ain't dissing you. Jus' having some fun, you know?"

Collin faced Reeshard. "Your turn, Reeshard. We've talked before about being thin-skinned, haven't we? About letting the jibe go? It's only the ones you hang on to which hurt you. I'd consider myself lucky to have feet the size of MJ if I were a dude and could walk and chew gum at the same time. And measured more than five foot six."

Reeshard couldn't help it. He smiled. "I seen you play hoops. You pretty tough for a white woman." He looked at Rory. "Sorry, man."

Rory shrugged. "Ain't nothing."

The situation having resolved, Collin nodded. "Okay, let's get back to camp. Everyone on board." Collin noticed Jeff studying her. Whether in approval or doubt, she didn't know.

Collin waited until the last camper boarded and climbed into her perch. She saluted Jeff. "Good to go, Cap'n." Jeff saluted her in return. Collin shut the wheels inside her brain down before they could read anything into his gesture. *He signaled you back. No big deal.*

Jeff announced, "Next stop on our tour will be what we lovingly call our marina. Six months out of the year, overflow from the river fills the area enough for swimming, boating, and a few other aquatic sports. In the winter, it's our ice rink for hockey and skating. The rest of the time, it's mud. But because God likes this group, He has seen fit to keep the river running high all summer, and we still have our 'lake.' It's a short hike from there to the lodge, and if we work this right, you'll have about half an hour to kill before lunch. Unless you want to take another swing around the camp?"

Cries and groans of, "No!" "No way!" "Help!" filled the tram.

Collin caught Jeff's eyes. The smile returned. Good. No permanent damage done.

Jeff laughed. "Guess not. I do hope someone got something out of this trip besides poison ivy. And a word of strictest caution: even if you don't think you touched any, don't be stupid. Wash your hands, your arms, and any exposed skin with warm water and soap as soon as you get back to your rooms. Change your clothes. Do not wear them again until they have been thoroughly washed. This is not a joke. And trust me, it will be quite obvious in the next day or two who listened and who didn't. We will know you by your rashes."

Jeff spent the remainder of the trip in silence. The campers continued to talk, battle, and jibe as kids will do. Collin listened to the drift and noticed Reeshard continued to be the focus of negative attention. At least Rory stepped, figuratively speaking, out of the crowd. For now.

Collin watched, trying to decide the best way to defuse the situation permanently and distract the young vultures from their chosen target. She slid forward into the bench directly ahead of Reeshard—and currently inhabited by his chief aggressor. The boy glared at Collin. She ignored him, turned around, and looked at Reeshard. "You never asked how I knew MJ's shoe size."

The boy beside her snickered. "Nike commercial."

"Good guess. But wrong. He told me."

Reeshard sat back. "He told you? When you see the man?"

Collin shrugged. "Summer camp a few years ago."

A few? Really? You're going there, aren't you? Your one claim to fame—

Shut up. Yes, it's more than a few. It still happened. "We suited up for a game, and I asked him what size he wore. He told me fifteen."

Her seatmate scoffed. "Yeah, right."

Reeshard's eyes widened. "He told you? You played ball with him?"

Collin nodded as if it were no big deal. "Yeah. I brought the pictures with me if you're interested in the truth." She stared at the boy beside her. He stared back in defiance. "Come see them anytime. I love showing them."

She slipped back to her seat and listened carefully to the dialogue which followed her exit. She knew, of course, how it would go— "She ain't for real."

"She is. You ain't been knowin' her like I do. She a straight lady. She says she knows MJ, she knows MJ."

"Ain't no white lady ever play ball with MJ."

"We go see the pictures an' we know."

"Ain't gonna be no pictures. She blowin' smoke."

"You 'fraid to find out?"

"I'll go anytime."

At least this she could resolve, and quickly if they wanted resolution and not simply aggression. Which could be a possibility. She'd know soon enough.

The tram pulled into the parking area by the docks, and everyone crowded to get off. Everyone except Reeshard and his three tormentors. They seemed determined to be the last ones off the bus. Collin tensed, sensing a confrontation. She noted Jeff got off the tractor but hadn't started up the slope with the others, as if he were waiting for someone. Or for something to happen, more like it. Maybe he knew kids, too.

All four boys rose at once. There came a moment of pushing and shoving. Collin stood up and strode forward, determined to prevent a full-on rumble. The shoving escalated. Collin caught the arm of the child closest to her. In her best gunnery sergeant voice, she yelled, "Freeze! Everyone now!"

Instant obedience. The boys turned to statues. But there came the sound of metal hitting metal, as a thin, shiny object clanged off the floor. Collin didn't know who's pocket it fell from, nor did it matter. She retrieved the ornately engraved handle and held it up for all to see. The sight of the knife kept the boys frozen.

Collin saw Jeff moving forward to intervene or maybe act as back up. Back up, she could handle. Interference she didn't need. Collin kept her eyes firm and cold on the boys, nailing each one with a look that drilled right through them. She didn't even look at the handle of the contraband instrument. "I've seen stupid in my time. But this—this is a winner. You got a free ride out of the hood to paradise, and instead, you carry the hood with you. Look around you. What did you expect to find up here that you'd need to shed blood? You gonna use a blade against a grizzly? What?"

Without even having to search, she tripped the mechanism and released the blade. It slid out silently and engaged without even a hint of a click. Collin saw the horrified and stricken looks on the boys' faces. She nodded. "You got it. Blade's been exposed, and blood has to be shed. Can't sheath it clean, can you? I crossed the line, and now someone has to pay in blood."

She saw Jeff moving forward as if he'd heard enough. She

called out, "Hold on, Fireman. The boys and I will be finished here in a minute." She looked around. "As soon as someone pays the price." She looked from boy to boy, from one panicked face to another. All machismo disappeared from their manner, wondering what this crazy woman would do next.

Her voice softened slightly. "Someone did pay the price, you know? You all stand there, guilty as sin, and someone needed to pay the price. And pay it in blood." Collin reached over and, in one smooth motion, sliced the palm of her left-hand open. Blood began spurting freely, and the boys cringed. Collin continued, "But He didn't just bleed a little to satisfy some gang ritual. He went all the way and died to save you." She held each boy in her steady gaze, challenging them. "Want to know more? Come talk to me after lunch. Now get out of here." All four scrambled headlong up the hill.

SATURDAY AFTERNOON

Collin closed the blade, cradled her wounded hand, and sank on the nearest bench. Not quite what she intended, but maybe it made an impact.

It made an impact on Jeff. He pounded into the tram, eyes blazing. Collin looked into his face and saw anger, disbelief, frustration, a tinge of disgust, maybe? He grabbed the first-aid kit, then her hand, and began trying to staunch the blood, but said nothing. Collin decided to lighten the moment. "Sharper blade than I thought."

Jeff glared at her. "Don't. Don't even try to make a joke out of this. How stupid...is that what they teach in counseling these days?"

Collin felt her hackles rise. "I know what I'm doing. I've been working with kids for a while now. It's my job. It's what I do."

Jeff's tone matched her own. "Since when does being a caseworker require self-mutilation?"

Collin jerked her hand away. "Listen, Mr. Fireman. I didn't ask for your help because I didn't need it. I know these kids. I will deal with them the best way I know. I don't need your judgment."

She started to brush past him, but he caught her arm. His tone softened. "You need stitches."

"No, I don't. I'll heal fine." She pulled her arm away.

Jeff repeated more strongly, "You need stitches. It's my job. It's what I do."

They locked eyes, but once again, Collin dropped hers. Collin sat on the bench seat. "Wrap it. I'll get them later." The wound began to sting. Collin forced her mind to overrule the pain. *Pain is weakness. No weakness. Never weakness. No pain. Ever.*

Jeff began dressing the wound. "Have you had—"

"—tetanus shots? Yes. Frequently. The blade was clean."

"How do you know? You said they can't put the knife away clean."

Collin shook her head. "This one hadn't been used." Jeff glanced at her face, then looked back at his work. Collin explained, "The mechanism slid too easily for it to have been used. You get to know the feel of them after a while."

The elephant on the bus trumpeted. Collin chewed the corner of her mouth. "You're going to report this, aren't you?"

"What do you think?"

Collin's eyes narrowed, reflecting her frustration. "Company policy, right? Anyone caught with a weapon is sent home immediately. Go directly to jail. No second chances."

Sarcasm edged her voice. "The camp's image as a wholesome, safe, family environment must be maintained above all else. I know the drill." Bitterness threatened to overwhelm her.

Collin took a deep breath, then caught Jeff's eyes. "Whoever brought this is a scared kid. I'm sure it belongs to an older brother, and the boy will get the snot beat out of him when he gets home. I won't give it back, but I won't try to identify him, either."

She stared hard at the man. "Do what you have to do. Report this. They can send me home. Get me fired. Whatever. I won't identify any of them. I want these kids to have this chance."

Jeff finished his work in silence. He sat down opposite Collin and studied her for a moment. "These kids mean that much to you? You'd take the hit professionally rather than see the guilty party sent home?"

"Yes." Collin lifted her chin. Her voice softened. "Someone did it for me. I can do no less for someone else."

She saw the corners of Jeff's mouth play slightly. His eyes, however, shone bright. "Grace isn't just our name, Collin. It's who we are."

He looked over the lake a moment, then leaned forward to catch her eyes. "I won't report this. I'm asking you to talk to Steve Parks. Tell him the whole story. He'll be the one to make the final decision. He's a godly man. You can trust him to do what's best for the boys." Jeff's eyes twinkled. He sat back. "However nameless they may be." Jeff stood. "I'll walk you to the infirmary."

Collin started to object but stopped. *More time for questions.* She nodded, then rose. She waited while Jeff put away the first-aid kit. As they exited the tram, Collin asked, "You won't get in trouble for not reporting this, will you? I'll tell Mr. Parks I asked you not to say anything."

They started the climb back to the lodge. Jeff shook his head. "No. Steve trusts his employees to use their discretion."

"What about the owner? Won't he be worried about the reputation of his camp?"

"God owns the camp, Collin."

Collin grimaced. "I know, but the man who signs the paychecks has to have some say in the matter." She wanted to say more but needed her breath for the climb up the hill.

Jeff shrugged. "He won't have a problem with any of this."

"You know him well? How long have you worked here?"

"I started during the planning stages."

Collin glanced at the man sideways. His answers…always enough to satisfy the question, but nothing beyond. *What is he hiding?*

Why should he be hiding anything?

Maybe he doesn't like the guy.

Maybe he doesn't like you.

They reached the top of the hill, then headed down the other side to the infirmary. It sat off to the left of the lodge, a building of its own. Jeff opened the door…

… or tried to. The knob didn't turn. Collin saw the puzzled look on the maintenance man's face as he knocked. "Doc? You in there?"

No answer. Jeff rattled the knob again, knocked, called. No response. He peered in the window.

A noisy group of campers walked out of the lodge, headed for the lake most likely. Two youngsters glanced over their way. Collin waved. One of the girls shouted, "Hey, Ms. Walker. We're going swimming. Join us."

Collin called back, "Maybe later. You have a counselor down there?"

The lodge door opened, and Mr. Lawler ran to catch up with the group. Collin turned away from the embarrassment of his neon

orange swim trunks. At least the kids would always know they
were being supervised.

Collin turned back to Jeff, still trying the door. "He's not there.
I'll be fine. I heal quickly."

Jeff pulled out his phone and speed-dialed. "You need the
stitches." He put the call on speakerphone.

"This is Dr. Wallace. I'm on an emergency call. For immediate
but minor issues, find Jeff Farrell, extension 111. Anything major,
call 911."

Jeff's shoulders rose, then fell. He shook his head. "Doc...why
do you do this to me?" He turned to Collin and said, "I'll take you
to the emergency room."

Collin's voice came down hard. "No."

Trust him.

What? Ignore him. You don't trust anyone. Never trust—

Trust him.

She cocked her head. "Have you ever stitched anyone?"

Jeff hesitated a long time. "Yeah. I've assisted Doc on
occasion. But he's always there to check it afterward."

"Then you do it, and I'll have Dr. Wallace look at them after he
gets back."

Jeff's eyes narrowed. "You want me to sew up your hand? I'm
the maintenance man. The janitor. Why would you think—"

"—because you're a paramedic. The doctor trusts you...the
director trusts you...the owner seems to trust all of his employees."
Collin paused, looked at the ground, then looked up at Jeff. She
shrugged her shoulders. "God trusts you. Why shouldn't I?"

Jeff pulled out a set of keys and unlocked the door. He didn't
open it but speed-dialed again.

A woman answered. "Yes, Jeffrey. What can I do for you?"

"Leeann, I'm at Doc's office. He's gone, but I have a camper
who needs stitches." Jeff turned to Collin, raised an eyebrow.
Collin nodded. "She wants me to put them in for her. I need a
chaperone. Can you send a female employee over to watch for us?"

"I'm sorry. Of course, Jeffrey. I'll be over in a few minutes.
Bye."

Jeff ended the call and put his phone in his pocket. Collin
scowled. "We don't need a chaperone. We're adults."

Jeff shook his head. "It's policy. When campers are involved, males and females don't go alone into any facility. We always have a third person present."

"Insurance liability?"

"Scripture accountability. No appearance of evil. And safety for all concerned. It's a good rule."

Collin's foot began inscribing small circles on the floor. "I suppose the owner set up all the rules."

"All the employees contributed."

Collin's eyebrows raised. "Really? Your owner values his employees that much? He lets you all in on the decision making? Wow. I'd like to work for him."

Jeff shrugged. Collin saw a twinkle in Jeff's eyes she didn't understand. "Maybe you will. One day. He's not a bad guy."

"Sounds like a wonderful guy. I'd like to meet him."

Only to investigate. Don't let this slick talk fool you. Keep your guard.

Trust me.

The lodge door opened. Campers came out. Campers went in. Excited chatter. Voices yelling. Raucous laughter. Sounds of home.

Except for the undercurrent of the river rumbling ever onward. Collin picked it out, even with all the distractions. Fear made her shudder.

Jeff saw. He touched her arm. "You okay? Maybe you'd better sit down."

Collin waved it off. "I'm—"

"—fine, I know. I know." Jeff smiled. "You're a fine woman, Collin. I realize."

Collin frowned. "I beg your pardon, sir."

Jeff turned his hands palm up. "What?"

Leeann walked from the lodge. She smiled at Jeff and Collin as she arrived at the infirmary. "I'm so sorry you got hurt, dear. Jeffrey will take good care of you, I know. He's the best."

Collin looked at Jeff sideways. "So it seems. Is there anything he can't do around here?"

Leeann laughed. In unison, she and Jeff said, "Cook."

Leeann added, her eyes shining, "Or find a wife."

Jeff groaned. He pushed the door open and held it as the director's assistant and Collin went through first. "I'll tell my own lies, Leeann, if you please."

Interesting.

Collin followed Jeff into an examining room while Leeann sat in the waiting area. Jeff left the door open. He motioned for Collin to sit and lay her hand on the table. She looked at Jeff. "I didn't plan that stunt, you know. Or maybe you don't know, but I didn't. It seemed to lend itself to the moment."

Jeff didn't look up, but his voice sharpened. "'Lend itself?' How does something like cutting your hand open just 'lend itself to the moment'?"

"I know the rituals these kids hold sacred. You put a knife back without drawing blood, it's your blood it will shed next. They believe it so strongly it terrifies them."

"You don't help a child overcome fear by participating in their blood rituals."

"You don't overcome it by telling them they don't exist, either." Collin's voice carried more heat than she intended, so she backed it down.

Jeff picked up a syringe. "I'm going to numb the area."

"You don't need to. I can handle pain."

Jeff stared Collin in the eyes. "I can't handle putting stitches in without it. One of us is going to be anesthetized, and I don't think you want it to be me."

Collin glared. Try as she wanted, she could not hold his gaze. She lowered her head. "Go ahead. Do it your way."

Jeff injected the pain killer, waited a few moments, then began stitching. He looked up at her. "This will be a rough patch job. You'll need a real surgeon to examine it when you get back to Oakton. I'll give you some recommendations."

Collin snorted. "Too expensive, and I doubt workman's comp will cover this."

Jeff chuckled. "Yeah, it might be a hard sell. Try the recommendations anyhow. It might not be as expensive as you think."

"You don't know my budget." *He doesn't need to know your budget.*

Or anything else about you. Quit giving him information about your life. He doesn't care.

He cares. Trust me.

38

Collin watched Jeff's surgical techniques. The man did know how to operate. Straight, tight stitches soon covered the cut. Collin nodded in approval. "Very nice work. Best stitching I've seen in a long time."

Jeff rebandaged her hand, cleaned up the area, tossed his gloves and gown. "You've had stitches in your hand before, haven't you?"

"Yes. And about everywhere else." *Stop telling him about you.*

Jeff glanced at her quickly, then turned back to sanitizing the space. Collin gazed out the window at the lake. Looked like the kids were having a good time. Mr. Lawler's swim trunks stood out even from here. Yep. No one could say, "I didn't see you." Maybe it had been the plan all along. Good plan, too.

Jeff waved Collin out of the exam room back to the waiting area. "I'm sorry I can't give you anything for pain. That's Doc's prerogative."

Collin shook her head. "I don't need it."

Jeff eyed her. "Superwoman?"

"No. But I learned early on how to control pain." She shrugged. "And if I can't, I've got my own secret stash of medications." *Which isn't secret anymore, idiot.*

Is there anything else you want to blab about? Hmm?

Leeann stood up as Collin and Jeff re-entered the room. "All finished? You didn't take long."

Collin smiled. "No, he didn't."

Jeff dashed off a note to the doctor, taped it to the reception window. He opened the exit door and waited as Leeann and Collin went out. Finally, he closed and locked the door behind him.

Leeann looked at her watch. "You'll still have time to catch lunch, you two."

Collin declined. "I need to go speak to Mr. Parks."

"Steve is in town until two o'clock. I'll put you on his schedule if you like."

"Thank you. I appreciate it." Collin bit the inside of her lip. "I should go check up on Rob and my other students." She noted Jeff studying her. "What?"

Leann joined a group of noisy youngsters who headed into the lodge. Collin eyed Jeff. "What's wrong?"

Jeff shrugged. "Nothing. Thought maybe we could have lunch

together, then you could go see Steve."

Collin bristled. "Are you afraid I'll skip out on seeing him? Leave you holding the bag for not reporting the incident?" The more she thought of it, the more her anger burned. "Is that it?"

Jeff did not rise to her challenge. "No. Do what you need to do. I'm inviting you to eat lunch with me. If you don't want to, it's up to you."

Collin eyed him. She wanted to be mad. Wanted an excuse to walk away and not be bothered with him again. His easy-going nature grated against her. *No one is that good. No one. He's hiding something.*

Go to lunch and find out.

Don't. Too dangerous. Go check on Rob. You're supposed to be working. You never work hard enough. Never near hard enough.

Rob is fine. Go. Eat.

Collin smiled. "Forgive me. I would enjoy having lunch. With you." *Investigation only. Nothing else.*

Jeff's eyes brightened. "Great. Chef Michael fixes a fantastic taco soup." The two walked the rest of the way to the lodge, through the doors and around bustling campers in bathing suits, campers in exercise gear, campers with exercise gear...busy place.

Collin noted the faces were all smiling or as close to it as stoic teens get. Had the camp begun working its magic? She hoped. Maybe there would be a change—and a chance.

Jeff led the way through the emerging crowd to the dining room. He looked at the clock and nodded once. "Five minutes to spare."

Collin looked at the serving line, still fully stocked, still steaming or still cold as needed. She shook her head. "This is so different. Five minutes to closing, they should be shutting things down, limiting the choices, putting stuff away. Why is this all still out here?"

Jeff shrugged. "Why should people who arrive at the end of service be treated different than those in the beginning?"

Collin picked up a tray. "They shouldn't. But that's not what usually happens."

Jeff smiled at the server. "Marie. How's the new puppy?"

The woman laughed. "Chewing everything. The pup has more

teeth than Tom's chainsaw. Sharper, too. What will you have?"

Jeff made his selections, Collin made hers, and the two went to a table near the windows. They both sat, and before Collin could bow her head, Jeff reached out and took her hand. "You mind if I say the blessing?"

Yes.

No.

Collin ducked her head. "Please." She listened as Jeff prayed, then added her "amen" to his. They started eating, and Collin began her questioning again. "It must cost a fortune to run this place. But I've never seen it advertised, and I don't see ads all over the windows and doors from sponsors. How do you stay in business?"

Jeff chewed on his answer, literally. "We have private donors who believe in the mission and the kids."

"Like who? I mean, that kind of philanthropic work is usually flashed around, or noted on a plaque somewhere. I don't see any."

"You won't. All of the donors here are private. They don't want publicity."

Collin moved the vegetables around her plate, so it looked like she'd eaten some. "Have they ever been here? Actually seen the place?"

Jeff smiled. "They're here a lot. They stay in the background, though. This really is all about the kids, Collin. If you're looking for ulterior motives, there are none. We are who we say we are."

He's lying. They always want something.

There's a catch here somewhere. You know there is.

Believe him.

Collin chewed on a bite of carrot. "I love how you talk about this camp as if you're a part of it, not a hired hand."

Jeff's eyes twinkled. "I couldn't love it more if I owned it." He looked around the room, then lowered his voice. "What are you going to do about the knife?"

Collin felt her body tense and knew her face reflected the same. "I don't know whose knife it is. I could find out, probably, without too much effort. The culprit should be shipped home, postage-due, to learn there are severe consequences to stupidity. Everyone else's baggage gets searched to teach the kids guilt by association is still a real element in life. Then—"

Jeff interrupted. "What are you going to do?"

She studied the floor. "I'm going to pitch the thing in the deepest part of your river out there." *You can't even look at the river. How are you going to throw anything in it? You're a fraud. A liar. A fake. A—*

"Or I'll ask someone else to pitch it for me. Then I'll wait and see if we need to deal with anything else this week. Everyone signed a paper saying they brought no contraband." She grimaced. "I wanted to believe them."

She looked at Jeff. "I still want to believe them. I'll pass the word among the counselors to keep their eyes open." She eyed the maintenance man sideways. "What would you do? If you were the counselor? How do you think the director will rule?"

Jeff sat back in his chair and pushed his tray away. "I've been trying to figure that out. If we send the culprit home, what does he learn?"

"He gets punished for getting caught. Just like home."

"But if we let him finish the week out…let him participate and go through the process— maybe, maybe he learns a different way. Grace is what we're about." He looked at Collin.

Those expressive eyes… Collin held them as long as she could, then dropped hers.

He continued, "That's what I would do. Me, myself, and I. But I'm not the director. It's up to him to make the final decision. He will want to do what's best for everyone. Including the culprit. Trust him."

Jeff looked at his watch. "I've got to get back on duty." He smiled at Collin, and his eyes twinkled with mischief. "You still haven't explained about the kangaroos. Maybe dinner tonight?"

He's moving too fast. Collin chewed her lip. "I can't. I've got to spend some time with my kids. Maybe another night?"

Jeff nodded. "Sounds like a plan. Have a good afternoon, Collin. It's been…interesting. You're a unique woman."

Collin stared at him a minute, unsure how to take the compliment. "Thank you." She stood. Jeff gathered both trays and bussed them to the counter. He waved as he left, disappearing into the kitchen.

Stay away from him. He's dangerous.

I thought we wanted information from him.

Keep your guard up. Always.

Trust me.

Collin let the internal voices fight it out while she headed to her room to change out of her blood-spattered shirt and jeans. Not the way to make a good impression. The halls stood empty, evidence the kids were enjoying the great outdoors. Good. It's why they came. Show them there is life beyond the streets.

Collin switched into her best "casual professional" attire she'd brought.

Looks the same as your play attire. Sloppy. Nothing professional about it. One glance at you and the director will kick you out.

Trust me.

The door to Steve Parks' office stood open, and Collin could see the director sitting at a desk mulling over some papers. She straightened her shirt, tapped on the door. Steve looked up. "Come in."

Collin-in-charge walked into the office. "Mr. Parks, I'm Collin Walker, one of the counselors." She paused. "I need to speak to you, but if now isn't a good time, I can come back later."

Steve stood. "No, no. Come in. Glad to have you." He smiled, escorted her to a chair, then sat down opposite of her. "How can I help you?"

Collin settled herself for the battle. "I want to speak to you about an incident this morning in which a camper dropped a…knife."

Steve looked grave. "Yes, I heard rumors to that effect. I refuse to act on rumors, Miss Walker. I prefer to wait until I hear all the facts."

Collin breathed out. "The facts are a knife, a switchblade, dropped during a scuffle between four campers after the morning tram tour. I don't know which camper it belonged to, and I didn't pursue the matter of ownership at the time."

"You saw it happen." Steve nodded to Collin.

"Yes, sir, I did."

"Please dispense with the 'sir.' It makes me think you're talking to my father."

Collin pushed ahead. "I decided to deal with the matter my way, much as I would at home. I know these kids. I know their motives and their fears. I believe I handled the situation correctly."

The demons screamed, *Liar! Fake! Fraud!*

Collin mitigated her statement. "Most of it, anyhow." She held up her bandaged hand. "Except this part."

Steve studied her a moment. "What about 'that part'? A significant part of the rumors I heard revolved around 'that.'"

Collin held her head high. "The streets have their legends and myths, Mr. Parks. One of those is if you expose a blade, you cannot sheathe it again without drawing blood, even if it has to be your own. I wanted to demonstrate because of their hatred, someone's innocent blood would spill."

She held Steve Park's gaze. "I wanted to give them something to think about." Collin lost the fire. "My intentions were good. My execution stunk."

Steve considered Collin's words. "You would have handled this the same way back home? Not turned the knife in or tried to find out who owned it?"

"I would have done the same. I'm trying to turn these kids around, not condemn them. Any angle I can use, I will." Collin wanted to shift in her chair but didn't. Shifting meant nervousness. Nervousness meant you were lying. "Mr. Parks, I am willing to be sent home instead of whoever brought the knife. I'll take his place. What happens to me doesn't matter. But I want these kids to have this chance." She lifted her head. "If someone has to go, let it be me."

Steve Parks cocked his head and eyed her sideways. "You'd go in their place?"

Collin nodded. "In a heartbeat."

"I see." Steve lowered his eyes and seemed to think for a moment. He looked up and asked, "You don't believe there's any further risk or danger to anyone else at the camp?"

"No, I don't."

Steve thought some more. "I'd like to take some time to pray about this. Will it offend you if I ask you to pray with me?"

Collin smiled. "You will not offend me."

"Good." The director bowed his head. "Lord God, nothing in my experience covers a situation like this." Steve paused. "Miss Walker believes she handled it correctly. Lord, we're here for one purpose: to reach these children with the truth. Show me what You want me to do. In Jesus's Name, amen."

Collin echoed softly, "Amen." She looked at the director. "Thank you."

"You're welcome. I expect I'll have an answer for you by this evening."

"That's fair. That's more than fair. I appreciate your understanding."

Director Parks stood and extended his hand. "Thank you for coming, Miss Walker. It took courage to come in like this. I hope the rest of your stay is more uneventful." His eyes sparkled.

Collin let the tension melt. "Me, too." She shook his hand, turned, and exited the office at a dignified pace. Then fairly ran down the halls back to her room. She dashed inside, closed the door, leaned against it, and sank to the floor. "Thank You, Lord."

He'll throw you out. He will. Watch. He doesn't care. No one cares.

Trust me.

Collin listened to the voices argue. She knew her father's voice well. But did she know her Father's? "I want to, Lord. I want to tell you apart. It's hard. Help me."

A light tapping on the door sounded. A young female camper called, "Ms. Walker, some of the guys want to see your pictures. I don't know what they're talking about, but they say you'll know."

Collin struggled to her feet. "I'll be there in a minute." Collin dug a small photo album out of her backpack. Once again, she thanked the Lord for the opportunity to attend that particular sports camp. And that they also provided a lasting memory in the photos. It cost her dearly in pain and sweat. But the experience had proven invaluable many times over. She grabbed her battered hat and went to the front.

A group of about five young men—Reeshard, Rory, and the tormentors on the tram— waited. Reeshard started the conversation. "There's some of us don't believe you, Ms. Walker. I said you'd have the pictures. Which one of us be talking truth?"

Collin motioned toward a small table in the foyer. "Over here. We'll settle this." The group gathered around the table, and Collin opened the album. The very first picture showed MJ towering over a group of teen girls, his arms surrounding the entire team at once.

Muted awes sounded. Collin pointed to a seventeen-year-old girl standing beside "The Man." "That's me."

Someone noted, "Don't say Walker. Say Winger."

"I know. I changed my name when I turned 18."

"Why?"

"Personal reasons. I haven't changed much. I'm still ugly as a mud fence. Anyone doubt me?"

One or two of the boys looked closely at the pictures then at Collin. Finally, they nodded. "It's you. Still wearing the same stupid hat, too."

"Thank you very much." Collin led them through the album, through the week at camp in North Carolina. From breakfast, practice, drills, lunch, practice, scrimmages, practice, clinics, practice, dinner, practice... Shots of MJ, Wade, Pippin, and other NBA notables permeated the scene. And coaches from Duke, Carolina, NC State, Kentucky. They were all there.

Rory looked at her with new respect. "Dag, woman. You met 'em all."

Collin smiled. "Not all, but a bunch. The most important thing they taught us: respect. Respect for ourselves, respect for our teammates, and respect for our opponents. Cop an attitude and you ride the pine. Best week of my life, up 'til then." She looked around at her audience. "I learned a lot. You want to play the game? Respect. Treat people the way you want to be treated. Got it?"

The boys looked around at each other, then dropped their eyes. Rory kicked at an imaginary hill of dirt. One of the younger boys looked down, then looked at the others, then looked at Collin. "Who you talkin' 'bout out there? Who died for us? Alex figured you talking about somebody back before we was born."

Collin held the boy's eyes. "Even before me, Trace. Long before me. Jesus."

Trace nodded. "Sorta what I figured, but no one believed me."

Alex objected. "But he ain't real. He jus' some story in a book Gramma keep on her shelf."

"Wrong, dude. Way wrong. He lived, He died, and He's alive now. And He paid in blood—His blood—for all the bad things ever done."

Collin stretched for a means of explaining. "What I did on the bus was first off, stupid. But God can use stupid, too, which is a good thing, 'cause it's what I have to offer most. But God's law is like the knife."

She held the gaze of each boy in turn. "Street law says when a blade's open blood has to be shed to make it right or else bad things happen."

The boys nodded. Rory said, "Yeah. Older guys told us. Guys who been on the street a long time."

Collin shifted her feet. Rory rocked back and forth on his heels. Trace's head went down. "When you break God's law, it doesn't cost a little blood. Someone gets the death penalty."

Alex muttered, "Vicious."

"So is breaking God's law. Murder and rape and drugs and fights and hate and lying and stealing all come from breaking God's law."

Collin watched the boys to see if anyone followed her explanation. The silence made it hard to interpret. She pushed ahead. "God knew if He enforced the death penalty on everyone who deserved it, there'd be no one left. He selected His son Jesus to die, to take the penalty for everyone who ever broke the law, born then or not."

No one spoke. "Of course, not many believed Jesus when He told them the Truth about God's law. They beat Him, spit on Him, whipped Him, and nailed Him to a tree. They even stuck a spear in His side to make sure He died."

Did they hear? "Jesus died so you wouldn't have to. Because He loved you."

Timmons, one of the fourteen-year-olds, yawned aloud. "I been hearin' all this at home. Ain't no real count in it. May mean somethin' to some but don't mean nothin' to me. I'm going to the game room. Anyone comin'?"

Reluctantly, almost embarrassed, the boys stood to leave. Collin saw a look on Reeshard's face mirrored in Trace and Alex. Their eyes darted back and forth from Timmons to Collin to Timmons to Collin. Trace dropped his head and mumbled, "Thanks, Ms. Walker. Maybe we can talk more later. You be around tonight?"

"Yeah. Ring the room or have one of the girls get me. I'll be around all week, too, you know." The boys smiled, then hustled to catch up with Timmons.

Collin took her book of memories back to her room and tucked it safely in her backpack. She debated stretching out on her bed for a quick nap. Ten minutes tops. Well, fifteen, maybe. Her hand would feel better, her head would feel better...

My head? When did it start pounding? Can't be a migraine. Tension. Has to be tension. Best remedy is sleep.

This trip isn't about you feeling good. It's for Rob. Remember him? A good counselor would check on him. But not you. You're not a good anything.

The voices were right. She'd come for Rob. Collin snagged one of the campers and asked him to check Rob's room to see if he could find him. Nope. Game room? Gym? Collin debated. On a hunch, she went to the gym.

Pay dirt. Four lanky figures—okay, three lanky and one short figure—battled in mortal combat on the pine. Collin watched for several minutes but couldn't tell who the teammates might be. It looked more like a free-for-all than an actual competition. Every man for himself and no one keeping score. When you brought the ball down the court, the score stayed the same: all tied at nothing.

Collin waited until the ball careened out of bounds. She called "Time!" and gave the referee's "T" hand signal.

The boys looked over at her. Rob broke into a wide smile. "Hey, caseworker lady! What you been doing all day, huh? Get your shoes on and come learn how the game is really played."

Collin laughed. "Not right now. Come here so I can talk without shouting."

Rob left the ball and came over. He looked at the bandage on her hand. "Guess they wasn't lying, huh. You cut bad?"

Collin shrugged it off. "No. What's the word?"

"You ain't playing with a full deck. I told 'em I knowed that long time ago. Didn't need to go slicing on your hand to prove it."

Collin felt her heart sink. *Marvelous. Great example. You're worthless.* "I see."

Rob dropped his voice lower. "Got 'em askin' questions, though. Asking who this Someone be you talking about, why He be dying for them, and stuff."

"What'd you tell them?"

"Told 'em go ask you."

"You think they will?"

Rob shrugged. "Don't know."

Collin let out a deep breath. "Well, if anyone wants to ask, I'll be in my room. Guys can ring, girls can knock. Hour doesn't matter, you know. I'll be up. Or awake, anyhow."

Rob motioned toward her hand. "Guess our match gotta wait, huh?"

"At least 'til Monday night."

"Ain't using pain as no excuse, now."

Collin stared at him, dead even. "Have I ever used pain as an excuse?"

"Used everything else. Still ain't beat me."

"Swagger on, my man. Your day is coming. You go on and practice with your friends there. You're gonna need all the help you can get."

Rob chuckled. "I hear the wind blowing. Later, caseworker lady."

"Later, Rob."

Collin made her way back to her room, closed the door, and sank gratefully on the bed. Her first full day at camp, and what had she accomplished?

Made a fool of yourself in front of the campers.

Got yourself in danger of being sent home. Real stroke of genius. You'll have to go a long way to top that one. Smooth. Real smooth.

Heard my voice and trusted two godly men.

Collin bowed her head. "I'm trying, Lord. I am."

Try harder.

* * *

Collin spent the afternoon reading and relishing the time to herself, with no one demanding anything from her. Quiet. Peace. She could get used to this. Maybe. Sometime. For a while, anyhow.

Three hours into her serenity, a knock hit her door. "Enter."

Leeann Baker, the director's assistant, stuck her head in the door. "Miss Walker? Steve would like to speak to you. Can you come to the office now?"

Collin drew in a deep breath, smiled, and got up from the bed. "Certainly." She resisted the urge to throttle the decision out of

Leeann and instead accompanied the assistant down the hall.

Leeann motioned to Collin's hand. "Does it hurt much?"

"No. Jeff did a good job of sewing it up. It's fine."

"Such a shame to be hurt on your first day. I promise this camp is safe. We take every precaution to keep our campers from getting injured."

Except banning stupidity.

Collin nodded. "I know. Sometimes things happen we don't plan." She slashed the demons into silence.

Leeann led the way into Steve's office. "I'm happy you ran into Jeffrey, though. He's an amazing person. I don't know how this camp would run without him."

Collin raised an eyebrow. "Oh?"

Leeann beamed. "Oh, Jeffrey backs up everyone here." She chuckled. "Except Chef Michael."

"Is cooking the only thing he can't do?" Collin kept as much of the sarcasm out of her voice as possible.

Leeann's eyes sparkled. "Like I said, he can't find a wife." She leaned forward and lowered her voice. "We're trying to find a match for the Prince of the Valley. It's almost a cottage industry around here."

Collin swallowed the giggle. "Prince of the Valley?"

"Oh, don't tell anyone what I said. It's what mothers with eligible daughters call him. Behind his back, of course. Jeffrey would be terribly embarrassed if he knew."

Collin felt a sense of pity for the man. Having been on the receiving end of such well-meaning friends, she could empathize.

Steve Parks rose from behind his desk as Collin entered. His eyes smiled. The corners of his mouth followed as he motioned to the chair opposite the desk. "Please, Miss Walker, have a seat."

I prefer to meet my fate on my feet.

"Thank you, Director." Collin sat and waited.

Steve Parks leaned against his desk, his arms crossed over his chest. "Rather than tell you how long and hard I've spent in prayer about this, I'll say we have agreed with your assessment. The boy, or boys, can stay."

Collin felt a surge of gratitude rush through her. Relief and gratitude.

The director continued. "As to your offer to go home yourself, well, not possible. We need your experience and expertise with these children." Steve's face became somber.

Collin lowered her head. "You've probably overestimated my expertise, Mr. Parks."

"But not your devotion. What you did for these boys—poor execution aside—is what this camp is about, Miss Walker. Grace. I hope you enjoy the rest of your stay."

Collin rose calmly. She reached out and shook his hand. "Thank you, Mr. Parks. I appreciate your decision." Her voice cracked. "Very much. Thank you."

It might be bad form to leave the director's office skipping and clapping, but Collin did it. One skip. One clap. And a whole lot of silent *Thank Yous.*

A new notice hung on the lodge door. Collin read it, and the emotional high she felt disappeared into a hollow of unknowns. The notice stated an all-camper meeting would begin at two p.m. Sunday at the pavilion with a list of the classes available. Collin felt a lurch in her gut but tried to ignore it. One challenge at a time. First, victory.

And then the agony of utter defeat. Get ready.

SUNDAY

Collin took Sunday morning to rest, eat breakfast, attend the chapel service, walk the perimeter of the camp, spend time with Jill and Marites, and do anything she could to not think about the classes. Fear whispered around the edges of her mind. What ifs and maybes crept along the edges of reason. Nameless probabilities darted in and out of her awareness. Collin tried exercising in the gym, but it didn't help. By one o'clock, she gave up. She showered, dressed, and headed to the pavilion.

Her watch said one-thirty when she arrived. The list of classes stared at her, daring her to read them. Collin scanned the list looking for something she might want to do. More to the point, what would Rob do? Basketball sessions might be a possibility but Collin's gut told her Rob would pass. He could play all the hoops he wanted to at home.

Some of the extreme sports, now, might interest him. Downhill rollerblading, maybe. Or street luge. *Not street luge, please.* Collin continued to read: horseback riding, canoeing, white water rafting, wilderness survival training, cooking, fishing, tree climbing, tree identification *(look, Dad, it's a tree!),* animal observation, avian tagging...the list seemed endless. Collin wondered how all this would tie to the real world. How could wilderness survival apply to living on the streets of Oakton? Climbing trees? Fishing? She frowned.

"Negative thinking on a Sunday afternoon? It's not allowed up here. It's in our constitution." Jeff smiled as he approached the pavilion, broom and dustpan in hand. His eyes twinkled.

Collin rolled her eyes. "Why am I not surprised you're here?

53

You turn up everywhere."

Jeff shrugged. "That's me all over, I guess. And the meeting doesn't start until two." He eyed Collin. "But I expect you know that. You're one of those people who'd rather be half an hour early than five minutes late to a movie."

Collin tossed her head. "If you miss the first five minutes, you might never understand what's happening."

"Classic type A personality." Jeff began sweeping down the seats.

Collin watched him a moment. "Can I give you a hand?"

"Nope. Already got two. And you don't have one to spare."

Collin grimaced. "Wise guy. Can I help you?"

"Why?"

"Because I'm standing here doing nothing and—"

"—and someone paid good money so you could have the privilege of doing nothing this week. This is my job."

"But I don't like doing nothing when someone else is working."

"Live with it. It might do you some good." Jeff seemed to enjoy her discomfort.

Collin looked at the board and the list, then began inscribing circles in the dust with her foot. "Can you talk while you work, or is it *verboten*?"

"If you mean does the employee handbook allow it, the answer's yes. If you mean can I walk and chew gum? That's questionable, but I'm usually up for a challenge."

Collin ignored the latter. "If you could choose one of these courses, which would you take?"

Jeff looked up, his brows raised, his eyes questioning. "Are you going to take one of the classes? Go with your kids?"

Collin shrugged. "I think so. It depends on what Rob chooses, I guess."

"What won't you do?" Jeff leaned his broom against the side of the notice board.

Collin stopped drawing circles. *Bad habit. Shows fear.* She straightened her spine. "I asked you first."

"Oh, yeah. I forgot. Let's see. What would I do? Probably hang gliding. I haven't tried it yet, but I've always dreamed of soaring with eagles."

"Why don't you?" Collin shifted her weight from foot to foot. *Stop! You're about to panic. Stand still.*

"Time. There's not enough time to do it during the day, and they won't let me go at night. Something about a lack of thermals and falling like a rock. I don't understand it. What about you? What scares you enough to want to challenge it?"

Collin chewed the inside of her cheek. "I don't know for sure." *Liar.* "It depends on Rob. We're not joined at the hip, but we do challenge each other to push harder. Whatever he takes, I'll probably tag along."

Jeff's eyebrows rose. "You don't 'tag along' on any of these classes. You're either in or out."

"Oh, I intend to be in all right. It's not a problem." Collin waited for Jeff to ask her about the conversation with Steve Parks. He'd want to know, right? They always want to know. *Why hasn't he?*

Ask him.

No. Why remind him? Let it go.

Campers and counselors began to arrive. Jeff smiled at Collin, gathered his tools, and left. The crowd gathered around the notice. Approvals sounded like "yeah," "oooh," "way cool, man," and the ultimate, "dude." The crowd jostled and elbowed and shuffled around so all could see.

Collin searched for Rob and noticed him standing a little off by himself. She studied him a minute, confused by his lack of enthusiasm. "Hey, my man. What's shaking?"

Rob's eyes remained firmly fixed on the ground, a scowl across his face. "Nothing."

"Got your game face on or what? Today's the day, little brother." Collin grabbed his shoulder and pushed it.

Rob scowled deeper. "What day? What they gonna let a kid like me do? I ain't hardly tall enough to ride the coasters at the Point. And they gonna let me steer a boat?"

Ted Johnson, the activities director, approached. He caught Rob's eyes with a firm look. "You don't steer a boat. You pilot one. And there are no weight or height restrictions at this camp."

Rob looked at him with suspicion. "They ain't?"

"No, there aren't. If you want to take canoeing, you take canoeing. But let's share this information with everyone, shall we?" He walked to the center of the pavilion, raised his voice to get the crowd's attention. "If you will all take a seat, I have a few things to cover before you start the selection process."

The teens and teen wannabes shuffled around for prime territory to listen. Mr. Johnson looked around at everyone present. "No long speeches. The choices are on the board. Choose whatever you want to try but understand this: every field there will require hard work, sweat, and extreme concentration. Even cooking." Someone snickered.

"Don't laugh. This isn't cooking for one or friends. This is banquet cooking, serving between 250 - 500 people every day. As a means of community service, we supply meals for shut-ins, homeless shelters, battered women and children shelters, the local community hospital, and the like. They deserve nothing but the best."

Mr. Johnson paused. "And we promise to deliver our best. So the pressure is on all the time, every day." He looked around. "But we want you to have fun along the way. Otherwise, we're using you for free labor, and that is not our prime directive." One or two of the campers nudged each other.

The man smiled. "So pick something which looks fun, looks challenging, looks like something you've never tried before and may never try again. There are no size restrictions other than Mr. Lawler here. I'd have a hard time finding a horse tall enough for him." The kids laughed; Mr. Lawler towered over the director. The counselor doffed his hat and waved it.

Voices buzzed with imagined possibilities. Ted continued, "But a word of caution: these classes are consecutive. What you learn on day one you will use the next day. There is no room for changing your mind."

Collin noted a few exchanges of uncertain looks.

"Once a class has started, you can drop out, but you can't join another class. Those who don't last can still enjoy the run of the camp—swim, hike, fish, whatever. Anyone who doesn't want to attend a class may sit out as well."

Mr. Johnson's voice took on a serious tone. "You've all been cleared to participate in anything we offer. We've got the waivers, we've got the permission slips, and we've got your guardians' signatures. Someone selected you to come because they knew you had the right stuff to make it through. Someone believed in you. Believe in yourself as well.

"One last promise. One person in class or fifty, it doesn't matter. No one gets shut out. If you already know what you want to do, hike up to the barn and register. Being first on the list gets you no special privileges."

He waved an arm at the expanse. "If you want to wander around and examine the equipment, the animals, the teachers—and yes, I'll be available to point out which is which—or the site locations, go ahead. You have until dinner to make your choice. Have fun." The director walked off, leaving the crowd to dissipate on its own.

Kids and counselors alike drifted back to the bulletin board to study the list with new respect. Collin watched Rob's face for any hint of what he might be thinking. He stared at the board. His eyes drifted off down the canyon. A chill ran up Collin's spine. "What are you going to pick, Rob?"

Rob looked at her. "You coming with me?"

Collin hesitated. "Depends on what you pick. I know my limitations, Rob. I'm not a kid like you. There are some things I can't do."

"You gonna let me say that?"

"Not until you try."

"You saying you tried all this stuff?"

"Not all of it."

"What?"

Collin's frustration increased with her fear. "Rob, pick something you want to do, man. Don't worry about me. I'll come or I won't. Don't base your life on what I do or don't do."

"I ain't." Rob seemed hesitant to continue. "But you're kind of fun to have around when you ain't being annoying or stupid."

Collin laughed. "I'm never stupid. Annoying, I'll buy."

Rob rolled his eyes. "Caseworker lady, you something else." He looked back down the canyon. "I want to ride it, caseworker lady. I want to ride the river."

Collin nodded, her stomach roiling. She kept her voice under control. "I think it's a good choice for you. You'll do well."

Rob looked at her. "You coming along?"

"I can't, Rob."

"Why not?"

Collin shuddered, her heart threatening to hammer its way out of her chest. "I promise you one day I will explain it. But I need you to trust me. I can't." She looked at him, her eyes begging his understanding.

Rob studied her a minute. "I'll hold you to that, caseworker lady. I'll let it slide this time, but you better have a good excuse."

"I do." She'd make one up if she needed to. Collin managed to quiet the shaking in her hands and gut. "So, you want to look at the equipment?"

"Naw, I want to know what you gonna choose."

Collin shrugged. "I thought about cooking"—Rob grabbed his throat and began making choking sounds. Collin continued, shoving him lightly—"but considering how I cook at home, I figured I wouldn't poison anyone while I'm here."

"Good plan. So what, then?"

"Thought about wilderness survival."

"Why?" Rob crossed his arms over his chest.

"Help me survive all the snakes and weasels I work with."

Rob gave her a disgusted look. "You ain't real, you know? You ain't for real."

Collin grinned. "Yeah, but you gotta love me." She rumpled his hair then shoved him. "Go on to the shelter and get signed up so you'll know where to go. I'll be along shortly." Rob grinned and headed to the hill toward the sign-up list.

Collin walked back to the bulletin board to stare at the list again. Most of the campers drifted off either debating their choices or hustling to register in case the director lied about everyone being allowed in the classes. Before long, Collin stood alone, staring at the board.

It wouldn't go away. Rationalize it all she could, it still wouldn't go away. But she couldn't do it. She couldn't.

What did Jeff ask? "What scares you enough to want to try it?" And Rob wanted to know her excuse. They didn't understand. They couldn't. She whispered, "But You do, don't You? You know what it's about."

The Voice inside intoned, *It's about trust. Do you trust Me?*

Collin felt the blood drain from her face and her knees grow weak. She sat down on a nearby bench. "Why? I'm perfectly happy not going near rivers. I can live my entire life in Your service and never have to come within miles of a river. Please don't ask." Collin looked up at the cathedral sky above her. "Please, please don't ask."

And the Voice didn't. The question repeated, *Do you trust Me?*

Collin gritted her teeth. She felt like a four-year-old about to have a tantrum but didn't care. "It's not fair, Lord. It's not why we're here. We came for Rob, remember? He's the one You're supposed to be working on." Silence. "I don't want to go on the river, Lord." More silence. "I can't go on the river."

Scripture echoed in her mind: *I am with you. When you go through the river, it won't sweep over you.* Collin ground her teeth in anger. "That's a cheap shot." Her defiance faded as quickly as it came. She slumped against the bench, defeated. "Father, please don't ask. Please."

She sat in silence for several minutes, unable to choose or move. The bulletin board remained impassive. The world became still, waiting for an answer.

There could be only one, and Collin knew it. He knew it, too. Defeated, she said brokenly, "You know I'll go. I do trust You. But can You take away the fear? Or the nightmares?"

No answer came. She got up, dusted herself off, and headed for the barn to sign up. Her feet felt like lead as she moved, unwilling to hurry the inevitable.

As she rounded a turn, she practically ran into Jeff, standing quietly in the path. Collin wondered how long he'd been standing there and how much he heard. Collin refused to meet his eyes, determined to brush past him.

His voice gentle, he called to her. "Collin..." She refused to face him. "I didn't intend to listen, and I'm not prying. I know a private conversation when I hear one. I want you to know if there is anything at all I can do to help, I will." He laid a hand on her shoulder; she turned at last. He smiled sadly. "I can't change His mind, though. I've tried enough times, but it doesn't work. I think you know that, too."

Collin ducked her head slightly. She looked into his eyes, filled with compassion. Her walls began to crumble as she whispered, "But I can't do it. Why can't He leave things alone?"

"Because He won't leave you alone, either." Jeff faced her

dead on. "Collin, I have no idea what you and God are fighting about. I don't need to know unless you want to tell me. But I do know He loves you. Everything He does is out of love for you."

Collin couldn't hide the sarcasm born of fear. "And what seminary have you been to?"

"The University of Life, milady." Jeff swept his arm around in a grand circle. "Everywhere, everything. It's all from living. I've been where you are, Collin. You've been where you are before. What happened the last time God challenged you? You got through it, right?"

Collin could feel her frustration rise as she listened to him talk. Yes, she knew what he meant. But this…this… God could bring her through everything else, but this...

Her mind snapped back into focus. What made facing the river any harder for God than any other experience she'd gone through with Him? He either loved her or He didn't. She either trusted Him or she didn't. Had He ever given her a reason to doubt His faithfulness?

Laughter swelled in Collin, and she let it out. Jeff's eyes sparkled. On impulse, Collin reached out and hugged him. Equally as fast, she let him go and straightened. "I'm sorry. Ignore the hug. I better get signed up or all this will be meaningless. Thanks, Jeff." She turned and hustled up the hill to the barn.

Jeff stood alone, watching her go. "No problem. No problem at all."

* * *

Rob caught up with Collin in the dining hall after dinner. Collin could see he'd given up the "I don't care" persona as he dashed across the room yelling, "Hey, caseworker lady! Where you been all afternoon?"

Collin shoved her plate of mostly uneaten meatloaf across the table. The first bites tasted wonderful. But the knots in her gut posted "No Admittance" notices on her stomach.

Rob bounced on the toes of his feet. "I looked everywhere for you. And I looked at all the lists. Your name ain't on none of them I saw. You gonna wimp out on me?" He smiled wide, but his eyes held a tinge of pain and disappointment.

Collin stared him down. "No, I am not going to wimp out on you. You didn't look at the right list."

"I looked at all the indoor stuff; made sure you not tryin' cooking." Collin sneered at him; Rob ignored her. "I looked at the hoops list figuring maybe you might finally want to learn the game." Collin narrowed an eye. The stern look seemed to encourage Rob. "You didn't sign up for horse stuff, either. I thought you might want to, seeing as how you sure can't drive them horses you got at home."

Collin arched her eyebrows. "If you are referring to my car and my driving abilities, I know very well how to handle them. And I did sign up."

Ted Johnson, activities director, called the campers to order. Collin motioned for Rob to sit beside her. He pulled up a chair, curiosity in his eyes. Collin lifted her chin to the director.

When it got quiet, Ted began, "I'm very, very pleased with the choices you've made today. I believe we have the broadest selection of interests I've ever seen. Which means some of you are going to get one-on-one attention in your chosen activity."

Ted looked at specific youngsters. "Others of you will benefit from additional staff help as we fill the requirements for the class."

Ted stopped. "Let me explain. If the activity you wanted requires multiple participants and not enough people signed up, you will still get to learn the activity. But it will be with the help of the staff and any local students we can recruit. I promised no one would get closed out of a class, and I meant it."

The campers cheered. Downcast faces began to glow again. Collin wondered briefly if maybe her class could be under-filled, and they would have several professionals with them. It didn't hurt to hope, did it? Or to ask? She sent up a silent prayer.

Ted looked around the room at the counselors. "I'm pleased to see some of you adults getting in the spirit of the camp." He looked pointedly at Collin and two male counselors. "I wish more of you signed up, however. Perhaps we can count on you to participate in other ways. Say, as taste testers. Or tackling dummies."

The teens roared with laughter and pointed to various counselors as candidates. Ted motioned for quiet. Collin continued her prayer. *Please, please, please.* Her jaw clenched, as did the rest of her body.

The director looked at his clipboard, then looked up with a

satisfied smile. "The most we have in any class is seven. And it's one of the tougher classes we offer."

Collin grimaced. Her prayer's answer? *No.* No getting off easy, it seemed. *Fine. Have it Your way.*

"All classes begin tomorrow at eight a.m. sharp. Your instructors will designate the meeting place; look for it on the board after eight p.m. tonight. On the mountain, down in the valley, or under the river, it's where you will meet the rest of the week."

Collin shuddered. She forced her body to relax. *Relax. We can do this. We can. He promised He's with me.*

Didn't promise to save you from drowning, did He? No guarantees. Some Savior.

Collin forced the door on the memories closed, battling the ghosts of ages past from slipping out around the edges. For every two she captured, another tried to escape. Only after she secured them all did her mind return to the cafeteria.

Ted finished up saying, "That's all I have. Meet your teammates where I told you and have a great time. Remember, you can."

Collin looked around, confused. She'd missed the directions. She looked at Rob, who studied her, concern on his face. "What?"

"Where you been? You kept zoning out, lady. What you thinking about?"

Collin shrugged. "What comes next, I guess. What are you supposed to be doing?"

"Meeting the team by the back doors, so we know who they is. Supposed to help us with 'bonding' or some such stuff." Rob looked at her sideways. "You got any idea what you supposed to be doing?"

"I do now." She stood up, took a deep breath. "Let's go. Let's do it."

Rob jumped up. "Go where? What did you sign up for?"

"White water, what else? You think I'm going to let you have all the fun and glory?"

"But you said—"

Collin cut him off. "I know what I said. But things change. I changed my mind, okay? I found a mind and changed it for my old one. It has a better warranty: thirty minutes or thirty questions, whichever comes first. So don't use them all up at once."

As they hustled to the back door, Rob said, "You ain't real, caseworker lady. You know? You ain't for real."

"That's what you keep telling me."

The team consisted of six campers and Collin. Three males and three females, ranging in age from twelve to fourteen. Collin recognized the brother-sister twins Niles and Nyla Pierson, who could be a gang by themselves. They honed their tough-guy attitudes—and their actions—to a fine art. Collin often saw the results of their handiwork on the bodies of her kids. Frankly speaking, Niles and Nyla were not nice people. But since they had come, someone thought them capable of change. *Or wanted a break from dealing with them.*

Harsh, isn't it? They're kids. They have souls.

Do they?

Along for the fun and excitement: Chonnell Rice and Lynn Pardner. The epitome of giggly preteens, Collin could not imagine why they would sign up for this class. Hopefully, the girls possessed more inside than Collin thought. The prospect of being on the river terrified Collin. Going out with the two of them as crewmates? Uh...no.

The final male besides Rob proved to be Ta'waan Gartson, a tall, gangly thirteen-year-old who Collin would have sworn to be at least sixteen. He'd polished his hoodlum image to a high luster and wanted everyone to know it.

What a crew. Collin felt her heart sinking even as the group talked together. *With this, we're going to challenge the river?*

I hope the instructor knows his stuff.

And we get lucky.

The meeting broke up just after nine with an agreement they would all meet for breakfast at seven, sharp. The kids moved off, trying to act as if tomorrow would be nothing special. Collin hung around the porch until the team left then walked over to the seats on the patio. The benches were placed for maximum viewing of the sunset.

Collin didn't have the heart to look. She curled up in a tight ball, pulled her knees into her chest, dropped her head down to her knees, and let out a very long, slow, shaky breath. *I can't do this. I can't. Thinking about the river gives me nightmares. What's going to happen when we get out there?*

Bet you can't even get in the boat.

The Lord thinks I can. My part is to obey. Okay? I'm obeying. It doesn't make it easy. I'm scared. I admit it.

You got no faith. You got nothing but talk.

First time you freak out, how do you explain it to Rob? What does your faith do for you then, huh?

Collin groaned inside. Outside, too, though she hadn't intended it. A warm hand touched her shoulder, and the getting-to-be-familiar voice asked, "Are you okay, Collin?"

Collin lifted her head. "Go away. No one sees me like this."

Jeff sat down on the bench across from her. "Like what? Curled up like a beach ball? Which you know, if you get stuck, it would take eight surgeons working twenty-four hours straight at least ten days to fix?"

Why could she not stay angry with the man? Collin uncurled enough to sit up straight but kept her arms wrapped around her knees. "What are you doing out here? Aren't you ever off duty?"

Jeff shrugged. "Technically, I'm on call twenty-four hours. We had a little plumbing problem over in the men's wing, and I fixed it. Took a little longer than I anticipated, but I got it finished. I was on my way out, saw this rather contorted figure, and thought I'd investigate." He smiled, and his eyes looked gentle. "What am I investigating? Is this some form of meditation? A new prayer position?"

Collin looked away. "It's the Collin Walker method of telling the world to go away and leave me alone."

"Does it work?"

She looked at him dead even. "Is the river still there?"

Jeff looked out to be sure. "Uh-huh."

She stretched out a little more. "Well, I can keep hoping."

Jeff lay his hand on her arm. "You don't have to go on the river, you know. I'm afraid of fire, but I don't go running through every burning building so I can conquer it."

Collin tossed her head. "You're a fireman. You should be afraid of fire."

"And for some reason, you're afraid of the river. Maybe you have a good reason." Jeff lowered his head to keep his eyes level with hers.

"I do." She barely whispered the words.

Collin's eyes met Jeff's. "But the Lord seems to want me out there. I don't know why, and yes, I've prayed and asked Him."

Collin struggled to keep the cynicism out of her voice. "He's a little short on 'why' answers right now. Asked me if I trust Him. What kind of question is that?"

Jeff chuckled softly. "He's never big on 'why' answers. But I hear, 'Because I love you,' a lot." The man paused and shrugged his shoulders. "Of course sometimes I get, 'Because I said so.' My dad learned it from God. Dad's a master of the phrase."

Collin shuddered involuntarily. Jeff tilted his head to look at her better. "Are you cold?"

Collin nodded. "Yes."

She left it hanging. She breathed out. "I suppose I should get back to my room and try to get some sleep. The crew wants to sit together for breakfast and storm the classroom early. They want to see if they can keep the book time to a minimum and the river time to the max."

"Which will suit Mitch fine. He'd much rather be on the water, anyhow." Jeff gave Collin a somewhat enigmatic look. "I hope you have a good time tomorrow. I'm serious. Mitch can be…a lot of fun, they tell me."

A thought nudged her. "Did you play hoops in school?"

Jeff cocked his head. "Yeah, I played some in college. Why?"

"Ever ref a one-on-one game? No time outs, no time limits, first one to 100 wins?"

Jeff whistled low. "I suppose I could hold my own. Why?"

"Rob and I are competing. I promised to beat him while we're here. We're on for tomorrow night if Doctor Wallace releases me to play. We need a ref."

"Is Rob any good?"

"He's got talent."

"Are you any good?"

Collin scowled. "I hold my own. I haven't beaten him yet, but I'm getting there."

"By choice?" Jeff raised an eyebrow.

Collin lifted her chin. "Trust me. Rob doesn't need my help to win. I always play him hard and fair." She stretched out her knees and bent at the waist to unkink her spine.

"You want me to ref. So you have rules?" Jeff sat back on the bench.

"Mostly inbounds kind of things. I'm trying to reinforce the 'within the lines' mentality."

"I thought the psychological rage is thinking and playing 'outside the lines.'"

"Maybe it is in some circles. But to survive in the real world, you've got to know there are lines in the first place. You have to know the limits before you challenge them."

Jeff nodded his approval. "Good thought."

Collin acted surprised. "You mean, I had one? Someone mark that down!"

Jeff grinned. Collin sobered up. "Can you come and ref?" She stopped. "Will you come is a better question. Unless you've already got plans." *Why did I ask him to come?*

Jeff smiled. "No plans. And I could use the exercise." He studied Collin a moment. "I can see where you would be a formidable opponent."

Collin deliberately ignored the comment. "We're competitive. We haven't drawn blood yet, but it's not for lack of trying. I promised him I would beat him one of these days. But beat him clean. And it has to be clean, Jeff. No tipping the scales one way or the other."

"Absolutely. I wouldn't do it any other way. How is Rob going to feel about having a third-party observer?"

"We've used refs before. Rob knows a win by anything other than pure ability, or dumb luck, isn't a win. If you gotta cheat you ain't a winner. We both want to win. But we want to do it right."

"What time and where?"

"Nine o'clock, on the backcourt."

"We don't have a backcourt."

Collin sighed, then measured her words. "Is there a court with lights?"

"Yes."

"Which one?"

"Court number two."

"We'll meet there. Understood?"

"Understood, yes, Captain."

Collin grimaced and stood. Jeff also rose. Collin said, "I'm going to my room now. You can carry on doing whatever it is you were doing before I interrupted you, and I'm sure I will see you in the morning."

Jeff saluted. "Thank you, Captain. Have a pleasant evening. Goodnight, sir." Jeff dropped the military bearing. "Sleep peaceful, Collin."

"Thanks, I will." Collin walked back to her room.

MONDAY

But while sleep she did, peaceful would not be the word to describe it. Harrowed, maybe. Nightmarish. But not peaceful. She flew. She fell. She drowned. Faces peered at her through the water. Some lifted her up. Some held her under. She felt fear, terror, panic, but overall, an incredible disbelief coupled with sorrow.

Collin tossed, groaned, and moaned through the night, unable to break the cycle. She drifted from dream state to dream state, always on the edge of consciousness but never allowed to cross the line. The five a.m. alarm became her salvation.

Collin sat, feeling battered and beaten, more exhausted than when she went to bed. The initial spasms of a monster headache reared its ugly face. Collin groaned. *Not now. Not today. Please. A little help and a lot of relief, please.* Collin prayed softly, "I'm doing this for You, You know. Please, help me. And be with me."

I am with you always. And I am doing this for you, you know. Because I love you.

The answer provided some comfort. Enough to get her out of bed, anyhow. She dressed slowly, wishing to forgo the breakfast ordeal altogether. She couldn't eat if she wanted to.

Suck it up, woman. Quit being a cry baby, quit feeling sorry for yourself. You'd think you are the only one out there who has problems!

Straighten up. You are Collin, the giant killer. Kill it and be done with it. Now move!

Collin accepted her marching orders, combed her hands through her hair, and strode purposefully out the door. *Time to finish this thing. Slay the beast and destroy the dragon. Reclaim my sanity…*

Well, the last one may be a stretch too far.

Collin cleared the mental musings and entered the cafeteria. She arrived about fifteen minutes early but knew the coffee would be ready half an hour before breakfast for those who like to slide into the day rather than greet it full force.

They think of everything here. Collin smiled with gratitude. She needed to find the owner and thank him. Or her. Or them. Collin poured a cup of coffee from the urn, then went to the window bench and sat. She stared into the depths of the mug. Her smile faded as the challenge ahead jeered at her. Where did the court jester go when she needed him? Being around Jeff…there was something different about the man. It brought back feelings she hadn't felt since—

The mental protective walls crashed down hard.

Don't. Don't go there. Not today, not ever. Over. Done. Leave it.

Collin turned to face the door, so she would see her crew coming. It would be a long day.

"I think I know what your problem is. You have too much time alone. You spend all your time thinking, and it leaves you miserable."

Collin's shoulders dropped, and she faced Jeff. "Why are you everywhere I am? Are you stalking me, Mr. Farrell?"

Jeff carried his toolbox in one hand and a cup of coffee in the other. He set the toolbox down. "Nope. I worked on one of the microwaves and saw you out here. You smiled at first. Then you looked sad. You think too much."

"And you don't? Sit down."

Jeff grinned as he pulled up a chair. "No. That's what everyone tells me. 'Boy, you don't think at all.' Usually, they're right."

Collin frowned. She hesitated. "Have you ever thought about taking white water rafting? You have so many hobbies. You want to add one more?"

Jeff's eyes became gentle, matching his tone. "You don't need me out there, Collin. You have the Lord."

Collin drew in a deep breath. She lifted her chin. "I will make it through. Done it before. Can do it now. Right." She smiled at Jeff. "See? All better."

Jeff lowered his. "Not like that, Collin. Not alone. No matter how strong you are."

Collin touched his hand. "I know, Jeff. I do. I appreciate the reminder. Now, are we still on for tonight? Backcourt, nine p.m.?

Jeff's eyes twinkled. "We don't have a backcourt. But I'll see you there." He gulped the remainder of his coffee, stood, and smiled. "I'm sure I'll see you around today." His face clouded. "Unless you honestly don't want me to."

Collin could hear the voices screaming inside. She lifted her chin. "I do want to see you, Jeff. You're a good man. And…" Why couldn't she finish the statement? Collin forced her mouth to form the words, to break through years of silence. She looked down. "I like you, Jeff."

There. She said it. The words were out, the barriers scaled.

Jeff touched her shoulder. "I like you too, Collin Walker. I care about—"

"Don't." It came out hard, fast, and bitter. "Not yet. You don't know me."

The door banged open. A crowd of campers came pouring into the cafeteria, Rob among them. He yelled and waved. "Hey, caseworker lady! You did get out of bed!"

Jeff patted her shoulder. "Have a good day, Collin. I'll see you tonight." He hesitated. His face lost its smile. "If things change during…well, after your class, I'll understand."

Jeff shrugged. His usual confidence seemed to have disappeared. "You'll know. It's been fun talking to you. If you still want me to ref, and only ref, it's fine, too. I mean it. Have a good day."

The man grabbed his toolbox and dashed out of the cafeteria. Collin stared at his fleeing back. *What was that all about?*

Worst brush-off ever. And you hear them all the time.

Collin cocked her head, puzzled. Before she could think more about it, she became inundated with crew members with voracious appetites. Pancakes, sausage, French toast, donuts, cereal, eggs, toast, bagels…all on Ta'waan's plate alone. The others' trays looked overloaded as well. The exception was Pardner, who ate light. She limited herself to only one of everything. Collin looked around. "You guys eat like this before going to the Point?" The Point was a well-known amusement park—with an infamous reputation for its killer coasters.

Rob stuffed a forkful of pancake in his mouth. "Don't get this kind of stuff at home, caseworker lady. Gotta eat it while we can." Nods and muffled, "Mmphs" voiced agreement.

Collin nodded. "I understand. I agree. But you don't have to try to eat it all in one morning. There's going to be some sick puppies out there if we hit the water."

"Naw!" "No way!" "Never happen," cries of protest met her statement.

Collin held up a hand in warning. "I hope you're right. I have a feeling barf bags are not standard equipment. Think about it."

Nyla sneered. "That why you ain't eating? Too scared?"

Collin looked the girl dead in the eyes. "Too smart. I know my limitations. Can you say the same?"

Nyla laughed harshly. "I ain't got none. Ain't that what they teaching us? I can do anything I set my mind to."

"Set your mind and train your body, Nyla. Don't forget the last part. It takes time to train a body to obey your will."

She should know. It took her years to learn how not to cry. To control her emotions. To ignore pain. To suppress the even simplest reaction to physical abuse.

Rob motioned to the others. "Caseworker lady be cool. She be knowing what it's like. She say chill out on the feast, maybe we should chill out."

Collin smiled slightly. "You're probably safe today. I don't think we'll be hitting the river first thing. But keep it in mind."

From the rude gestures which followed, Collin gathered Niles, Nyla, and Ta'waan disagreed with her. Pardner and Chonnell seemed less sure, torn between the image of the three and the sense of the one. So they did what most girls their age would do: they compromised. They only ate about half of what they had on their plates. More than they should have eaten, but less than they could have.

So call it a half a victory. I'll take it.

The crowd finished, bussed their trays, and headed for the docks to meet their instructor. Towering trees shaded the area, leaving only stabs of sunlight here and there. Water slapped against the moorings, a reminder of the power and proximity of Collin's nemesis. *You're gonna freak out. You can't do this.*

I will do this. Now shut up.

They found the instructor sitting on a stump seat, kicking his heels in the sunshine. He smiled as the six campers and Collin approached him. His eyes seemed to linger on Collin's bandaged hand. Would the injury disqualify her? *You wish.*

Mitch Kellum might be thirty, maybe younger. Tan, well-muscled, and yes, what you would call drop-dead gorgeous. Collin smiled back to let him know she was alive.

The guide motioned toward the ground. "Sit. You will come to appreciate the feel of solid ground under you before this week is over."

He waited until the group arranged themselves on the ground in front of him. "My name is Mitch. I will be your teacher." He stopped. "Teacher is a misnomer. I will be your guide. The river will do the teaching. I'm here to show you how to get to know her."

His eyes played over the assembled group. He made each one stand and tell him their names. Finally, he looked at Collin. "Who are you, and why are you here?"

Collin returned his gaze. His intensity made her uncomfortable. "Collin Walker. And I'm here to learn white water rafting."

"What did you do to your hand?"

Collin tried to shrug it off. "Had an accident with a knife and cut it."

Niles chortled. "Ain't what I heard." Nyla matched her brother's derision.

Collin caught the eyes of the brother-sister twins but spoke to Niles. "You've been talking to Macon, haven't you? He likes to tell stories."

Both Niles and Nyla froze. Collin's use of the "Macon stories" would warn them off in ways none of the Southside gangs would dare contradict. Niles backpedaled. "Uh, yeah. Maybe it just a story. Don't mean nothing."

Mitch didn't miss the interplay between Collin and Niles. "No, go on, Niles. Even if it's a story, it must be a good one."

Rob stepped in. "He heard the same one I did. Caseworker lady playing some stupid game called Mumble logs or something—"

Collin offered, "—Mumbly Peg."

"Yeah, whatever. She don't got sense enough not to play some knife-throwing game. Trying to impress someone, right, caseworker lady?"

"I was not trying to impress anyone. But that's about as close to the truth as we're going to get here."

Mitch's eyes narrowed as he studied Niles, Nyla, Rob, and Collin. He motioned to the hand. "Let me see the cut."

"There's no need. I got stitches, and it's fine. It won't be a problem, I promise you."

Mitch's eyes narrowed further. "Let me see the hand. I'm the one who will decide whether you're fit to be on this crew or not." He held out his hand, waiting for Collin, daring her to refuse.

Collin stared back at the teacher. After a moment's consideration, she held out the injured hand and let Mitch unwrap the bandage and look at the wound. The man's eyes widened as he noted the length of the cut. Collin endured the examination as long as she thought necessary, then pulled her hand away. "See? Healing nicely. Not a problem. Satisfied?"

Mitch seemed to come back to himself. "Yes, I suppose I am." He looked at her and smiled. "Just making sure. Everyone has to pull their weight, you know."

"I can pull my own, thank you."

Mitch nodded. "Good. Good."

He motioned for the class to stand. "Hmm. This could be a problem." The height variance again. Rob stood out as the shortest of the males. Collin could read the pain in the boy's face as he prepared to be singled out once again.

But Mitch proved better. "No problem with who has the helm: has to be you, my man." He slapped a hand on Rob's shoulder, and the boy looked at him in surprise. Mitch nodded. "Yeah, you. You look strong enough. What's your name? Do you know what the helm does?"

"Rob. And he steers the boat."

"I'll buy that. You will stand in the back and take instructions from the lookout upfront. Are you good at following instructions?"

Rob glanced at Collin. "Yeah, I am."

Mitch saw Rob's look at Collin. "What is she to you, helmsman?"

"She's my caseworker. She's the one brought me up here."

Mitch stared at Collin a moment. He looked back to Rob. "Do

you want her here with you? You don't have to, you know. Those are the rules of the game."

Say no. Please, please, please say no. Please.

Rob hesitated. "Naw, she can stay. She's pretty cool for an old white lady." He grinned at her.

Collin formed her hands into a circle a little smaller than the size of a fourteen-year-old's neck. Rob got the picture in record time. "But she's cool, you know? Crazy, vicious, but cool."

Collin relaxed her fingers and smiled. She wished she could loosen the knot in her gut as quickly. "I didn't take the class to supervise Rob. He's a free agent up here, and he answers for himself. This trip, we're independent individuals. And I will say he's living up to the independent part quite nicely."

Mitch nodded. "Okay by me. I wanted to make sure we all know what's coming down." He turned his attention to the remainder of the crew, issuing them their assignments. "Niles, you will paddle with Ta'waan in the front of the raft. Nyla, you and Collin will partner in the middle, and Chonnell and Pardner will row in the stern position."

Which prompted the first revolt of the day. Nyla slapped her hands on her hips and sneered, "I ain't being partner with no white lady." If she spit in Collin's face, she couldn't have made the phrase more insulting.

Rob jumped in immediately between Nyla and Collin. "She ain't no white lady. She cool. She one of the brothers."

Niles threw his head up and hooted. "Eastside brothers! All they got is ladies. Ain't a real man—"

Mitch called, "Enough! This is not a democracy. I said you row together, and you will row together."

Nyla continued to protest. "She ain't near strong enough to pull with me! We be rowing in circles, and I be carrying all her load." The girl jerked her head toward Ta'waan. "You row with him. He more your speed."

Before Ta'waan could join the fray, Mitch scowled so deep all the offended parties quit talking. "There's an easy way to settle this and decide our pairings. A test."

Nyla's eyes filled with concern and doubt. She moved her hands to her sides. "What kinda test?"

"A test of strength, endurance, and focus. Each of you will take a paddle. Hold it in front of you, vertical to the ground."

Mitch demonstrated, grabbing the oar in the center. "If you are right-handed, use your left hand. Left-handed do the opposite. We can see from there who has the kind of strength we need." A twinkle glinted in the man's eye. He looked at Collin. "I'd let you do it right-handed, but I wouldn't want to give you an unfair advantage."

Nyla barked, "She gonna fall out and claim it cuz she injured."

Collin leveled her gaze at Nyla and held the girl's attention. "There will be no excuses, Nyla. Injured or not, it doesn't matter. We're all starting on the same footing."

Mitch ordered, "Everyone spread out." The group moved into a semi-circle. Mitch nodded to the two youngest. "Chonnell, Pardner, you two need to stand on the bench. Otherwise, your paddles are going to touch the ground to start with."

Rob didn't wait to be told but jumped on the bench between them. "I'll stay here and keep an eye on them." He glared fiercely at the two girls who both went into fits of giggles.

Mitch instructed, "We'll stay 'til the last man—or woman— falls. Once your paddle touches the ground, lay it down, and have a seat."

Nyla crowed, "We be here all day. Me an' Niles. We be the last two here."

Ta'waan's voice carried heat. "You want to place a bet?"

Mitch interrupted. "No betting. No mouth. Now's the time to prove yourselves." He looked at his watch. "Ready...now. Paddles up." Obediently, eagerly, and yes, defiantly, seven paddles rose into the air.

Collin expended a small amount of energy watching the way the others gripped their paddles. Niles, Nyla, and Ta'waan all throttled theirs tightly, a sure sign of an early exit. Rob held his with a more gentle grip, reflecting a part of her teachings. Good. He might be learning something.

The two younger girls were harder to see. But from the rock-steady manner in which Pardner's paddle hung, Collin guessed the girl had some training in stamina. Could be a good thing.

Having scouted the competition and finding it as she expected, Collin closed her eyes and retreated to her inner circle. She flew to the island kingdom she and Erin created sixteen—*sixteen?*—years ago. It had been their hideaway, their mental refuge from the twisted reality around them.

Collin made some changes since Erin…since Erin. A separate wing housed all the books she'd read. So much solitude since Erin. She busied herself sweeping the floors, dusting off the shelves, and generally repairing what her neglect damaged.

"Seven minutes."

Collin risked a quick peek to see which competitors remained still in the game. As she guessed, Niles and Ta'waan had fallen down, and Nyla would be going soon. The fierce grimace on her face, the sweat dripping down her cheeks, the rather violent shaking of the paddle… Stick a fork in her. She's done.

As if in reaction to Collin's thought, Nyla slammed the paddle into the ground and let out a grunt of pure frustration and disgust. She stomped over to where her brother parked, flopped down beside him, and sat glaring at Collin.

Collin returned to her castle. *Ocean breezes cooled her. She lifted her head to smell the salt, to hear the gulls screeching, to feel the waves tickling her feet, burying her toes with sand.*

"Ten minutes."

The crack of a paddle hitting the ground brought her back to the river. A second paddle followed. Chonnell and Rob fell out, too, though with far less malice. Which left only Collin and Pardner.

The youngster looked at Collin. Her face shone with sweat, her bangs pasted to her forehead. She grinned. "No gimmies 'cuz I'm youngest."

Collin offered a solemn nod. "No gimmies. You got it." *Must be more to the girl than I thought.*

Without looking at Mitch, Collin retreated to her beach.

"Fifteen minutes."

The sun beat down on Collin's shoulder. Strangely, only on the left shoulder. Maybe she should stretch it out.

"Sixteen."

Collin commanded an ice pack to appear on her sore joint. Ah, yes. That got it.

"Seventeen."

Who was doing all the counting? Go away. You bother me.

"Walker, snap out of it, woman. Game's over. Wake up!"

Collin opened her eyes to see Mitch standing in front of her. His eyes glinted with a satisfaction Collin distrusted. She peered around the riverboat captain and looked over to Pardner.

The girl jumped up and down, beaming. "Seventeen minutes! Longest I ever held anything up like that. You good, ma'am. You real good."

Collin grinned, stepped around Mitch, and crossed over to where Pardner stood on her bench, minus her paddle. Collin slapped hands with the girl and risked a hug. Pardner returned it happily.

Collin pointed to the child. "You are good. Get a little older, get a little muscle on you and there's no one gonna beat you. But you know what? You put your mind to use on something real, something that matters, girlfriend, and there's nothing you won't be able to accomplish."

Pardner ducked her head slightly, probably having heard the same speech before. But this time, it came from an equal. Which might make all the difference. Maybe.

Again, Mitch took control of the class. He drawled, "If there are no further objections, I'm going to assign rowing partners. Strength is not the only criterion you now know."

He smiled sweetly at Nyla, who merely gave him an icy stare in return. Mitch ignored it. Collin hated to think he discounted Nyla's anger. Only a fool dismisses so blatant a warning sign. But the river guide rubbed his hands together. "Since we've settled such a minor disagreement, we can get on with more important business."

As Mitch turned to continue his instructions, Collin grimaced in disgust. She looked over to see a look of equal distaste on Nyla's face.

Nyla turned from glaring at Mitch to glare at Collin. Collin held the girl's eyes in a long, steady gaze, neither mocking nor condescending. After several moments Nyla's gaze lost its fierceness and took on a measure of, if not respect, at least mutual understanding. It might not be peace, but it could be at least a truce. Preferable to war, anytime.

Rob sidled over to where Collin stood. His eyes darted back and forth, almost not meeting hers. Collin guessed the problem. "Thanks for letting me stay, Rob. I appreciate it."

Rob shrugged. "I figured way down inside you wanted to do this. I didn't want to get in your way."

Collin squeezed his shoulder. "Believe me. I won't get in yours. I'm nothing more to you than Chonnell up there is. Crewmates. Mitch is the boss."

Mitch overheard the comment. "The river is the boss. Never forget it. The river is the one entity you must never, ever overlook. She'll talk to you, sing to you, show you beauty beyond your dreams. She may forgive you for your little mistakes. But the one thing she won't forgive is being ignored. Never, never, never take her for granted."

Collin could feel herself pale as Mitch talked. She noticed the puzzled look on his face as if uncertain about her reaction.

Ta'waan challenged, "Man, you talk like it's alive or something. It's water."

"How old are you?"

"Thirteen."

"You want to live to see fourteen?"

Ta'waan stared back defiantly. "Yeah."

"The river is alive. She moves. She breathes. She changes constantly. If you don't respect her, you'll never be able to ride her. She'll spit you out then swallow you in a heartbeat."

If possible, Collin paled even further. She started the slow breathing she'd taught herself years ago. In, out, in, out…

As long as you're breathing, you're living.

Mitch looked around, and Collin caught his eyes lingering on her face again. She forced a smile. Maybe she shouldn't have.

Mitch finished his survey of the class. "How many of you are scared?"

Collin's hand shot first in the air. Chonnell looked at Pardner; the two girls giggled and raised their hands. Rob looked at Niles and Nyla, looked at Ta'waan, looked at Collin. Finally, he must have looked inside. He raised his hand slowly, as well.

Mitch nodded. "Good. Good. I have something to work with, with you four." He turned to the remaining three. "You, though, have a long way to go to be proper river riders. The first thing you learn in any venture is to respect the power and the will of your opponent. Perhaps if we take a walk down to the water, you'll begin to understand." Mitch directed the class down a footpath toward the roaring rapids.

Not all at once. Please, please, not all at once.

Mitch led the class around a curve in the footpath. The river lay open before them. Surging rapids threw foam balls to the trees and rocks lining the banks. Waves mounted three, four, five feet high, and raced by with tremendous speed and power, twisting into convoluted shapes and dimensions.

Collin closed her eyes and backed up against a small fence. Internally she curled into a small, tight ball as if to hide from the monster. Externally, life drained from her as the shadows danced between her and reality.

She could hear Mitch yelling over the thunder of the rapids. She heard him explain the names of the turns. How you navigated it. How many boats lost their crews at which point. She understood the words but could make no sense of them. They washed over her, becoming part of the flood threatening to drown her.

Collin's fingernails dug trenches in her thighs, drawing blood. She felt nothing. She heard nothing but the song of the river. Calling…

Someone took her arm. Someone led her away from the thunder of the river. Collin opened her eyes and acknowledged Mitch as he directed her steps.

A scowl masked his face as he looked at her. "What is that all about?"

Collin drew in a shaky breath. "It's something I need to deal with."

The rest of the class filed past with looks of curiosity, disdain, and outright disgust. Rob's face reflected confused hurt. Mitch directed them back to the shelter. "In the shed is the equipment we'll be using. Find a helmet, a life vest, and a paddle to fit you. I need a word with our counselor here. I'll be right with you." The crew began digging out the equipment, leaving Collin alone with Mitch. His eyes narrowed. "Explain."

"I have a problem with rivers."

Brilliant answer. Got any more?

Mitch's tone became stern. "I'm sorry, but we don't have time for psychotherapy. This is not a carnival ride, counselor. I need people out here I can count on, who won't wig out on me at the first sign of a bubble." He jerked his head toward the crew. "I can't have you endangering the lives of these kids because you're trying to exorcise some personal demons."

Collin matched her tone to his. "I came to learn to raft. It's why I'm here, and the only reason I'm here."

She wondered if telling Mitch God wanted her to be here would get the same response as it did from Jeff. *Wanna make a bet?* "You won't have to worry about me putting anyone's life at risk, including yours. I'll jump overboard long before that happens."

Mitch's eyes softened. "What happened? Some sort of boating accident?"

Collin kept the shudder out of her voice. "Not exactly. Let's leave it there, please?"

He rubbed her arms. "No problem. If I can help, let me know."

Collin hesitated. "There is one thing."

Mitch smiled. His eyes danced. "Name it."

Collin sensed an instinctive urge to shove Mitch across the clearing and away from herself. She stomped it hard. "Rob doesn't know about this. He knows I'm scared, but nothing more. I'd like to keep it that way."

Mitch began massaging her shoulders. "You are terrified, aren't you? You need to relax."

When Collin could handle it no longer, she carefully took Mitch's hands off her shoulders. She smiled. "I'm fine. I think some of the class needs a little help with sizing." She motioned to where Pardner stood in a life vest reaching below her knees.

Mitch laughed. They walked over to join the crew.

* * *

The remainder of the day became an emotional blur for Collin. They marched as a group to lunch and, at Mitch's insistence, sat together. It "reinforced teamwork."

Too much togetherness reinforces disharmony.

Ah, but Mitch knows how to build a crew.

So he says.

Collin saw Jeff sitting by himself, studying through a pile of books. A tiny smile crossed her face. She turned to see Mitch staring at her. "Is there a problem?" she asked.

Mitch arched a brow. "You've met our janitor?"

"Jeff? Yes. Do you know him?"

"Eh. We don't have much in common. I'm more a 'get out, have a good time' guy. This town may not have any real nightlife, but there are a few cozy places. I could show them to you if you're interested." He flashed her his most winsome smile.

Collin shrugged him off. "I appreciate the offer, but I'll pass. This is more of a working vacation for me." She cocked her head. "Isn't there some rule about staff and campers fraternizing?"

Mitch never lost his smile. "We're adults. I think we can handle our own affairs."

All the while Mitch talked, Collin noticed Rob's eyes never left her face. She lifted her chin, stretched her neck, and nodded. Rob dug back into his lunch, making the mountain of sweet potato fries—with cinnamon and sugar—disappear.

As they finished up, Collin looked at the clock. "I've got enough time to run by the infirmary, have the stitches checked, then meet you all back at the dock."

Mitch frowned. "I looked at the stitches this morning. They were fine. You don't need them looked at again unless you felt something pull. Did you?" He caught her hand while he waited for an answer.

Collin tried to retrieve her hand. Mitch held it tight. *You gonna make a scene already?*

She stopped resisting. "No. Nothing has changed. I received instructions to see the doctor on Monday." She smiled. "It's Monday, and I need to see him. I'll be back before you know I'm gone."

Mitch's eyes narrowed. "Who told you to see the Doc? Who put in the stitches?"

Collin could see the interest in the crew's eyes at this discussion. Street kids could sense a confrontation before it happened. She chose her words carefully. "The EMT who stitched me when I cut my hand."

Mitch snorted. "EMT's can't sew people up."

"They can in an emergency or when the distance to the hospital is too great. I refused to go to the hospital, so they stitched me up and told me to see Doc on Monday. Which is what I'm doing. Now. May I have my hand back?"

As Mitch released her hand, Collin heard the collective sigh of the crew. Conflict avoided.

Mitch, however, wasn't going down without a fight. "Doc takes lunch from one to three. His office is closed. He'll be open 'til six, so you can get it checked after class." He smiled at her. "And you won't have to miss a moment of my instruction."

Collin's eyes flared. *You really want to do this now, in front of everyone? You're supposed to be showing the kids a different way, remember? Smile, nod, say thank you, and let it go.* Collin smiled, nodded, and said, "Thank you, Mitch. I'll go after class."

Ego restored, Mitch looked at the crew and waved his arms wide. "That's how you build unity, crew. Let's get back to work. I have so much more to teach you. And you have so much to learn." Collin could see his eyes linger on her a moment longer than necessary. *Wonderful. There goes the week.*

Seven crew members and one instructor returned to the dock, where they learned proper boarding and disembarking procedures. They practiced throwing life ropes. They received instruction on the correct way to grab a drowning victim, how and how not to tow an unconscious person and the required CPR.

The lessons piled up swiftly. Collin grudgingly admitted Mitch did know how to relate to the kids. Or at least keep them moving.

Eventually, five p.m. came. The class adjourned for the day. Mitch gave them one last instruction. "Everyone sit together at dinner. Spend as much time with each other as possible. We'll build this into a great team. You'll see."

Contrary to Mitch's wishes, the crew scattered upon arrival at the lodge. Before everyone got away, Collin grabbed Rob and reminded him, "Nine o'clock, my man. Court two. Come with your crying towel, 'cause you're gonna need it, mister."

"Yeah, yeah. I hear the wind blowing. I'll be there and have you whipped by nine-thirty."

Collin grinned. "Talk is cheap, my man."

Rob waved her off as he headed for his room, laughing. Collin chuckled and headed for the infirmary.

Closed. Hours: eight a.m. to five p.m. After-hour emergencies should call Jeff or 911. Nothing about lunch. Nothing about staying open 'til six. Collin's teeth ground together. *Round one to Mitch.*

He'll pay for this. I promise he will.

Can you wait until the week is over and not ruin everything for the kids? Huh? Can you?

Collin drew in a deep breath, let it out slowly. "I'll wait. But he will pay for this."

She made her way to her sanctuary and sighed as she collapsed on the bed, too tired to move further. *I could stay here all night—*

—if you weren't so stupid as to challenge someone half your age to a young person's game.

I do it for Rob. He learns from the competition. He loves the game and so do I. What's wrong with it?

Collin decided she'd go to the court at eight-thirty, warm up, get the feel of the asphalt, check the resilience of the backboards. She'd use any edge she could find. Preparation meant everything.

Which included renewing her energy levels. Food would be a good idea. Food would be a great idea. She should eat. She should. Eating might take her mind off the throbbing in her head. The headache continued to hang around. Fine. She ignored it.

Collin pulled out her Bible and opened it to Psalms. She needed to refresh her spirit more than her body. Reading would help. Reading always helped.

I'll eat. I will. Later. Now shut up.

At eight-twenty, she rose, dressed for the game, slipped a sweatshirt and jogging pants on over her outfit, took her basketball, and headed for the health bar. She debated whether to go for endurance or the sugar high, settled for two bananas, a granola bar, and a can of juice.

As she walked out the door, an overly familiar voice said, "Now, why did I know you'd skip dinner and come here instead?"

Collin leveled the bananas at him. "Don't move, mister, I've got you covered."

Jeff grinned. "She's playing. Nice switch."

They walked over to one of the picnic tables so Collin could eat. Collin noted Jeff wore a University of North Carolina blue warm-up suit with the number thirty-seven on it. Interesting. She sat down. "I survived my first day."

"Congratulations."

Collin repeated, "I survived, Jeff. We went down to the water, and I survived. I never thought it could happen."

Jeff's tone became gentle. "I'm happy for you, Collin. Does it…"

She looked up at him. "No, it doesn't take care of the problem. It means I survived being near it. Sort of."

"Sort of near or sort of survived?"

"Both. I'd probably still be standing there if Mitch hadn't pulled me away. But I kept breathing."

"How did Mitch get on with the kids?"

Collin shrugged. "No serious problems. He seems to relate well with them. A bit antagonistic. Maybe a bit too much know-it-all, but they know how to handle him. I think the class will do fine." She eyed him. "Why?"

"Curiosity. People react to Mitch in different ways."

"I'm sure they do."

Jeff studied her. Collin ignored his look, lifted her chin slightly and admitted, "I didn't have my stitches examined by the doctor today."

Jeff's scrutiny deepened. "Why?"

How much to tell? Would telling the janitor something about a teacher make any difference? "Bad timing. Missed communication. It didn't happen. But they feel fine."

"Let me see the hand."

Somehow, coming from Jeff, it wasn't an issue. Jeff peeled the bandage back and examined her hand. "You're going to take a beating on your palm playing tonight."

Collin shrugged. "I don't dribble with my palm."

Jeff scowled. "I'm familiar with the dynamics of the game. You could tear them open, you know. I'm not sure—"

Collin thought fast. "Compromise. We'll take a half-time break, and you can look at it again. If it's broken open or looks like it's going to, you call the game, and I'll quit, I promise." The corner of her mouth smiled. "I may never speak to you again if I happen to be winning, but I will quit. Deal?"

Jeff sighed a deep put-upon sigh. "You get one half."

Collin finished her bananas and juice and dumped her trash. "I'm going to the court, now, to warm up. Are you still working, or are you free?"

Jeff bowed deeply. "Madam, I am yours to command." He waited for her to rise. Together they headed to court number two.

The courts sat on a rise apart from the main lodge. Collin looked at the layout as they walked. Trees to the left; trees to the right. A small brook created a divide between the field of the camp and the basketball courts. It looked like a great place for an evening stargazing. *Next trip. This is business.*

Once there, Collin stripped down to shorts and shirt and began to dribble slowly, getting the feel of the ball on her hand. Not bad. A little twinge now and then, but not bad. Jeff looked at her, questioning. Collin shrugged. "It's fine. No problem." She paused. "Warm up with me?"

Jeff shucked his sweatshirt revealing a North Carolina Tarheel's jersey underneath. Collin studied the name and number carefully. Farrell. 37. Why did it spark a memory? She tried to make the connection, but it would not stand and be recognized.

Jeff noticed her scrutiny. "What?"

Collin dismissed for the moment the unformed thought. "Nothing. Trying to remember something." She intoned. "'Old data. Pay it no mind.'"

"Uh-huh." Jeff took the ball from Collin and began up the court at an easy jog. Collin followed him; he passed her the ball, she sent it back. Jeff picked the pace up slightly; Collin matched him. He bounced her the ball; she returned it.

At mid-court, Jeff fired the ball to her and broke for the basket. Collin hit him with a near-perfect strike. He caught it mid-stride, bounced it once, and executed one of the prettiest lay-ups Collin had seen in years. The ball made nary a sound as it slipped through the basket, dropping home for the two. He caught it and waited for Collin to finish her jog down the court.

Collin said with respect, "Nice. Very nice. You've played more than a few hoops in your time, Mr. Maintenance Man."

Jeff tossed her the ball. "Your turn. Let's see what you've got."

Collin shot up the court, taking him by surprise. She crossed the court diagonally, threw the ball to Jeff. He caught it, pirouetted, returned it. Collin did a touch pass; Jeff lobbed it above the rim. Collin leaped, brought the ball down gently, and swooshed it through the basket.

It felt so good to be active again! To be moving and not thinking. She dribbled the ball slowly until Jeff joined her at the end line. "Not bad for an office worker. You've worked the pine some yourself."

Collin shrugged. "Unrealized passion. I can't let it go." She motioned to his jersey. "I used to follow the ACC, especially the Tarheels. Knew all the players, all the stats…"

The bell went off in her brain again, the "I know I know something, but I don't know what it is" bell. She studied Jeff once more, trying to figure it out.

Jeff saw her scrutinizing look. "What? Is my shirt on backward? What is it?"

Collin banged her head as if to clear the cobwebs. "I'm sorry, Jeff. It's one of those fragments of memory which won't connect to anything else."

Jeff rubbed his chin, and his voice became deep and introspective. "I see, I see. Fragmented memory connections. Very interesting. And how long have you experienced this problem, ma'am?"

Collin decided to get into the game. "Since birth, I think. Is it significant?"

"It could be. It could be."

"Is there any hope, Doctor?"

Jeff stroked his chin again. "I don't know yet. We must dig for the answers. Tell me, how do you feel about your father?"

An innocent question and in line with the spirit of their game. But it hit Collin like a brick. She blanched. She looked away quickly, shielding her face from his eyes.

Jeff bailed her out. His tone became gentle. "What a dumb game. And a stupid question. How about another lap around the court?"

Collin regained her composure. Mostly. "I think that's a great idea."

Before they could complete the lap, Rob came running on the court. Collin looked at him sternly and stated the obvious. "You're late. I could have scored ten points by now."

Rob pulled off his sweatshirt. "Yeah, and I'd still beat you."

Collin warned him off. "Don't get cocky, dude. Because you ain't been beat yet don't mean it won't happen."

Collin began dribbling slowly, trying to plan her attack. She studied Rob often as he played on the courts behind the trailers where she lived. Collin developed a feel for the young man's rhythm and style. But could she put it into use?

Information without application is useless.

Time for some real-world application. Collin feinted to her right and quickly reversed field, spun once, and broke toward the basket.

Rob shadowed her, not caught at all by her juking. He knew Collin's opening move in every game they played. Rob could follow her in his sleep. Precisely what she counted on. She took the usual two steps toward the basket as if to hit the lay-up. Rob waited, timing his leap to her motion. But at the last possible second, Collin pulled the ball back in, whirled, reversed direction, and came up behind Rob, lightly kissing the ball off the backboard and into the cylinder. She dropped down, drew her elbow back sharply in exultation. "Yes!"

Rob stared, dumbfounded. "What was that? You ain't never made a move like that before."

Collin grinned evilly. "Yeah, and I never drew first blood before, either. Live with it." She looked over at Jeff standing on the sidelines. He merely shook his head. Collin looked back at Rob. "I warned you I've been practicing. Never take an opponent lightly, my man. He might jump up and bite you."

Rob seemed neither intimidated nor impressed. He dribbled the ball to half-court. "Yeah, yeah. I hear the wind blowing. You talk good. But one shot don't make no game. You get ready, caseworker lady." Rob turned at the midline and blasted back toward the basket. Collin waited, bouncing on the balls of her feet. Rob's typical move would be to spin at the top of the key if his opponent came out to meet him. But if the man—or woman—held back, he would shoot it from there. *If you came out halfway, however…*

…maybe you could alter the trajectory of his shot, causing a misfire.

Better still, fake…

Stop. Too much thinking, not enough acting. Collin stepped forward to intercept. Rob dribbled twice and started to slide around her to the right. Collin refused to take the bait. She stood her ground as he rotated back to his left.

Rob hadn't anticipated her countermove and left the ball dangerously exposed. Collin slapped the ball away. They raced after it. Rob got there first but couldn't press the advantage with Collin all over him, refusing to let him advance. The young man realized his proximity to the out-of-bounds line. He saw Jeff silently waiting to make any call necessary. In near desperation, Rob slammed the ball at Collin's foot, hoping for a rebound.

The ploy worked, and the ball careened off her shoe out-of-bounds. Jeff blew the whistle. Collin glared at him. "It never touched me!"

Rob ran after the ball. Jeff warned, "Arguing with the ref will get you thrown out, you know." He looked down at the whistle. "I've always wanted one of these. I've had enough of them blown at me."

Collin continued to argue. "It never touched me. It didn't."

"Would you like a little cheese with your whine?"

She glared. "Cute. Real cute. Who invited you to this party?"

Jeff thought a moment. "I believe it was you. Something about fair play and learning where the lines are."

Collin grumbled. "Yeah, yeah, yeah. Throw the ball in." But she smiled and his eyes shone back.

Rob returned with the ball. He accepted the throw-in from Jeff and brought the ball up the court with deliberate steps. Collin shut the brain down and began to let her training, instincts, and most recent practices control the motion of her body. For every action, an equal and opposite reaction. For every reaction properly executed: two points scored or a defensive victory won. Spin, block, shoot, run...

An hour flew by. The lights dimmed. Jeff blew his whistle. "Half-time; take a break. I've got to reset the timers."

As he jogged to the far end of the court, Collin and Rob took the opportunity to double over and try to breathe. They both puffed hard, harder than they should be. Between gasps for air, Collin declared, "Tie score, my man. Mark it down in history."

Rob waved her off. "I hear you. Ain't worried."

Jeff made his way back. "Don't you two think you might want to call it a night?"

Aghast, Collin asked, "Quit, now? When the score is tied? Are you crazy? I'm not about to let this man off the hook."

Defiance marked Rob's reply as well. "No way, man. Have her telling everybody how she tied me to end a game? Ain't happening, dude."

Jeff frowned. "Let me see the hand."

Collin hesitated only a millisecond then extended the left hand. "It doesn't hurt at all, Doc. It doesn't."

Jeff muttered, "You're so high you couldn't feel it if it did."

Collin laughed. "Come on, Jeff. We're having fun. Just for a little while longer. Until I beat him." Rob snorted. Collin rephrased her supplication. "Until one of us wins or one more hour, I promise. Please? No pain, no gain, you know."

Jeff re-bandaged the hand. "I believe the correct rendering is 'no pain, no brain.'"

Collin stuck her tongue out and instantly regretted it. Well, almost instantly. And somewhat regretted it. *You are so far over the line. What do you think you're doing?*

Having a good time. For once. Now shut up.

Collin took a long look at Rob to see how he was doing. Ah, youth. He looked fine. Winded, but okay. "You good to go, my man? I mean it seriously. Because I'm acting the fool doesn't mean you have to."

Jeff added, "Amen."

Collin glared at him but asked Rob again, "You want to call it a night?"

Rob snorted. "I ain't tired. And no old white lady gonna tie me in hoops."

Jeff cautioned, "One last warning. Do you know what altitude means?"

Collin laughed. "Yeah, it's how high above the rim my man Rob gets when he's trying to block one of my shots. Now give me the ball." She held out her hand.

Jeff gave her a deep, penetrating look. One she would need to learn to interpret. But tonight, tonight she would prove old caseworkers could still compete.

Back at it.

Another hour went with no clear winner. Spin, block, shoot, run…argue with the ref… run, run, run.

Collin regretted the "no time out" rule more than ever before. Her lungs burned from lack of oxygen for reasons she couldn't fathom. She noted Rob fared no better. The young man leaned over, clutching the bottom of his shorts, waiting for Collin to bring the ball inbounds. Exhaustion poured from him as Collin knew it did from herself as well.

Only Jeff seemed untouched by all the exertion, though he ran up and down the court all night with them. *Superman in the flesh, maybe?*

Collin stepped inbounds, dribbling the ball. Rob stood halfway between the midcourt line and the top of the key, panting. Collin picked up her dribble. "I can't breathe. Let's finish this tomorrow."

To Collin's everlasting relief, Rob gave no argument. "Right, lady. I'm there with you." He looked at Jeff. "Okay, ref, what's the score?"

Jeff looked surprised. "You didn't tell me I needed to keep score. I thought you two kept it yourself."

Collin groaned. "Don't tell me we've done all this for nothing!"

Rob joined the protest. "An' I be beating you good, caseworker lady."

Collin's eyes narrowed. "You were not! The score is tied, or maybe I'm a few points ahead of you."

"You ahead? In your dreams, caseworker!"

Side-by-side, in simultaneous strides, the two combatants stepped off the court. The three collected their belongings and walked back toward the lodge.

Collin decided to pull Jeff into the debate. "Well, I would have been if the ref did his job instead of watching the cheerleaders."

Jeff said haughtily, "I call them like I see them."

Rob sniped, "Yeah, you couldn't see them for nothing."

Jeff entered the play. "May I inform you, I am held in the greatest regard by many of my peers."

"Oh, really?" Collin gave Jeff a sidelong look.

Jeff nodded. "Quite correct. I've been told there has never been another referee quite like me. I've been assured after God made me, He destroyed the mold."

Rob looked from Jeff to Collin. "You two related? You both weird."

Collin chuckled. "Aw, Rob, you know you love me."

Rob threw up both hands as if to ward off evil and ran off screaming. Collin looked at Jeff in innocence. "Did I say something to upset him?"

Jeff shrugged. "Kids. Who knows these days?" He slowed his pace considerably. Collin noticed and appreciated the change.

Jeff seemed hesitant, as if wanting to say something but not finding the right words. Collin waited patiently. At length, Jeff said, "You're good, you know? At hoops, I mean." He added the last almost as an afterthought.

Collin shrugged. "Thanks. I used to love the game. I wanted to go to Duke and play for Coach K. so bad I ached."

"Why didn't you?"

"I'm not a guy. Technicality, maybe, but it kept me on the sidelines."

Jeff nodded. "I see. Why didn't you play women's ball?"

Collin looked shocked and offended. "Play hoops with a bunch of females? Are you out of your mind? Only guys play real hoops. Girls only pretend."

"Where did this bit of intellectual garbage come from?"

Collin dropped the outrage. "Here and there. It doesn't matter. I missed the chance to do something I dreamed about..."

Collin stopped and studied him intently. "Why am I boring you with all of this? Why are you so confounded easy to talk to anyhow?"

Jeff shrugged. "I don't know. I guess I'm non-threatening." He gave her a sad puppy dog look. "Would you ever feel threatened by this face?"

Collin shuddered. "Yes! It's you innocent types who get me in trouble."

Jeff straightened. "You mean, you've been with others?"

"No, I mean, I've met others. And I refuse to say anything else." They reached the door of the lodge, but neither made as if to go in. Collin leaned against the wall and took a deep breath. "It hurts."

"It's supposed to hurt to let you know when you've pushed too far."

Collin shook her head. "But I've played with Rob a dozen times for a lot longer than this."

Jeff looked at her, frustration in his voice. "Collin, look around you. Where are you?"

Collin did the perfunctory round-the-world glance. "At Camp Grace."

"Which is in the middle of the mountains, right?"

Unsure what direction Jeff intended with this, Collin nodded.

"Uh-huh."

"Try and stay with me here. You live in Oakton, elevation between minus ten and a hundred feet, depending on where you're standing. This is Camp Grace, elevation 4000 feet at the bottom of the canyon."

Collin began to see the light. "Ahhhh."

"'Ahhh' is right. Thin air, lack of oxygen, lungs burn..."

Collin finished the sentence for him, "...brain cells go dead. I'm sorry, Jeff. You tried to tell me earlier, and I ignored you. How could I be so stupid?"

Jeff dipped his head. "Practice, maybe?" Collin scowled but said nothing. Jeff let her off the hook. "It's easy to get caught up with things here. And you looked like you were enjoying yourself."

Collin continued to frown but at herself. "Maybe too much. I forgot what I'm here for."

"A chance to unwind, right? That's what this is all about for you. The camp will take care of Rob. It's what we're here for."

Collin couldn't help herself. She half-smiled. "How come you're so smart?"

"It's a mystery. A great mystery."

Collin stretched and groaned. "The mystery will be if I can get out of bed in the morning. Getting up to face the river is not enough incentive, believe me."

Jeff hesitated. "How about breakfast with a friend?"

Collin studied him a moment.

Don't do it. Don't get involved.

He's not your type.

No one's your type. You deserve no one.

Collin ducked her head. "I'd like that. I'd like it very much."

"So would I. Is six too early? I can get us a special dispensation to get in then. I have to be at work at seven."

Collin loosened up her shoulder muscles. "You're not making this easy, you know." She looked into his eyes. "Nothing good comes easy, right?"

Jeff shrugged. "I don't know. Sleeping comes easy."

Is he reversing his field? Changing his mind?

Not after asking you. Say, "Six it is" and go with it.

"Six it is. I'll see you then." Jeff held the door for her, and she added softly, "Goodnight, Jeff. Thanks for putting up with me."

The man smiled. A genuine, honest smile. "Goodnight, Collin." The door closed as he walked away.

TUESDAY

Collin's alarm went off at five. She rose, showered, dressed, and went to the cafeteria, arriving early, maybe ten minutes to six or so. She wanted to assess the situation first. See who all got this "special dispensation" Jeff claimed to be able to arrange. As she rounded the last corner, she saw Jeff standing in the hallway leaning against the wall looking at his watch. He had an ornery grin on his face as she walked up. "Yep. Early."

She grimaced. "Would you rather I came 'fashionably late' to everything? Though I never could figure why being late is fashionable."

Jeff shrugged. "No clue. But I find your enthusiasm for punishment delightful." He pushed off the wall. "The cook has consented to fix short-order breakfast for us. I'm the apple of her eye, as she has three daughters of marriageable age."

He stage whispered, "None of whom I'd consider if they were the last females on earth, but I haven't got the heart to tell her." Jeff led Collin down the corridor and into the dining hall. "Besides which, she knows I'm the only one who can keep her beloved coffee urn going. It's at least fifty years old, and you can't find parts for it anymore, but she insists it's the only one which will make decent coffee."

"If you can't find parts, how do you keep it going?"

"Charm and good looks." Collin scowled and Jeff grinned. "When it fails me, as it most often does, I resort to salvage, spit and glue, and magic. Since she still offers me breakfast, it must be working. You drank the coffee yesterday, right? I know you didn't have anything else other than the banana."

Collin picked up a tray and silverware from the line and slid it down the rails. "Two bananas."

"Oh, excuse me, two bananas."

Collin eyed him. "Are you spying on me, Mr. Farrell?"

"Nope. Keeping an eye on a friend." He looked at her, slight confusion in his eyes. "I can say friend, can't I?"

Collin paused. "That's why I'm here, right? Breakfast with a friend."

"I didn't want to be presumptuous. Forward. Pushy. Overbearing." He looked at her for help. "Stop me anytime. I'm running out of synonyms, and my thesaurus won't fit in my pocket."

Collin gave him an approving nod. "I like a man with an expanded vocabulary. It's a refreshing change from those whose entire linguistic repertoire is 'yo.'"

The cook smiled at Jeff. "Jeffrey! You didn't tell me your friend is a female friend. I'd have put out the good linen."

Collin noticed a little color appear in Jeff's cheeks. A good sign he didn't do this often. Jeff said, "Mom O'Brien, this is Collin Walker, one of the counselors for the week. An exceedingly dedicated counselor. To a fault, even." Collin glared at him, but Jeff ignored her. He continued, "She bleeds for these kids. She's so—"

Collin dropped her tray on the rails for effect, extended her hand. "Hi. I'm Collin Walker. He's an idiot if you didn't know."

Mom O'Brien laughed. "Oh, I've known that for years. Our camp idiot. But we love our Jeffrey. Nice to meet you, Ms. Walker. I don't think I've seen you here before."

Jeff sniped, "Good eye, Mom."

Collin glared at Jeff. "I've been in the dining room several times. But with the fresh air and change in altitude"—she glared at Jeff, daring him to say anything. The man merely whistled softly and looked over and up and around the room. Collin looked back to the cook— "I haven't had much of an appetite. Everything always looks and smells delightful."

Ms. O'Brien beamed. "It's a team effort. Chef Michael plans the meals, and I fix them. But this morning, you get to choose your poison."

Collin paused. "I'll have whatever Jeff has but less of it. A lot

96

less of it. A whole lot less of it."

Cook laughed. "She knows you, Jeffrey. She's seen you eat."

Jeff sniffed. "I'm a growing boy."

Cook snorted. "Growing fat on my good cooking."

"And you know you do it so well, Mom."

"Enough with the charm. What do you want to eat?"

Jeff ordered wheat toast and eggs, fruit, juice, and coffee. Collin added a glass of milk to her order. It took only a few minutes before they received their food and went to sit down.

Collin noticed two or three other camp workers in the room. The cafeteria must open for the early shift. Nice touch. Depending on what it cost, of course.

As they sat down, Collin asked, "I know this can't be part of the regular camp service. It has to cost extra. Who do I pay for it?"

"Don't worry about it. It's covered."

"No, Jeff. I'll pay for my breakfast. You shouldn't—"

Jeff repeated evenly, "Collin, it's covered. We don't charge extra for early morning meals. No employee pays for the meals they eat. They can eat anywhere they like, of course, but meals here are free. Even to the campers, meals are free. I can't see inviting someone to visit, putting them off someplace without transportation, and then charging them for food. You wouldn't do it to a guest at home; we won't do it to our guests here."

Collin gave him a half-smile. "I love the way you say 'we' and 'our.' You feel like you're part of this camp, don't you?"

Jeff grinned. "I couldn't love it more if owned it."

"It shows. The owner must be exceptional to get such loyalty."

Jeff looked off to the side. "Oh, I don't know if I'd call him exceptional. People do, I know, but I have a harder time with it."

"Why? What do you know everyone else doesn't?" Collin pushed. Maybe she'd found the chink in the armor.

Jeff looked down at his food. "I've known him longer." He looked up at Collin. "May I pray for our food?"

Impelled by some force outside her own, Collin reached out and took Jeff's hand. "Thank you. Please."

Jeff bowed his head. "Lord, watch over Collin today. The river scares her. You telling her to go out on it scares her even more. Hold her close. Keep her safe. In Jesus's Name, amen."

Collin looked down at the table. "Thank you." Jeff said

nothing. Collin looked up.

The man's eyes studied her, but with gentleness. After a moment, he dropped his gaze and attacked his breakfast.

Collin cleared her throat. "What is it you have to do which requires such an early start?"

"Our dairyman's wife suffered emergency surgery yesterday, so I'm filling in as the milk machine."

"Are you everyone's back up here?"

"Only in a pinch. There's a 'real' man starting this afternoon. I'm only covering the morning shift."

"They expect too much out of you, I think."

"No more than I'm willing to give. I could always say no."

"Have you?"

"On occasion." Jeff stuffed a forkful of sausage into his mouth. He chewed around it. "I do know my limits, Collin. And the Lord has creative ways of reminding me if I forget."

Collin threw in a heartfelt, "So I've experienced." She hesitated. "How'd you come to know the Lord if that's not too personal a question?" *Too personal. And immaterial. Stick to the interrogations. Everything should be about the owner. All this is useless. Who cares?*

I care.

Jeff smiled slightly. "It should never be too personal to ask. My parents raised me in the Lord. I got carried to church from the time I was a week old. All the nursery rhymes I remember were Bible verses. Mom didn't sing lullabies; she sang hymns and praise choruses. I accepted him as Savior when I turned five."

Jeff scooped up some of the eggs from his plate. "I rebelled in my early twenties. Got far enough away from God to know it wasn't where I wanted to be. Made Him Lord of my life then. I've been walking with him—or as close to it as I can—ever since."

Jeff shrugged slightly. "Not very dramatic, I'm afraid. But it's a path I hope my children take someday. Except the rebellious part. I'd love to see my kids go straight from the cradle to the grave loving and serving Jesus. Am I selfish or what?" He grinned and swallowed half of his juice.

Collin moved the eggs around with her fork. "Why selfish? Isn't it what the Lord wants anyhow?"

"Wants, yes. Gets, no. Or at least not that I've ever heard.

Unless you're the exception?"

It should have been the perfect lead-in for Collin to tell her story. Except how did she condense a story which spanned her whole life? How much could Collin share without having to go into all the gory details? Would Jeff follow up with questions she didn't want to answer—yet?

He watched her, waiting for her reply. Collin's silence wasn't the answer she wanted to give Jeff. She lowered her head. "No, I'm not an exception. My...parents didn't know the Lord. Our mom died...when we were about five. I didn't hear anything about the Lord until I turned...fifteen?"

She thought a moment. "Yeah, soon after my fifteenth birthday. I... got involved, I guess you'd say, with a street mission in Oakton. I heard God loved me. Didn't need me to clean up my act first, change, or do anything. Simply loved me."

Collin lifted her head. "Loved me and forgave me everything. He knew all I had been, all I became, and He still loved me."

Collin's voice tightened. "I couldn't pass up His kind of love and still live, so I gave Him my heart. I asked Him to use me wherever He could, and we've been together—mostly—since then."

She smiled, relieved she'd gotten through it. "Also, not very dramatic."

Jeff seemed to study her a moment. His voice became soft. "Maybe not. Someday maybe you can fill in the details for me." He hesitated, looked down, looked back. "May I ask one question? You said, 'when we were five.' Can you tell me who 'we' is?"

"My twin brother, Erin." And rather than have him agonize over whether to ask or not, she said, "He died when we were fourteen."

She paused. "He broke his neck." She offered nothing more.

Jeff again studied her face. "I'm sorry." He finished eating, then looked at the food still left on Collin's plate. "At least eat the eggs, so Mom O'Brien won't think it's her cooking you don't like. She's very sensitive."

Collin nodded obediently. "Yes, Mother. Thanks."

Jeff shrugged self-consciously. "No problem. One of these days, if you want, you can tell me. But only if you want."

Collin nodded but did not answer. She finished off her eggs, glared at him in mock anger. "There, I finished them. I know how to eat."

"Finish the fruit and the toast, and you'll have actually eaten something."

Collin scowled. "You are pushy, you know?"

"What are friends for?"

Before she could answer, two hands caught her shoulders from behind. Mitch's voice said, "Well, surprise, surprise." His voice sounded smooth and friendly, but Collin thought she sensed something more in it, something she couldn't interpret. Mitch continued, "The counselor and the janitor. How democratic." He began massaging her shoulders lightly.

Collin kept the irritation from her voice. "Jeff and I are old friends. Ever since Friday night, right?"

Jeff nodded. "I believe you're right."

Mitch scowled at Jeff. "Is this what you've been doing the last couple of days instead of working? Hitting on the clients?"

Jeff grinned, apparently not intimidated in the least. "Maybe. What did you need?"

"The moorings on dock seven you 'fixed' last week have come loose. Again." The river guide's voice held more than a tinge of sarcasm.

Jeff cocked his head. "Again? That's a problem. Which dock are you using this session?"

Mitch's eyes narrowed. "That's not the point. The point is you said you fixed it last week and you didn't. Whether I'm using it or not isn't the issue."

Jeff motioned, palms up. "If you're using it, I'll tighten the moorings down this morning and keep them tightened down through the week. If you're not using it, I'll close it down, tear the moorings out and replace them. It'll take a couple of days to get the parts in, but it would be ready for next session. It depends on what is most convenient for you."

Mitch's eyes cast back and forth. "Hum. I suppose I could use one of the other docks until you get it fixed right." He raised an eyebrow. "Assuming you know what you're doing, to begin with."

Collin watched Jeff for his response. How would he handle this attack?

"If you don't find it safe, we'll bring in someone who does

know." Jeff rose from the table. "I'll go check it right now." He smiled at Collin. "Thanks for breakfast, Collin. I'll see you later." He picked up both their trays and walked off humming quietly.

Mitch let go of Collin's shoulders and quickly sat opposite her. He gave her his most winning smile. "So, breakfast with the janitor. How noble of you to condescend to the little people."

Collin kept her voice even. "He's good people. I like him. What can I do for you this morning?"

Mitch chuckled. "Such a loaded question. I have so many needs."

"Well, let's start with any having to do with our classes."

Mitch laughed. "Okay." He became more serious. "I thought I encouraged you to eat as a crew. Why would you come down by yourself?"

"Jeff and I arranged to meet for breakfast. I'm here for the crew when they come in. I'll sit with them."

"You won't be eating."

"They don't care. The bonding idea is wonderful, Mitch. But as essential as you think it is, these are street kids. Independence is a very hallowed concept for them."

"But what about the gang idea? Gangs hang together."

"Gangs are built or grown by careful selection. You don't throw a bunch of strangers together, call them a gang, and expect gang loyalty or interrelatedness to appear overnight. It takes longer than a week to get cohesion on the streets, Mitch."

"And I suppose you would know all of this." The man snorted.

Collin raised an eyebrow. "It's my job, Mitch. It's what I do all day, every day. You've got at least three different gangs on your crew, maybe four. And you and I are outsiders trying to fit in. When the kids come in, see if you can pick them out."

Mitch leaned closer, his voice deepening with empathy. "I know my crew, Collin. It's not the kids who worry me. It's you. You're the one who's not fitting in yet." Mitch picked up her right hand. "Your fear can bring this whole crew down. You need to tell me what it's all about." He gave her a look of intense compassion. "You can trust me, Collin. For the good of the crew, tell me."

Collin studied his face while chewing the inside of her cheek. "No, Mitch. My fear will not impact the rest of the crew. No one knows about it but you, and unless it bothers you personally, it's not going to be a problem."

Mitch continued to hold her hand, twisting it one way then another, admiring it. "You have beautiful hands, you know?"

Collin pulled it away. "Thanks. It's a matched set. Had them all my life." To distract him, she asked, "Are we going on the water today?"

"Not out on the river, no. Not yet. The crew needs to learn to paddle together first. Why?"

"I'm going to prove to you there will be no problem. I can do this, Mitch."

He looked at her with curiosity. "It means that much to you? You fear it so much you'll put up with all this?"

Collin drew a deep breath, unsure of how to answer. "I do and I don't. Let's leave it there, okay? If there comes a time I need to tell someone, I'll consider your offer."

Mitch tenderly patted her hands. "I'll hold you to your word, Collin."

To Collin's relief, the doors opened, and ravenous campers came pouring in, intent on the destruction of as much food as they could consume in one hour. Nyla, Niles, and Ta'waan descended on Mitch and Collin, hooting and laughing. Insults of "Oooo…teacher's pet" and "Trying to score already?" and a few other comments equally offensive were bandied around.

Collin watched Mitch's face closely and noted an almost pleased look in his eyes. She debated whether to deflate his ego all at once or let him continue in his delusion.

Let it go.

God will uphold your honor.

Such as it is.

Collin rose and moved to a larger table so her crew could join them. She looked for Rob and spotted him among those in line, his tray already full even though he hadn't reached the "good stuff" yet. She smiled. Watching him get the "good goods" in life tickled her.

Mitch's voice buzzed in her ear. "What makes you smile so much?"

Collin reflexively moved away. "Rob. He is enjoying this camp."

Mitch sat down close beside her. Collin slid her chair away a few inches to give him room. His advances were going to get real annoying real fast. She'd have to come up with a plan and soon.

Lay him out.

Report him.

You do, you'll end up ruining the week for everyone.

Ask Jeff. He'll know what to do.

Yeah, right. As democratic as Camp Grace might be, Jeff was maintenance and Mitch, a teacher. There would be some insulation of layers there. No, she would handle it her way. For now.

If he crosses the line, I'll lay him out, and then tell someone.

Again the kids saved her from further overtures as Chonnell and Pardner came to the table and sat down. Chonnell looked around to see if anyone could see her, dropped her head briefly, prayed quickly, and looked up again to make sure no one caught her.

Collin smiled. She remembered those days. *Poor kid.*

Chonnell's devotions went unnoticed. She began to ply Mitch with questions, all the time shoveling food into her mouth. "We going on the river today?"

"Not yet."

"We going in a boat today? How we gonna learn to tackle the river if we don't get in the water?"

Pardner quipped, "We don't want to be in the water, moron. We want the boat to be in the water and we're in the boat. Ain't that right, Mr. Mitch?"

Mitch laughed. "Well, that is the plan."

Chonnell fired back. "Okay, smartie. When we gonna get in a boat? We ain't even seen no boat yet." She swallowed a tremendous mouthful of food. "We got all this stuff assigned to us and no place to use it. When we gonna get our rowers wet?"

Mitch grinned. "Paddles, Chonnell. They're called paddles. And I hope today."

"You hope? You the teacher. You supposed to know this stuff. How come you don't know what we gonna do?"

Collin stifled the giggles threatening to escape her lips. Mitch stared at his pint-sized persecutor, as if unsure how to respond to this tiny tormentor.

Deal with it, Mr. Mitch. They're going to be like this with you all week long. These aren't your usual Boy or Girl Scouts. These are my kids. Be sharp or go home, man.

Collin kept a straight face. "Chon, it probably depends on how quickly we learn what we need to, so we don't end up in the water or look like total idiots in the process." She looked at Mitch. "Right?"

She saw a combination of resentment but also relief in the man's eyes. But who did he resent? Chonnell for questioning him? Herself for trying to rescue him? Either way, she felt uncertain about the implication.

Mitch merely laughed. "You got it! Chonnell, I love your spunk."

Chonnell gave him the side-eye. "What you talking about, spunk?"

"Courage. Determination. You aren't afraid of anything, are you?"

Chonnell hesitated. "No, I ain't. Got no reason to be."

Niles, Nyla, and Ta'waan arrived, followed by Rob. With the four new arrivals, the questions of their day's activities were repeated, readdressed, rehearsed, rehashed, and re'd to death. The campers soon cleared their plates, cleared the table, and cleared out of the dining hall.

Mitch took them to an area behind the boat docks where an eight-man raft sat. They practiced entering and exiting the boat, falling out, reboarding, paddling positions, changing paddling positions, etcetera, etcetera, etcetera. They worked hard at it until lunch, but Mitch provided sandwiches, chips, and drinks for everyone, so no one needed to leave.

Collin took the proffered fruit juice but declined the sandwich. *I'm too tired to eat, anyhow.* "Mitch, I need to run to the infirmary."

Mitch's eyes widened. "The stitches again? I thought you got those checked last night."

Collin let only a hint of spice pepper her words. "Doc wasn't there. His hours are on the door: eight to five. Nothing different."

Now Mitch looked surprised. "You're kidding! He's always been open until six. This must have been a recent change. I'm sorry, Collin. I'll call up and make sure he stays late tonight. He's done it for me before."

"I'd like to go now. Nothing says he's closed for lunch."

Mitch rolled his head. "Collin, Collin, you have got to learn to trust me. If you can't trust me on land, how will you ever trust me in the boat on the river? Especially when she gets wild and wooly? Grabs hold of the boat and spins you around like a top, folds you up in half, and spits you out like a bad taste in your mouth?"

If Mitch wanted to invoke images of terror in her mind, he failed. Nothing in Collin's nightmares involved a boat. She raised an eyebrow. "I'm pretty sure I know how much to trust you, Mitch. May I go, please?"

Out of the corner of her eye, Collin noticed both Rob and Nyla following the conversation with interest. Rob, she understood. Nyla? Why?

"After class, Collin. If you'd have asked me before we ate, I could have let you go. But waiting this long… Sorry, but we're out of time. And I can't have you missing anything vital in the lessons. You leave and I'll have to ground you from the class. It's the rules. Your choice."

Take him down. Show him no one's in charge of you.

Nyla is watching.

Collin refused to fume or bluster or give Mitch any satisfaction at all. She smiled. "You make the rules. I'll follow them. For the good of the class."

Collin watched Rob steam. Nyla stared at her with a more measured look. Extension of the truce? Or had Collin made some ground with the youngster? *Lord, whatever You're doing, use this. Don't suppose You'd take Mitch out for me, would You?*

As expected, silence followed.

Mitch looked around at the crew and rubbed his hands. "Let's try all these exercises one last time, then put this boat in the water."

Six campers began cheering. Collin grinned as she realized even the laid-back older ones yelled approval. They were as tired as she was of climbing in and out of their blasted rubber bowl. She looked at Mitch. "I think you've got a winner."

Mitch smiled back. "I know I do."

Collin studied the boat captain as he turned away. *What does he mean?*

Paranoid. What would anyone want with you? Get over yourself.

And so the afternoon progressed. The group did all their multitude of position changes, shifts, and etceteras until Mitch satisfied himself no one would capsize the boat.

They carried their gear to the docks where a second identical craft waited for them in the water. With all the skill one morning's training could impart, they climbed aboard, got settled and situated, and pushed away from the dock. With some measure of difficulty, they paddled out onto the "lake" area and spent the remainder of the day circumnavigating its perimeter.

If Magellan tried to circumnavigate the world with this crew, he never would have left Spain.

Ta'waan proved woefully ignorant of the proper way to recover a paddle from the water without it splashing on the crewmember behind him: namely Collin. The first time it happened, he apologized profusely. "Hey, lady worker, sorry! I didn't mean to get you all wet. Jus' can't get the hang of this paddling stuff. Never done it before, you know?"

Collin smiled. "No problem, Ta'waan. We've all got a learning curve to master." She chose to ignore the smirk on Niles's face and the swallowed giggle from the young woman beside her.

Three strokes later, Collin caught another face full of water. Ta'waan looked around to her. "Sorry, ma'am."

Collin grinned. "You're getting better. You're catching more water with each stroke."

Nyla sniggered. "So's you."

Collin laughed. "You could say that. I wouldn't say it too loud. Brothers can be notorious for treachery and deceit."

Nyla looked at Collin curiously. "You got brothers?"

Collin bit her lip. "One."

Nyla snorted. "Yeah, well, having a brother don't let you know nothing 'bout having a twin brother. Niles wouldn't never turn on me."

"Never's a very long time, Nyla."

"We'll see what you know." She yelled forward. "Hey, Niles! Tell this know-it-all white woman you—"

She never got to finish the sentence. A face full of water hit her between her sneer and her gloat, putting authoritative punctuation on the discussion.

Nyla spit and sluttered and rained curses on Niles. She

eschewed the water and went after him with her paddle, jumping up to get better leverage.

And of course, jumping up in a boat is number one on the list of "Never, never, nevers," which come with the owner's manual.

Mitch thundered, "Sit down!" Nyla lost her footing and pitched over the side. Niles screamed in pure panic. Collin started over the side to bring Nyla back. Mitch thundered again, "Sit down, everyone!"

All eyes fastened on the riverboat captain. Mitch ordered, "Everyone look to your right."

Which everyone did. The crew saw Nyla calmly dog-paddling in place, letting the life jacket carry her weight. Mitch instructed, "Nyla has it perfectly figured. No panic, no floundering around, quietly waiting to be rescued. Right, Nyla?"

Nyla jeered. "No, I'm waiting for someone to throw my fool brother over so he can join me."

If no one else saw, Collin did. The interplay between the twins powerfully reminded her of the many she and Erin shared. Niles's eyes colored with fear, doubt, and regret. Nyla's burned with anger, malice, but behind it all, forgiveness. The two shared a secret here, one Collin could deduce with only a little effort.

But Mitch missed it. "Maybe we should. We can teach him a lesson in life-saving."

Collin stood abruptly and jumped into the water. Diving makes a much more dramatic statement but is awkward in a life jacket. She swam up to within a few feet behind Nyla and, ignoring the look of frustration on Mitch's face, called, "Always approach from behind."

Collin waved the crew into a chorus. Together they chanted the instructions for rescuing swimmers (conscious or un), towing said same to shore or safety (whichever proved closest), and then recovering them from the water.

Only after Nyla and Collin climbed back in the boat did Collin look at Mitch with her most winning smile. "Did we get it right, Cap'n? Huh? Did we? Did we get it the way you taught us? Miss anything? We want to make you proud of us. Are you proud of us? Huh? Are you?"

She refused to take his scowl as a final answer. She might be on the edge of total insubordination, and by rights, he could throw her out of class.

Hmmm...now, there's a thought. Maybe if I agitate him enough...

Mitch laughed.

Drat.

He nodded and included the entire crew in his accolades. "Yes, you all did it right. You all did it perfectly. I'm very proud of you." He shook his head. "You've proved you can rescue each other. Now let's get back to learning how to paddle, so we don't have to."

Everyone resumed their proper positions, and the circumnavigation resumed. After a few quiet minutes, Nyla leaned toward Collin. "Why'd you jump in? I know how to swim."

Collin debated for a moment. "You do. Niles doesn't."

Nyla stared hard at Collin, shocked. "How you know?"

"I read his eyes. Read yours, too. You never thought Mitch would take you up on throwing Niles over, did you?"

Nyla continued to stare at Collin, unsure whether to trust her or not. "Never." She hesitated. "You going to tell Mitch?"

Collin snorted a little. "Tell him what? Niles needs to wear a life jacket?" She fanned her vest. "Gee, no. I don't think so. If Niles falls over, he floats like the rest of us. If he can kick his feet and wave his arms, he'll be fine. We won't put his name first on the life-saving roster, though. Deal?"

Nyla gave Collin one last long look. "Why? Why you do this?"

Collin shrugged. "I had a brother. I know what it's like."

Nyla's eyes narrowed but she said nothing else. She returned to concentrating on her stroke, working slightly harder to match her pull to Collin's. She did, however, seem to be having a little extra difficulty on the forward recovery: she kept flipping water on her brother's back.

Collin noticed her own paddle seemed to possess an additional zing at the end, one which caused plentiful droplets of water to fly off the end and land in a shower on Ta'waan's neck. The boys turned and glared at their tormentors. Collin and Nyla looked at each other and grinned. "Sorry."

* * *

By the end of the day, the crew could have paddled the lake in their sleep. Chonnell and Pardner did. Collin noticed even Nyla and the boys looked tired. Mitch pushed the kids hard. He finally directed the boat back to the dock and looked at his watch. "Good job, crew. Good job. I'm proud of each of you. Great technique. It's six-thirty. Go up, get your showers. Chow hall is open an extra half an hour for you."

Moans and groans greeted him. The idea of food roused most the crew. As everyone filed out of the boat, Mitch called out, "Walker, would you stay behind, please? I want to work on your stroke a little more."

Collin turned away from him to hide the frustration across her face.

Rob stepped back between Mitch and Collin. "Hey, man, caseworker lady and I got an appointment an' I need her. Can't she do what she got to do with you tomorrow? This is important stuff we gotta do, real important."

Collin picked up the ball Rob threw her. "Mitch, the kids aren't just here for fun. We're still working with them as counselors, too. Rob and I scheduled this time a while ago. I'll work twice as hard tomorrow if you say so. But I need this time with Rob."

Mitch stared hard at both of them. After a moment, he nodded. "Go on. Get out of here. I'll see you early in the morning. Crew eats together, remember."

Collin nodded. "Right. Together."

"Seven a.m. Dining hall. Be there. Crew only."

"I understand." *I understand a lot more than you think. Maybe.* Collin nodded. "Let's go, Rob." As they rounded the corner away from the docks, she said in a low voice, "Thanks, my man. Nice job."

Rob grinned. "An' I ain't lying, either. We got an appointment. I got to finish whipping your sorry butt in hoops tonight."

Collin smiled. "After what you did, I should let you win." She paused. "Should. But I won't. Some things you just don't do. And giving you a win in hoops is one of them."

She wanted so badly to reach out and hug him but knew she couldn't. Not because of a state directive but by Rob's parameters for their relationship. Some day. Some day she would give him the hug he needed and deserved and wanted. But not yet.

Rob kicked the dirt with his shoe. "He been hitting on you most the day. Why you ain't put him in his place?"

"He's in his place, Rob. He's the teacher. If I bring him down, what about the rest of the crew? If I try and fail, he takes vengeance on everyone. I can ride it out. We only got three more days. I've dealt with worse than him, believe me."

"Montgomery?" Collin nodded. "He was a dirtbag."

Collin chuckled. "I should disagree with you on principle's sake. But I can't. You're right." She hesitated. "It would help if you kind of kept an eye out, you know? Like you did just now. I'll do everything I can not to get left alone with him. But if I get in trouble, I can use all the backup I can get."

"You got it, caseworker lady. I don't want to be breaking in no new counselor. I'm just getting you trained."

Collin laughed and shoved him lightly. "Get out of here. Go wash up and eat. I'll be in later."

Rob warned, "You better be eating some power food yourself. You're gonna need it tonight."

"Yeah, yeah, yeah. I hear you." She headed up the hill toward the infirmary. If Mitch had been correct, the Doc should still be there, and she would be in good shape with her promise to Jeff.

But the "lights out, no one home" appearance of the office left her grinding her teeth in anger. *Power-hungry little—*

Say nothing in anger you wouldn't say out loud.

Oh, I'd say it. You bet I'd say it. Collin headed back down to the lodge. She debated to eat or not to eat, bandied the question about, and decided finally to eat. And get the nag in her head off her back. At least another banana, a protein bar, and an apple for a change of pace. She needed to go back to her room and stretch out her muscles. Not as in stretching out to sleep. No matter how tempting the thought might be.

She ate as she walked, pitched the peel and core at the can by the dining hall, and went to her room. A good, hot shower loosened up most of the knots she would re-inflict on them later. Maybe she would go to the gym to finish the job. Safer than going to her room and listening to her pillow's siren song. Much safer.

Collin changed clothes, took another set with her, and headed for the gym. Mr. Lawler and Mr. Tremont were already there working out. Good. Safety in numbers. Not that there would be any real danger. Guys like Mitch worked daylight hours and primarily at the office. Opportunity takers, not seekers.

Collin selected a mild series of pulls and stretches on the universal gym. Something to ease the muscles, not extend them beyond comfort levels. She kept one eye on the clock, however, to make sure she didn't risk missing her deadline and showing up late on the court. *When one is trying to teach responsibility to a child, it behooves one not to be a poor example oneself. No matter how good one's intentions or excuses may be. Right?*

Right.

* * *

Collin worked until a little after eight, changed into her hoops duds, grabbed a last banana from the snack bar, and trotted to the ball court. Jeff arrived and brought a five-gallon cooler with ice water, hauling it on a small wagon. Collin noticed plastic cups lying beside the cooler. She grinned. "You think of everything, don't you?"

Jeff bowed low. "We aim to please madam." He straightened. "How did the day go?"

Collin shrugged. "It went." Not wishing to sound negative, she added, "We got to paddle around the lake a few times. That was educational. We worked hard." She grinned. "I swear, though, if Mitch ordered one more boarding drill, he would have a mutiny on his hands. And I'd have led the charge."

Jeff grinned. "Oh my, rebellion in the camp? Maybe I ought to warn Mitch."

Collin shook her head. "Naw, let him figure it out on his own. He could stand to learn a few things." *Oops, shouldn't have said that.* Collin looked at Jeff and saw him studying her. "Sorry, not what I meant to say. Or at least not how I meant it to sound. Or I meant…"

Collin stomped a foot in frustration. *Bad enough to stutter mentally. Do you have to do it out loud, too?*

Collin pulled herself together. "Disregard. How did your day turn out?"

Jeff studied her a moment longer. "Busy. Full. I took care of the dock. I hope. Someone has been tampering with the moorings, though why they would is a mystery. It's not like it hurts anything at the camp."

Jeff tossed a basketball to Collin. "We're not in full operation. We can switch docks with no problem. It's more an irritation. But

I'm going to keep an eye on it for the next week or so to make sure."

He pulled his whistle out of this pocket and hung it around his neck. "Other than the deck, the ladies and I had a terrific milking session this morning. They told me they hadn't been milked like that in years. The fact I have warm hands probably helped some. A little quirk of theirs, I guess. They hate cold hands."

Collin chuckled. "You're a nut."

"Pecan or cashew?"

"Filbert."

"Filbert?" Jeff looked surprised. "Filbert? What's a filbert?"

"I have no idea. Which is why it reminds me of you. I have no idea about you sometimes."

"Is it a bad thing?"

"Not at all. It makes you intriguing."

Jeff looked concerned. "So to keep you interested, I have to be crazy? This could be tough."

"No, you have to be you." *Honesty?*

Say it.

I don't remember how.

Try. "You don't have to 'keep' me interested. I…uh, I…" Words failed her as did every other mental process. She fought valiantly for some intelligent way to finish the thought. Failing intelligence, she searched for any way she could find to close out the sentence. That, too, failed. Finally, she looked at Jeff and shrugged haplessly. "I like you, Jeff. I want to get to know you better."

Jeff's eyes sparkled. "I think you're a special woman, Collin. A little demented, maybe, but something we can work with."

Jeff was saved—or barred—from further disclosure as Rob came running up the hill yelling, "Caseworker lady! Caseworker lady! Where you been all night? Me and the crew been looking for you. Mitch called us together after dinner. He got a bonfire going down by the docks, and he be telling stories about the river and how he ridden it. It's sweet, lady. Really sweet. You gotta come down and listen. You gotta. Mitch acted real disappointed when you didn't show up."

Collin's mouth hardened. "I'll bet."

Rob shrugged. "Whatever. I told him you probably be up here.

He said he'd come get you, but I told him I'd be there faster. He really wants you to come."

Collin shuddered involuntarily, keenly aware Jeff missed none of the nuances. Hadn't commented or questioned, but hadn't missed it, either.

She squeezed Rob's shoulders. "You did good, my man. Why don't you go on and listen for both of us? You can fill me in later."

Rob went to strip off his sweatshirt. "We got a game to finish."

"We can finish it anytime, Rob. Go. Listen to Mitch. You'll have a good time, I'm sure. Hang with the crew."

"You sure you don't want to come? Man may be a lowlife, but he tell a good story."

"I'm sure he does." *You bet I'm sure.*

"Ain't gonna upset you, me not having to beat you again?"

Collin pointed downhill in mock anger. "Out. Go. Vanish. Disappear. Take your sorry self and be gone."

Rob laughed and ran off. "Later, Jeff! Bye, caseworker lady."

Collin turned to Jeff. "I'm sorry I messed up your evening for nothing."

Jeff shrugged. "I didn't have any plans, anyhow. Are you sure you don't want to go down with him?"

"I am sure I don't want to go down with Rob."

"If it's not down by the river?"

Collin tried to keep her voice even. "I don't care where he set up. I do not want to spend this evening, or any evening, with Mitch. Can we leave it there?"

But Jeff couldn't. Or wouldn't. "Is there a problem?"

"I can handle it. It's personal, and I'll deal with it. Okay? Let it go, Jeff." To lighten the moment, she placed both hands on his shoulders and looked him straight in the eyes. "I would much rather spend my time with the janitor than with a blowhard ship's captain."

Whatever levity she intended disappeared in the depths of those eyes. And the longer she looked and read the emotions there, the less of a jest her statement became. Finally, as her own emotions began to jumble and swirl, she dropped her eyes and turned away. She cleared her throat. "I did want to play ball tonight."

Jeff must have found something in his own throat as well. He coughed slightly. "You know, to tell the truth, I kind of wanted to play, too. Some two on one, maybe."

Collin looked at him in surprise. "Really?"

"Yeah. It gets boring playing by myself. You always know who's going to win."

Collin frowned. "Not when I play alone. There are too many personalities out there with me."

Jeff grinned. "Caseworker lady, you are something else." He stopped. "Why does he call you caseworker?"

"Because I am his caseworker. Rob's been saddled with so many workers in his life he vowed three workers ago not to learn anyone else's name until they'd been with him at least a year. I've got about two months to go."

"Tough kid."

"Good kid, tough upbringing."

"You care a lot about him, don't you?"

"I'd adopt him if I could."

"Why don't you?"

"His mother won't give him up. She'd lose some of her support money. And I can't give him the one thing he needs most: a strong male influence."

Collin felt her frustration rising. "If he could have one male role model who would show him you can be strong and still love, win without cheating, and succeed in life without all the bells and whistles, I think he could make it. I can show him, but he only says, 'yeah, but you a woman. Ain't true for us dudes.'"

"Sounds like he needs a father."

Collin heard the heat rising in her voice. "He needs someone who will care about him."

Jeff looked at her a moment. His brows arched. "I think we've established the river and fathers are problem areas. Are there any other topics I should know not to bring up?"

Collin slapped at him in frustration; Jeff ducked. She threw the basketball at him. "Yes. My weight and the way I dress. Are we done with our analysis, yet?"

Jeff backed up, baiting her but his eyes shining. "What's the matter, caseworker lady? You can handle everyone else's problems, but no one better touch one of yours?" He threw the ball back and it stung.

Collin's eyes glinted. "You don't get it, do you? I make the rules. I call the shots. I'm in control. That's how it works." She fired the ball back.

Jeff trotted toward half-court. "So, what are the rules, lady?" Again he passed her the ball.

Collin joined him. She enumerated tersely, "One: first man to 100 wins." She passed the ball back to him, hard.

"How high does the woman have to score?" Jeff fired the ball back.

Collin ignored him. "Two: no time outs. First one to walk off the court loses." Ball.

"Anything else?" Ball.

"One more rule." Ball.

"What?" Ball.

"I win." Collin broke for the basket, catching Jeff flatfooted. He raced after her but couldn't stop her before she laid the ball in cleanly. As the ball dropped through, she yanked her sweatshirt off, threw it violently to the ground, and stood ready for Jeff's first assault on offense.

Jeff cruised to the end line and stared at Collin.

Is he trying to read me?

Let him try.

She stared back defiantly. Jeff took the ball and bounced it. "So that's how it's played, is it?"

Collin nodded curtly. "That's how it's played."

"Then give it your best shot." He dribbled slowly and deliberately back to the midline, turned, pointed, and started back up. Collin watched him for a moment then went out to battle. The war began.

But the next six points belonged to Jeff as Collin couldn't pick up his rhythm. After his second bucket, she began to see a pattern, however. Before shooting, he faded to the right as if favoring the left knee ever so slightly.

It didn't slow him down any. Collin stretched to stay with him. His crack the other night about the office worker hadn't been far off the mark. She did need to get serious about staying in shape.

As his third basket in a row sank, Collin nodded. She knew now. Collin brought the ball to mid-court and dribbled up slowly, studying him. What did her coaches always say? The eyes. Watch the eyes.

And Jeff's eyes danced, taunting her. "Study long, study wrong, they always say."

Collin asked coolly, "And who would they be?" She faked to her left; Jeff mirrored her. Spinning around, she moved right, then came back to her left. As Jeff moved back, Collin slapped the ball over his head, bouncing it high enough to dodge around him, catch it, and break away for an easy two points. She let the ball fall and retreated to midcourt.

Jeff retrieved the ball and nodded with respect. "Very creative. Don't think I've seen that move in the NCAA." He dribbled past her. "Wonder what the Dean would have thought of it?" Jeff crossed the half-court line, turned around, and started back up, intending to shoot by her as in past engagements. But Collin slid to her left, blocking his path. Jeff dodged left, but she anticipated him and stood in his way.

Ducking and weaving, Jeff fought up the court but couldn't elude Collin's defense. He gave her a shake-and-bake move and drove toward the basket, firing the ball at the last moment.

Collin timed her leap perfectly. She caught the ball at its apogee and smashed it away with a carnal pleasure that surprised her.

Jeff eyed her with new respect. "You been sandbagging."

Collin retrieved the ball and fired it to him. "You gonna talk or you gonna play?"

Jeff's eyes narrowed slightly. "Play."

They were back at it.

And at it hard. Neither kept time, neither kept score. Each basket became a mini-game all in and of itself. Collin stretched again and again to her limit and beyond, fighting to keep up, stay even, and sometimes maybe pull ahead.

She thought the score might be close but would never swear by it. She desperately wanted a break but seeing as how she'd made the rules, couldn't bring herself to admit she wanted one. The fire inside burned down to glowing embers, ready to be re-ignited if required, but equally ready to die if allowed. But no matter how tired she got, she would never admit it to Jeff.

Not that he fared much better than Collin. Number thirty-seven hadn't had the opportunity to strip down out of his warm-up suit.

He sweat profusely. His breathing came hard, and he developed an increasingly apparent limp. What hadn't he told her?

Jeff waited at mid-court, slowly dribbling the ball. As Collin set herself on defense once again, he asked, "No time outs, right?"

Collin stiffened her game face. "No time outs." No mercy. Not yet.

Jeff eyed her carefully. "Have it your way." He broke up the court; Collin stumbled and chased him, always a step behind.

Jeff put in the lay-up, caught the ball as it fell through the net, and heaved it as far down the court and out of bounds as he could.

Collin yelled angrily, "Hey!" As she chased the ball down, out of the corner of her eye, she saw him quickly shuck the warm-up suit and stand ready for her return. *The snake. Well played, but still a snake. He'll pay for that one.*

Or maybe he already had, once. Jeff limped in earnest but smiled at her as he met her at midcourt. "Sorry."

"You certainly are." Her eyes moved to his knee and its web of surgical scars. She looked up at him. "Blow out?"

Jeff shrugged. "Ancient history. You gonna talk or play?"

Collin stood dribbling the ball slowly, deliberating.

The voices in her head lined up pro and con:

Beat him while he's down. Take full advantage of the opportunity handed to you and crush the vermin.

Let him know right now who's the strong one here.

Strong in mercy. Strong in kindness. Strong in not having to prove your prowess through someone else's pain.

What would Jesus...

Collin laid the ball down. "Talk. You're hurting."

"What, you find what you think is a weakness, and suddenly it's time for analysis?"

"No. I just—"

"Let's play ball, woman. You were ready to beat my brains out two minutes ago. I'm the same man. These scars don't change anything."

In frustration, he picked up the ball and launched it in a high rainbow arch, which swished silently through the net.

Vanna White turned over the last consonant on the board, and the answer became clear. I'd like to solve the puzzle, Pat. Collin whispered, "Jeff Farrell. Number thirty-seven. North Carolina.

You were going to be the next MJ."

Jeff grimaced in disgust. "Press hype."

"I watched you play. You were good."

Jeff retrieved the ball. "Were. Past tense."

"You still are good, Jeff."

"Against shadows in the street, maybe."

Collin sensed the game was over, or at least on hold. Side by side, they walked over to the water jug. "What happened? The doctors talked about a full recovery."

Jeff snorted. "The doctors' ideas of recovery and the coach's ideas of recovery weren't quite the same. He knew I wasn't listening to the therapist. I wanted to play ball, period. So he protected me against myself."

Jeff looked at the ground. "He didn't cut me from the team. But he didn't let me play until he could be convinced I was 100%. Which I never got back to." Jeff sighed slightly and shrugged. He smiled sadly at Collin. "But God knows I love the game." Collin found her throat tight, unable to speak. Jeff touched her cheek lightly; she looked at him. "I guess we've all got a few demons yet to master."

Collin poured a cup of water for Jeff and one for herself. Both chugged them greedily and went for refills. Collin poured a second cup for Jeff and one more for herself. Jeff drank his, but Collin dumped hers over her head, splashing the remainder on her face. It felt deliciously fresh.

Jeff watched her, grinning. "What's that all about?"

Collin smiled. "It feels great." She poured another cup. "You ought to try it." She raised the cup as if to repeat the shower but, at the last second, dumped it over Jeff's head.

Jeff jumped back in surprise. "You!"

Collin grabbed another cupful of water and threw it at him before he could recover. She took off running.

Jeff grabbed the water jug, disdaining the cups, and chased after her.

Collin headed for the grass, figuring there would be less chance of harm if this game went awry. She ducked and dodged, but with the slippery footing, could not shake him. Even with a limp, the man could fly.

Think, think. Element of surprise, maybe?

Collin slowed enough for him almost to catch her, then spun on her heels, and doubled back. She guessed Jeff would empty the contents of the jug at her as she passed. She might get a little wet, but it wouldn't kill her.

She didn't anticipate his counter-attack. As Collin sped past him, Jeff dropped the jug, reached out, and tackled her. In a flash, he reached back, grabbed the cooler, and emptied the remainder of its five gallons over her. Collin spat water. "Foul! Technical foul! You can't do that!"

Jeff stood over her, laughing. "Another one of your rules?"

"Yes." Collin reached out and tripped the unsuspecting maintenance man, dragging him to the grass with her.

She caught Jeff by surprise, and he landed with a thud beside her. He started laughing and couldn't stop. Collin lay beside him, laughing with him.

Jeff finally gained control of himself and rolled on his side, looking down at Collin. She looked up at him and smiled gently. Again, she stared into those oh, so expressive eyes. Their emotions drew her in.

Jeff hesitated. He reached out and very tenderly kissed her, tentatively, as if not sure how she would respond. Collin put her arms around his neck and kissed him in return.

It was long. It was intense. It was everything Collin ever thought a kiss should be.

And it scared her. Collin broke off suddenly and sat up straight. She looked at Jeff, who wore a stricken, guilty look on his face. "Collin, I'm sorry. I…"

Collin grabbed him, hugging him hard, burying her head in his shoulder. Jeff cradled her in his arms and rested his head lightly on hers. She whispered, "You big dummy, don't apologize. Don't ever apologize." Sitting there felt very warm, very natural, very right. Like she could sit there forever…

Suddenly the court lights went out, and they sat in total darkness. Collin gasped, Jeff chuckled. "Timer. Supposed to mean time's up and everyone goes home. We probably ought to take the hint."

Collin nodded. "I think you're right. It's been a long evening."

Jeff stood, helped Collin to her feet, but did not release her hand. They gathered up the ball, their assortment of sweatshirts, and the remains of the water jug. Hand in hand, they walked back to the lodge. A crowd of campers stood at the door. There could be no goodnight kiss, only a gentle squeeze of the hand, a smile, and a whispered, "See you tomorrow." Then he left.

Collin entered the lodge alone but, for the first time in many years, not lonely. And yes, she smiled all the way to bed.

WEDNESDAY

Seven a.m., however, found Collin sitting in the dining room, off by herself, as alone as she could manage in a place bustling with campers. She clutched a cup of coffee, swirling it more than drinking it, lost deep in thought. Last night had been the first night since they'd arrived—the first night in years—Collin didn't dream of the river. Not that dreaming of Jeff proved any less disturbing, but at least with him, she wasn't drowning. At least not in the literal sense. Or at least not—

A voice startled her, commanding sharply, "Stop it!" Collin turned around quickly. Jeff stood there with a tray of food and a stern look on his face. He set the tray down on the table. "Stop. Stop analyzing, bisecting, dissecting, or whatever you're doing to take apart what happened last night and accept it for what it was. I loved it. Every muscle in my body aches, but I had fun. Did you?"

Collin nodded, feeling properly chastised. "Yes, I did. And yes, I ache too. I need to get out of the office more often."

Jeff grinned. "I need to do a lot of things more often. Here." He set a toasted bagel with cream cheese in front of her. "Eat. It's good for you."

"Jeff…"

He mimicked her tone. "Collin…you have to eat to stay healthy. And you need to get your strength up if you ever hope to beat anyone at basketball."

Collin glared. "What do you mean 'hope to beat'? I whipped you pretty handily last night."

Jeff smiled. "You have to do something about these delusions, milady."

Collin started to protest, but Jeff silenced her. He took her hand, bowed his head, and again asked the Lord to bless the food and their day. Collin added some silent thanks of her own, looked up at Jeff's "amen," and smiled. "Okay, maybe I wasn't ahead, but I didn't lose."

Jeff started in on his breakfast. "Who walked off the court first?"

Collin stared at him in disbelief. "What?"

Jeff shrugged. "You made the rules. I simply followed them."

Collin looked for something to throw but had only her coffee and the bagel at hand. Her personal religion forbade the wasting of a good cup of coffee, and she feared doing Jeff serious bodily harm if she hit him with the bagel. Which left her no recourse other than to steam. "You wait. You wait."

Jeff smiled, then got serious. "Listen, I've got to tell you something. I don't want you to take it for anything other than face value, okay?"

Collin felt a too-familiar twisting in her gut. The defensive walls began to rise. Her voice got quiet. "What?"

Jeff held his hand up. "See, you're doing it already. You don't even know what I'm going to say. If this relationship is going to go anywhere, you have got to learn to trust me." He kept his tone light, almost as if he'd anticipated her reaction.

But Collin's defensives came to full steam. "Does one kiss make a relationship?"

Jeff reached out and took her hand. "There were two. And I hope so."

Those eyes. Those cursedly intense eyes. Collin softened. "What's wrong?"

"I have to leave this morning. I'm flying out in about an hour. Dad called me last night, and some deal he's been working on for the last six months is suddenly ready for closing this afternoon. He needs my help."

Fireworks went off in Collin's brain. *You knew this would come. It always does. They're all the same.*

Listen. Hear him.

Collin exercised supreme maturity and restraint. "It's good you two are close."

Jeff shrugged. "We're business associates. He runs the

business, and I get to associate with him. Works for me."

Jeff must have noticed levity wasn't scoring points. He changed his tactic. The maintenance man squeezed her hand tightly. "Collin, if for any reason you need me, or maybe want someone to talk to, I left my numbers on your dresser." Collin looked up at him sharply. "I went in to fix the vent screen. Someone complained about it rattling at night."

Collin relaxed slightly. She lodged the maintenance request in the first place, after all. Of course, he wouldn't have been in her room without a legitimate reason. "I didn't complain. I mentioned."

"Collin, I'm coming back. Thursday evening or Friday morning at the very latest. I promise."

Collin held up her free hand to stop him. "Unless you've become God since last night, don't promise me anything."

Jeff squeezed her hand again, then, in a unique gesture, placed his palm upright against hers. "I give you my word I will try to be back here before you take the river ride. I will also try to call you every evening and every morning until I do get back." He stopped, hesitated. "If you want me to."

Collin needed time and space to sort out the emotions boiling inside her. She shrugged. "If you have the time. I imagine you're pretty busy while you're home."

Jeff snorted, dropping his palm from hers. "Busy? Let me detail a day in Oakton for you. I'll get there around eleven. Dad will pick me up at the airport, take me to lunch somewhere he dislikes, but knows my mom will approve. Then we'll go to the property site."

Jeff swallowed some of his coffee. He took a large bite of the eggs, swallowed. "I'll do as thorough an inspection as I can get access to, which is never thorough enough, but it's the best we can do. We go back to the office, spend the next couple of hours hashing out whether his plans for the site are feasible, logical, practical, economical, or profitable."

The man swallowed more of his coffee. "The last hour there, we spend praying about what the Lord wants us to do with all of this. We'll get home, and Mom will have forgotten I'm coming home, so she hasn't fixed enough to eat, and we'll all go out to dinner."

Collin cocked her head, sensing something wrong with the scenario. Jeff continued, "Mom had a stroke about five years ago. She hasn't been herself since. She's regained most of her functionings, but something in the brain never quite made it back. It's tough to explain. She's not all Mom."

"I'm sorry."

"We all are. But the Lord has His time and purpose. Everyone loves the new Mom."

"But misses the old?"

"Yeah." Collin saw the flash of longing in his eyes. He looked down at his breakfast and continued his description of the events at home. "After dinner, I'll help Mom with some of the housework, listen to Dad rehash the decision of the day, feed the dog, water the cat, feed the cat to the dog…"

Collin shook her head. "You're so bad."

"Wanted to see if you were listening. We don't have any pets. Let's see what else? Dad will end his evening watching a little television, usually some documentary about alligators or the mob or something educational."

Jeff finished the eggs and attacked the sausages. "Mom will sew or needlepoint or do something creative with sharp objects until Dad finally decides it's time for bed. He informs Mom, she puts everything away in specific places and order, which takes about half an hour, then they go to bed."

"What do you do?"

I don't care.

I do.

"I spend most of my evening helping Leesa' with her homework."

"Leesa. Is she a younger sister?"

A look of pride filled Jeff's eyes. "She's older than me. By about three years."

"Is she in college?"

"No. Leesa has Down Syndrome. She's a senior in high school this year." His eyes beamed. "She told me she doesn't care how long it takes. She wants to graduate. And she'll do it, too."

Collin tried to think of something to say. She found her throat inexplicably tight. "Sounds like a full day. I envy you."

Jeff shrugged. "It's family. It's my family, anyhow." He took a deep breath, let it out. "I'd better get going. I've still got chores to do before I leave."

He handed her a piece of folded paper. "Would you give this to Rob? I told him last night I had to leave. I said I'd give him my number if he got stuck on anything. He'll know what I'm talking about. He can use the camp phone." He grinned. "He's one great kid."

Collin nodded. "Yeah, I know." She lifted her chin in dismissal. "I'll miss you, Jeff." *Now and forever.*

Jeff's eyes questioned hers. She stared back, freezing out all emotion. Jeff's voice became uncertain. "I'll miss you, Collin." His tone turned serious. "This 'personal thing' between you and Mitch. I know you can handle it all by yourself. But if by some minuscule chance you do need help—not that you ever would, mind you—but on a one in a million chance it happens, Steve Parks is always on call. Trust me. He will listen to anything you have to say. Day or night, it doesn't matter."

Collin nodded curtly but offered nothing more. Jeff studied her as if expecting a response he didn't get. Finally, he said, "Take care of yourself, milady. I'll see you soon."

Collin gathered in all her runaway emotions. "Goodbye, Jeff." The man disappeared out the door.

On cue, the crew came jamming over to the table hip-hopping and be-bopping to someone's singing at a table across the way. Rob slid his tray across the table and chimed, "Hey, caseworker lady. Heard you got beat at hoops last night, and I wasn't even there to do it."

Ta'waan sat beside Niles, who sat beside Rob. Nyla sat with Chonnell and Pardner on the other side of the table. Chonnell doodled with a pen, drawing googly-eyed characters and showing them to Pardner. Pardner giggled as she stuffed food in her mouth.

Collin kept her voice restrained. "Who told you such a bald-faced lie?"

"My man Jeff. Ain't he telling it straight?"

"When did you see Jeff?"

"Last night after we got back from the bonfire. And Mitch is still upset you didn't come down." Rob drained his milk in one gulp. "Anyhow, Jeff came to the game room to fix one of the units. I got talking with him and then we got playing around. He showed me fifteen different ways to beat Thrones of Honor. He cool."

Collin raised an eyebrow. "You think so?"

"Yeah. He told me you beat him, but then walked off the court, so he won." Rob looked at her, his eyes questioning. "You going soft on me, caseworker lady? You ain't never walked off the court."

"Call it a mental lapse never to be repeated." *Never.*

Did Jeff use Rob to get information about her? "What else did you talk about?"

Rob answered between bites of pancake. "Me, mostly. Where I's from, things I like to do, what I thought about school, that kind of stuff. He asked me why I chose white water."

Collin felt the ice in her soul tempering. "And you told him...?"

Rob chewed thoughtfully. "Power. A man who can ride it can do anything."

Ta'waan nodded. "He ain't lying. You should have heard the stories Mitch told last night 'bout all the rivers he's rode, all the places he been. Sweet, sweet stories, man."

Collin pushed the untouched bagel aside. "Great, guys." She looked at the diminutive duo. "So why did you two choose the river?"

Chonnell spoke around swallows of biscuit and bacon. "I seen this show 'Reading Rainbow' and this guy, LeVar Burton, went down a river in a boat. It looked so cool I wanted to try it. It looked like fun, like the rides at the Point."

"Did Mitch tell you it would be all fun?"

Pardner frowned. "Course not. I know it be hard work. I ain't afraid of working. I been toting Mama's laundry baskets full of people's wet clothes since I's old enough not to fall in 'em. Washer's in the basement. We live on the third floor. I can pull my own weight."

Niles laughed. "Yeah, but you don't weigh nothing, so it don't count for much."

Collin interceded before Pardner could draw blood. She looked at Niles and Nyla. "What about you two? Joint decision or someone lose the draw?"

Niles's eyes narrowed slightly. "How you know 'bout the draw?"

Collin smiled a little sadly. "I had a brother. I know how these things work." She noted the curious look on Nyla's face but let it go and looked at Niles. "I'm guessing you won. Why white water?"

"Like the dudes said: power, man. It's all about power."

Ta'waan looked at Collin. "Why an old lady like you sign up, huh? You working for the Man, so you got all the power you want. Why you out here? My counselor didn't sign up for nothing."

Nyla added roughly, "Can you see Mrs. Pelfry doing any this?"

Niles chuckled. "Like to see her on the luge, man. She be doing barrel rolls down the mountain."

Collin started to intercede, stopped, thought about it again, started again, stopped again…all in the matter of less than a second. She chose to say nothing and let her silence speak. Combined with a look of stern disapproval. If those carried no weight, well, too bad. Let the counselors' lives speak for themselves.

Pardner said, "I think Mr. Tremont is doing the rappelling. Saw him yesterday, an' his hands is all torn up and bandaged. He laughed like it weren't no big deal. Say he havin' a great time."

Chonnell snorted. "Ms. Peacock brought a ton of books with her. She say she got no intention of getting dirty, wet, or otherwise 'inconvenienced' by this. She come to babysit, nothin' more."

Collin corrected the girl. "It's Ms. Petcock, isn't it?"

"Not the way she go strutting. She too high class for this. Told me over an' over if she could find a job where they'd pay her what she worth, she be long gone."

Collin ached inside. Role models. What models did she and her kind present to the kids? What did Rob see in her? Did he see anything worth following? Worth imitating? Did he see Christ in her?

Nyla brought Collin out of her soul-searching and repeated the question. "So why you choose rafting?"

Collin hesitated. To speak or not to speak? Reveal her secret fear or continue to hedge and pay the consequences later? Who had a coin when she needed it?

What would Jesus…

Collin looked around at the group. "I signed up because the river scares me."

Niles said, "Say what?"

Collin looked in Rob's eyes as she explained. "I had a bad experience with a river as a little kid, and I've been afraid of going in, or even on one, ever since."

Rob studied her eyes as if trying to discern fact from fiction. He asked, as if trying to understand, "You were scared? Ever since you been a kid? Of a river?"

The two littlest girls giggled. Ta'waan and Niles laughed harshly, but Nyla stayed silent.

Collin answered Rob. "Yeah. Of a river."

Rob snorted. "I ain't believing it. Not you. You ain't afraid of nothing. I seen you out on the streets, lady. I seen you face down Jaegger's lieutenant. I seen you standing 'tween the Snakes and the Skins when they gonna rumble. You ain't telling me you afraid of water?"

"You think I didn't get scared those times? Come on, Rob. It terrified me. But I needed to go out there. I didn't go alone, either."

Rob muttered, "Look like it to me."

She smiled. "Because you could only see on the outside. It's Who's on the inside that counts."

"Yeah, well, ain't He still on the inside? What be the difference 'tween now and then?"

Collin thought the question over a moment. A long moment. "Nothing, I guess. I've never faced it before." She nailed him with a glance. "Oakton is not exactly blessed with raging rivers, you know."

Niles began mocking to Ta'waan, "How anyone be scared of a river?"

Ta'waan's voice took on a falsetto. "Oh, my, the river's gonna get me."

Collin saw the blood rising in Rob's face. She laid a hand on his arm in warning. To Niles and Ta'waan, she said, "I hope you never have to find out. I hope you never run across anything which scares you."

The social worker chose to forgo nailing Niles with a knowing look; he'd figure it out soon enough. Collin looked around instead. "You better finish up. Mitch will leave without us if we're late."

Ah, but at least they would be late as a whole crew. He couldn't complain on that count!

The crew crammed as much food in their mouths as they could, half-chewed it, and washed it down with colas, as is the manner of teens and teen wannabes. Not five minutes passed before they cleared the table, returned the trays and seatbacks to their full upright position, and everyone headed for the door.

Rob held back slightly, enough to drop him and Collin out of earshot of the others. "You ain't afraid, lady, you only think you afraid. I be knowing you. You can't quit."

"I'm trying, Rob. I really am trying. But this is big, man."

Rob cocked his head. "You bigger. Or the One you always be telling me about is. Ain't He?"

"Yes, Rob, He is."

"You can do it. I know you can."

Collin put both hands on Rob's shoulders. "If you can pilot the boat, I'll stay in it."

"Your word?"

"My word."

Rob grinned wide and slapped her fist. "You got it. Let's catch up." He raced off to join the others.

Collin closed her eyes. *Don't let me let him down, Lord. Please, don't let me let him down.* She walked on toward the dock, fear whispering at her steps.

Mitch waited patiently, the camp van behind him. His eyes lit up as Collin approached. "You did come. We missed you last night. Thought you might have bailed on us. I wanted it to be a crew thing, you know."

"I already made other plans. But I hear you're a great storyteller."

Mitch refused to let it go. "Plans with who, the janitor?"

Collin kept her tone even. "Plans with Rob and Jeff, yes. When Rob canceled, I saw no reason to cancel on Jeff, too." She went back to her diversionary tactic. "Rob did a great deal of bragging on you. He liked your style."

Appeals to ego are usually great mollifiers. Mitch's proved no exception. "Oh, I don't know. You'd have to hear me in person to judge. How about tonight?"

"I don't know, Mitch. We'll have to see how today goes. Yesterday took a lot out of me."

But you put in over an hour on the court anyhow.

Let's not mention it, shall we? Mitch doesn't need to know everything we do.

Mitch raised an eyebrow. "I suppose it depends on what Jeff is doing, too."

Collin answered truthfully, "No, it doesn't." She didn't add Jeff left the camp. And her heart.

Mitch's eyes lit up. "It doesn't? You mean the fling is over? A real man has a chance to turn your head?"

Collin warned, "Mitch, you've got six bored campers getting antsy. Where we come from, that's asking for trouble. You better get these kids directed toward something, or they're liable to practice dismantling your engine to keep up their skills."

Mitch turned around and saw all the teens poring over the van's motor like vultures. He shouted, "Okay! Let's go. Everyone in the van. Adults upfront."

The river guide smiled at Collin, a man with hope reborn. "This is going to be a great day."

Collin's gut niggled at her.

Paranoia. You have nothing he wants. Trust me. You're nothing to him. Collin growled inwardly, but only smiled at Mitch. "Let's hope so."

The group piled in the van with the usual amount of heffing and heefing over who sat where. But once they settled and the vehicle started moving, Rob called, "Hey, Mitch? Where we going anyhow?"

A chorus of seemingly disinterested voices echoed his question.

Mitch smiled in the rearview mirror. "Oh, I thought we'd go for a ride up in the mountains."

Pardner called, "We in the mountains now. How far up we gonna go?"

"Up to where our river is born."

A buzz of discussion started. "Rivers don't get born, do they?"

"Naw. Ain't no such thing as a baby river."

"Sure they is. Ain't you never heard nobody talkin' 'bout 'The Mother of all Rivers'?"

"Yeah, an' Mama use to tell me 'bout 'Ole Man River.' Some song they use to sing an' play when she knew Moses."

"Yo mama never knew Moses."

"Did too. Daddy say she older 'n Moses an' meaner than Satan. Then he laugh."

"Be laughing while he running, he be my daddy an' call my mama old."

Mitch refocused the attention of the group. "In order to get to know a river, it's important to understand where she came from, where her roots are."

Nyla slapped Collin lightly on the shoulder. "First, this river born, now it got roots. I don't think the man know what he talking about."

Collin saw a flash of…rage? Hostility? Irritation? How many synonyms for "anger" did she know? However many there were, they all showed in Mitch's eyes. She'd seen it when Pardner challenged him at breakfast the morning before. *Maybe this class needs to come with a warning label: "No negative personal comments about the teacher." For these kids, it should read, "No dissing the man." Either way, this could be a problem.*

But Mitch managed to bury his wounded pride. "Oh, you'll be surprised at all the things I know." He hummed to himself, a look of satisfaction on his face.

Collin exchanged confused looks with Nyla; they both settled back in their seats, leaving Mitch to himself.

They spent the remainder of the two-hour trek in relative silence. Twice Mitch managed to brush Collin's knee while changing gears. The first time she ignored it. The second time she debated before making a suggestion. "You know, it's pretty tight quarters up here. Can we move this water jug to the back? It would give me more space for my feet, and you wouldn't be fighting my knees for fourth gear."

Mitch smirked. "Sorry, Walker. Jug's full, and there's no way to shift it while we're moving. Maybe after the rest stop at the top of the ridge. It's only another ten miles or so."

Collin swung her knees as far to the right as she could manage, twisting them around and under her. No possible chance for an encounter now.

Mitch looked at her. "You can't be comfortable."

Collin smiled. "I feel no pain, Mitch. Trust me."

"No? None at all?"

"When you're dead from the neck up, you feel no pain."

Niles called from the back. "Yeah, but they say fear be all in your head. How that be, huh?" He nudged Ta'waan, and both boys began laughing.

In the mirror, Collin saw Nyla's eyes boil. But before the girl could mount an attack, Collin said softly, "Nyla, let it go. It doesn't bother me."

Nyla stared at Collin, studying her. After a few moments, she nodded and settled back in her seat.

Mitch lay his hand on Collin's arm. "Does he know how afraid of the river you are?"

Does anyone know how afraid of the river I am?

Other than the Lord?

Maybe one person, and he died at fourteen. Collin took in a slow breath. "No. He knows I'm afraid; they all do. I told them."

"Did you tell them why?"

Afraid I told them something I haven't told you? "No, I didn't. I have enough nightmares without bringing it up voluntarily. I simply said I had a bad experience. No one needs to know anything else." *And it's more than I want to remember.*

Mitch rubbed her arm lightly. "I really could help you, Collin."

She disengaged his hand politely. She patted it firmly. "No, Mitch. It will be fine, I'm telling you."

Mitch put his hand on her shoulder. "It'll destroy you, you know. Hiding fear inside. It will kill you."

Again Collin repositioned the errant hand. "I guess I'll have to take my chances. It's been a lot of years, and I'm still breathing. Between the Lord and I, I think we've got it covered."

Bingo! The magic Word, which stops most advances. Mitch turned away, looked in the mirror. "Another hour, and we're there. Or we're at the parking lot. We've got a short climb, and we'll be at the birthplace of our river." He grinned at Collin. "And all its nightmare secrets."

The Lord is on my side. I won't be afraid. What can a man do to me? The Lord is my helper. The Lord is always with me. Being away from the river made a difference. Content. She would be content.

They covered the last few miles with only one final disruption. Ta'waan and Niles jabbed each other in the ribs, whispering and laughing. Collin could tell they were planning something. She could only guess whether she or Mitch would be the target. Most likely herself. With their plans finalized, Ta'waan called out, "Hey, Mitch, you know the lady here afraid of the river?"

Mitch nodded. "Yeah, I knew. So what? Everyone's afraid of something."

Nyla drawled snidely, "Yeah, bro. Everyone 'fraid of something. Ask Niles. He know 'bout being afraid."

Niles snapped, "I ain't afraid of nothing. You know that, Nyla. Of course, I ain't saying you got nothing you 'fraid of."

Collin started to intervene, but Mitch cut her off. "No, you're wrong. It's a proven fact. Everyone has a fear of some kind." He looked in the mirror and called, "Hey, Chonnell, what scares you? Things going bump in the night? Monsters under your bed?"

Chon called back, "It's the monsters on the street get me worryin'. Pusher down on the corner. I seen how he got my sister hooked an' how he got her walking the street. I wonder if I got what I need not to get taken, too. That's the monster I worry 'bout."

Collin's voice caught. "That's not fear, Chon. That's good sense."

Pardner chimed in with a fear less intense but more communal. "I don't like it when it get dark outside an' Mama done left the window shades open. Ain't never sure what be lookin' in."

Nyla nodded. "Yeah, I hate it, too."

Collin offered, "Open closet doors at night. Lets the bogeyman out."

Niles hooted. "Bogeyman?"

Nyla looked at her brother. "Yeah, you know. Kin to the ghost in the attic."

Niles paled slightly. Ta'waan started to howl, but Collin cut him short. "Be a real man, Ta'waan. Admit it. You've got things that scare you. Maybe it's your aunt Thelma's spinach pie. Or those bottlebrush kisses from Uncle Mo. 'Fess up, bro."

"How you know I got an Aunt Thelma? And how you know 'bout her pie?" Ta'waan remained staunch, however. "Ain't scared of nothin'. Real man ain't scared of nothin' no ways."

Mitch drawled, "Snakes? Ever been locked in a room with a handful of hissing, slithering, agitated snakes?"

"Ain't gonna bother me. I'd stomp 'em."

"Ever seen a rat up close? Those beady little eyes staring you in the face?"

"I'd pitch him cross the room." The machismo in Ta'waan's voice dropped a level.

Collin decided she should change the course of this discussion. Even if it meant sacrificing her knees. She stretched out slightly, drawing Mitch's attention from his imagery and asked in a little girl whine, "Are we there yet?"

Aha! A universal unknown they could all share. All seven crew members, regardless of age, race, or gender, began to raise the calls of a parent's worst nightmare: "We there yet?" "How long 'til we be there?" "I gotta go!" "He's touching me!" "I wanna sit by the window!" "Aren't we ever going to be there?"

Collin kept a close eye on Mitch's face, especially on his eyes and the muscles of his jaw. But the catcalls seemed to not bother him. Indeed, he hummed to himself, smiling and chuckling. He looked happy, and it bothered Collin. She didn't want him unhappy; an unhappy Mitch could be hard to handle.

But a happy Mitch? Come on.

Yeah, couldn't we have an in-between Mitch? A not too morose, not too sunny riverboat captain?

The van jerked to a stop as Mitch yelled, "We're here!"

Collin looked around. "Where?"

They stopped in an abandoned parking lot, or more to the point, a "panoramic turnout." Mitch said, "From here, we go on foot." He pointed to a ridge, maybe a mile down and away from their present position. "Our river starts over there. There's a fairly smooth trail, so no one should have to work too hard getting there or back."

Mitch led out, accompanied by Chonnell and Pardner. Ta'waan, Niles, and Rob held the middle ground while Collin and Nyla brought up the rear.

Collin sensed the younger woman wanted to say something but didn't try to guess what it might be. They walked along in silence for several moments before Nyla broached the subject. "Twice now when you talk about your brother, you say you 'had' a brother. Like he gone or something. And you look sad when you say it. Your brother, is he dead?"

Collin took her time getting herself together. "Yes."

Nyla refrained from the customary, but meaningless, "I'm sorry." "He been gone long?"

Collin smiled sadly, realized what she'd done. "Somewhere between twelve years ago and yesterday."

"He older or younger?"

Collin hesitated. "Younger. By fifteen minutes. He was my twin, Nyla."

Nyla stared at her, speechless, unable to process the information or the horror.

They lagged slightly. From the head of the pack, Mitch yelled, "Walker! Nyla! Pick it up! Let's go!"

Nyla snapped out of her nightmare. "Someone need to shorten him."

Collin grinned. "You do, I'll watch."

Nyla's eyes took on a mischievous twinkle. "Yeah, I know how you is with a knife."

Collin swatted at her accuser, but Nyla ducked out of range and trotted to catch up with her brother. Collin grinned and followed suit, joining up with Rob and Ta'waan. Collin noticed Ta'waan's face looked a little pale, a little strained, a little, dare she say—fearful—as he looked out and down the sheer cliffs. He marched on the outside of the three-abreast formation, putting him closest to the edge. Granted, a rock wall acted as a barrier, but it stood slightly less than waist-high. It did nothing to obscure the view of how far down someone might fall to the base of the ridge.

Collin debated letting the boy suffer for his arrogance earlier. But a remembered rumble of her fear put her in action. "Ta'waan, can I have the outside? I can't see over you. Tall people need to be on the inside."

Ta'waan looked at her. His face held a mixture of shame, gratitude, and relief. But he said only, "Yeah, no problem."

Rob looked at Collin, question in his eyes. After ten months with Collin, she knew he learned to read both her eyes and her actions. He would know she had a purpose in her request. Collin held his eyes only momentarily—long enough to tell, not long enough to show. He nodded imperceptibly.

The three walked on in silence for a few moments. Rob said, his tone conversational, "You know, caseworker lady, I been thinking 'bout the fear stuff Mitch be throwin' 'round in the van. I figured out it's pretty easy to say you ain't scared of something you ain't never faced, ain't it? When he asked Ta'waan 'bout them snakes, I thought the same thing. I ain't afraid of snakes. Never seen one 'cept in the zoo. They's behind glass. How'm I gonna know what I'm afraid of 'til it happens?"

Collin nodded. "Good point, little brother." It pleased her to watch Rob's teaching technique. Pleased her more Ta'waan seemed to be listening. Now, if he learned from it, well…

Rob continued almost as if Ta'waan weren't even there, "You afraid of the river, but you got a reason. You been in the river, somethin' bad happened, an' now you afraid. Makes sense." He stopped. "I use to be afraid Tulle's daddy would come back and finish what he promised." He looked at Ta'waan. "Tulle be my half-brother. His daddy killed him and tried to kill my mama before the police killed him."

Collin knew the history…knew Rob left out a great deal of the horror of that night. She wondered he would even bring it up. But Rob's motives were his own.

Rob shrugged. "Fact is, I knowed the police killed him, knowed he couldn't hurt me, but I still got scared. Still am scared sometimes. Is that stupid?"

Collin worked to keep her voice from cracking. "No, Rob. That's not stupid at all. Whether you're afraid or not doesn't make you more or less of a man. It's what you do with the fear makes the difference. I'm afraid of being stung. When a wasp or any other flying critter comes in the office, do I run for the woman's room and hide until it's gone? Or do I kill it and get on with my day?"

Rob grinned. "Don't know. What do you do?"

Life returned to Ta'waan. He decided to jump in on this one. "She hide in the bathroom."

Collin smiled sarcastically at Ta'waan. "Wrong! I get out the longest flyswatter I can find or Marne's hair spray, and I kill the bugger. Scared or not, I got work to do. I can't be ducking shadows all day long." She glared at them both. "Can't hide in the bathroom, either. It'd get very crowded in there."

They walked on some more. Ta'waan asked slowly, "So what if it's not something you can kill?"

Collin hesitated. "I remember a summer, once, when I went out barefoot. There's a path between our house and the river made up of a bank of flat rocks. They baked in the sun all day. Didn't hurt when I started out walking on them, but by the time I got to the middle, I realized my feet burned. There wasn't any place to get relief and no grown-up in sight."

Except the one who sent you out on the rocks in the first place.
Let's stick to the point.

Collin continued, "I had two choices. First, flop down, cry, and wait to be rescued. And in the meantime, more of me would be getting burned, and I'd be even more miserable. Second, suck it up, keep walking, and no matter how it hurt, get it over with."

Collin looked from boy to boy. "The solution to fear is to face what you have to, avoid what you can, and get through it. I've been afraid of rivers, but since I haven't gone on or near one, it hasn't been a problem."

She looked pointedly at Ta'waan. "People who are afraid of heights shouldn't look down from tall buildings. But if they are ever in a place where they have to be up high, they need to take a deep breath, and keep doing whatever it is that brought them there."

The trio walked on in silence for a few moments until Ta'waan asked, "How old you be when you walked them rocks?"

"Ten."

"An' you walk on out?"

"Didn't see much choice."

"Why didn't you call for you mama or daddy?"

Collin chewed her lip. "My mom died by then. My father…my father is a whole different story. One which I'd rather not discuss." She smiled. "Sort of like avoiding those fears if you can."

But Ta'waan couldn't let it go. "He mean to you?"

Collin closed her eyes as a series of vivid flashbacks rolled past her consciousness. "You might say that."

And now Rob jumped in, apparently realizing his caseworker lady had opened up—or fallen down. "You afraid of him?"

To which there could be only one answer. One honest answer. "All the time. Every moment I lived with him."

Not living with him is no picnic, either.
Knowing he's still out there, somewhere. Still hating…

"How'd you live?"

"I wouldn't let him win. I wouldn't let the fear stop me from living. I would not give him the satisfaction."

Collin shut down anything internal, refusing to debate, remember or otherwise continue the discussion. She looked pointedly at both boys. "You make up your mind whatever it is won't beat you, and you go on."

"WALKER!" Mitch thundered from his point position. "What is the matter with you, woman? We're at the head of the river, not the river itself! If you're going to fall behind, at least let the kids get past you! I'd like to get back sometime tonight! Move it!"

Collin smiled and waved. Under her breath, she muttered, "I'm gonna feed him to the grizzlies. So help me, before this trip is over, I'm going to feed him to the grizzlies."

Rob cleared his throat. "Uh, caseworker lady, ain't no grizzlies—"

Collin cut him off. "I'll find some. I'll hire some. I'll buy some if I have to. I don't care if it's Smokey Bear, I will feed him to the bears."

Ta'waan grinned. "That I'd like to see."

Rob slapped hands with him. "I'm down with you, bro."

Collin grinned on the inside. *A Southsider and an Eastender agreeing on something. Will the wonders of this camp never cease?*

They will if we don't catch up to Mitch.

The eccentric side of her nature wanted to link arms with the boys and skip forward, singing, *"We're off to see the Wizard."*

Might be fun, but the boys won't understand the connection.

Besides, the choreography could fail. You'd end up falling the rest of the way and land at Mitch's feet.

He will throw you off the boat.

Play it straight.

Collin smiled with genuine pleasure. "Let's go, boys. We've got a river to birth."

WEDNESDAY AFTERNOON

With a little extra effort, the front trio caught up to Mitch, followed almost immediately by the back duo. Mitch sneered. "Nice you could join us."

Collin smiled at Mitch. "It's too beautiful up here to walk fast, Mitch. We don't get to see mountains, much less be in them. Tallest thing out my window is a telephone pole. Or a billboard." A chorus of general assent backed her up.

Mitch sighed. "Okay, I forgot. It is beautiful up here. After we get our lesson in river origins, you can climb or look around if you like. But let's do what we came for first."

He led them to a point on the side of the hill where a small stream bubbled happily from between two boulders. Mitch explained, "This is an outlet for an underground lake deep inside the mountain. Water flows out, but no faster than the lake fills."

He pointed down the hillside. "You can follow the path as it curves to the left, there. It's pretty tame up here, but it gathers speed as it goes down, picking up rocks and pebbles along the way. They scour out the creek bed and let the waters flow faster."

Mitch continued to point upstream and down. "When the snows melt, they not only feed the underground lake but feed the stream as well, giving it volume. Smaller feeder streams join it near the bottom"—he pointed to the south end of the valley— "over at Three Forks.

"From there, it gathers steam with each thunderstorm which smashes through here. And we can have some wild storms, believe me." His eyes flashed with excitement. "Then is when you want to be on the water. Spring is best for rafting but only for the experienced. This time of year, the levels are down, and the current slows considerably. Which is why you, my crew, are here now instead of in spring." He smiled and clapped his hands. "Okay, so much for the outside view. Now I want to take you to see the underground lake. There are caverns around the point there where we can investigate a little. You should enjoy this. I know I do."

Something in his eyes bothered Collin. Of course, not much about Mitch didn't bother Collin. The idea of actually walking underground, in the dark, with him behind her, proved a daunting thought. One she would not allow.

Collin slipped forward to walk with Chonnell and Pardner. After further consideration, she called back, "Nyla, come join the female contingent. Girls against the guys." *Tale as old as time.*

Nyla skipped forward happily, put an arm around Collin's waist, and murmured, "Safety in numbers?"

Collin murmured back, "You got it, girlfriend."

If Nyla objected to the term, she didn't show it. Instead, she tousled Chonnell's hair and said, "We'll teach you two how it be. Us women got to stick together."

Collin grinned. "Until we find a man of our own. Then it's every woman for herself."

Nyla laughed out loud. "You got it, girlfriend."

They reached the entrance to the caverns. Mitch went to the head of the line, showed his Camp Grace ID, and the group passed through without comment. Other than the customary "Welcome."

A designated professional guided the tour. The Camp Grace team walked along narrow passageways, squeezed through even narrower passageways between massive boulders, slid under boulders, around boulders, between boulders…all to reach a limestone cavern somewhere near the heart of the hill. Lamps along the way bounced crystal reflections of light off the ceilings and floors, reflecting in small pools of silent mineral waters.

Once the group reformed, the guide began giving a basic history of stalactites and stalagmites. Collin's mind began to wander.

The guide recited, "Stalactites are formed first, by water laden with lime and salt dripping from the ceilings of the cavern. Stalagmites form from stalactites and are on the floors of the cavern. When the two grow together, we call it a column."

Hey! Hey, everybody! I got it! I got it! Stalactites come first. They come first in the alphabet, too. Now I can remember which is which! I got it!

Does anyone care?

Internally, Collin sighed. *It's the little things.*

The guide talked, pointing out the beauty of the caverns, the salt formations, the cascading waterfalls. "Remember, this is not what the explorers saw when they discovered this place. Their first glimpse looked like this."

He plunged the cavern into utter darkness, darkness you can touch and feel. Someone screamed, and Collin felt small arms grab her from all sides. She whispered, "Close your eyes. It'll be over in a minute."

The guide chuckled, and as quickly, the lights returned. "Until they lit up the cave, all this beauty remained entombed in darkness."

The tour concluded with a walk around the underground lake, large enough to row across, or maybe even float their raft. Collin decided she could forgive many—well, not all, but some—of Mitch's sins for bringing them here. Once again, he showed them something the city-dwelling campers and their counselor might otherwise never experience. She should thank him.

Of course, maybe we should wait until the trip is over.

Or maybe when the week is over.

Maybe we can send him a letter after we get back to Oakton.

Maybe...

"WALKER!" Collin snapped out of it, to find herself the loose caboose on the train, and the rest of it left the station. Mitch berated her. "What is it with you? Are we boring you? Not good enough for your company? Not interesting enough to merit your attention? Explain yourself!"

Collin banged her head lightly to clear the cobwebs. "It's a character defect. I lose touch with reality sometimes."

"Sometimes? Walker, you haven't been in touch with reality since you got off the bus. I swear I ought to slap you on permanent shore duty and relieve the crew of your influence."

Collin studied Mitch a moment, trying to read the man's eyes. She saw anger in them, far out of proportion to the crime. Did he want her to grovel for forgiveness? Expect her to beg to be allowed to stay? Could this be a bid to regain power in the kids' eyes?

Collin chose her words with care. "I apologize for my lack of attentiveness, Mitch. I don't deliberately tune out. Being near the river has me unbalanced, and it's a defense mechanism my brain uses."

The light in Mitch's eyes switched from anger to interest. "Defense mechanism? Defense against what?"

Collin shrugged. "Pain. Fear. Memories. It's sort of an all-purpose tool." She hesitated. "I promise I will do all I can to stay with the class, mentally and physically. I admit I've been a little worse today than before—"

A little?

"—but I'll pull it together. Write today off as an aberration." She adopted a sober, solemn expression and waited for Mitch's decision. The man continued to stare at her. Collin guessed she hadn't given him the response he expected. Or wanted. *Deal with it.*

After a moment, the man's eyes moved from anger to one of measured interest. "Defense mechanism, huh? Maybe we can test it before the week is over. See how good it is."

Collin sensed the challenge or—maybe more correctly put—the threat. Two worlds collided in her brain.

Take him. You know you can. Take him.

Don't be a fool. Sure, you can take him, but what do you prove? You don't feel pain?

You know how the game ends up. Smile, say, 'Maybe' and leave it there.

Be smart. For once.

Collin smiled at Mitch. "Maybe." Without further comment, she hustled to join her crew.

The trip home passed without event. As they pulled into the camp parking lot at the end of the day, Mitch instructed everyone, "We meet early tomorrow. Six a.m. at the boathouse."

Rob groaned; Ta'waan protested. "What about breakfast? Cafeteria don't even open until then!"

Pardner and Chonnell joined the chorus. "Yeah! What about breakfast? When we gonna eat?"

Before mutiny could ensue, Mitch laughed. "It will be open! I promise you. I'll get special permission for you to go in early.

Would I let my crew starve? Come on, people. You've got to learn to trust me."

Pacified, the crew grumbled and mumbled out of the van back to the lodge. Collin had a distinct feeling there would be an attempt to double up on dinner in case Mitch failed of his word. *Hope the cooks are ready!*

Collin climbed out of the van. "Thanks, Mitch. I enjoyed today."

Mitch followed behind her. "Hold up a minute."

Collin took a slow, deep breath and let it out equally slowly. She turned to face Mitch.

The man waited until the kids cleared off a respectable distance. "I'm glad you told the crew about your fear. I believe in getting everything out in the open. No secrets."

Collin nodded. "Right. No secrets."

"So you'll share why you're so afraid. You don't have to tell the crew, and I certainly won't say anything. But we need to get this out in the open."

Inwardly, Collin grimaced. How many times can you repeat a refrain?

Make something up. Something horrid. Maybe it will keep him happy and off your back.

Collin kept her tone even. "Mitch, what happened doesn't matter. What matters is I'm here. With your help, I intend to stay here."

Mitch's face brightened. "So, you're going to stick it out?"

"As long as I can. Rob wants me to stay, and I'm going to give it my best shot."

Mitch's smile broadened. "Great. Wonderful. You'll get the chance to get to know me better. You'll find out I'm not a bad guy after all." His hand slipped on her shoulder.

Collin slipped out from under it. "I already know what kind of guy you are, Mitch." She kept her tone measured. "You're a terrific person, and you're great with the kids."

"So you'll have dinner with me? I'll take you somewhere in town. It'll do you good to get away from all the kids."

She tossed her head. "I can't, Mitch. Not at night. The kids are why I'm here. They're my responsibility."

"Other counselors leave. I think you're the only one who hasn't

144

left for at least a few hours."

Collin didn't bother correcting him. "I can't speak for anyone but myself, Mitch. I have a job."

Mitch scoffed. "Oh, right. A job. Give me a break. You use it as an excuse not to let people get close, don't you?"

Collin would not be baited. "It's who I am."

"No, it's not. I've watched you. You know how to play, how to have a good time." Mitch dropped his hand from her shoulder to her waist. "It's what I'm offering you, Collin. The chance to have a good time. We could have a good time together, you know. Like adults." Mitch's voice dropped lower and softer.

Collin stepped back. "I'm not up for anything but friendship with you or anyone else. My life is too complicated as it is."

Mitch didn't seem to hear her. He moved closer to Collin. "Even friends can enjoy each other's company, Collin."

Take him. Take him.

Collin stood her ground. "Mitch, don't make me hurt you."

Mitch stopped, looked at her, and laughed. "You? Hurt me? Are you joking?"

Collin stared him in the eyes. "Let it go, Mitch."

Mitch continued to laugh. "No, this I got to see. Give it your best, shot, Walker. Your move. Hurt me."

Rule number one: karate for defense only.

Rule number two: first, learn rule number one.

Collin continued to stare at him, neither angry nor intimidated. It would be Mitch's call.

The man eyed her sideways. "You honestly think you could hurt me? Could take me in a fight?"

"I'd rather not have to find out. I want our relationship to be teacher to student. Nothing more. Can we leave it there?" Collin waited for Mitch to resolve the issue himself.

Mitch's eyes glazed, then came back to focus. He smiled. Or smirked. Whichever way she wanted to read it. "You're right. We can discuss anything more after the week is over. When you and the river come to terms. If you can."

He nodded his head. "Have a pleasant evening. Collin." He turned and walked toward the lodge.

Collin watched him go, half expecting him to turn around. He didn't. She waited a few more minutes, then walked to the lodge and turned down the corridor to her room.

A note hung on her door. A call came in for her at the reception desk. Jeff. Collin took the slip of paper down and stared at it. *He promised he'd call.*

I didn't expect him to follow through.

You going to call him back?

No.

Yes.

Why should I?

He's a good man, and he's interested in you.

There are no good men. Especially men who would be interested in you.

Call him.

NO.

Call him.

NO.

Collin stared at the paper. She turned it over and over in her hand, looking at the phone number on the reverse side.

Throw it away. Shred it and throw it away. You don't need him.

Collin walked up the hall, still turning the paper around and around. She hesitated at the exit doors leading to the lobby. Hesitated again at the entrance to the reception area. Hesitated before she keyed the combination to the phone lockbox. Hesitated before she took the phone to a corner of the room and sank to the floor. Hesitated before she punched the digits of the phone number on the keypad. Hesitated before she entered the last numeral.

Her finger hovered over the magic button. Connect the call? Hang up and walk away? Voices in her head screamed for both options. Collin stared at the phone.

She pushed the send button.

Three rings and a slightly lisping voice answered, "Fae'll residence. Jeff's phone. May I help you?"

Collin remembered Jeff talking about his sister. She took a chance and asked, "Is this Leesa?"

"Do I know who you are?" The voice filled with confusion.

Collin assured her, "No. I'm a friend of your brother Jeff. He told me about you." Collin forced the words out. "Is he home? May I speak to him?"

He must have left his phone sitting around, she guessed.

The voice came back formal and proper. "Jeffrey cannot come to the phone right now. May I take a message for him?"

Collin sagged. Leaving a message after all this build-up? "No. I'll call back." If only she'd been able to bring her cell on the trip, she could've just texted him.

She heard an older woman's voice in the background. "Leesa? Darling, who is on the phone?"

"It is for Jeffrey. It is a girlfriend."

Collin started to jump at the term but stopped herself. Maybe to Leesa, it made sense. Collin was a girl and a friend.

The older woman's voice approached the phone. "Oh, Leesa. You know Jeffrey doesn't have any girlfriends. You must be mistaken. Let me have his phone, dear. I'll talk to whoever it is."

Collin waited as the older woman took the phone from Leesa and said, "Hello? May I help you?"

"My name is Collin Walker, and I'm a friend of your son's from up at Camp Grace. May I speak to Jeff, please?"

The voice brightened. "Oh! I see how Leesa could be confused. Females don't call for Jeffrey. When you said you were his friend, Leesa must have thought you meant you were a girl and a friend."

The woman laughed, a light, lilting laugh that struck Collin as off. Not fake. Not forced, but somehow off. What did Jeff say about his mom? She'd had a stroke and hadn't made it all the way back? Collin listened hard to the tones. The woman chirped, "I'm sure Jeffrey will be sorry he missed your call, young woman. He so rarely gets calls. Jeffrey is always busy with his work at the camp and the fire station and helping his father. It's a wonder he has time to have any friends at all. And he's always helping Leesa and me. I don't drive anymore, and when he's home, he takes us wherever we need to go, and he never complains about it at all."

A deep male voice sounded in the background. "Lacey, my love, who are you talking to?"

"Oh, Harmon, I forgot her name already. But she's a friend of Jeffrey's. I told her he wasn't able to come to the phone."

"Dear, instead of running up the woman's minutes telling her he can't come to the phone, why don't you go get him? If this is that Walker woman he's been talking about ever since he came home, I do not want to live with him if he misses the call. Please."

Collin swallowed a smile. She heard Lacey saying, "Now,

dear, you were young and in love, once."

There came the sound of a kiss. Harmon said, "Now I'm old and in love. Go get your son."

Collin ached for the simplicity of it. Could there honestly be a relationship so beautiful? One she would ever know?

The phone apparently changed hands again. Harmon's voice came over the line, pleasant and warm. "Thank you for waiting so patiently. May I ask who is calling, though I'm sure you've told both my wife and my daughter."

"Collin Walker, sir."

Silence. "I see. It's a pleasure to speak with you. My son has done little else than talk about you since he came home. I'm looking forward to making your acquaintance, Ms. Walker."

Collin chewed the inside of her lip. "He has told me some about you as well, sir."

Harmon chuckled. "I doubt in quite the same glowing terms. Ah, I see him coming in now. Thank you for holding for him. It's going to make him so much easier to live with."

Jeff's voice sounded sharp but respectful. "Dad. Mom said I have a call. May I have my phone? Please?"

"In a moment, son. Ms. Walker, when you return to Oakton, you must come out to visit us. Don't wait for Jeffrey to invite you. We're in the book. The only Farrell on Lewiston Road."

Collin projected a quick mental map, trying to remember Lewiston Road. On the east side, to be sure, divided north and south by the river.

North boasted flashy new money: condos and townhomes and mansions too modern to have trees of any size. South of the river, the houses remained big and comfortable, built before Oakton became a city.

South were homes you wouldn't want to heat in winter, nor cool in summer. The kind developers always wanted to tear down to make way for more condos and multi-family units. Collin asked, "South of the river, sir?"

Mr. Farrell sounded impressed. "Shrewd guess, Ms. Walker."

Collin could hear a still respectful but slightly more pressing, "Dad, please, may I have my phone?"

Harmon's voice took on a light, bantering note. "Ms. Walker, I believe Jeffrey is available to take your call now. Do you still wish to speak to him?"

"Yes, sir, I do. It's been a pleasure talking to you, Mr. Farrell."

"And to you, Ms. Walker."

Collin heard the phone changing hands, a muttered, "Thanks, Dad," and then, "Collin? Are you still there?"

Collin swallowed her smile. *What a family.* "I'm here. I got the note you called."

"I'm sorry about that. I forgot I left my phone sitting in the living room." Jeff's voice lacked his usual confidence. "I didn't know if you'd call back. You were upset this morning, and I can't blame you. I wasn't happy about leaving, either, and I'm sorry."

"I'm sorry I sounded short with you."

Jeff chuckled. "We're two sorry people. Not the best foundation for a relationship, I know. But at least we can admit it."

Collin leaned her head against the wall. "Okay. How has your day been?"

"Busy. Dad's been bidding on this piece of property for months now, since Christmas, I think. Owners took it off the market in May. Then yesterday, it shows up again as a new listing at a reduced price, and Dad needed to move on it. Which is why I got the 'come home, Jeff' call. He wanted me to inspect it before we put in another bid to make sure nothing changed."

"Had it?"

Jeff's voice became sarcastic. "Changed? Of course not! Nothing changed. Except there'd been a fire that melted some of the HVAC conduits. And there was water damage where they put out the fire. Which the owners inferred we saw and accepted last year." Jeff snorted. "I pulled the records of the responding fire units. Yeah, no. The fire happened the end of April."

"Won't your dad offer a lower bid, then?"

"No. He withdrew his bid altogether. Dad won't enter into a contract with anyone he knows has lied about the condition of a property. There's never only one lie."

Collin felt a chill run up her spine. "Is your dad like that with people, too? No forgiveness? No second chances?"

"No! No, he's not like that with people. And not even in business. He knows we're all human, and we all fall short. That's not what I meant. In contract matters, if Dad knows someone has lied to cover something up, gets caught, and still lies about it, he won't do business with them. Who knows what else they may have lied about?"

Collin wished this were a video call. She wanted to see Jeff's eyes when she asked him the next question. "With people?"

Jeff's voice became earnest. "He knows we all fail. We all make mistakes. Bad decisions. Bad choices. He's made his share, and he admits it. The Lord forgave him. He has to forgive others."

Collin's thoughts darkened. "Easy to say."

Jeff's voice took on an urgency. "Easy to do when we remember who we are inside. Collin, whatever someone has done before, it doesn't matter to my dad or me. It's who they are now that's important. What they do with their lives." Jeff paused. "Whatever happened in the past doesn't matter." He paused. "I don't mean it doesn't matter, because likely it does. But it doesn't make a difference in how I feel about you. Or...about anyone. And I learned that from my dad. It's how he lives his life."

Collin stared at the floor. She whispered, "Maybe you'd better hear what it is before you say that."

Jeff's voice became gentle. "Has the Lord forgiven you?"

Collin's eyes filled with tears. She closed them and turned her face up to keep them from falling. "Yes."

"Then I can't hold anything against you, either. You need to believe me."

Collin chewed hard on her lip. "I... I want to try." She tossed her head to throw off the fear. "It's hard, Jeff. It's hard."

"Harder than first man to one hundred wins, no timeouts, no time limits?"

Collin laughed. "A little bit. Maybe."

Jeff's voice seemed to relax. "I understand, Collin. I'm going to prove it to you, though. Stay with me. I don't mean 'stay' like live with me or anything. I mean, don't give up on this relationship. Hang with me, okay? Let me show you. Trust me."

Never trust anyone!

Never trust anyone. Never trust anyone. Never trust never trust never trust never trust...

"I'll try. I am trying." Collin closed her eyes.

"Did class go okay?"

"Yeah. Mitch took us up to the limestone caverns. It's a beautiful place. Very educational." Collin chuckled. "Until they turned the lights out. But I suppose they thought that educational as well."

Jeff's smile came through the phone. "Yeah, caught me off guard the first time, too. About jumped out of my skin into my dad's." Jeff's tone became more guarded. "How are things with you and Mitch? Any...problems?"

Collin kept her tone even. "None that haven't been resolved."

You hope.

I hope.

"I hope that's a good thing." Jeff sounded less than convinced.

Which matched Collin's mood. "So do I."

Jeff hesitated. "Remember Steve Parks will always listen. To anything. Got it?"

"I got it, Jeff. I do." She closed her eyes. "I miss you."

"I miss you. I'll be back tomorrow night or Friday morning at the latest. I'll try to be there before you take the river ride."

Collin nodded. "No promises. It would be good to see you before I go out, I know. I should get off. We're supposed to meet at the docks at six tomorrow morning." Collin smiled. "The crew became pretty upset about possibly missing breakfast, but Mitch assured them the kitchen would be open." She looked at the phone. "Would they open up the whole cafeteria for six kids, a counselor, and an instructor? Isn't that asking a lot of food services?"

Jeff seemed hesitant. "It might be unless Mitch arranged it beforehand. Chef Michael likes to have twenty-four hours notice, but he's been known to do it with less. Doesn't particularly like it, but he takes it up with the instructor, not the campers. Your crew will get plenty of food to eat." Jeff paused. "You're missing dinner, aren't you?"

Collin bristled. "What I eat or don't eat doesn't concern you, Mr. Farrell."

"As a friend, it does. I know you're stressed, but——"

Collin saw a face in the office window and guessed someone else needed the phone. She waved at the figure. "I have to go. I'll talk to you tomorrow, okay?"

Jeff said quickly, "Collin, take care of yourself. Please, milady? There are a lot of people who need you. They...I need you, milady. I care. Please?"

Collin couldn't get the words out around the lump in her throat.

The best she could do was whisper, "Bye." She pushed up off the floor, put the phone back in its lockbox. She kept her head down as she walked past Ms. Peaco...Petcock. Collin muttered, "Nite." It's all she had left.

She walked around the lodge, too restless to go back to her room. She needed action. Needed to be moving, not thinking. Too much thinking going on. Thinking about Mitch. About the river. About Jeff. So much not settled, so much unknown. If she sat, all the doubts would catch her. Fear would overwhelm her. No, better to keep moving.

Maybe Rob could help. She'd see if he wanted to shoot some hoops. It might help her settle. Collin went down to the game room and found Rob noisily playing video games with a mob of campers. All eyes stayed glued on him as he revealed move after move, beating the enemy in spectacular fashion.

Collin heard one camper say, his voice incredulous, "Jeff taught you? The janitor taught you? Janitors ain't cool, man."

Rob said hotly, "Don't matter what a man do on the outside, dude, long as it's honest. It's what he got on the inside makes him cool. And Jeff is one cool dude. Watch this."

Collin slipped quietly back out of the room. Rob needed to be here. Somehow, he was learning. And now even passing it on to others. Cool. Way cool.

Collin sighed. While cool though it might be, it didn't solve her restlessness problem. Maybe a walk. Maybe a run.

Maybe not. There were no lighted paths outside. Only the lodge had perimeter lights and walking around and around the building didn't cut it. The only other outside lighted area Collin knew happened to be the basketball court. She could go there, shoot a few hoops, practice a few moves, think about the night before...

Collin didn't waste time finishing the thought but headed back to her room. She changed into her sweats, grabbed her ball, and headed toward the court.

The glow from the lodge provided enough illumination to reach the court without difficulty. Collin snapped on the court lights, set the timer, and slowly began dribbling up and down the court.

It didn't feel nearly as restful as she hoped it would. Maybe if she pushed a little harder, it would.

Harder. Always the answer. Don't understand a problem? Work harder. Can't get the hang of something? Work harder. Falling behind? Work harder. Don't ask for help, don't look for excuses, don't try to analyze the situation, work harder.

The familiar demons began whispering in her mind.

Harder. Work harder.

You're only afraid because you're not working hard enough.

You should have stayed at work. You never work hard enough.

You're out here playing. You should be back at home, working harder. How will you ever please anyone if you don't work harder?

Work harder. Work harder.

Collin began to pound the ball against the blacktop as anger and frustration built. She started jogging around the court, running laps as she dribbled. The demons continued to hound her, echoes of her father's voice.

Harder. Work harder.

You're a girl, a worthless girl. You want to win? You want to be as good as your brother? Work harder. Harder. Harder.

You can't cry. You don't have time to cry. You have to work harder.

The laps came faster, the ball rising and falling with each step. And still, the demons mocked.

You'll never be anything. You're a girl. A worthless girl.

Girls don't know how to work hard. Your brother works hard. Your brother makes me proud. But not you. You don't know anything about working hard.

You want love? You want respect? Work hard. Harder. Harder.

And know no matter how hard you work, it will never be hard enough. Never be hard enough. Never...

Collin made no sound as she ran. Her teeth clenched, her face devoid of emotion. Run. Run. Don't stop, or they'll catch you. Run. Run. Harder. Harder. Run. Run...

Collin pulled up abruptly and shouted, "No! I will not run anymore." She began moving again at a slow jog, trying to cool down. The voices in her head continued to jeer and mock, but she ignored them.

She bounced the ball slowly, keeping pace with her steps. "I did work hard. I did everything you asked me to do. I couldn't be Erin. Erin couldn't even be Erin for you."

Her pace slowed to a walk, then to a halt. She turned and faced to the west, looking in the direction of the lodge but seeing a distant mile beyond it.

The lights on the timer went out, but Collin didn't move. She stood alone on the hill. "I wanted to love you. But you wouldn't let me. I tried. I really tried."

But did you try hard enough?

Collin looked up at the stars and asked, for neither the first nor the last time, "What else could I do?"

No tears came; none remained. The deep silence of the heavens came as her only answer. Collin dropped her head in defeat, acknowledging once again the futility of the inquiry. She closed her eyes and stood motionless.

An explosion went off in her brain as someone or something struck her from behind. She dropped to her knees. Another blow hit her in the back, and she curled to the ground. A savage kick cracked against her ribs. A frantic voice in her head urged, *Roll right! Roll right!*

Collin responded out of instinct, barely dodging the blow aimed for her head. Adrenaline masked any pain. She rolled to her feet, keeping the attacker between herself and the lodge in an attempt to see him. A tall, misshapen figure loomed in front of her. *What is this?*

The figure grabbed her arms. She grabbed its. They grappled together for a moment, then in one smooth motion Collin twisted, stepped back, ducked and threw her foe over her head. She heard a sharp "crack" as a head hit the pavement, and a loud "oof" as oxygen exited its lungs. *Human. Male.* Any other observation would have to wait.

Collin crouched low and ran, holding her side to steady the ribs she knew were broken. The lights ahead would be both her worst enemy and best friend. At the hill's crest, she slid flat to the left, knowing better than to make a straight run for cover. She listened for the thud of her assailant's feet but heard nothing. Collin risked a quick look over her shoulder and saw the form outlined against the sky.

Anger, hate, rage all radiated from the dark outline. Collin moved as silently as possible to her left, angling away from the lights of the lodge.

The hill bottomed out then rose gently again, forming a narrow creek bed. If she could gain the far shoulder, she would be invisible to the menace above her. But to cross, she would risk detection by sound. The man hesitated at the top of the hill as if unsure how or if to proceed. Collin wished on him all the mental confusion and uncertainty she could. *Maybe he can take some of mine.*

Collin's heart dropped as she realized the lodge doors were still open. She could hear the young campers laughing and talking. If she broke for the lodge, what would prevent her attacker from abandoning her as prey and choosing someone less feisty? Collin could not let that happen. She desperately wished she knew what the time might be. The doors closed at ten-thirty, after a camper headcount.

Collin looked back up the hill and realized she'd lost track of her opponent. She carefully picked up a handful of stones and prepared to throw them as a diversionary tactic. But where to throw them? Would he be stupid enough to fall for the oldest trick in the book, or would he head the opposite direction, knowing the stones as a ruse?

Do you have time for this debate? She strained her senses to pick up any sign of the man but received nothing. He could be gone for all she knew. The prickling at the back of her neck and the twisting of her gut told her otherwise. Collin drew in a silent breath and threw the stones in as hard and as broad a pattern as she could. At the same time, she leaped across the creek and began running hard to the right.

The stones made excellent sonar. The thuds off the grass sounded muted and gentle. The thuds of a padded object a mere two feet or so away caused her heart to surge. Any pretense at strategy disappeared, and Collin bolted for a line of trees.

She could still hear the voices of campers. How many children out there? Enough to be a deterrent or just enough to be an invitation? Could she risk it?

Can you live with yourself if you're wrong?
Can you live if you don't?

Too many questions and no time to answer them. Collin dashed between the trees seeking cover in the brush. She made herself as small as possible and waited. Her lungs burned, but she couldn't risk the gasp for air, which might reveal her position. Slow, shallow breaths didn't get it, though. Collin drew in a deep breath, willing herself to exhale slowly, quietly, ever so slowly, ever so quietly...

She heard the snapping of the tree branches as her attacker forced his way into the brush. He abandoned all pretense of stealth, smashing through the underbrush in a vain attempt to find her. Collin remained still. *Father, blind his eyes to where I am. But keep him away from the others, please.*

Words hissed. "Come out, coward. Face me."

Collin willed herself not to move, not to breathe, not to let the pounding of her heart give her away. *Please, Lord. Help me.*

"I am your fear. I am your nightmare. You will face me sooner or later. And I will win. I always win."

The bell rang at the lodge, signaling curfew started, and all campers and counselors needed to come in for a headcount. It left Collin fifteen minutes to report in, or be counted as missing, and a search would ensue.

The attacker swore under his breath, then seethed, "You will face me. Tonight. Tomorrow. One day. I am patient. I will wait. You will come to me, and we will finish this. Pleasant dreams."

The man backed out of the brush and ambled back into the darkness of the hills. He even whistled as he went. Collin could see his silhouette moving away, headed back up the hill and away from the lodge. Collin's eyes narrowed as she studied the figure. Padding? Did he have on a padded suit? Why? To hide his real dimensions?

To keep from being marked. No scratches. No DNA. No proof. Your word against his. Clever. Well-conceived. Practiced.

Practiced. He's done this before. How many times?

Collin left any further deliberations for later. Now, right now, she needed to get in for the headcount. And report the attack. She limped to the far entrance of the facility, closest to her room. She pulled the exit door closed behind her and leaned against the wall for support. Gritting her teeth, she stood as straight as she could and walked to Jill and Marites's door. She banged on it and demanded her customary, "Show me two faces."

Both girls came to the door. Marites popped her head out, then in again without comment. Jill looked at Collin, her face drawn with concern. "Ms. Walker? What happened to you?"

Collin leaned against the wall and managed a smile. "I looked in on a cooking class, and it got out of hand. I'm fine. You two need anything?"

Jill's eyes widened. "No, ma'am. What did they cook?" The girl's voice reflected her incredulity.

"Collard greens. Nasty buggers. Tried to fight back." She nodded her head. "But we got 'em under control. I think." She squeezed Jill's shoulder. "Good night, girlfriend. I won't see you in the morning. Class is meeting early. Early early. Set your alarm."

Jill nodded repeatedly. "Oh, yes, ma'am. We never miss breakfast again. Learned that one quick." She smiled. "'Nite, Ms. Walker."

Collin waited until the door closed, then doubled over in pain. Now came the painful walk to the reception desk. She slid along the wall when she could, stopping at each door to catch a shallow breath, then pushing on forward. Six doors.

Five doors. *You gonna report this?*

Is there a choice? He's done this before. I need to stop him.

Why you?

Four doors.

He picked me to attack. He won't get to pick any others.

Three doors.

Like you can stop anyone. You're weak. You're useless. You can't even stand up straight.

Two doors.

Collin stopped and lay her head against the wall. She breathed in and out, shallow breaths, not daring to expand the lungs against the possibly shattered ribs. Collin shoved herself to a full-upright standing position. Under her breath, she seethed, "I can. I am. I will. Watch me."

Collin keyed the entrance to the reception area. She pulled out the attendance ledger from its place, marked her two charges present and accounted for, then moved to the phone box. She unlocked the case, took out the phone, then collapsed in the corner of the room.

Same place she'd been four hours ago. Four hours? Really? Collin cradled the phone in her hand, closed her eyes, and sighed. "Father, what is this? What is this all about? Why me? Why now? Why here?"

She dropped her head. "I know, I know. Don't ask why. Ask, 'what do You want me to do about it,' right? Okay, I'm asking. What do you want me to do? Call the police? And tell them I got attacked by a nightmare? Right."

Call Steve Parks. Jeff's voice in her head. *Steve Parks is always on call. Day or night.*

Did the camp director need to know she'd been attacked?

Would you want to know?

Collin pulled the paper Jeff gave her out of her pocket and keyed in the number.

Steve's voice sounded as if receiving a call from the camp phone happened all the time. Maybe it did. "This is Steve Parks. How can I help you?"

Collin closed her eyes. "Mr. Parks, this is Collin Walker."

"Yes, Ms. Walker. Is everything going okay?"

Collin cleared her throat. "Uh, no. No, sir, it's not. There was an…an incident out on the basketball court. I… I think… I'd like to discuss it with you in person if it's not too much trouble."

Now the man's voice reflected concern. Not panic, but deep concern. "Where are you, Ms. Walker?"

"In the reception area, sir. I'd like to move to somewhere else, in case someone needs to use the phone, or…or something." The adrenaline levels dropped. Her brain began to fog.

"Leeann's office is just across the hall. The key code is 5574. Wait for me there. Mrs. Parks and I will be over in fifteen minutes."

Collin nodded. *He can't see a nod, idiot.* "Yes, sir. I'll be there." She disconnected the call, slipped the phone back into its case and put the case back where it belonged. She pulled herself to her feet, using every shelf and ledge she could find to support her climb upward. It took all she could do to not groan with every movement. But the sharp pain cleared her head for the moment. Collin stood, remembered to turn out the light, and left the room.

She leaned against the closed door, estimating the distance

across the hall. *Eight feet? Ten feet?*

What difference does it make? You have to cross it sometime. Unless you want to slide the length of the corridor and back again.

You can't do it. You're weak, and you're selfish. You could do it if you wanted to, but no, you only think about yourself.

I will help. Do it.

Collin sucked in her bottom lip, bit down hard on it, stood as straight as she could, and began walking. She closed her eyes and counted. "One."

One step forward. "Two."

Two steps forward. "Three."

At the third step, a rib shifted, sending a cascade of pain through her body. Collin clamped down on her lower lip, drawing blood in her agony. "Four."

"Five."

"Six"

"Seven."

"Eight."

Collin opened her eyes. Two more steps. She could do this. She could.

"Nine."

"Ten."

Collin sagged against the wall. She wanted so badly to curl up in a ball on the floor but knew she couldn't. Not yet. She still had work to do. She keyed the lock, opened the door, closed it behind her, and sank. That's all there was.

Except...

Except Steve and Mrs. Parks were coming, and she didn't want them seeing her splayed out on the floor. Or curled up in a corner. No, she needed to climb into a chair, sit up relatively straight, and act like she controlled the situation.

Fat chance.

Collin crawled across the floor to the desk and its complement of chairs. First order of business: find a chair with no wheels. Collin inched her way off the floor, inch by inch, into the seat. Only after her rear settled securely did she let out the moan that threatened to undo her. Collin wrapped both arms around her middle and breathed. She didn't move, didn't think, didn't do anything but sit and breathe.

Time passed. The door opened, admitting Mr. and Mrs. Parks. Steve took one look at Collin and reached for his phone. Collin stopped him. "I don't need a doctor. The ribs are bruised, and that's the most they'll tell me. I already know that part. Help me understand the rest of it."

Steve and his wife sat down opposite Collin. Steve leaned forward slightly. "Is there a danger to this camp, Ms. Walker?"

Collin paused. "No. I don't believe there is. Whoever this is, they're focused on me."

"Tell us what happened."

Collin went back over the story piece by piece. Telling it solidified details. She subtracted the fear, leaving only facts as she observed them. "He wanted me to think he might be some sort of surreal monster, maybe born out of my imagination." Collin's eyes narrowed. "But when I flipped him, he had solid muscle and bones." She ducked her head to the side. "And his feet were real enough. A mugger in a costume. That's all."

Steve put a hand on her shoulder. "I believe you. This isn't the first time he's been seen around here." He sat back in his chair. "But it's the first time he's hurt anyone directly." He looked at his wife, then back to Collin. "We need to call the sheriff."

Collin held up a hand. "No. Or yes, I'll talk to him. But I don't want the police out here. These kids are having the week of their lives, and I don't want it ruined because of some nutjob." She implored, "Please. Don't bring the police here."

Mrs. Parks pulled out her phone and connected to someone immediately. *Speed dial to the sheriff's office?*

Is that a good thing?

While Mrs. Parks spoke to whoever answered the phone, Steve assured Collin, "It's going to be okay, Ms. Walker. Sheriff Lodi is very good at keeping a low profile. The campers won't know they've been here."

Collin nodded. "I need a ride to the sheriff's station, then, so I can give them the report. For all the good it will do." She snorted. "There's no proof any of this happened."

Steve pursed his lips. "Don't sell Bo short, Ms. Walker." He stood, offered his arm to his wife, then extended it to Collin so she could stand.

Collin pulled in a deep breath, took Steve's elbow, and pulled herself up. It surprised and pleased her she could stand straighter and without as much assistance. The three walked out of the office, out of the corridor, and out of the lodge.

The drive to the sheriff's station took less than ten minutes. Steve parked the car, opened his wife's door, then Collin's, and stood back as Collin slid out and stood unaided. He stepped back and let Collin enter first, announcing as she did, "Bo, this woman has a story to tell you need to hear."

A uniformed man in his early sixties met them in front of the check-in counter. Balding on top, bulging slightly in the middle, he looked the epitome of the bumbling backwoods law enforcement caricature. But the hard eyes and the grim set of the mouth vanquished any such foolish misconceptions. Steve made the briefest of introductions: "Sheriff Bo, this is Collin Walker. Ms. Walker, Sheriff Bo Lodi."

Collin reached out to shake his hand. "Sheriff."

Bo eyed Collin up and down, measuring her for...what? *Veracity? Stability?*

Sorry about that, Chief. Collin didn't know what the standard of approval might be. She held his gaze evenly, neither cowering nor attacking. After a moment, he nodded a trace, and Collin guessed she passed the initial test, whatever it meant.

Bo looked at Steve. "I appreciate you and the missus bringing her to me. I'll see she gets back to the camp when we're done."

Steve nodded to Collin. "I'm sorry this happened, Ms. Walker." He looked at Sheriff Lodi. "We need this guy off our backs, Bo. He's escalating."

Bo "humphed." Steve and his wife left the station. Bo motioned for Collin to follow him to an inner office. One wall was adorned with a 12-point buck. Next to it hung a bass, pushing legal size. Collin could just make out the date beneath it. Must have been the sheriff's first bass ever.

A yellowed wall calendar from 1975 hung on a bulletin board. Little League trophies lined bookcases. Desks, chairs, tables, bookcases, all crafted from oak, and so well worn, no ridges remained anywhere. Collin noted a young woman with a stenographer machine already in the room, ready to take down everything. Collin cocked her head in surprise. Sheriff Bo said, "It's for your convenience. So you don't have to tell the story twice."

"In case it changes?" Collin took a seat against the wall, leaning back to support the ribs that still protested.

The man smiled. "That, too. What is your connection to the camp right now?"

"I'm a counselor. A social worker. I work with these kids every day, where they live in the streets."

"For how long?" The sheriff made a note on the yellow legal pad lying on his desk.

"I started volunteering with an intervention team after high school and began fulltime work after college. Eight years." Collin looked the sheriff in the face. "Eight long, grueling years of trying to teach these kids there's a better way to live." She stopped. "Or a way to live, period. These kids are my life, Sheriff."

The man didn't react. "Where were you, and what happened, exactly?"

Collin stepped into her observer role. "I went to court two to practice some hoops and to get exercise."

"What time?"

"I'm guessing around nine."

"Alone?" More notes.

Collin realized this would be an interrogation as much as a deposition. She warned her brain to be prepared to shift gears mentally as often as necessary. Some rumbles of disagreement sounded from the boys in the back, but they agreed they would try. Still, it would cost her dearly down the road. "Yes, alone. I needed some time to clear my head."

"Of what?" Bo's eyebrows lifted.

Collin managed to keep the irritation out of her voice, but barely. "Of being around teenage kids all day every day for the past week. I wanted someplace quiet to decompress. Okay?"

The man chuckled. "I'll buy that. What then?"

"I lost track of time. The lights on the court went out, and something hit me in the back of the head."

"Any idea what it could have been?"

"My guess is his fists, doubled up. Then he hit me in the back, and I fell to the ground." Collin went through the attack step by step, relating anything she could remember, whether she felt it mattered or not. She finished with the man's threats and his walking back into the shadows.

Sheriff Lodi's eyes narrowed to slits as he studied Collin. "What did he mean about being your fear?"

Collin dropped her eyes for a moment. She looked up. "I have a fear of the river. It terrifies me. Somehow he knew about that and wants to use it against me."

The sheriff sat back in his chair. "Who knows about this fear?"

Collin shrugged. "It's not something I particularly spread around. My crew knows. Mitch Kellogg, the rafting instructor." Collin paused. For one moment, her heart sank. "Jeff Farrell."

He's out of town. Can't be him. No.

Wanna bet?

Collin looked back at the man. "That's all I know. Crew doesn't talk about stuff with anyone else, so that leaves them out. And leaves Mitch and Jeff."

Sheriff Lodi shrugged. "We checked off Mitch Kellogg after the last incident."

Collin hated herself. "Farrell?"

The sheriff about split a gut laughing. "Farrell? Are you serious? Jeff Farrell attacking anyone is ludicrous. You've been on the streets too long if you think for one moment Jeff could be involved in this." He rocked back and forth in his seat in time to his chuckles.

Collin stared back. "Maybe I have. But I'm still alive because I don't take anything for granted."

The man stopped rocking. "Okay, so you say your crew knows, but they don't talk about it to anyone. And Jeff Farrell knows, but he's hardly a suspect. Mitch Kellogg knows, but we've eliminated him before. Who does that leave us?"

Collin looked at the sheriff sideways. "Eliminated Mitch from what? And what did Steve Parks mean about getting him off the camp's back? And what's escalating?"

The man stretched, settled in his chair, eyed Collin carefully. "There've been a few incidents like yours in the past few years. No one has been attacked before, so we haven't pursued it beyond taking the report. It started with kids being scared by some lumbering apparition chasing them out of the woods." He raised an eyebrow. "Where they didn't belong in the first place. And never went back again."

Collin shrugged. "West Virginia flavored Big Foot."

"About what we thought. No traces, no footprints, nothing. Chalked it up to imaginations or pranksters and let it go."

Bo stood and walked to look out the window. He turned. "Six months later, a female counselor took a horse out for a ride. The horse came back alone. We searched and found the counselor five miles from camp. Seems the horse bolted when a shadowy figure roared out of the trees at them. She couldn't get the horse under control. It carried her out to the middle of a field, dumped her, and walked back. She twisted an ankle when she fell, but otherwise, no permanent injuries."

Collin listened closely. Her eyes narrowed as the sheriff continued. Bo leaned against the wall. "Four months later, a group of campers got the wits scared out of them by this thing showing up at the movie theatre, jumping in front of the projector, shrieking and screaming. No evidence of a break-in and no forensics to give us anything to go on."

Collin bit the inside of her lip. "Big Foot moving indoors? Still doesn't equate to any real harm, right?"

"Other than the mayhem of people stampeding out of a crowded theatre. Two people ended up with broken legs." Sheriff Bo moved back across the room and sat down again.

Collin looked at the floor. "What's he learning with each attack? He can scare more people? Or he can hurt people? What's his end game?"

The sheriff leaned back and crossed his arms. "We don't know. But you're the first person he's physically attacked, and the first person he's spoken to. What makes you special?"

Sheriff Bo's eyes bored into Collin, perhaps daring her to answer. Collin sat perfectly still. "I have no idea. Maybe I'm the first person who fought back."

"No. He didn't come at you to scare you. He assaulted you from behind. He intended to bring you down." Bo pulled forms from the drawer in his desk. After he thumped it to get it to open. "Whoever this is, you made him mad."

Collin snorted. "Well, that makes two of us. I'm not thrilled with him, either." She looked at Bo. "What happens now? He threatened I would face him sooner or later. Which means he's coming back after me."

The man raised an eyebrow. He tossed the forms across the desk to Collin. "How do you feel about protective custody?"

Collin gave him a jaundiced eye. "No. And no bodyguards, either. If this creature is after me, I'll face him." She slid the forms back.

"Don't expect him to fight fair."

A cold thought washed over her. Collin looked at the floor, then looked up to hold the sheriff's gaze. "Would he endanger the kids?"

The sheriff thought a moment. "If he thought it would give him an edge, probably."

Collin shook her head. "That can't happen. I'll call him out first. It doesn't matter what happens to me, but the kids…"

Collin stood abruptly. "I've got to go back to camp. Maybe I can find him before morning and end this." She began to shake with anger. "He's not going to hurt my kids. None of them. I won't—"

The man pulled Collin's chair closer to her. "Sit down, Ms. Walker. We're not going to let anything happen to the kids at the camp, or to you if we can help it. Tell me what your day will be like tomorrow. Where are you meeting, and with who?"

Collin sat down. She checked her anger. "We meet at the boat dock at six. Kids will eat breakfast at five, I'm sure."

"Names?" Collin gave him the names and ages of the crew. The sheriff wrote them down on his legal pad, then stopped and looked at them again. "Seems like a lot of inexperience to take on the river. You sure about this?"

Collin shuddered. "No. I'm not. I'm not sure I can even go on the river. But I promised Rob I'd try, so I'm trying."

"Good luck. You'll need it."

Collin scowled. "Thank you for the vote of confidence, Sheriff. It does a whole lot to lift my spirits." Collin crossed her arms over her chest.

Bo put up his hands. He chuckled. "Don't take it personally." He looked at Collin sideways, studying her. "You say he called you out about your specific fear. When you're rafting, is there ever a time you're alone? Could he get you alone during the day?"

"Not unless he capsizes the raft, and then there's no guarantee who ends up where. I don't see how it can happen during a class."

"What about after?"

Collin thought. "Kids usually scatter. Nyla and Niles will go to the game room. Rob will either go there or go to the gym to shoot hoops. Chonnell and Pardner tell me they spend time in the kitchen." She smiled. "Seems they both want to learn to cook, and since they can't take two classes, Mrs. O'Brien has been teaching them after dinner."

"You?"

Collin looked at the floor. "I would have gone up to the outdoor courts and played ball by myself. But I suppose that's out of the question now, right?"

Sheriff Lodi nodded slowly. "Exactly." He hmmed to himself for a moment. "Ms. Walker, I'm going to put men in the field to follow you and your class." He held up his hand. "You won't see them, I assure you. They are going to shadow your moves and see if anyone else is out there doing the same. I want to put an end to whatever game this guy is playing before he goes any further." He eyed Collin sideways. "Can you act like nothing's different?"

Collin closed her eyes. "Sheriff, I can act any way you want me to. You tell me what you want me to do, and I'll do it. Just make sure nothing happens to my kids."

The man stood up. "We have a deal, then. I'll take you to the ER then back to camp."

Collin gritted her teeth. "No ER. I already know the ribs are either cracked or busted. I'm not wasting hours of my time sitting in an examining room, going in and out of X-Ray, having someone constantly checking my vitals, only for the doctor to say, 'I'm sorry, but there's nothing we can do for cracked ribs.' I've cracked ribs before, and I can live with them. Take me back to camp, and I'll be fine."

He raised an eyebrow. "You sure about that? You don't want them to check out any other possible injuries? Like a missing brain?"

Collin sneered at him. "Cute. No, Sheriff. I'm good." She paused. And paused. "Sheriff, you eliminated Jeff Farrell without a second thought. You know him pretty well?"

The man smiled. "I've known him since he was old enough to steal gumballs off the counter at the movie theater." The corner of his mouth twitched up. "How well do you know him, Ms.

Walker?"

Collin looked at her lap. "Not as well as maybe I should." She raised her head to look Sheriff Lodi directly in the eyes. "Is he real? I mean, the inside and the outside match?"

The man's eyes smiled. The corner of his mouth twitched a bit higher. "Yes, Ms. Walker. Jeff Farrell is real inside and out. He's a good man. Now, let me ask you a question. Are you pursuing him? Or is he pursuing you?"

Collin lowered her gaze. "I'm not sure." She sighed. "Take me back to camp. You might want to sneak me in, so 'Fear' doesn't know I've reported this."

"Why wouldn't you?"

"Because if he knows me at all, he knows I'm a self-reliant, hard-nosed female who takes nothing from no one and certainly wouldn't ask the police to intervene in a personal matter."

He raised both eyebrows. "He'd know all that, would he?"

Collin dropped the conceit. "It's what he'd see on the outside. Let's hope he's banking on that image."

Sheriff Lodi chuckled. "Agreed. I'll take you back."

THURSDAY

Morning came with a predawn wakeup call of the obnoxious kind. Fierce pounding on her door jarred her to wakefulness. Fiercer pounding in her head threatened to knock her out again. Collin sensed she could stop the outer pounding much more rapidly than the inner, so stumbled out of bed, limped to the door and hissed, "What?!"

Chonnell and Pardner sang in chorus, "Time to get up! Rob say stop moping and get moving. He say you missed breakfast, again, and now you gonna be late to practice. He say if you ain't woman enough to admit you don't want to go, least you could do—"

Collin seethed. "You tell Rob..." Flashes of reason returned to her brain before she could get herself in too much trouble. She looked at the clock: five-forty. She told the door, "Tell Rob to meet me at dock one in ten minutes, and we'll have a talk about being late. Ten minutes, dock one. Got it?" In response, Collin heard giggles, followed by scuffling, laughter, and silence. Oh, to be young and foolish again. Okay, oh, to be young again. Foolish, she'd never given up.

Collin slipped on her bathing suit, donned a pair of elastic-top shorts, pulled on a pull-over, and looked in the mirror. When did she get all the scrapes and cuts? *I don't remember them being there last night.*

Did you look?

Probably not.

Remember playing in the trees, huh? Or rolling around on the blacktop? Might you have picked up a few marks then? Hmmm?

Collin muttered, "Great. Something else to explain to Rob."

She yanked a hat over her head, pulled it down low, grabbed her sunglasses, shoved them on her face, and left the room. Holding her ribs, of course. Which would take some explaining, too. Today would be a thrill a minute.

Collin arrived at the dock and found Rob lounging around, trying to look cool. She walked up to him, keeping her head down and said, "Hey, dude."

Rob took one look at her and stared. "What did you run into, a '57 Chevy?"

"'49 Ford. Does it look bad?"

"You should be wearing a sign says, 'I got the snot beat out of me.'"

Collin sagged. "Give me a break, man. What am I supposed to do?"

Rob reminded her of the finer arts of abuse-camouflage. Arts Collin gradually forgot over the past twelve years. "Lose the glasses. You never wear them. It makes people look at your face when you got something different on. Pull your hair out on the sides like you too late to comb it or something."

Rob stepped back and looked at the finished product. He shrugged. "I guess you pass." He studied her face. "Know who done it?"

"He didn't leave his name. Dressed all in black, boots, gloves, mask..."

"White guy, huh?"

"Yeah. White guy. Rob, this is serious, man. Let's get to class, and I'll explain on first break." They started walking. "Work with me, dude. The sheriff's people are gonna be in the hills with us today: in the trees, the bushes, playing commando. Don't let it spook you, and if anyone else says anything, divert them, okay? Got it?"

Rob's eyes clouded with concern. "I got it." To his credit, he asked no questions. Yet.

"Go nowhere unless it's with a group. And I mean nowhere, Rob. As in absolutely nowhere. The bigger the group, the better it is. Got it?" Rob took this silently but nodded. "Last thing. Do you remember battle code red?"

"You Xena, I'm Ares? I remember it. Dumbest code we ever did."

Collin smiled wryly. "Yeah, but no one ever guessed it, did they? They might guess you could be the god of war, but—"

Rob finished the justification, "—no one ever gonna suspect you no warrior princess. I got it. You ain't near as strong as she is. Ain't near as ugly, neither."

Collin grinned. "Why, Rob, that's the nicest thing you've ever said."

Rob kept his head down. "Yeah, well, look like you could use some nice things about now." He looked up at her. "You better have one good explanation for all this, caseworker lady."

"I do." She had all morning to think of one.

They arrived at the dock and found all members of the crew present and accounted for except Mitch. Collin leaned against a piling. "Morning, crew." Her standard opening. If Rob remembered right, the more routine she followed, the less attention she'd garner.

Niles grumbled. "Teacher be late. Teachers ain't supposed to be late. Kids supposed to be late, not teachers."

Nyla sniped. "You'd be knowing about being late. You ain't been on time since you born."

Collin smiled inside. It sounded so familiar it hurt. "We had a rule in college if the professor hadn't shown up in fifteen minutes, class got canceled. We can wait until then before we go back to the lodge and see if anyone knows what's happened to him. No one knows, we go back to bed or back for another breakfast." She knew which one got her vote.

They waited another ten minutes, and excitement began to stir about whether Mitch would make it or not, and whether there would be anything different for breakfast the second time around. But to the chagrin of the majority, Mitch suddenly came pounding down the path, yelling, "I'm here, I'm here! I'm coming."

Boos and jeers greeted him, but he waved and bowed. Collin raised an eyebrow. "We contemplated mutiny."

Mitch grinned and looked around. "Not my crew. You'd wait for me forever, wouldn't you?"

In unison, the kids answered, "No way!"

Mitch smiled. "That's what I like. Solidarity. Come on, people. Let's find a river where we can practice. Show me you got it together, and tomorrow we do the real thing." That won him approval and support of the most vocal kind.

Collin studied the man's eyes and saw something different in them: a spark of energy, maybe, or a light which hadn't been there before. A cold tingle started in her gut, raced through her, and just as quickly died.

We're talking about Mitch, here. He's obnoxious, lecherous, maybe.

Okay, no maybe. But he's a talker, not a doer.

Sheriff Bo said he'd been cleared. Mitch didn't fit the profile.

As the instructor grabbed supplies from the shed, Collin and crew slid into position. Collin experimented with the paddle, trying to find a stroke she could manage, and not end up screaming in pain from her ribs tearing at her insides. Nothing proved entirely satisfactory. She finally settled on a variation of the original and left it there. She'd have to be tough.

Collin saw Nyla watching her closely. Collin shrugged. "It'll work."

"You want to switch sides?"

"Thanks, Nyla. I appreciate the offer. If Mitch says we can."

Nyla hesitated. "What you do?"

Collin needed to work on an answer. An honest but not-too-involved answer, which would avoid further questions. "I fell."

"On what? How?"

Not the right answer. "I went to play hoops"—*or thought about playing, anyhow*— "things got intense. I got knocked down and stepped on."

Nyla's eyes narrowed slightly. "You saying the truth?"

Collin lowered her voice. "All I can."

The answer seemed to satisfy Nyla. She studied Collin a moment. "Guess your face got stepped on, too, huh."

"Yeah. A little."

Mitch came back with a cooler and a load of supplies, secured them in the boat, and said brightly, "Well, are we all ready to rock and roll?"

Nyla's hand shot in the air. "Mitch, me and the lady here wants to try switching sides."

"Why?"

"Cause she ain't worth nothing on her side. We got to pull even, and she can't pull near as good as I can on the right."

Mitch seemed uncertain. "I don't know. We've been practicing it this way and doing pretty good. What about it, Collin?"

Collin did not turn to address him but shrugged. "Fine by me. I think Nyla's jealous. All the cute guys on the shore have been on my side of the boat." She grinned at Nyla. The girl threatened her with her paddle.

Mitch harrumphed. "Well, it's settled. We must, by all means, keep you from ogling any cute guys except me."

The male contingent hooted, and Mitch smiled broadly. Collin and Nyla switched sides without further ado. Collin whispered to Nyla, "Thanks. I owe you."

Nyla shrugged. "Twins got to stick together. Even if they ain't same blood."

The boat pulled away from the dock at Mitch's command. Paddling on the opposite side was painful, but at least on this side, she could do it and scream inside, rather than not do it and scream outside. As they pulled with steady, even strokes, Nyla matched her stroke to Collin's, and Collin matched hers to Niles's in front of her.

Collin swallowed her fear. They were on the lake, nothing more. Like all day yesterday. On the lake. She kept her head down, focused on paddling. She would not acknowledge they headed out through the small channel into a tributary of the river itself, leaving the safety of the familiar, into the fear of the unknown. Head down. Eyes on Ta'waan. No looking around. Focused.

Nyla broke Collin's concentration. "How you live, your brother being gone?"

It took Collin a moment to connect Nyla's question to the girl's comment about "twins stick together." And what struck the chord in Nyla. Contemplation of life should she lose Niles. Collin kept her eyes down. "I almost didn't." She kept her voice low, intended for Nyla's ears only. "I lived in agony for two years until I met a Man who could fill the emptiness Erin left behind. A Man who knew me better than Erin did. Who knew everything I'd said and done and loved me anyhow. A Man who promised to be with me forever; to never leave me no matter what, to stay with me and help me wherever I am."

Nyla snorted. "Ain't no man can do that."

"One Man can. And He has."

"Yeah?" Nyla's voice dripped disbelief. "Where he be last night when you got 'stepped on?'"

"Right there, Nyla. I'm not dead, am I? I'm not laid up somewhere in a hospital." She silenced the voices, which started to protest. "Nothing's broken but the ribs, and they will heal. My Friend never promised me nothing bad would happen. He promised me He would always be there to help me when it did."

Nyla's conversation, and the knowledge of Who held her, served as welcome distractions from the fear wanting to mount in Collin. She managed a weak smile.

The girl asked, "This friend got a name?"

"Jesus." Collin decided to lay it out with no apologies. Speak the Name and let Him do the rest.

Nyla snorted again. "Thought so." She hesitated. "But I ain't seen one of you religious types so real before. Sure ain't seen none cut they own hand open to prove a point, neither."

"Don't take me as a good example, Nyla. Knowing the Lord doesn't exempt me from being stupid on my own. The Lord did all the bleeding for us. He's never asked us to repeat it."

Nyla pointed to the look on Mitch's face and said, "He gonna yell at us for talking, we don't quit. We get a break, and maybe you answer some more questions for me."

Collin ducked her head. "I'd be happy to, Nyla." Both females lapsed into silence, and Mitch's countenance cleared.

Collin focused on her paddling, trying hard to keep up with the young man in front of her. The ribs throbbed, even though she carried the brunt of the stroke's force through both shoulder joints. Even then, some strain could not be avoided. As the morning progressed, Collin hurt more and more. She forced herself to concentrate, to focus all her attention away from the pain and outward to her paddling. *Focus. Concentrate. Shut out all distractions and focus.*

Focus hard. Focus harder. If you focus hard enough…

You forget where you are and what you're supposed to be doing. Rob's foot nudged her in the back sharply. Collin came to with a start and looked at him. He hissed, "Wake up, lady. You zoning out and getting Nyla all messed up."

Collin blinked her eyes to clear the cobwebs and mentally swatted at the spider as he jeered at her. "Thanks." She looked at

Nyla. "Sorry." Rob grunted in response, the male equivalent of "No problem." Nyla only shrugged.

Collin took a furtive look around, trying to get some sense of their location, what time it might be, and how far they were from a break. The answers all seemed of the "who knows?" variety.

Suck it up, woman. Do the deed and get on with it.

Collin let out a sigh. She began chanting the strokes in her mind as a diversion. *Up, forward, dig, pull, retrieve. Up, forward, dig, pull, retrieve. Up, forward, dig...* It became a rhythm in her head, a mantra to ward off pain. And if you do it hard enough...

Rob's foot in her back couldn't save Collin from detection this time. She came to with Mitch literally in her face, shouting, "Walker! What do you think you are doing? This isn't nap time!"

Collin jerked to attention. "You're right. I'm out of line."

Mitch huffed a couple of times. "Do you want off?"

"No. But I could use a break. I strained some ribs last night, and they're killing me right now."

Mitch's eyes held concern. "How? What did you do?"

Collin stuck to her story. "I went out to play on the basketball court, fell and bruised my ribs."

"Let me see."

Collin frowned. "Uh, no. They're purple and blue, and I'm not stripping down for anyone."

"Let me feel them, then. Like I told you before, I've got some medical training."

Collin repeated with more force, "No. I've broken, cracked, and bruised ribs before. I know which is which. They're bruised. And I could use a break."

Mitch wouldn't let the matter go. "Who were you playing with?"

Collin jutted out her chin, pointing over his shoulder. "Mitch, if someone doesn't start paddling, we're going to be hitting a hole sideways, and you taught us that's the wrong way to start a run."

Mitch turned and realized they were headed crosswise into a trench. He yelled, "Niles, pull hard starboard. Ta'waan, backstroke. Helmsman, get us out of here!" The crew jumped back to life, and the boat turned back to its proper heading.

They spent the rest of the morning's trip in silence other than terse commands and even terser responses. Mitch forgot—or ignored—Collin's request for a break. She passed the time in private agony. To Nyla's looks of concern, Collin responded with tight-lipped smiles, or when she could manage it, a pain-filled grin. The rest of the time, Collin spent praying and rolling her fear over to the Lord.

At noon they reached a "beach" Mitch promised them. A shallow, flat point had been hollowed out to use as a jumping-off spot for river cruises. Mitch ordered the boat run up on shore. They unloaded coolers, divided lunch, distributed drinks, and everyone spread out to relax. Mitch called, "One hour break. Make good use of it, crew. We've got hard paddling ahead."

Collin found a smooth boulder to lean against, shoved her sandwich back into its bag uneaten, and closed her eyes. Maybe she could catch a few winks; however long a wink might be. *How do you measure forty winks?*

Well, let's see. The traditional forty winks equaled a full night's sleep, so say eight hours. Twenty winks would be four hours, and ten winks, two hours, five winks one hour.

Sixty minutes in an hour, so five winks into sixty equals...

Collin couldn't get her brain to do the math and then couldn't get it to stop trying. But even thinking about math couldn't divert her attention from how miserable she felt. She ached everywhere, and where she didn't ache, she hurt.

Her head pounded, keeping pace with the throbbing in her side. She wanted very badly to crawl in a corner and cry but knew she did not have the option. No corners in the wilderness. And it would hardly be becoming of an adult of her professed strength and maturity.

Collin laid her head back against the rock and tried to drain all feeling from her system, starting at the top and working down.

She'd gotten as far as her hair when a hand on her shoulder stirred her insistently. She looked up. Rob stood beside her, looking more concerned than she'd ever seen. "You okay, lady?"

"I'm beat, Rob."

"Who beat you?"

She motioned for him to sit down, looked around to see where Mitch settled. "I don't know for sure. I got tagged out on the court last night. Never saw more than his shape, like some giant, shaved, Big Foot..."

"But you chased him off, right? I mean, you're here, so you must have whipped him good."

Legends die hard. "He gave up, Rob. He's some kind of head case into scaring people. But the sheriff thinks he's got a vendetta against me."

"Then why you still here?"

Collin's eyes narrowed, and she tossed her head. Carefully. "No freak's gonna run me off. I've got to ride this cursed river, first. Bus don't leave until Saturday, and neither do I." She looked at Rob. "You want to leave?"

Rob snorted. "I ain't afraid of no Big Foot." He thought a moment, trying to put it all together. "So what you mean about staying with the group?"

"I don't want someone using you as bait to get to me."

The thought of genuine danger to Rob stabbed through her. *You want to put his life on the line, too?*

Of course, you do. You're too much of a coward to face anything alone.

You're not alone.

Collin squeezed Rob's shoulder. "Stay with the group, Rob. Whatever happens, stay with the group. Or a group. Or any group. Don't get caught alone."

"Yeah? What about you? You being a target, ain't you?"

Collin frowned. "Not a chance. I'm not out here wearing a sign saying, 'Come and get me,' am I?"

"No." He frowned. "Don't mean you ain't, neither. What's the Man doing about all this? Why ain't he out here looking?"

"Looking for what?" Nyla joined the discussion. "Who you be talking about?"

Rob looked at Collin, not sure how much he could share. Collin said quietly, "Rob wanted to know if the Man was out looking for the guy who 'stepped' on me."

"Is he?"

Collin nodded. "Man's out there. Sheriff said we wouldn't see him, but he's there." She looked at Nyla. "Sort of like my Friend. Can't see Him, but I know He's there."

Nyla plopped down beside Collin. "How can I ever be knowing Him? People say I gotta clean all up on the outside before He'll take notice of me. How'm I gonna get clean enough, huh?"

"You can't. No one can. He doesn't expect you to, Nyla. That's what Jesus came to do for us."

Collin twisted around inch by inch to catch the young woman's eyes. "It's like you're standing there in old dirty threads, and God says, 'Nyla, I want you to come to be with me. But Nyla, you got to put on a clean shirt, first.' He didn't say 'Take off all the dirty stuff first.' He said, put on a clean shirt."

Collin waited until Nyla nodded. Collin continued, "So you look through all you got, but you know you haven't got anything clean enough for God. And Niles hasn't got anything good enough to borrow, even if he'd let you."

Nyla snorted. "You know brothers better than that."

Collin smiled. "I remember. Anyhow, you can't find a shirt anywhere. Jesus comes along and says, 'Nyla, I've got a shirt for you. You take this one I give you, and you can be with God anytime. I'm the only one with a shirt clean enough for Him.'"

Nyla nodded slowly. Listening, maybe, but not fully believing. Collin continued, "When God sees the shirt, He says, 'That shirt belongs to My Son. And if He gave it to Nyla to wear, He accepts her. So I do, too.' "

Collin held Nyla's gaze. "We can't clean ourselves up. God does it for us. Our job is to accept the shirt Christ gives us."

Collin hesitated. "Except Jesus doesn't have spare shirts laying around. He died. Jesus gave everything because He loved us. His death is the only way we could ever be clean enough for God. Once we accept Him, He promises never to leave us alone again."

Nyla looked at Rob. "You been around this lady awhile?"

"Most part of a year." Rob gave Collin a half-grin. "Longest ten months of my life."

Collin smiled sweetly. "Ah, Rob, you remembered."

Nyla ignored the interplay. "But you be knowing her, right? She straight on this stuff? You be believing it?"

Ah hah! Let's see how Rob handles this one.

Rob hesitated before answering. "Lady be straight on this stuff. She believing it, she trying to live it. I seen it make a difference in her. Am I believing it? I believing it can be; I just ain't accepted the shirt from the Man, yet."

Collin smiled. "Thank you."

But Nyla remained unsatisfied. "Why ain't you? If it so great and all and make such a difference, why ain't you?"

Collin said quietly, "Nyla, everyone has a reason why not until they're ready. Taking the shirt means more than getting to be with God. It means you're gonna start living the way God does, the way God says. Like loving your enemies. You'd have to give up hating the Southside gangs and learn to love them instead."

Nyla's eyes narrowed. "Ain't no way."

"God says there is, and He'll teach it to you when you become one of His. But not until then."

Rob admitted to Nyla, "Got some enemies I ain't done hating, yet."

Before anyone else could say anything more, Mitch stirred from his napping spot. Lunch officially ended.

Nyla jumped up. "Gotta go wake that good-for-nothing brother of mine. He sleep all day if you let him."

Collin looked at Rob. "Watch out for yourself, my man. I promise I won't put myself in unnecessary danger, and you promise me you won't be stupid and think you are Ares. Got it?"

Rob nodded. "I got it. I ain't no fool."

"I know you're not. You're my main man, Rob. You always will be. I don't want anything to happen to you. I'd hate myself forever if something did, and I could have prevented it. I don't know what I'd do without you. And I don't want to have to find out." Collin's voice cracked.

Rob stared at her for a long minute. "You something else, Collin. You know that? Crazy man out after you, Mitch hitting on you, and you worried about me. Where they come up with you? And why they give you to me?" He reached out and, in one quick motion, hugged her, then equally as quickly let her go and headed back to the boat.

Collin stared after him. Unexpectedly, her vision clouded with moisture. "First time. First time he ever called me by name. If that's Your reason, Lord, bring on the muggers. Thank You. Thank You."

"Thank me for what?" Mitch came up behind Collin without her noticing.

"Thank you for the break just now." She stretched gingerly. "I think I can manage the rest of the trip."

Mitch patted Collin on the shoulder. "I think we should give you a long break. Why don't you take the point, and I'll paddle with Nyla."

Collin shook her head violently. "I don't think it's a good idea. I don't know the river as well as you do." She tried to put more confidence in her voice than she felt. "You know where all the rocks and stumps are submerged."

Mitch chuckled. "You mean where all the bodies are buried?"

Inwardly Collin shuddered. Could this be some twisted attempt at macabre humor or the idiot's poorly timed joke? Or could he be jibbing at her fear of the river? Whatever the purpose, Collin said evenly, "Something like that. I can keep paddling."

Mitch scowled. "This fear you have about the river has you so spooked you're practically useless. You froze twice this morning. You didn't think I saw it the first time, did you? I did. If I didn't like you so much, I'd ground you here and now."

Collin counted to ten slowly. "Is that your professional evaluation?"

Mitch nodded. "It certainly is. I should leave you here and send maintenance after you when we get to base camp." He stopped. "But you might enjoy it too much. Maintenance would mean a long drive back with the janitor. Wouldn't it?"

Mitch's eyes taunted her. Collin stayed under control. "Jeff and I are friends, period. If I'm not fit to crew, tell me."

Why this sudden attack? What did he want her to do?

Get mad and stay behind.

Then what? I walk back?

End up alone out here where he can finish you.

Mitch?

Who else? Not the kids, not Jeff. Who's left?

The sheriff said not Mitch.

Wanna bet your life on it?

Collin realized Mitch wanted an answer. She pulled out her most diplomatic side. "Mitch, I don't know why you suddenly think I can't carry my weight as part of this crew. If you think I'm a detriment, I'll take point position. Or I'll sit in the middle and be ballast. Either way, I want to finish this class with my crew."

The four older crew members gathered around, listening to the discussion. Nyla stared hard at Mitch. "She ain't doing so bad. Only thrown me off once."

Niles unexpectedly jumped to Collin's defense. "Yeah. For a white lady, she got good rhythm. We might could make a rapper out of her yet."

Collin said dryly, "When pigs fly."

Ta'waan stepped in front of Mitch and did everything but put his hands on his hips. "You weren't making no noises about how she pulling her strokes earlier. What's the deal?"

There followed a chorus of, "Yeah, what's the deal? What you trying to pull? What's going down?" from all six crew members, young and older.

Mitch's face broke into a wide grin, and he began to laugh and clap his hands. "This is great! This is fantastic!" To the suspicious faces, he said, "The 'deal' is you all passed the test with flying colors. A real crew needs to pull together and not only on the water, either. You've got to stand and defend one another. I wanted to know if you all learned it yet." He slapped Ta'waan, Niles, and Nyla on the shoulders. "Good job, crew. Good job. Now let's get loaded and back on the water."

He moved off, his arms around Niles and Ta'waan. Nyla looked at Collin. "You believing him?"

"I don't know what to believe about him, Nyla."

"I be believing he a snake. I ain't trusting him. What your God got to say about that?"

Collin phrased her answer carefully. "I believe God would say keep your eyes open but treat him like an honest man. He's innocent until we prove him guilty."

"Or he proves hisself guilty."

"Amen." Nyla took herself back to the boat, leaving Rob and Collin alone once again.

Rob looked at her, his face dark with concern. "Collin, lady, you be watching your back." He corrected himself. "I be watching your back. I don't got a good feeling about him."

Neither did Collin, but she wouldn't admit it. "Don't hate a man for being a fool, Rob. He is what he is. But I appreciate the support."

Collin did the unthinkable: she put an arm around his shoulders and hugged him. Rob wrapped his arm around her loosely, and together they walked to the boat.

The crew launched the raft with as much expertise as four days of training could give them. Mitch stood in the front and looked ahead. "We've got white water ahead."

Nyla lowered her voice. "White water. You okay?"

I am with you.

Collin nodded, keeping her eyes down. "I'm not alone. I'll be fine."

The rapids proved to be less than her fear made them. Fast, yes. Precarious, yes. Swiftly angling from side to side, pitching the raft back and forth…of course. But everyone stayed in the boat, and no one lost their seat, which made it a success to Collin's mind. Or parts of it.

Baby rapids. The real ones come tomorrow. You'll be crying in the corner.

There are no corners in a raft. I'll be fine.

Mitch seemed pleased with the effort, laughing and clapping his hands in approval. "Well done, crew! Well done! You managed so well, I've got a surprise reward for you."

The raft rounded a curve and came upon another landing site where a crew with a flatbed truck and a van waited for them. The rubber boat drifted up on the shelf in the water and everyone bailed out. With practiced expertise, the ground crew loaded the watercraft and its contents, but not its occupants, onto the flatbed and pulled away. Gratefully, the porters left the van behind. Collin didn't know how far from the lodge they might be, but one mile or twenty, she didn't have the reserves to walk back. Her head and her side throbbed. She controlled the pain as long as she could.

Mitch told the crew, "I promised you a surprise at the end of the run. I don't want you thinking I'd cheat on a promise. We have to hike over the rise and we're there."

He drove them forward up a barely discernable path, unmarked save for one recent track where the grass had been stomped down. Wherever they were going, no man had gone before. Or at least not in recent history.

Collin struggled along the way, and each step became more and more uncomfortable. And although they left the river well behind, she could still hear the faint hint of water rushing. Would this never end?

Mitch dropped back to join her, giving up his sheepherder duties. Collin waited for him to broach a subject. After several moments of silence, Mitch said, "You did great this afternoon when I baited you. I knew I could count on you to help me."

Collin's eyes narrowed. "Do you attack all your guests without warning?"

"Not usually. I don't always find someone as sharp as you to play with." Collin got an uneasy sense of his meaning but let it go. Mitch plucked a high stalk of grass as they continued their walk. "Someone roughed you up last night, didn't they? You want to tell me about it?"

"No, Mitch."

He shrugged. "It's good to talk things out, you know."

"I know, but it's still too...close."

"Did he hurt you anywhere else?"

"Just my pride."

Mitch smirked. "Yeah, you're the one who's always in control, aren't you? It must have been terrifying having someone else calling the shots."

Collin's eyes narrowed as her gut squeezed closed. She kept her voice steady. "It happens, Mitch. I don't win every game. I roll with the punches."

Sometimes not fast enough, though. Ask your ribs.

Collin ignored the not-helpful thought. "You learn to adapt to whatever happens."

"Adapt to being attacked from behind in the dark? I don't think so. No one is that cool, Collin. Not even you." Mitch's eyes shone with delight.

Collin's breath slowly squeezed from her lungs as he talked. *How did he know I'd been attacked from behind? I never said anything about being attacked, either. I said I'd been playing ball.*

Told you so.

Collin forced her hands not to clench at the thought of throttling Mitch here and now. She cleared her throat. "It's not a matter of being cool, Mitch. It's a matter of doing what you've got to do."

"Fear never stops you? There's nothing you're afraid of?"

"I'm afraid of the river. But I'm doing something about it."

Mitch caught another stray weed and yanked it out of the ground. "You still haven't told me what makes you so afraid. Is it the fact you almost died? You're afraid of death?" Mitch's eyes turned an unhealthy shade as he probed for her answer.

"I'm not afraid of death, Mitch. I know where I'm going when I die." Collin threw up a *Thank You, Lord.*

Mitch hadn't finished. "But the dying part...scares everyone. I've never met anyone who wasn't afraid of the dying." Mitch laughed. "Everyone has a fear, Collin. I think yours is drowning."

The kids' excited shouting saved Collin from having to answer. They reached the rise and pointed downslope at something. Calls of, "Way cool, man!" and "Dude!" and "Sweet!" indicated to Collin whatever they saw met their approval. Which meant something extreme, hazardous, and otherwise radically different. She puffed up the last few feet of the trail and took one look. "Oh, joy. A waterslide."

A long expanse of plastic covered the ground, laid out to resemble the river. It dipped and rose and fell in river fashion, curving and meandering over small humps, all the while descending the steep slope. The glistening of the surface said whoever set this up used something more than water as a lubricant. It would mimic a pace slower than the river, but move crisply enough on its own.

Mitch came up behind her. "Here it is. Your last test before you reach the Holy Grail. Let's see you handle this one." His eyes never lost their unholy light. "We'll see who's laughing when we're done." He hustled down to where the others gathered. "Okay crew, here's the deal. This may look like your ordinary waterslide, but it has a purpose. A pilot may say any landing you walk away from is a good one, but for a riverman, it's not so simple."

Mitch rubbed his hands together. "If a riverman lands, he lands in the water, and there's only one way to do it correctly. This is to teach you exactly how to ride the river in the unlikely and dreaded event you fall overboard. Some of us may already know the experience, right, Collin?"

Collin shrugged. She never said she fell out of a boat, Mitch did. And if he preferred to believe his explanation, why would she say otherwise?

Mitch continued, "Let me demonstrate the proper position. I need a volunteer. Collin, why don't you come down..."

Niles bounced forward. "Naw, she a grown-up. I be the dummy this time."

And in true sister fashion, Nyla quipped, "You be the dummy all the time." Niles glared at her; she gave him the sister smirk that said, "I love you, too."

Mitch grumbled, "We're losing daylight, people. Do we do this or don't we?" Niles hustled forward and stood in front of Mitch. Mitch instructed, "You've all been taught there's a right way and a wrong way to get into a boat. But there's a right way and a wrong way to fall out of a boat, too. The right way is when the river smacks you so hard you get airborne and land feet first in the water."

Mitch held each crewmember's eyes. "The wrong way is to get airborne and land headfirst. I know there are some pretty thick skulls out there, but none of you, with maybe one exception, has a skull petrified enough to be a match for what the river has in store."

Collin let it slide.

Mitch continued, "Under the surface, she has boulders, trees, tree stumps, tree limbs, rocks, and anything else Mother Nature cares to deposit. And of course, there is humanity's contribution to our river's ecology: bottles, washing machines, freezers, 69 Mustang..."

As Mitch continued listing the submersible hazards found in a river, Collin began to flashback. Weary as she felt, there were no reserves left. Objects whizzed past her eyes. Or, did she whiz past them? She saw car parts, though the make and model escaped her. Ghostly and ghastly trees reached out to snag her, sharp rocks cut, and bruised her. A large white appliance of some kind crushed her arm as she flailed in panic... The river held her. Once again, it held her.

A hand grabbed her arm and pulled it sharply. "Collin! Snap out of it! Did you hear one word I said? Did you?" Mitch's voice filled with disgust.

Collin fought her way up from the bottom of the river, gasping for air. Still disoriented, she floundered for an apology. "I lost it for..." She didn't know how long she'd been out so repeated, "I lost it. I'm back now."

Mitch snapped, "You're putting these kids' lives on the line. They need to know they can depend on you, and you're going to be there for them, not off in la-la land fighting some private fantasies.

Tell us what scares you now. Or sit out tomorrow."

Collin answered with a tinge of heat. "Mitch, it's been a very long day, preceded by a very short night. I'm tired, I'm hurting, and I lost it. Tomorrow I'll be rested, a lot less sore, and it won't be a problem. We spent all day on the river, and I didn't lose it to fear once. Lost it to pain a couple of times, but not to fear. I'll be fine."

"Not good enough, Collin. Not even close. Your choice: tell me now or you're grounded. This crew will sail without you."

Collin looked around at her crewmates. "You agree with him?"

Mitch snapped, "Don't ask them. It doesn't matter what they say. They know you can have them punished for speaking up and telling the truth. I'm the one in charge here. I'm the only one who matters."

Collin's voice matched her mood. "I think my crew knows me better than that. They've never been afraid to tell me what they thought before. They're not going to start now."

Ta'waan stepped forward. "Lady got that right. Ain't never been afraid of her or nobody else." He glared at Mitch. "Ms. Walker's crew. Rob here, he see her from where he standing. He know if she zoning. Nyla see her, too. Nyla slap a paddle upside the lady's head if'n she start freaking out."

Rob stepped up in defense as well. "Caseworker lady showin' us what happens when we sleeping stead of learning. Ask Niles."

Niles shoved Rob. "Besides, who gonna keep my other half straight to paddle, huh? Nyla go paddling on her own, she ain't never gonna keep in time." He grinned sweetly at his sister. "Can't tell time, let alone keep time."

Nyla rushed across the clearing and smacked her sibling. He ducked. The two proceeded to have a hand-to-nose-to-wrist-to-ear-to-gut discussion about the superiority of the sexes.

Watching the two wrestle brought an ache to Collin's soul and loneliness to her being. But the ache and the loneliness were tempered by the knowledge she no longer walked alone.

As the fight looked to be a draw, Mitch waited until the dust settled, then glared at each member of his crew. "She stays on one condition. She has to pass the river test, ride it to the bottom, and do it right." He glared in triumph. "Otherwise, she stays behind."

Collin nodded. "Fair enough."

Mitch played his trump card. "And you ride it first."

Collin felt her stomach lurch. She'd missed the instructions and felt sure Mitch would not repeat them for her private edification. She swallowed hard, nodded. "If that's the way you want it."

"That's the way it is."

Or would have been. Chonnell and Pardner whispered together and giggled in secret. Suddenly they took off running toward the starting point at the head of the slope. Chonnell yelled brightly, "I'm first! I'm first!"

Pardner yelled, "Me next! Me next!"

Mitch yelled impotently at the scampering sprites, "Get back here! Chonnell! Pardner!"

Chonnell jumped into the slide position: arms across her chest, feet crossed at the ankles. She laid her head back in the water and yelled, "Watch me! Watch me, everybody!"

Beside Collin, Ta'waan said softly, "She got it right, lady. Gotta put your head down. Gotta lay down and gotta put your head down."

As the child swooshed by her, totally submerged, Collin felt all the life drain from her. No way. No way.

Find a way. Make a way. Fake a way if you have to, but do it.

These kids put it on the line for you.

Don't say you can't. You can if you want to. If you want it bad enough.

If it matters more than your puny ego.

But you're too weak, too selfish. You don't want to do it. Not can't, won't.

I am with you.

A voice outside her ear buzzed softly with satisfaction. "You can't, can you? You can't do it. You're terrified of this. Why? What power does it have?" Mitch stood behind her watching her reactions as Pardner followed Chonnell down the slide.

Collin smiled at Mitch with all the bravado she could muster. She turned to the teens. "Our turn. And I will go first this time." She grinned. "I refuse to be shown up by a twelve-year-old. Two of them no less."

Nyla chuckled. "Yeah. Little twerps. Think they so smart."

The crowd walked to the top of the slope, but Mitch stayed near the landing point, waiting for Chonnell and Pardner to climb out and join him.

At the line, Collin stopped. "Thank you guys for getting me another chance. If anyone wants me off the crew, say so. I told Mitch I'd be better tomorrow. I don't know for a fact. All I can do is try."

Rob shrugged. "You been saying it's all anyone can do, caseworker lady. Ain't expecting you to do more than just try."

Collin looked at the other three. "Anyone?"

Niles rubbed his cheek. "Not me, man. Uh, lady."

Nyla pointed to her brother. "What he said."

Collin's eyes rested on the last man standing. "Ta'waan?"

The boy kicked his foot in the grass. "Used to think it uncool to be scared. Like it made you a coward. But grown-up like you be scared and still do what scares you… Be something to think about. If old lady can beat her fear, maybe I can, too."

Collin grinned. "No maybe, Ta'waan. You can."

Mitch yelled up the hill. "We haven't got all day! Unless you want to walk back to the van in the dark. Move it, Collin!"

Niles grumbled, "He is one uncool dude, you know?"

Suddenly Rob stepped in front of Collin. "Wait 'til I be halfway down then go. I be waiting for you at the bottom. Understand? I be waiting for you." He jumped on the run, gave a war hoop, and went rocketing down the slide.

Collin looked skyward. He covered all the bases, didn't he? Friends at the top, friends at the bottom. What more could she want? Collin waited until he passed the midway point and slid into position. She exclaimed, "Cold!" then laid her head back, breathed a thousand silent prayers in a moment of time, and let go.

Her body took off like a rocket down the slide, twisting and turning as it conformed to the contours of the run. But her mind went instantly out of control, careening back in time. She bounced and skipped along the river bottom, flashing helplessly past the outstretched arms of would-be rescuers. Screaming, gagging on water, retching, screaming more, carried endlessly on and on and on… Finally, staring up through the water at the face of an angel, ready to go home, wanting to go home, praying to go home…only to have the angel pushed aside by a well-meaning stranger who dragged a half-dead five-year-old from the river's clutches.

Back on the run, Collin felt no sense of panic, only the calm assurance she would die, this time, and he would win. Water splashed across her face. Collin held her breath, knowing to breathe, to swallow water meant drowning.

How long the run would last, she didn't know. Her defenses vanished; resistance was futile. She only needed to take one liquid breath, and everything would be over. One little breath…

Many hands grabbed her and pulled her off the grass at the end. Someone pounded her on the back, yelled. Collin drew in a deep, painful breath of air as the present returned to her slowly. Rob's hands rested on both her shoulders, shaking her sharply and demanding, "Come on, lady, come on. I know you in there. Come on. You did it, Collin. You did it. You made it."

A large body swooshed past behind them, followed in rapid succession by two more human torpedoes. Ta'waan, Niles, and Nyla vaulted up, cheering and hollering. Collin reached out and hugged Rob. He neither stiffened nor pulled away but returned the hug warmly and tightly. Collin roped in the others for a group hug and repeated over and over, "You guys did it. The four of you. I couldn't have done it alone. You saved me."

Chonnell and Pardner did little victory dances back to where the others stood, leaving Mitch by himself. The girls joined the celebration as Collin pointed to each of them. "You two. You two are something else! What am I going to do with you two?" She hugged them individually and corporately then let all the emotions flow.

Nyla's face darkened. "Here comes…"

Collin kept her voice even. "Whatever else he is, he's still our instructor, Nyla. One more day. Keep it cool one more day." *And then we nail his hide to the wall.* How someplace as beautiful as Grace could hire someone as unbalanced as Mitch remained a mystery. How had he been eliminated as a suspect? *Or…* Collin parked the theory for further examination at a later time.

Mitch walked up to the group, a picture of contented accomplishment. He smiled. "No hard feelings? I needed to give you this final test, and you passed it with no problem."

Collin fixed Mitch with a dead-even stare. "No more games, right? No more little tests, no more phony fights. No more harassment?"

Mitch nodded. "Well, the river itself is the final test. I wanted to see if you were ready." He looked at Collin. "Especially you, Collin. I've never seen anyone so relaxed. You looked unconscious. Or dead. Amazing."

He paused, then clapped his hands together. "Okay, everyone. Back to the van and back to camp. Tomorrow is the big day, the one we've been waiting for." His eyes sparkled as he looked at Collin. "I know I'm looking forward to it." He looked at the crew. "We meet at eight-thirty sharp on dock two. Everyone hear me? Eight-thirty, dock two."

They arrived back at the camp around five. Collin noted with wry satisfaction the spring in everyone's step seemed to have sprung a mite. Even the youngest of the crew could barely drag their exhausted bodies out of the van.

Only Mitch seemed unaffected by the day's toils. As the tired bunch dragged up the hill to paradise—hot showers, hot food, and stationary beds—Mitch called cheerily, "Eight-thirty, dock two. Latecomers walk!"

Nyla groaned. "Can I stuff him, please? Just one time, I promise."

Collin assured her, "Tomorrow. Tomorrow you can stuff him."

Niles added, "And I get to help."

"I'm in."

"Mark it." Ta'waan and Rob weighed in.

Collin nodded. "Tomorrow."

THURSDAY EVENING

The group split up at the hall, guys to the right, girls to the left. Collin went straight to her room and collapsed on the bed. *I'm not moving. Ever.* She stretched out as far as she could to give her battered ribs room to simply be. And she didn't hurt. She could breathe without the constant scraping of bone on muscle. She would stay like this the rest of the night. She would...

A knock sounded at the door. Collin grumbled, "Go away. I'm not here."

She heard Jill's voice giggle. "Ms. Walker, Rob say you need to come to the cafeteria and eat. Say a few other things I'm not repeating, but say you a bad crewmate if you don't."

Collin counted to ten. "Thank you for delivering the message, Jill. You don't have to run messages for Rob."

"I ain't. I finished my dinner already. He really want you to come, Ms. Walker."

Collin groaned. "Thank you for letting me know, Jill. I'll..." *I'll what? Tell him to mind his own business? To take a hike? To leave me alone?*

You gonna make Jill carry a message back to the cafeteria? Put the poor child in the middle of your fight? What kind of example are you setting?

Collin rolled her eyes. "I'll tell him myself when I get there. Have fun tonight."

"Thanks, Ms. Walker. You, too."

Collin rolled carefully off the bed, trying to make sure all the pieces moved at approximately the same time. *I was having fun. I wasn't moving.*

Collin stood, feeling very much like the Tin Man, trying to keep everything in its proper place. She went to the sink, dashed water in her face, grabbed a ballcap to cover her hair, and headed out of the room. Collin took a small piece of paper, folded it over, and placed it between the door and jamb just above the floor. She made sure the door locked behind her.

She arrived at the cafeteria with fifteen minutes left for service. She saw Rob and the crew sitting together near the back of the room. She heard them laughing and chattering. An extra person occupied the table. At first glance, Collin thought maybe Mitch came to dinner as well. *Not how I want to spend tonight. Or any night.*

But she looked closer. The man faced the window so she couldn't get a hard look. But the silhouette looked vaguely familiar. She studied him a long moment, willing him to turn around.

He did. Jeff's face bore a look of concern, caution, uncertainty, maybe? But his eyes...those eyes. Collin lowered hers, dropped her head, and walked to the table. Rob put his hand to his chest in mock amazement. "She came. She actually here."

The crew began applauding and cheering. Collin sighed, shaking her head. "Okay, okay, maybe I deserve some of that. But not all." She looked at Jeff and kept her face from betraying any emotion at how she felt about seeing him. "Hi."

Jeff held her eyes with his gaze. He pulled a chair beside his and offered it to her. Collin sat down carefully, swallowing the little grunts of pain threatening to escape her throat. Rob jumped up. "I'll get you dinner. One of all of it, right?"

Collin sneered. "Two." Rob laughed and raced to the serving line. Collin looked in Jeff's eyes. "When did you get back?"

"About noon. Since Dad's deal fell through, I figured I should come back here, in case I'm needed. This place can't run without me."

The man smiled, but the words sounded forced to Collin's ear. Niles jumped into the conversation. "You shoulda seen the rapids we crossed, dude. We were rocking!"

Ta'waan joined in. "Yeah, man. Almost lost my seat! Mitch told us the river we practiced on wasn't nothing compared to what we gonna do tomorrow. Gonna be a sweet ride."

Chonnell bounced up and down in her seat. "We even caught air! Me 'n Pardner. It's scary!" The joy in her face belied any fear.

Pardner chimed in. "Yeah. I'm gonna carry rocks in my pockets and tie some horseshoes to my feet to hold me down tomorrow."

Nyla laughed. "Them rocks you got in your head should be enough to keep you in your seat. You tie horseshoes to your feet and fall overboard, you gonna sink. Even your lifejacket can't keep you floating."

Pardner's eyes darted back and forth as she considered what Nyla said. A moment later, her face brightened. "We can put seatbelts on the raft! That'd work. Right?"

Everyone laughed, except Jeff and Collin. Collin smiled gently. "I don't think they have them for a reason, Pardner. If the boat flips, you'd be hanging upside down in the water."

Pardner humphed. "Well, I gonna put some extra padding on my bottom anyways, so it don't hurt so much when I bounce. Them benches are hard after a while."

Collin agreed. "Yes, they are, Pardner."

Rob returned with a tray and a plate of stewed chicken, mashed potatoes and gravy, peas, and a Jello salad. He set it in front of Collin. "Eat. I get you ice cream if you clean your plate."

Collin grimaced. "You're enjoying this, aren't you?"

Rob smiled a wide smile. "Ain't often I get to tell you what to do. Feels kinda good." He resumed reliving the day with the rest of the crew.

Collin rolled her eyes. "Enjoy it while it lasts, little brother." She looked at Jeff and saw the same look of concern in his eyes. She closed her eyes, said a silent grace, then looked back at him. "What's wrong, Jeff?"

He kept his voice quiet. "We need to talk. After dinner?"

Collin nodded. "Of course." She began eating, mixing the peas in with the potatoes.

Pardner jumped to her feet. "You shoulda seen me on the waterslide, Mr. Jeff! I went so fast I thought I'd shoot right offa the bottom of it all the way back to camp!"

Four voices joined hers in exclaiming the fright, the thrills, and the sheer joy of riding the waterslide. Niles asked, "How come no one else even knowed about it, huh? No one I talked to even heard about it."

Jeff's eyes widened in surprise. "Waterslide? We don't have a waterslide."

Multiple voices all responded, "Yes, you do!" "Yeah, it's cool!" "We rode it, has to be one!"

Jeff held a hand up to still the crew. "Where is this? Where did Mitch take you?"

He looked to Collin for answers. She shrugged. "I don't know, Jeff. I don't. We came off the river, walked over some rolling hills, and it was down in a flat area."

Nods backed her story. Jeff's eyes lost the surprise. He tapped his hand on the table. "And you all rode this waterslide?" He smiled, but Collin saw deepening concern on his face. "With water and everything?"

Niles leaned forward. "Yeah, man. Mr. Mitch said it's the final test to teach us how to ride the river if we fall out of the boat. You mean you don't know about this slide? I thought you know everything about this camp."

"I thought I did, too." Jeff's brow crinkled. "How far did you have to walk?"

Pardner and Ta'waan both answered at the same time, but with different estimates. "Forever!" "Not far."

A genuine smile crossed Jeff's face for the first time since she'd seen him. "Okay, okay. Never mind. I'll talk to the owner about it."

Collin cocked her head. "Are you really concerned there's something here, and the owner hasn't told you about it? Does he tell you about everything?"

Jeff hesitated. "I'm his...safety advisor on stuff like that. He shouldn't be putting in rides I don't know about. Especially ones that...exciting."

Niles laughed hard. "You just jealous you ain't got to ride it first!"

Jeff laughed with Niles, but Collin could see the concern returning to his eyes. "Right, Niles."

He stretched a little and looked at Collin's plate of food. "No ice cream if you don't finish it. You heard the man."

Collin shoved a forkful of chicken and potatoes in her mouth. "Smeemmsh?"

The crew began the process of clearing their tables. Collin swallowed and looked pointedly at Rob. "I want that report on Ares done tonight. Got it? And yes, use all the help you can get. The more people, the better."

Rob's eyes narrowed slightly, but he nodded without losing a beat. "I'm gonna ask Jeff if you clean your plate. Better be getting some power food in you, you wanna beat me." He snorted. "Think you Zena or somethun. Huh."

Collin pointed at him, then hit her chest. Rob looked down and tried to hit his in return, without the others seeing.

Collin swallowed the choking sensation she felt in her throat. She stuffed another portion of her dinner in her mouth, swallowed, then looked at Jeff. "Hi."

Jeff's smile crinkled the corners of his eyes. "Hi yourself. It's good to see you." He leaned closer, tapped her shoulder with his. "Missed you."

Collin closed her eyes. *Say it.*

Don't say it.

"I missed you, too." She opened her eyes and held his. "I missed you, Jeff. I haven't missed anyone in a very long time. But I missed you."

Jeff placed his hand on hers and squeezed it. They sat silent for several moments. Jeff motioned to her half-full plate. "No ice cream."

Collin chuckled. "Yes, Mother." She admitted, "That's the most I've eaten in a few days. I think I deserve ice cream for the effort."

Jeff chuckled. "I'll think about it." He looked at Collin, question in his eyes. "What was that between you and Rob? Ares and Zena?"

Collin stuffed half a bite in her mouth. "It's a code we use. Rob and I have to get him out of some tough situations with his mother's succession of live-ins. There have been times I've tried to check in on him, and his mother or someone else will send me a note supposedly from him saying he's fine and leave him alone." She shrugged. "Without the code word Ares, I know it's not from him. When we talk to each other, if he's being coerced or threatened, we use the names to let each other know."

Jeff studied the table. "Okay, I see why you would want him to use Ares. But why are you Zena?"

Collin let out a deep sigh. "There have been times when I pretend not to be his social worker. Where I've taken on a gang persona. He tells someone Zena is going to pick him up. Let's me know I need to bring back-up or come prepared to rumble." She shrugged. "It happens. We like to be prepared."

Jeff looked at her sideways. "Okay, then. I see where that might come in handy. I think." He motioned to her plate. "Two more bites, and I'll concede." He amended his condition. "Two full bites."

Collin rolled her eyes. "Why do I put up with you?"

"You trust me? You like me?" Jeff hesitated. His voice became soft. "You love me?"

Collin's hands trembled. Her eyes widened. She stared at the table, not seeing it or anything else. Emptiness. Darkness. She closed her eyes.

Jeff touched her hand. "Collin. It's okay. I'm here, you're here. God has us, milady."

Collin swallowed hard, lifted her head, breathed in slowly, sighed, and relaxed her shoulders. She opened her eyes and gave Jeff a weak smile. "It's been a tough week. I'm not all here right now."

You're never all here. You've never been. You're—

Jeff interrupted the debate. "Tell me what happened on the basketball court."

"How do you know about that?"

"Let's say I have friends in high places. And low ones, too, for that matter." He smiled to take any sting out. "How bad are you hurt?"

Don't tell him anything. He doesn't need to know your business.

You don't need his help. You're too weak to fight your own battle?

Tell him the truth.

I want his help.

Coward.

"He cracked some ribs on the back of my left side." She hesitated. "One may be broken." She looked at Jeff with defiance. "But they don't do anything for busted ribs, so there's no use in me

196

going to a hospital or a doctor. They will immobilize it, which I will do when I can get to a drug store and get a wrap."

Jeff dipped his head. "I hear you." He paused. "Any idea who it might have been?"

Collin nodded. "I know who it is. Mitch Kellum."

Jeff's eyes narrowed. "You know this for a fact?"

"He said I'd been attacked from the back. I never told anyone about that." She sat back in her chair and pushed the plate away. "I know the sheriff said Mitch had been eliminated as a suspect in the 'Big Foot' incidents. He also told me I'm the only one's been assaulted and the only one who heard Big Foot say anything."

Collin turned and looked at Jeff, question in her eyes. "What if they're not the same people? What if Big Foot is some nutcase who gets his jollies out of scaring people? And what if Mitch decided to copy him so he could get to me?"

Jeff's eyes lowered, then he looked up. "Why would Mitch want to hurt you?"

"Because I stood up to him. I challenged his manhood."

Jeff's eyebrows went up a notch. "What did you do?"

"Turned down his advances. Threatened to hurt him if he didn't stop." Collin recounted the last incident with Mitch. "I think he attacked me to prove he was better than me."

Jeff mused a few moments. "Do you want to call Sheriff Bo and tell him?"

Collin cocked her head. "Sheriff Bo? First name basis with the local Mountie?"

Jeff grinned. "He's known me since I was tall enough—"

"—to steal gumballs off the counter at the movie theatre. I know. He told me." She looked down at her lap. "Tell him what? I think Mitch Kellum attacked me? What proof do I have? My word against his. I know how that game is played." Collin felt her face burning. "Woman accuses man of assault. He claims she initiated it or made it up. Without proof, the homeboy has the advantage." She ground her teeth. "Not how I want to be remembered here. Not the image I want my kids to have of me, either."

Collin looked up at Jeff. "He'll come after me again. Tomorrow, tomorrow night. It doesn't matter. I'll be ready."

Jeff kept his voice soft and gentle. "Like you were last night?"

Collin sagged. "What do you want me to do?"

Jeff took her hand. "I want you to trust me. To trust Bo. To trust Steve Parks. To trust God we are in your corner. It's not you against the world, milady. I know it has been."

He picked up both of her hands and made her face him. He lowered his head, so Collin would look him directly in the eyes. "Collin, I don't know what you've been through in your life. I don't know what happened to get you where you are. But I know you're not alone. You love the Lord. He is with you. He wants to help you. I want to help you. But you have to let us. Please."

Collin closed her eyes. Her face twisted as she fought the tears threatening to burst out after so many years. Voices screamed in her head.

Trust no one! Let no one in! No one loves you. No one cares.

He's like all the others. He'll take what he wants and leave.

Trust me.

You're worthless! You're weak! You're a coward! Can't even fight your own fights, huh?

Collin dropped her head. She whispered, "One voice. Only You, Lord. I have to hear only You. No one else. Your sheep...I'm scared. Please. One voice."

Trust Me. Trust him.

Collin leaned against Jeff, her eyes still closed, her head still down. Jeff put his arms around her and held her.

They sat that way for an eternity. Or five minutes, whichever someone counted. Collin opened her eyes, looked at Jeff. "I bet they want us to get out so they can close up and go home, right?"

Jeff shrugged. "I'm sure they'll get overtime."

Collin cocked her head. "Your boss is that free with money? He won't care some weepy counselor kept an entire shift after hours while she melted down?"

Jeff grinned. "He's covered other meltdowns, believe me. He's very understanding."

Collin stood with Jeff's help. "I'd like to meet him before I leave. Is he here? I mean, does he watch the classes? It must get old seeing people doing the same thing over and over. One class gets to looking like every other one."

Jeff frowned. "Not true. Classes are as unique as the people in them. He never gets tired of watching what this place does for the campers."

Collin eyed Jeff. "You know him that well?"

Jeff chuckled. "He's said that more than a few times. I know how he feels about Grace. It's his passion. Sort of like you and the kids you serve."

Collin snorted. "Poor guy."

Jeff and Collin left the cafeteria and went into the main lobby area. Jeff sat Collin down in one of the straight-back chairs near the fireplace, then sat down next to her on the floor. "We work this out together, milady. You say it's Mitch. I believe you. What do we do about it?"

Collin stretched her neck to relieve some of the tension. "I don't know, Jeff. I don't. If I tell the sheriff and I'm right, he arrests Mitch, and the kids lose their shot to ride the river. If I'm wrong, or the sheriff doesn't believe me, I spoil the day for them anyhow. Mitch won't want me on the crew, and the kids will have to take sides. It's not what I want."

The words sounded quiet. "Who's side wins?"

Collin dropped her head. "Mine." She looked at Jeff. "And then I've ruined an innocent man's reputation, and my kids still get cheated out of their last day."

Jeff's eyes looked sideways, then looked back at her. "What if…" He trailed off.

"What if what?"

"What if I go with you all? What if I make the ride, too? If he's guilty, he won't try anything with another adult there. If he's innocent, we all have a great time on the river. No harm, no foul."

Collin chuckled without mirth. "Easy for you to say. I still have to face the fear."

"Surrounded by people who love you and will make sure you stay safe. Your crew won't let anything happen to you, and neither will I."

For the first time that evening, Collin felt hopeful. "Could you actually do that? Won't Mitch be upset and think you're crashing his party? Would he have to let you go with us?"

Collin sensed Jeff making this plan up as he went. "If the owner and Steve Parks and Ted Johnson all signed off on it, Mitch would have to either take me along or refuse and quit."

"But if he quits, the kids don't get to ride the river, and we're back where we started." Collin dropped her head against the back of the chair. "And it's only an 8-man craft anyhow. You'd be out of place, or he'd insist one of the kids stay behind." She looked at the floor. "I'd volunteer."

Jeff touched her arm. "You've come this far. You're not going to stop now." He sat back against the wall. "There's a way. I know there is." He caught hold of Collin's hand and laughed. "Uh, I think we're going about this the wrong way." She looked at him in question. Jeff closed his eyes. "Lord, You know the problem. You know the solution. Show us, please. We need you."

Collin added a whispered, *Please. Help me. Help us.*

The male side of the dorm's doors opened, and a trio of young campers came out, laughing and jostling one another. Collin recognized Rory but didn't try to get his attention. He looked busy enough.

But Rory saw Collin and dropped back from his companions for a moment. "Ms. Walker, I got a note here for you." He dug a folded piece of paper out of his pocket and handed it to her. "It's from Rob."

Collin looked at him sideways. "Rob gave this to you?"

"No. Timmons give it to me to give to you. He said Tyler give it to him, an' Tyler got it from someone else who got it from Rob. All I know is I's supposed to give it to you."

Collin took the paper, looked at it, looked at Rory. "Thanks, Rory. I appreciate you taking time to run messages for someone else."

Rory shrugged. "Not really a problem. It's a thing back there. Anyone headed up to the front takes a message for someone else. It helps."

Collin nodded. "Yes, it does. I'm glad you men have figured out cooperation works."

Rory laughed, "Yeah, yeah. We know. We learning." He looked at Jeff and said, "Hey, Jeffman. You know Ms. Walker?"

Jeff nodded. "I'm learning to."

Rory grinned. "She pretty cool for a caseworker. Crazy sometimes, but cool."

Collin pointed down the hall. "Go. Begone."

Rory laughed and ran to catch up with his buddies. Collin looked back at the paper. She didn't open it immediately. Her brow furrowed. Her eyes narrowed. She looked at Jeff. "Fast answer."

"Depends on what it says."

Collin felt a tensing of her muscles as she opened it. She read aloud, "Collin, want to shoot some baskets? Meet me at court two by nine, and we'll practice together. You have to teach me the 'bounce the ball over the other guy's head' trick. Rob."

Her eyes glazed as she looked at the words. Jeff's voice brought her back to the present. "Collin. Talk to me. What's going on?"

Collin looked up at him. "It's not from Rob."

"Because he didn't mention Ares?"

She nodded. "And because he doesn't call me Collin. And we never 'practice' together. We always compete." She looked at Jeff. "And he taught me that move, anyhow. This isn't from Rob."

Jeff got to his feet. "I'll call Bo."

"No. There's no crime here. All we have is a note asking me to come to the court. Not worth bothering the Mounties."

Jeff's face darkened. "You're not going out there alone, Collin. At the very least, I'm going with you. If Mitch is there, he won't dare do anything. He'll have to explain the note, but he doesn't lose face, and maybe he figures out we're on to him, and he leaves you alone."

Listen to him.

Collin drew in a deep breath and let it out slowly. "Okay. What time is it now?"

Jeff looked at his watch. "It's 8:05."

Collin nodded. "Let me go to my room, change into my sweats, and I'll meet you back here in ten minutes." She started to stand, struggled to get up, rose finally, and looked at Jeff. "Fifteen. It's a long hall. My room's at the back by the exit door."

"Wait. Collin." Jeff reached in his pocket and pulled out a small hair clip.

Collin looked at it with skepticism. "What is that?"

Jeff's face hardened. "Don't laugh. It's a listening device." He placed the clip in her hair. He pointed to the clip. "It's connected to my watch. The watch is connected to Bo's. All you have to do is talk, and we can hear you."

Collin's eyes narrowed. "Where did you get these? And why?" She stared at Jeff in confusion. "Who did you talk to you could even get equipment like this?"

Jeff pursed his lips, took Collin's hands in his, and looked her dead in the eyes. "I will explain everything after we get through this tonight. I promise. For now, please trust me I'm on your side. I care. I want to help. Okay?"

Collin took the clip from her hair. She turned it over and over in her hand. She looked at Jeff. "What kind of range does it have?"

"About a mile. Then it has GPS tracking, even if you're not talking."

Collin stared hard at the clip. She kept her head down but looked at Jeff. "You didn't buy these on a janitor's salary. Or a paramedic's, either."

Jeff repeated, "Trust me, Collin. Please?"

She stared at him a long moment. "Okay." She looked him in the eyes. "You will explain everything." Jeff nodded. Collin swallowed a chuckle. "And I make no apologies for what I may say under duress."

Jeff smiled, and Collin saw a look of relief on the man's face. "I'll take that chance."

She squeezed his hand, tucked the clip in her hair, and said, "Fifteen minutes." Collin walked gingerly to the corridor doors, opened the girls' door, and went inside. She counted doors the same way she did last night. At least tonight, she could walk without leaning against the walls.

Close inspection indicated a somewhat muddy pattern across several stretches of one side. Housekeeping would not be happy at week's end. Ah, well. Job security, right? She reached her door, looked down, and immediately froze. The paper tell she placed at the bottom of the door lay on the floor. Someone had been in her room.

Was in her room now? Collin's breathing slowed, and her body came to full alert.

Signal Jeff.

Collin muttered, "I sure hope Rob got his report on Ares done. I might have to go all Zena on him if he doesn't." She snorted once. "Like I could ever be the warrior princess for real. Can't even remember to lock my own door. Worthless. Totally worthless." *What now, Lord?*

Wait.

Collin waited. Her door flung open, and Mitch stepped out,

knife in hand pointed at her throat. Collin kept her voice even. "Mitch. Not surprised. I figured since you—"

Mitch's eyes danced with anger. But his words came out barely above a whisper. "Shut up. Unless you want me to drag one of your precious kids with us."

Collin lowered her voice. "No. I'm the prize. Do what you came for. Kill me. Leave the others alone."

Mitch snarled, "Kill you? You think I'd make it easy on you after all your mouth?" He mocked her tone, "'don't make me hurt you.' Like you ever could. No, I've got better plans." He motioned toward the exit door. "That way. Move."

Collin moved toward the door.

Keep him on your side, not behind you.

Collin prayed, *Okay, Lord. You gave me the training. Tell me what to do with it.*

Stillness flooded through her. Not frozen panic, but peace. God held this. Collin pushed the door open and stopped. "Left or right?"

"Straight ahead. To the docks."

Collin's peace slipped a step. *Lord?*

I have you.

Clear of any campers or intrusion, Collin asked, "Where are we going?"

Mitch's eyes narrowed to tiny strips. "Oh, I think you know."

"The river, I got it. You want to see me cower and crawl and beg you for help. Right?"

"No. I want to see you die screaming in fear."

Collin tossed her head. "That ship sailed, Mitch. I'm not afraid to die. I told you."

"You lie. They always do."

"'They?' Who is 'they?'" Collin looked at Mitch in genuine surprise.

"The others. The ones before you. Drifters, runaways. People no one would miss. Most of them said the same thing." He mocked their tones. "'I'm not afraid to die.' But they all screamed in the end. So smug. Just like you."

Collin felt her stomach turn. "How many others?"

"What's it matter?"

Collin kept him talking. "Hard to hide a whole lot of bodies.

One or two, maybe. But more than two? I don't know, Mitch." She looked at him. "These Big Foot sightings. Was that you, too?"

Mitch snorted. "No. Stupid amateur. Scaring people, then letting them go? Why bother?"

They reached the lower end of the docks, nearest dock two. A lone figure loomed ahead of them, coming off of dock seven.

Mitch caught Collin's arm and said, "Stay calm, or he dies, too."

Jeff smiled a winning and confused smile. "Hey, Mitch, Collin. Mitch, I checked those moorings on dock seven. They seem to be holding. I didn't know if you needed it tomorrow, so thought I'd—"

Mitch slashed the knife to Collin's neck. "You'll do exactly what I say, got it?"

Jeff held his hands out in surprise. "What's going on, Mitch? I thought—"

Mitch pressed the knife harder. "Shut up." He looked from Jeff to Collin and back again. Then he laughed. "Oh, I see." He motioned to Collin. "You got suspicious, didn't you? And told your hero about it. And he comes down here alone to save the day."

Jeff warned, "I'm not alone, Mitch."

Mitch laughed harder. "Save it, janitor. You're here because no one else believes her. Who would? She's a deranged counselor who slits her own hand in front of kids. Then she tells the sheriff she got attacked by Big Foot, who she now claims is a respected teacher, namely me. No one is going to buy her story."

He drew Collin closer. "Did you try telling the owner, too, huh? He didn't believe you either, did he? Of course not. He's concerned about the reputation of his camp. What does he care about one camper's wild story?" Mitch looked at Jeff. "But you, you'll believe anything, won't you? Especially when a female gives you more than the time of day. I saw the two of you. It's disgusting. Her picking you over me."

Jeff dropped the pretense. "You can't take us both, Mitch. You go after one, the other drops you. Give it up."

Mitch continued to sneer. "I don't have to. I have my ace in the hole. Your boy Rob. You'll do anything to keep him safe, won't you? Anything at all."

Collin went cold. *Trust me. Rob is safe.* "What do you mean, Mitch? Where is Rob?"

"I have him. He's safe for now. But only while you cooperate."

Collin's eyes narrowed. "You're lying. You don't have Rob. He's smarter than you."

Mitch pulled a paper out of his pocket, still holding the knife against Collin's windpipe. She could feel trickles of blood from the pressure he exerted on her skin. He threw the wad of paper down and told Jeff, "Pick it up and read it. Show it to her, but stay back."

Jeff read, "'Collin, help me. Mitch told me to write this, or he'd kill me. I want to go home, please. Help.' It's signed, 'Rob.'"

Jeff held the paper at arm's length so Collin could see it clearly. Collin's eyes narrowed as she studied the script. Not Rob's. But a child's handwriting, nonetheless. Collin could see artwork from the other side shadowed through the note. Artwork of googly-eyed characters. *Lord, does he have Chonnell?*

No. She is safe. But do as he says.

Collin looked at Jeff. "I know the artwork." She turned to Mitch. "We'll do anything you say."

Jeff nodded without looking startled or surprised. Good acting job. Who was he, anyhow? Collin looked at Mitch. "Now what?"

Mitch motioned toward a small canoe. "Can't leave blood and bodies lying around the dock. Looks bad. We're going on a trip." He smiled again. "The river loves to hide bodies for me. She's accommodating that way." He stepped in first, dragging Collin along. Jeff kept his eyes firmly fixed on Collin's and followed Mitch into the boat.

Mitch pushed the knife up tighter against Collin's neck. His eyes narrowed as he stared at Jeff. "Paddle. Paddle us out to the junction."

Jeff wielded the paddle awkwardly, making only shallow dips, pulling little water or distance. Mitch hissed, "I said, paddle."

Jeff barked back, "I am paddling. I'm the janitor, remember? I clean the boats, not use them."

Mitch glared at him and seethed, "Just paddle. Dig it deeper."

Jeff complied, and his stroke improved. Barely. Collin watched the man's uncoordinated efforts. At this rate, they would reach the junction in fifteen minutes or so. Time enough for Sheriff Bo to reach them?

Collin decided they needed more information. "Where are you keeping Rob?" Another thought chilled her. "Why would you keep him alive?"

Mitch loosened his grip on Collin's throat, but only enough so he could move into a better position to see both her and Jeff. "Why wouldn't I? Lots of people pay good money for a kid. Girls bring more, but a boy still fetches a good price."

Collin's stomach nearly leapt out of her throat. Hatred, anger, rage, revulsion...she experienced them all in a moment. She wanted to jump on Mitch and pound him into the bottom of the canoe. Only the Lord and the knife stopped her.

Vengeance is mine. I will repay. In full.

Collin forced herself to relax all the tensed muscles in her arms and shoulders. She would not kill him. Yet.

Love your enemies. Pray for those that use you.

I'm working on it. I can forgive those that use me. But using a child is a whole 'nother level of atrocity.

"Where are you holding him?"

"He's safe. I have a place up the river where I keep my visitors." He smiled. "You'll see soon enough." He looked up and glared at Jeff. "If this fool ever figures out how to paddle." His eyes narrowed as he looked from Collin to Jeff. "I wonder how much your stroke would improve if I started cutting her every time you miss one?"

Jeff struggled to keep the paddle under control in the increasing current. "I'm doing the best I can. Don't hurt her. I'm trying!" Jeff practically begged.

Mitch preened. "Oh, listen to the big man. Begging me not to hurt his precious love." He pulled the knife away from Collin's neck. "There, see? I believe you. You're doing all you can." He nodded. "Sure, you are."

In one swift move, Mitch stabbed the knife deep into Collin's shoulder. Her eyes widened, but she made no sound. Jeff started forward. Mitch jerked the knife out and poised it over her throat again. "Paddle. Now."

Mitch patted Collin's shoulder. "Sorry, sweetheart. But he needed to be taught a lesson." He cocked his head and studied her. "Don't you feel pain?"

Collin kept her head straight. "I feel pain, Mitch. I don't show pain."

"Really? How much pain can you keep in? Might be a fun game."

Collin started to respond but received a sharp, *Don't. Just don't.* She chose silence instead.

Jeff seemed to make more progress with his paddling. Maybe being with the current helped. It certainly moved them along with greater speed. They reached the channel's junction, and Mitch ordered Jeff to pull across the sister stream to the main river.

Collin kept her eyes fixed on the man in front of her working the oar, maneuvering the too-frail craft into the center of the current. The boat kicked and bucked precariously. Collin lifted the only prayer she could. *Help me. Help us.*

A small child sat on the ground beside her Father in Heaven. She clung to His leg. "I'm scared, Abba Daddy."

"What did I promise you?"

Collin recited, *"When you go through the fire, I am with you. When you go through the flood, I am there. I'll help you."*

"Right. Now, what's the first part say?"

"Don't be afraid."

"If I'm right there with you, and you're holding My hand, what can hurt you?"

"Nothing."

"What can pull us apart?"

"Nothing."

"What is there to fear?"

"Nothing."

Collin opened her eyes. She lifted her focus from the bottom of the boat, now filled with water. She studied the man fighting the currents and rocks. He strained and pulled and dodged rocks and boulders and eddies that would spin the craft sideways into deadly hydraulics. Collin lifted her gaze further up, to the river itself. She stared into its waves, its pools, and washouts.

Her mind began to flashback to another river, another time. *The images flowed as they ever did. Except this time, she held her Abba's hand. He walked with her through the memories, reassuring her all would be well. She would be rescued. She would live to see her mother and brother again. Yes, she would be with the bad man for a while longer. But God knew his plans for her future. Plans to save her. To bring her to Himself. To give her Life and Joy and Peace. Plans which included bringing Collin to a camp to meet a man she could love and who would love her back.*

Collin relaxed and smiled. No fear. No monster. Only water.

Mitch noticed the difference. He glowered at her. "What's so funny?"

Collin looked down, then looked back at Mitch. "The fear is gone."

"What?" Mitch barked. "You're lying. This terrifies you. You said so, and I saw your face the first time. Now you're telling me you're not afraid? You're a liar. And a bad one."

Collin waggled her head. "Suit yourself." She could feel herself beaming with a light no one could take away.

Mitch glared at her in fury. "You think this is a joke?"

"Not a joke. Just not scared anymore. God took the fear." She smiled at her kidnapper. "Sorry to disappoint you."

Mitch's eyes burned. His fists clenched, the veins in his neck stood out. He reached back to strike her, but Collin headbutted him in the chest, knocking him backward. He grabbed at her; Jeff jumped to help. The river dropped the boat into a hole, then shot them spinning. Mitch grabbed for Collin, Jeff grabbed for Mitch, Collin grabbed for the gunwales.

All three missed. The boat flipped, pitching them into the water. Mitch yelled. Collin grabbed as much air as she could before being shoved under the surface by a wave roaring over a boulder. She let the force carry her along until it bobbed her back into the air. More boulders lay ahead. The trick would be to grab one and hold on; maybe even climb on top of it. Either way, she needed to be prepared.

It's not the fall that kills you. It's the sudden stop at the bottom.

Translation: don't tense up. Don't lock knees, feet, elbows, arms...but keep your feet downstream. Better broken ankles than a crushed skull.

Collin tried to anticipate every dip, every drop, every sudden stall. But the current proved too swift. The river pummeled and pounded her, thrashing her like a laundromat washing machine. How long she struggled, she didn't know. Half-drowned, she tried to angle toward a bank, either bank, it didn't matter. The waning moon did nothing to illuminate any avenue of escape. The river alone would determine her fate.

And the Creator of the river. With a sudden "whoosh," the river tossed Collin out sideways over a shallow wash. She rolled away from the following wave, further in and higher up, to avoid being swept back into the river's grip. She gagged and coughed against all the water she'd swallowed, too weak to stand, too weak to do anything but lay in stillness and breathe.

Collin closed her eyes to whisper, *Thank You. Thank You. I love You.* She could have lain there and been happy the rest of the night, except she began to shiver from cold and exertion. Time to get moving.

Right. Where? How?

You're resourceful. You'll figure it out. Do it. Move. Don't ask—

Collin blocked the litany. "Lord, what do You want me to do?"

She felt the approving smile. *Crawl up the hill. Shelter under the bushes. You will be warm.*

Collin waited until she felt steady enough to climb to her hands and knees then began the ascent. It took only a few moments but cost her dearly in bruised kneecaps, wrists punctured from sharp rocks, and her shirt ripped by the unyielding branches. But under the limbs, she found a warm haven. Some river creature hollowed out a bed or den, lined it with cast-off feathers and fur, and only recently vacated the premises. Collin didn't care if it came back; it would simply have to find another spot. "Done. I am done," she muttered. "And Rob says they ain't no grizzlies in West Virginia." She curled into a ball, closed her eyes, and slept.

THURSDAY NIGHT

Jeff's first thought when he hit the water: *Collin!* He hugged the bottom while he could, knowing the current would be stronger, but less violent under the waves. He bounced off a large boulder, fought his way around to the far side, and came up briefly in the hole created by the waves parting, then coming together again. Long enough to inhale a lungful of air before diving down again to fight his way cross-stream to the near bank. He scanned downstream as far as he could see, but it proved futile. Between the dark and the bend in the river, nothing could be seen. Jeff crawled up the bank. He knew the direction to the camp lay upstream. But Collin... Collin would be downstream. And hurt. And bleeding from where the... Jeff choked on the words he wanted to use... Mitch stabbed her without any warning or chance to defend herself.

Jeff's thoughts took a dark turn. He should track the scum down. Should beat him to an indistinguishable pulp and then—

He pulled himself out of the tirade before God did. *Sorry. I'm wrong, I know it. No excuses. What do I do now?*

No words, but the distinct knowledge he should backtrack, find Bo, and let the sheriff be the justice-keeper. Jeff felt torn. *She's out there, Lord. Alone. Hurt. She needs help.*

Jeff got the overwhelming vision of God raising an eyebrow, saying, *Really?* Jeff dropped his head. "I got it. I got it. You'll take care of her. I'll go get Bo." He started tramping back to the docks, but muttered, "At least have Bo headed this way, please? And for once, let me join the search party? If she's going to be my wife, I should be allowed to find her. Or at least look for her. Right? This once?"

Jeff swore he could hear the chuckle in his mind.

* * *

Collin woke to the sound of shuffling nearby. She listened carefully. No sniffing. Not an animal. Not in the physical sense of the word. Then came the muttering. "I'll find her, I swear I will. I don't need my eyes. I'll find her." He added an unfavorable description of Collin's parentage. Collin resisted the urge to shake her head. *Move nothing. Stay absolutely still.*

More muttering. More swearing. Collin tried to sort out anything useful. Not much. But the man continued to shuffle around the area. "She'd get out here. It's the only place she could. Not strong enough to go anywhere else. Unless she drowned."

The shuffling stopped. "No. She wouldn't drown. She's not lucky enough to drown. She's around here. I know she is." Mitch raised his voice. "Walker! I know you're here. You'll die without my help. Come out to me. I'm the only one who can help you now."

That would be a big fat noooo…

"Walker! If I wanted to kill you, I would have done it before now. Come out."

Collin took slow, shallow breaths. Nothing to give him any indication she hid anywhere in the vicinity.

The shuffling began again. As did the swearing. And the muttering. "…rocks. Need to find a long stick. Not crawling on the ground to feel my way. Never crawling again…"

Collin filtered out the negative references to Mitch's own ancestors. But the "crawling" held her interest. And he'd said he didn't need his eyes. Presumably, Mitch could see the same shadows Collin saw. Why did he feel the need to crawl?

Why do you care? If he's blind, let the sheriff's people find him. He's their worry, not yours. Maybe he'll fall into the river and drown. It would be a fitting end to his miserable existence.

Considering how he's tried to end yours. And others, so he says.

Collin heard the voices but knew One was missing. The One that would quote, *If your enemy is hungry, give him something to eat. If your enemy is thirsty…*

Collin lowered her head. *Tell me what to do, Father. I can't walk out of here by myself, I know.* She reached to check for the hair clip Jeff had given her. *Gone. Figured. Too far, and not enough strength left.*

If he's gone blind, he's not walking anywhere by himself, either. Is that why we're here? So we help one another?

She chuckled to herself. *Couldn't you have stranded me with Jeff instead?*

Silence. Amused silence.

I know, I know. Okay, tell me how to do this, and I will. I still need only Your voice, but I am beginning to hear the difference. I hope.

The muttering moved away from her, but not far. Collin heard a "snap," a "whoomp," a yell of pain, and a string of words she'd not heard in many years. Mitch thrashed and yelled and screamed in pain and frustration. The sounds did not move away but stayed firmly planted in one place. Did he step in a hole? Collin's eyes widened. *A trap? An actual steel-teeth and spring-loaded trap? Now wasn't that convenient?*

Mitch's howling and flailing around covered the sound Collin made as she slipped from her nest. She managed to step within five feet of Mitch without him hearing her. In the dim moonlight, she saw the man sitting on the dirt, pounding on something at the base of his right ankle. He pulled and pushed and cursed and swore and yanked and hammered…and nothing changed.

Collin waited until Mitch ran out of curse words and energy. The man stretched out full on the ground in defeat, sobbing in his pain. She said, "I'm here, Mitch. I'm going to help you."

Mitch rolled to a sitting position, still trapped at the ankle. His voice echoed supreme sarcasm. "Of course you are. What else would you do?"

Collin shrugged. "Leave you here for the bears to find. Or the sheriff's people. I'd make my way back to camp sooner or later."

Mitch's voice sneered. "How? You'll be crying for help before you get ten feet. Your only hope is getting me loose and following me."

Collin pursed her lips. "That would be a no, Mitch. I won't follow you anywhere. I suspect you banged your head in the river, and you can't see. And the trap has most likely broken your ankle. Which means you're not moving anywhere fast. Looks like I'm the only help you're going to get tonight. Like it or not."

Mitch sat still. "Fine. Get my leg free. I'll let you lead."

Collin remained out of reach. "Throw me your knife."

"I lost it in the river."

"Throw me the knife, Mitch. I can't open the trap without it."

"I told you I lost it in the river."

Collin frowned. "Don't believe you. Can't help you if you don't give it up."

Mitch yelled, "I don't have it!"

Collin shrugged. "Can't help you then. Sorry. You're on your own." She turned and began to work her way along the bank of the river heading upstream.

She got about five yards when Mitch cursed. "Fine. Here." He pulled the knife out of the sheath inside his shirt and threw it on the ground. "There. Happy now? Get my foot out of this thing."

Collin returned and picked up the knife. She buried it under a bramble bush, after tying some of the branches in a knot for later identification. She then made sure to stay out of range of Mitch's arms, in the event he planned more surprises, and knelt down at his foot.

The trap had no teeth, but the steel bars closed on Mitch's ankle gave no indication they intended to move. Collin felt along the length of the trap and reached the release mechanism. She prayed, *Help me do this Your way, Lord. If I'm wrong, make sure this doesn't open. And being honest, I hope it doesn't. But Your will be done.*

Collin instructed Mitch, "Grab hold of the mouth. When I press the release, you need to push the sides apart. Make sure you push them all the way down. Otherwise, they'll snap closed again."

"What do you know about traps? You're a city rat."

Collin cleared the dirt and leaves off the release, so nothing would prevent it from working. "A city rat that can't afford cable. I watch a lot of nature shows. Ready?"

Mitch caught hold of the mouth of the trap and prepared to pull. "Ready."

Collin hammered the release with a rock and held it down. "Now."

Mitch pried the mouth open wide enough to free his foot. As he pulled his ankle free, he let the mouth go, and it slammed shut on his fingers. He screamed in pain and let fly a string of invectives. Collin yelled, "I told you to push it all the way down!"

Mitch yelled, "You did this on purpose!"

Collin took a deep breath and waited until Mitch stopped cursing again. "When you're done, we'll try this again. You'll have to hit the release, and I'll pull the mouth apart. Got it?"

Mitch growled his assent. Collin appreciated the darkness. She didn't have to see the glare she knew she'd be getting. She wedged her hands above his to be able to grab the mouth and force it open when Mitch pushed the release. If he pushed it. She tapped his foot to get it into position to stomp the release. Mitch grunted and stretched and finally worked his foot onto the round plate that served as the release. He nodded to Collin. "Got it."

Collin prayed aloud this time. "Lord, give me strength to open this. And the ability to keep it open so we both can stay free of it. Please. In Your Name, Lord." She nudged Mitch's shoulder. "Now."

Mitch stepped hard on the plate. Collin felt the slight give of the jaws and pulled them open. Mitch yanked his hands out. Collin pushed the bars 180 degrees apart and set the trap on the ground. Mitch cradled his broken hand. "You want me to thank you, don't you?"

Collin picked up a rock and threw it against the spring of the jaws. They snapped shut. *No temptation. For either of us.* "No, Mitch, I don't. I don't want you to tell anyone I helped you. Ever."

She searched the area for a suitable tree limb Mitch could use as a crutch but found nothing that would work. *I'm it, aren't I? I get to be his support. Lord, You're not making this easy. I don't trust him as far as I can spit, and You want me to let him lean on me as I take him back to be arrested for attempted murder and kidnapping.* She looked skyward. *I know You're God. I trust You. Help my un-trust.*

Collin approached Mitch, standing over him. "You'll have to either hop, hobble, or lean on me. Your choice."

Mitch sat without moving. "I'll hobble. Help me up."

Collin reached down to grab Mitch by the arm. As she did, he swung out hard with his elbow, trying to catch Collin in the jaw.

He missed. And Collin anticipated it. She stepped back away from him. "Nice try. Not stupid. I'm going to help you, but don't think that means I trust you."

Mitch glared up in the direction of her voice. "Why would I let you take me anywhere?"

Collin frowned. "Um, you're blind, you have a broken ankle, and you can't use your hands. Jail or starvation seem to be your options right now."

Mitch snorted. "I've got a third option. You help me get to my cabin, and I don't report the camp for all its shady dealings."

Collin closed her eyes. "What shady dealings?"

Mitch laughed. "Ah, that's the rub, isn't it? You want to know so you can warn McFa'ell to hide the evidence. Won't work. I'm not telling you anything. But what I know could close this place down for good. So, if you want to protect your little happy place, you'll get me to my cabin."

Collin stared at the ground in disbelief. "Right. Mitch, if you have accusations against the camp, if you have proof of accusations against the camp, I'll help you shut it down. Who's McFa'ell? Never heard of him."

"The owner. And I have all the proof anyone needs. The sheriff has been investigating this camp for years, and I have what he needs to put every last employee there in prison for life. Including your precious janitor." He cocked his head to look at Collin, or in her direction, anyhow. "You still want to help take me back?"

Collin shifted from one foot to another. She needed to sit. Standing took more energy than she possessed. But sitting in range of Mitch seemed like a bad plan. She backed up and leaned against a tree, considering her words. "Yeah, I still want to take you back. If you have proof, you should bring it out, get it out in the open. I'm sure Sheriff Bo would be happy to see what you have."

Mitch pulled back slightly. "I don't know. He might be investigating to see if anything implicates him. I might do better going to a higher authority like the Feds or something. If you're serious about helping stop the camp, you'll take me to my cabin where I can get my proof. Then we take it to the Feds in Charleston."

Collin rolled her eyes. "Right. This gets better all the time." She pushed off from the tree, walked back to stand over Mitch again, and said, "We're going. Take my arm."

"You believe me, don't you?"

"Should I?"

"Smart woman like you. You know this camp is too good to be true. Bringing all these kids up here. Kids no one cares about anyhow, for what? To show them a better life? Right." Mitch's voice dripped with disgust. "They're prospecting these kids for pimps back in the city. Trying to sort out which ones are worth selling and to who. That's all this sports camp is for. And I've got the proof in my cabin. Your boy will fetch a great price. And who's going to notice a handful of street rats go missing?"

Collin stared hard at Mitch. "Their counselors."

"I'm sure you'd be well compensated if you even mentioned it. Most counselors are so overworked, they're happy to have one less kid around. Wouldn't you be? Admit it."

Collin grabbed Mitch's arm below the shoulder. "Let's go."

"To the cabin?" Mitch's voice turned to pleading. "It's all true, Collin. All of it. I have the proof—names of kids who have gone missing since being here. Records of who bought them and for how much. I have the proof. But you're too in love with the janitor, aren't you? What if I told you he set up the whole thing? His 'interest' in you? Pretense. Anyone could tell you were the 'clean one' in the bunch. You would be the one to expose the whole plan. Someone needed to neutralize you. That's why Jeff pretended to be interested in you. To keep you from finding out about the whole deal."

Collin pulled Mitch up to his foot. "This all sounds very incriminating. Very suspicious. Which is why we're going back to the camp so you can lodge your accusations in front of my fellow counselors. Seeing as how you're implicating them as well. We'll all be very happy to listen to what you have to say and to make sure you get the chance to prove it. After you answer for kidnapping, admitting to killing others and trying to kill me."

She knew he couldn't see her glare, but she gave it to him anyway. "You have an answer for those charges?"

Mitch leaned on her to keep from putting his weight on his injured ankle. He managed less than a hop, but more than a step as Collin pulled his arm around her shoulder to complete the support. He remained silent for several minutes while they tramped through the brush, staying close to the river, but not so close they might slide down the bank and end up in its grasp once again.

Collin saved her energy for breathing and carrying Mitch. Prayer took no muscle power, however, so she engaged in it. *He's going to attack me before we get there. I know it, You know it, he knows I know it. Why are we doing this?*

Silence.

Okay, forget the why. I can ask, but You don't have to tell me. You're God, I'm not. I get it. Am I doing the right thing? All those accusations he brought. They're all lies, aren't they? Aren't they?

Collin went back over her interactions with Jeff. She initiated contact, not him. She approached him in the cafeteria. She decided on the morning tour, not him. And she asked him to sew up her hand. She asked him to be the ref, and she asked him to play basketball that night. *Over and over, You said, 'Trust him.' You've never once told me to trust Mitch. If You wanted me to, now would be a really opportune moment.*

Silence.

Collin could hear faint echoes of voices in the background of her mind telling her she chose poorly, she was wrong, and would always be wrong. But over it all, silence ruled. She nodded to herself. *Right. I'll trust Jeff. I'll trust You, first, and then I'll trust Jeff.*

The rest of the night turned to a blur of exertion, exhaustion, and increasing pain. Mitch remained unable to bear the least amount of weight on his broken ankle. He leaned more and more of his weight on her shoulders. Collin could feel the knife-wound trickling blood as the rubbing, jarring, pulling motion reopened it.

She made the first halt their only halt. The temptation to lay down and simply stop intensified in front of her, singing strong and clear of rest, sleep, relief. She sat long enough to catch a second wind, but not so long as to lose the drive to keep going. She had to make it back. To see Jeff. To assure Rob Zena lived. To ride the whitewater final examination. So many things to do. Keep going.

* * *

"Son, we have to stop. We're going to miss her in the dark. We can resume in the morning."

Jeff spun on Bo, desperation in his voice. "Bo, we won't miss her. I know she's out there, and I know she's trying to make her way back. If Mitch is still alive, I'm sure he's chasing her, and she's going to need my... our...help. I'm not giving up, Bo. I'm not."

Bo put his hand on Jeff's shoulder. Jeff slumped, then drew himself upright. Bo stared him in the eyes. "Jeff, you nearly drowned yourself. You've been hiking these woods for a couple of hours now, and you can't keep going like this. We'll call it for tonight, come back in the morning when we can see what we're looking for, and then we'll find your uh... friend."

Jeff waved Bo off. His fists clenched, his body shuddered. "No." He took a breath, got himself under control. "I understand. You've got men to think about. I don't. I'm going to keep looking. I'll find her, Bo. I will."

Bo stared at Jeff, his eyes patient and sad in the lantern's light. The sheriff turned around and directed, "Okay, men. Mark your positions so you can come back and start fresh. I want everyone out here by first light, you got it?" He looked at his senior deputy and ordered, "Tell the men on the other side the same thing. First light, they better be in the field searching."

Bo turned back to Jeff. "Let's go, son."

Jeff's eyes flared. "I told you, I'm not—"

Bo interrupted him. "I know, I know. I'm going with you. Someone's got to keep you from falling in the water again. Don't want to fish more people out than I have to."

Jeff's whole being flooded with relief and gratitude. "Thanks, Bo."

Bo shrugged. "I'd be the same way. Let's find your lady."

* * *

For Collin, time didn't exist. Distance didn't exist. Putting one foot in front of the other mattered. Nothing else. *Keep going. Keep going.*

Until she had nothing left and simply quit. She let Mitch down as gently as she could, which didn't mean a whole lot. The man passed out from pain a while ago. Collin arranged him on the ground, trying to make sure his crushed hands lay on his chest and not in the dirt, then collapsed against a tree trunk. "I can't, Lord. I can't go any further. Or farther. I'm done. If it wasn't enough, I'm sorry. I hope Mitch lives. I do. Not because I want him tried and convicted, but because he's a human and deserves a chance to live, too."

Collin closed her eyes, lifted her chin to the sky. She hummed a chorus that came to mind. Then she smiled and sang the gentle melody barely above a whisper. "I will follow where You lead me. Where You put me I will stay. I will do the things You ask me. What You tell me I will say... You are my life." The words felt right, whole, healing, and filling. She repeated the chorus, because what else could she do?

Her eyes remained closed. She sang it one more time as she faded out of consciousness. In her dream, she heard Jeff calling—yelling, actually—her name. She didn't try to reply. It was her imagination, anyway. Let it go. Sleep.

* * *

Jeff crashed through the underbrush, yelling, "Collin! We're here! Keep singing, lady. Keep singing!" He barely heard the strains of the song, but he could guess which direction they came from. Jeff shouted, "Bo! Up this way! Come on, man!"

Bo climbed the bank to rejoin Jeff. "What? Did you hear something?"

"She was singing. I could hear her. She's close, Bo. She's close." Jeff started to dash forward, but Bo grabbed his arm. "Wait, son. You say she's close. Good. But now it's time to slow down and search carefully. You get all worked up, you'll miss her." Bo looked around, cocking his head to listen. "I don't hear anything."

Jeff breathed deep, let it out slowly. "She stopped. I heard her, Bo. I'm not crazy. I heard her." He pointed in the direction downstream. "That way. I know it was her, Bo. I do." Jeff began to shake in frustration. He needed Bo to believe him. *Collin's life depends on me.*

Collin's life depends on Me. Be at peace, Jeffrey. I have her. Always.

Jeff dropped his head. Tears stung his eyes. He looked skyward, crying out his heart. *But I want her with me, Lord. For a while, anyhow. The rest of my life, maybe? That's not too long, is it?*

Bo shone his light over and around the undergrowth lining the riverbank. Low branches reflected back, casting shadows on the mounds of dead and decaying leaves and brushwood. Jeff moved forward slowly, feeling his way through the bushes. He pushed aside loose debris with his feet, shuffling more than walking. Bo did the same. One painful inch at a time. They both cast their lights back and forth, up and down, crisscrossing the area.

Nothing.

Nothing.

Paydirt. Jeff's light shone on something pale, something not vegetation. A body. A body sitting against a tree. Jeff's heart stopped. "There. She's there." Jeff dropped down beside her, moving her so he could hear a breath, get a pulse, find some sign she still lived. He put his ear to her chest. Tears stung his eyes as he whispered, "Thank You. Thank You." Jeff didn't bother to shake the tears off. He looked at Bo. "She's alive. Thank You, Lord." He buried his head in her chest to listen to the most wonderful sound on the earth right then.

Bo continued to move his light around. He called out, "I've got another one." Jeff jerked up and looked where Bo pointed. He could see the sprawled-out figure of another body. Bo's light shone on the face. *Mitch. That—*

Let no corrupt language come out of your mouth.

Jeff bit his tongue. Literally. He waited. "Mitch. It's Mitch."

Bo checked him out. "He's breathing. Looks like he either got attacked or put his hands where they shouldn't be. Nasty wounds. Lost a lot of blood, I think."

Jeff examined Collin's shirt in the light. "She has too. We need Search and Rescue."

"I'm on it." Bo pulled his radio from his belt and called. "Mountain Rescue, we need transport for two injured people, and we need it yesterday." Bo looked at his phone. "And the coordinates are…"

Jeff heard the crackled "10-4." Pause. "ETA thirty minutes."

Bo ordered, "Make it less. These two are in bad shape."

Jeff went into paramedic mode. He checked Collin's limbs for injuries. She barely moaned as he felt along her ribcage. His hands could feel the breaks that once were cracks. But nothing else appeared to be broken.

Mitch hadn't fared as well. Besides the crushed and torn hands, Jeff discovered the mangled ankle. Bo's eyes narrowed. "Bet he tangled with a trap of some nature. Illegal, of course. There's no trapping allowed this time of year. Must have been a big one to cause that much damage. Probably bear. And we don't allow bear trapping any time of year. We'll have to go looking for the trap."

He patted Jeff on the shoulder. "But that will be my men's job. You have enough to do with caring for her." Jeff saw a twinkle in Bo's eye. "You sure you're up to it?"

Jeff sat down beside Collin. He cradled her in his arms and answered, "No. But I'm going to give it my best shot." He rested his head on hers. "I've got you, milady. I've got you."

FRIDAY MORNING

Collin drifted up through the fog and slowly opened her eyes. She stared at the ceiling above her. Nothing there indicated where she might be. She looked to her right. An IV bag hung on a pole. The IV attached to her arm. *A clue.*

She turned her head to the left and looked into two sets of worried, anxious, troubled...how many synonyms did she know for concerned? Collin stared at a young man and an older man, probably not related. Both sat on the edge of chairs as if waiting for her to speak. Or move. Or do anything except sleep. They looked vaguely familiar. Like she should know them. Her eyes narrowed. Thinking made her head hurt, but she stared hard at both of them. She looked at the man. "You're... you're Jeff."

The man's face broke into a huge smile. Relief washed over his features. "Yes. I'm Jeff."

Collin turned her attention to the young man. "You're...you're...the pain in my neck who keeps me employed, aren't you, Rob?"

Rob dove onto the bed and buried his head in Collin's arms. "Oh, caseworker lady! Don't ever leave me like that again." He pulled up, tears dripping down his cheeks. "You ain't Zena. Ain't supposed to even think you are. Why you go off with Mitch thinking you gonna bring him in on your own, huh? I try something like that, you'd skin me alive. After you chewed me out and tried to beat sense into my head!"

Collin hugged the boy. "I wasn't trying to be Zena, Rob. Things sort of got out of hand."

Rob sniffed. "Got out of Mitch's hands, too, they say. Both

broken across the knuckles. He ain't gonna be doing nothing to nobody for a long time."

Collin looked at Jeff. "Is he going to be okay? He's not going to lose his foot, is he?"

Jeff shook his head. "It's going to take a skilled surgeon to put all the pieces back in place. Not sure they have anyone so gifted in the state penitentiary system, but he might get lucky."

Collin heard the bitter notes in Jeff's tone. She held out her hand. He took it. She pulled him closer to the bed. "Let it go, Jeff. I have. God will take care of Mitch."

Rob sat and looked at Collin. His eyes narrowed, his face darkened. "You forgive Mitch? After what he done to you? He try to kill you. He beat you up, kidnap you, try to drown you, and you still forgive him? Ain't no way."

Collin squeezed Jeff's hand. She hugged Rob. "Yes, there's a way. Jesus. Same way He forgave me. Forgives me." Pain began to creep in around her eyes. She clamped her lips shut as a wave of nausea and agony swamped her. She dropped her head back, lifting her chin to try to keep from making any sound. She heard Jeff talking to the wall. "Yeah. Ms. Walker needs pain meds. Right now."

His voice became soothing. "It's okay, Collin. It's okay. Yell if you want to. No one's going to stop you."

Collin closed her eyes and panted in time to the throbbing in her head. She could hear Rob's frightened, "What's wrong? What happened? Did I do something?"

Jeff's voice continued to be smooth and calm. "You didn't do anything, Rob. Her body is letting her know all the places needing attention. It's probably a longer list than she thought."

Collin wanted to lash out at his smugness but knew if she opened her mouth for anything, she'd scream and never stop. She heard a body enter the room. Someone looked at the band on her wrist, then she felt the bite and blessing of medication seeping into her veins. She sighed, relaxed all the muscles on high alert. "I'm going to take a little nap. You two are dismissed. Go do something. Anything. I'll see you later." With that, she slept again.

* * *

Jeff put an arm around Rob's shoulder. "Let's go. You need to eat. Mom O'Brien told me you and the crew didn't eat breakfast this morning. About brought the whole shift to tears." Rob glared at Jeff. "I'll take you and get you an early lunch or late breakfast or something not on the schedule. But don't tell the rest of the crew. It'll be our secret."

Rob chuckled. "Right. They's out watching the other classes finish the courses."

Jeff sensed the regret in the boy, though Rob would never admit it. "Yeah. About you and the crew missing your final. Um…the owner said to tell you he feels really bad about what happened with Mitch, and how he turned out. He wants to make it up to you. He's going to call all your guardians and see if he can get permission for you to stay later than promised. He may not have to depending on how the permission slips were written. But he's going to bring in an experienced guide this afternoon. The guide will work with the six of you, see what your strengths and weaknesses are, then tomorrow morning, he or she will take you out for your run at the rapids."

Rob's eyes widened. "You serious? You ain't jiving? He for real said that?"

Jeff nodded. "Yes, he did. And because you will have to be here later in the day to finish the trip, he's decided he'll fly you all home in the company jet."

Rob fairly jumped into Jeff's body. "He what? A jet? Dude, you got to be lying to me. Ain't no one gonna fly a bunch of street rats in they company jet anywhere! Come on, man. Don't be lying to me."

Jeff grinned. "No lie, Rob. I know how much this means to the owner. He has to get permission from you to stay later, but it shouldn't be a problem, should it?"

Rob dropped his head in defeat. "My mom didn't want me to come to start with. She ain't about to give me permission."

Jeff studied the younger man a moment. He asked, "She didn't want you to come, but you're here. That means she signed something that allowed you to come."

Rob shrugged. "Maybe. I guess. Collin took a paper to her month ago when she first heard about this camp. I heard her and my mom going round and round about it. My mom finally did sign, I guess. Collin told me I was her ward for the week." Rob looked at Jeff, his eyes growing wide with hope. "Ten days. She say ten days. Say would be the longest ten days of her life, but she gonna do it. So I ain't even supposed to be back until Monday. I can stay!" Rob began to jump up and down again. "I get to stay! Jeff, dude! How sweet can it be? Collin gonna be okay, Mitch gonna go away, we get to ride the rapids, and we get to fly in some dude's company jet! I'm gonna explode!" Rob grabbed Jeff around the middle. "Let's go tell the rest the crew! Nyla gonna freak out, I know she will."

Jeff laughed, enjoying Rob's exuberance. "Let's go back to camp and get something to eat first. I'm starved."

Rob grinned. "Yeah. Suddenly I am, too."

As ever, Mom O'Brien took delight in fixing food for Jeff and Rob. Rob curtailed his normal vast selection of choices for simpler fare: bacon and eggs and sausage on the side. And a cinnamon roll, since Mom offered. Jeff requested the same. The two men took their trays to the back of the room and sat down. Jeff bowed his head to bless his food. When he opened his eyes, he saw Rob staring at him, a puzzled look on his face. Jeff started in on his food.

Rob stirred his eggs around. "Jeff, you a man, right?"

"Last time I checked."

Rob turned his head slightly. "You tell me straight. All them stories Collin be telling me 'bout God and love and loving your neighbor and about some carpenter's son. They be the truth? I mean, how could some dude tell me to love the punk what stole my ride and is trying to make a hooker out of my little sister? How you gonna love Mitch after what he done to the lady? Ain't no way. Man say that don't know the streets." Rob tackled the bacon. All eight strips of it.

Jeff swallowed down the sausage he'd been chewing. "He knew the streets, Rob. The streets He walked weren't much different than ours. And people didn't believe His words any more than you do now. He got beat up, spit on, mocked, cursed, you name it. In the end, His enemies killed Him by whipping Him, nailing Him to a cross, and hanging Him up to die a slow death from suffocation and loss of blood. They even drove a spear in His side to make sure the deed got done."

Rob tossed his head sharply. The young man pointed his fork at Jeff. "Don't make sense, man. Lady told me all that, and it don't make sense. She told me how He could'a come storming down and fry every one of them in the crowd—in the whole place, even—but He never raised a finger. Why? Why not fry them all?"

"Did Collin tell you who made up that crowd?" Jeff made short work of the eggs. Maybe he could get those down before they got too cold.

"Yeah. She said a bunch of murderers and thieves and liars and pushers and cheaters and people that hate other folks and..." Rob's list grew and became inclusive. Suddenly he stopped. He looked at Jeff, then looked at the floor, then looked back at Jeff. "People like me."

Jeff nodded. "And me. And Collin. And Ta'waan and Nyla and Niles and even Mitch. The Bible says every person ever born is in that crowd. We all reject what He said."

Jeff eyed Rob carefully to see if the boy understood. The light in Rob's eyes said yes, so Jeff continued. After he chewed and swallowed his bacon. "God knew anyone who broke His law would die. He told us from the very beginning of time. Whoever sins dies. And the only way not to die is for someone else to take your place."

Rob nodded. Jeff guessed Collin shared much of this before. But this time, Rob seemed ready to listen. Jeff said, "It can't be any old person who has to die. It has to be someone perfect, someone who's never done anything wrong. And there isn't anyone. Never has been; never will be." Jeff looked at Rob. "You know anyone perfect?"

Rob looked down. "No. No one." He finished the last of the sausage, then started working on the giant cinnamon roll.

"God sent Jesus to live and die and take our place. Jesus is the only One who can. And when we accept Him—when we believe He took our place and we give Him control of our lives—then God's law is satisfied. We give Him our rotten selves, and He gives us new life. Jesus's life."

Jeff leaned forward. "That's how we can learn to love our enemies and forgive those who hurt us and hate us. Collin did it, and that's why she can forgive Mitch. I did it, and I'm still a work in progress. I'm having a harder time forgiving Mitch. But when I start thinking about hating him, the Lord holds up His hands for me to look at. I see the scars in His hands He took for me, and I stop. God promises we're never alone." Jeff smiled sadly. "Even when we maybe should be."

Rob still looked puzzled. "But how you know? How you know God ain't still mad at you? Or he be talking with you?"

"Because Jesus didn't stay dead, Rob. They buried Him, but He didn't stay there."

Rob sounded out the unfamiliar syllables, "The Resurrection? Him coming back from the dead? Lady told me 'bout that, but I ain't believing. Ain't no one comes back." Rob guzzled his milk.

"Jesus did. The people closest to Him didn't believe, either, until He let them touch His hands and feet where the soldiers put the spikes in Him. And He ate food with them, too, to prove it was Him."

Jeff searched for the right words. "If God hadn't been satisfied—hadn't accepted what Jesus did—Jesus would never have come back to life. But He did. God let Jesus take the rap so anyone who asks can trust in Jesus and never have to worry about God turning away from them."

Jeff could see Rob thinking, trying to put the pieces together. Jeff continued, "Even when we mess up, and mess up big time, God still loves us because of what Jesus did. Jesus stands between God and us and says, 'Look, Dad, I know Farrell screwed up again, and he does deserve to be blasted out of existence.'"

Rob chuckled. Jeff nodded. "'But Dad, he's one of My friends, and I promised I'd take care of him. So for My sake, let him go. I'll deal with him. And I know exactly how to do it. I'll send hard-headed Collin Walker to him. She'll make his life so miserable he won't ever stop talking to you.'"

Rob grinned. "She gonna bust you, you know."

Jeff grinned in return. "Yeah, but truth hurts."

Rob studied the floor. "I seen the lady get through some mean times an' always give the credit to God like He some kind of real friend. You talking 'bout him the same." Rob hesitated a long time. "Can I be knowing Him like that, too?"

Jeff nodded. "Anytime you want to, you can. It's a matter of asking Him. Of admitting you can't live life your way. You want to live it His way, through Him. In Him. You ask. He'll answer." *Lord, anything I'm leaving out, fill in for him. He's Yours. Always has been, always will be. Keep him, Father.*

Rob swallowed the last of his breakfast/lunch. His eyes flicked from side to side. After a moment, he looked up at Jeff. "I gotta be in church to ask Him?'

"No. Anywhere, anytime. He hears your heart." Jeff finished the food on his plate, pushed the tray back, and sighed. "Good food. Rob, I've got some work to finish up. Would you mind if I dropped you back so you could check in on Collin and make sure she doesn't try to go over the wall? No running off before the doctors let her go."

Rob nodded. The younger man looked reserved, pensive. Jeff picked up both trays. "Thanks, my man."

They rode in silence to the clinic that served as a hospital for the local area. Jeff dropped Rob at the front. "I'll be back later and relieve you of your warden duties."

Rob nodded again but still said nothing. Jeff asked, "You okay, bro?"

Rob nodded. "Jus' need to think, that's all. Lots to think about." He slapped Jeff's jeep, a signal Jeff could leave.

Jeff drove off slowly. *Lord, if I said anything more, it would have been me talking to You, not Rob. He needs to use his own words, his own way. Your will, Lord.* Jeff turned the jeep into the parking lot in front of the camp administration building.

An hour later, having finished up all his requisite duties, Jeff returned to the clinic. He checked in at the nurses' station then went down to the room Collin occupied.

Rob sat beside Collin's bed, a look of peace on his face. All the tension, all the fear, all the worry disappeared. The boy looked happy. He smiled at Jeff, and his eyes glowed. He jumped up and met Jeff halfway across the room. Jeff caught Rob in a bearhug and looked toward the sky. "Yes! Thank You, Lord!" He grinned at Rob. "Welcome to the family, brother. It's great to have you with us."

Rob ducked his head but grew serious. "Don't tell Collin. I want her to see it in me, not hear me tell it. I want her to see I changed."

Jeff smiled. "She's going to take one look at you and know, Rob. You've got the 'shekinah' glow. Every person I've ever seen come to the Lord has it. At least for a while. But I won't say anything. I'll let you do it your way."

Rob sat down again, but cocked his head and looked at Jeff. "What I gotta do now?"

"Live. Collin can help you with the particulars. But the biggest thing is getting to know the Lord." Jeff held up a hand in warning. "Don't listen to what other people say about Him. Get to know Him yourself. Makes a difference."

A sleepy voice asked, "Difference in what?"

Jeff smiled. He crossed to the bed and took Collin's hand. "A difference in whether you stay in the hospital another day or not."

Collin didn't open her eyes. "Oh. I don't want to stay here. If all I'm going to do is sleep, I can do it better at camp than anyplace else."

She pried her eyelids open. "Besides, I want to be there when the crew rides the rapids this afternoon." She looked at Jeff, and a fire smoldered in her glance. "We are going to ride the rapids. The camp promised, and we're going to go. We'll go without a guide if we have to, but we are going." Collin shifted in the bed and slowly tried to sit up.

Jeff looked to Rob. "You tell her."

"Tell me what?"

Rob grinned. "We got us a guide. We gonna face the rapids tomorrow." Collin settled back in the bed. Rob's voice went up a notch. "And then the owner is going to fly us home in his jet! Ain't that so cool, Collin? We gonna fly home in a jet! All the other brothers and sisters gotta go home on the bus, but we get to fly home!"

Collin looked at Jeff. "He's not joking, is he? The owner is honestly going to fly this crew back to Oakton?"

Jeff nodded. "He told me so himself." Before Collin could object, he added, "Mr. McFa'ell knows I've gotten to be good friends with Rob and some of the other crew. He couldn't be there to tell them, so he asked me to relay the message."

Collin chewed her lips, narrowed her gaze, but didn't object. Yet. Jeff continued, "He contacted all the guardians and explained the kids would be in later in the day and would be taken directly home instead of having to be picked up at the bus station. No one objected."

Collin shook her head. Carefully, Jeff noted. "That's amazing."

Rob looked serious. "You ain't fit to go, Collin. You know it.

You hurt all over and trying to crew ain't gonna happen."

Collin drilled Rob with a glare Jeff knew would melt the tundra. "I am going. I'm part of the crew. I trained as hard as anyone, and I'm not going to be left behind."

Rob frowned. "We gonna have to take a vote, then. Whole crew gotta say yes, or you stay on the dock." He picked up Collin's hand, and his voice became softer. "You ain't got to prove nothing to no one, caseworker lady. We all know you toughest one out there. Know you ain't afraid of nothing. I don't want you getting more hurt than you is now. Understand?"

Collin sagged. "Who are you and what have you done with the real Rob?"

Rob grinned. "I's here. I gonna be here for a long time. You'll see."

Collin squeezed his hand. "Said it before. You're my main man, Rob."

Rob looked over his shoulder at Jeff and half grinned. "Yeah, well, I know someone who'd like to change that. For him, maybe I step aside."

Collin looked from Rob to Jeff. Her brows went up. "Um…do I have a say in the matter?"

Together, Rob and Jeff said, "No" and "Yes" respectively. Rob laughed. "You got no say in me stepping aside. You only get to choose who takes my place. Got the feeling Jeff here wants to be the candidate."

Jeff glared at Rob. "I'll tell my own lies, please." He looked directly at Rob, then looked down. He hoped Rob understood Jeff's meaning. Jeff looked at Collin and said, "Kids know I went out after you, that's all. No wild stories."

Collin's eyes reflected concern. Then her face softened, and she gave him a gentle look. "I understand."

Rob looked from Collin to Jeff, then back to Collin. He sat up a little straighter and said, "No, you don't." Rob looked at Jeff. "I heard the sheriff called off the search, and you wouldn't stop looking. Went walking off by yourself 'til you found her."

Collin cocked her head to look at Jeff. "You did what?"

Jeff shrugged. "I wasn't alone. Bo came with me."

Ted, the activities director, popped his head into Collin's room. "Hey, Jeff. Ms. Walker. Rob, Nyla told me I'd find you here. The whitewater guides will be at camp in half an hour for practice. You need to get back to camp, suit up, and be ready when they get here." He looked at Jeff. "Mind if I take him off your hands?"

Jeff looked at Rob. "Any objections to riding with Ted, here?"

"Course not." Rob looked at Collin, gave her a hug. "You rest up. We'll see you tomorrow after the run and tell you all 'bout it."

Collin's eyes narrowed. "I will make you vote on this, Rob. I want to know who is on my side."

Rob waved her off as he walked out with Ted. Jeff watched the two leave, then turned back to see Collin grimace. "You need to ring the nurse for more pain meds?"

She snipped, "No, I need to ring a taxi, so I can go back to the camp." She sighed. "Please, Jeff? They're not doing any actual treatments. Observation, that's all. Someone can observe me sleeping in my own camp bed. Which is a thousand times more comfortable than this thing. Your owner does not skimp on the details, does he?"

Jeff looked down at the floor but smiled. "No, he doesn't. Not fair to bring someone up here for a week, then make them sleep on hard beds. If he can't do it himself, he won't make anyone else do it, either."

Collin closed her eyes. "I do want to meet him."

"You will. I'll make sure you see him before this week is up."

Collin repeated her plea. "When the doctor comes in, I'm going to put in my request to go back to camp. Will you back me up that I can rest there better than I can here?"

Jeff nodded. "No doubt about that. Question is, will you?"

Collin paused. "Yes."

"Promise?"

Collin nodded. "I promise."

Jeff mistrusted the twinkle in her eye, but it could have been from lighting, or pain, or who knew what. He grumped, "I guess, then."

Collin held out her hand. Jeff took it and sat closer to the bed. She closed her eyes. "Fill in the blanks for me. What happened after we got thrown in the water?"

"I'll fill in mine if you fill in yours. Mitch has given us some bizarre stories, but none of them match up to reality." Jeff chuckled slightly. "Oh, and they found Mitch's knife. The sheriff said finding a bramble bush with a bow tied in it was 'unique.' Never seen that in nature before. They searched under it and found the knife. Preliminary tests say the blood on it is yours. How did you get it away from him?"

Collin asked, "Has his vision come back?"

"Didn't know he lost it, but yeah."

Collin settled back and told Jeff her side of the story, up to the time she collapsed on the way back. When she finished, she said, "Your turn."

Before Jeff could start, Doctor Wallace walked into the room. "Good afternoon, Ms. Walker. Wonderful to see you awake and alert."

Collin gave him a wide smile. Jeff chuckled to himself. *Watch out, Doc. She'll have you signing her discharge papers before you know what hit you.*

It actually took surprisingly little wheedling and cajoling on Collin's part, with Jeff's backing, to get the hospital release signed, and Collin made back into a free woman. Free to go back to camp and rest.

NOT free, however, to go whitewater rafting. Jeff held the distinct feeling her not having medical clearance to go would only be a minor impediment to her determination to ride the river. Medical and insurance waivers existed, too, you know.

Jeff transported Collin back to camp. He pulled the jeep into the parking lot at the lodge. "Wait here. I'll get someone to take you down to your room and help you get settled back in your room."

Collin answered by opening her door and sliding out of the jeep. She leaned against it for support. Jeff saw the anger, the determination, and then the surrender in her eyes as her shoulders dropped. Jeff came around to the passenger's side and let Collin use him as a temporary crutch to get into the building and seated in front of the windows.

Yells and victory whoops sounded up and down the corridors. Excited and exuberant campers dashed in and out, shouting their mastery over field, stream, cooking utensil...

Jeff took a moment to revel in the joy. *Yes. This makes it all worth it. All of it.* He felt an ear-to-ear grin and unspeakable joy cross his face. Didn't matter he felt this way after every challenge camp. Some things never got old.

He noticed Collin studying him. "What?"

She grinned. "You're as excited as they are. You love this, don't you?"

"Absolutely. Nothing better. Until the Lord returns."

Collin smiled. "Amen." She stretched her head back. "I yield to you having someone help me to my room, and to getting settled." Her eyes twinkled. "Then they can help me back to the cafeteria so I can get food, and they won't have to bring it to me like you'll want."

"We're getting to know each other, aren't we?"

"I hope so." Collin hesitated. "Will you sit with me while I eat? So I can prove to you I am eating? And then you can fill me in on your side of our joint venture."

Jeff looked at the clock on the wall. "It's nearly dinner time. You want to rest up first, then come down around seven, when the campers are done? There's going to be a whole lot of adrenalin pumping around in there."

Collin nodded. "Probably a good plan. But make sure you have someone come get me. None of this, 'you were sleeping, and I didn't want to wake you' garbage."

Jeff swallowed a smile. "What about the 'you were sleeping, and we couldn't wake you' scenario?"

"I'll wake up. I'm good, Jeff. Not fine, but good."

"Okay. I'll get help."

* * *

Collin rested without sleeping. Too many places ached to find a truly comfortable position. She could take the pain pills Dr. Wallace prescribed, but then she might sleep through her dinner call. *After dinner. After I talk to Jeff.*

She needed time to sort out all the comings and goings of the past twenty-four or more hours. Why did she turn to him for help? Why did he practically jump in the boat to save her from Mitch? Could the Lord really have taken her fear? Forever?

Collin wished she could get on her knees, but the odds of not being able to get up again prevented her. And the Lord understood anyhow. "God, I feel like everything is so far out of my control right now."

It was never in your control, dear one.

"But it's always my decision. And it's always wrong."

Stop. That lie comes from your past. You are a new creation. Camp Grace is teaching the children they can start over. Can be new people in the same old circumstances. You are not trapped in your past just as they are not trapped in their present. Life is yours. Love is yours. What isn't yours is fear. You hold it because it's safe, predictable. Let go. I have you.

Collin stared at the wall, seeing the past, seeing the present, seeing the possibilities, seeing the doubts, fears, traps. *How would it all be different without the fear? Without having to be in control, without having to be responsible for everything in life?*

Would things even get done?

Would they get done right?

Would I have to work twice as hard to fix them than if I simply did it myself?

It would mean trusting someone else. Trusting someone else could be as capable, as conscientious, as dedicated and devoted as I am.

And they would share the same standards of perfection...

The Lord pulled her up short. *Perfection?*

Collin backtracked. She waved her hand to erase the statement. "I don't mean perfection. I mean—"

But you do. If it's not done your way, it's not right. Your way becomes the standard. Anything else is less than. Anything else falls short. Only you know the right way.

And who does that make you?

Collin went silent. She stared at the floor, letting the Lord's words sink into her being. *Is that what I'm doing? Being my own god? Trusting only myself...*

A knock sounded on the door. Collin called out, "I'm here."

A muffled voice said, "Jeff says it's safe to come down, now. He said you might be needing help."

Collin's eyes narrowed. She threw back the covers from the bed and tried to stand in defiance of his perception of her as weak. Of—

The knees held, but the legs wobbled. Collin caught hold of the bed frame and waited until she felt some stability return to her lower half. She ducked her head. "Thank you. The door isn't locked. I can use help."

A young woman, one of the foodservice workers, came in. She looked at Collin, and her eyes grew wide. "What did you do? What sport did you try?"

Collin held out her hand for the woman to come help her to the sink. "Needlepoint."

The girl laughed. "We don't offer that skill, Ms. But you might think about taking it up over whatever you tried."

Collin splashed water on her face, dragged a brush—carefully, very carefully—through her hair, then turned around. "You're probably right. What's your name?"

"I'm Trilby McShane. I'm one of the dieticians here."

Collin revised her opinion of the young woman's professional skills. "Collin Walker." As the two of them walked up the hall, Collin leaning on Trilby's arm, Collin asked, "How did you come to work here?"

"I worked summers in the kitchen, cleaning up mostly. Jeff nagged me about doing something more with my life." She smiled. "I told him to stuff it."

Collin chuckled. "I can see that."

Trilby nodded. "But then the word came down the camp would fund college for anyone wanting to go if they're specialty would benefit the camp. Full ride scholarships, room and board, you name it. All we needed to do was maintain a ten-hour workweek at the camp during the summers." Her eyes shone as they reached the end of the corridor. "It's amazing how many fields ended up benefiting the camp. I don't think anyone ever got turned down."

Collin whistled low. "Those are some fantastic benefits. People like working here, then? Pay is decent?"

"Pay is good. Oh, we could earn more if we went to the cities to work, but anyone wanting to stay close to home and still be able to live and raise a family can make it on what Mr. McFa'ell pays us."

"You've met him, then?"

Trilby nodded. "Yeah. Well, we haven't been introduced face to face and shaken hands or anything, but I've seen him from a distance at the company picnics, and a few of the farewell dinners. He's a good man."

Collin nodded. "I'm getting that opinion from everyone I've talked to." *Except Jeff. Remember? Jeff said he doesn't know if he likes him sometimes or not.*

Hmmm.

The women passed through the halls without being accosted by still frenetic children regaling each other with all the glory they experienced that week. Collin decided the prevailing theme was who worked the hardest. Kids.

Trilby supported Collin to the table where Jeff sat by himself. A linen tablecloth and a thin vase with a single daisy decorated the space. Collin saw color in Jeff's cheeks. *Ah hah. This wasn't his idea, then. Thank you, Mom O'Brien.*

Jeff stood and took the handoff of being Collin's support staff from Trilby. The young woman pointed her finger at Jeff. "You be nice to Ms. Walker. I've never seen one of our guests this beat up." She smiled at Collin. "I'm happy I could help you out. Nice talking to you."

"Thanks, Trilby. Maybe we'll see each other again before I leave."

Jeff seated Collin at the table, then hugged Trilby. "Thanks, Tril. I owe you."

Trilby's eyes twinkled. "You certainly do. I've got a lawn needs mowing. You can pay me back when camp is over."

The woman turned and headed to the kitchen. Jeff sighed and sat down. Collin looked at him. "You taking on side jobs, too? Maintenance for the whole town?"

"No, not the whole town."

"Just the ones working here, right? Part of the employee package?"

Jeff frowned. "I am not maintenance for the whole town, and no, it's not in the employee benefits package. Trilby's husband moved to Charleston to find work last year." Jeff's voice darkened. "He found another woman instead. Trilby is raising her three children by herself. If I can help out, I do."

Collin grew serious. She studied Jeff a moment. "How many, Jeff? How many people are you helping?"

Jeff met Collin's eyes. "Anyone the Lord brings my way. I don't keep count."

Collin dropped her eyes first. Jeff cleared his throat. "Mom O'Brien saved us some of the beef and gravy if you like."

Collin nodded, feeling rebuked. "That would be wonderful."

Jeff got up to retrieve the plates. Collin whispered, "I'm sorry, Lord. Sorry I ever doubted him." She'd come here looking for a man like Jeff for Rob. And spent the better part of the week trying not to get involved with him. She dropped her head, eyes down, surrendered. *Your will what happens from here, Lord. I've messed things up, trying it my way. Take charge. Always. Be God.*

She looked up and smiled at Jeff as he returned with the food. He set her plate in front of her, set his down as well, then sat. He asked, "May I say grace?"

Collin extended her hand. "Thank you."

Jeff asked the blessing on the food, then began eating. Collin moved her food around, then took a fork, stabbed a hefty portion of meat, and began eating it. Jeff noticed and nodded, approving. Collin waited until she'd finished over half the food on her plate before she asked, "You promised to tell me what happened with you." She touched his arm. He looked at her. "Start with why in the world would you throw yourself into the middle of a kidnapping? He could have killed you right then and there."

Jeff shrugged. "Seemed like the thing to do at the time. I knew Mitch wouldn't kill me." He lowered his eyes. "I'm sorry I got you stabbed. I—"

Collin rapped the table. "Stop. Right there. You did not get me stabbed. Mitch stabbed me. He wanted to have an excuse, and he used you. You are not responsible for anything Mitch did. Nothing. You got that?"

Jeff looked up, and the hurt remained. Collin squeezed his hand. "Got that? Not your fault."

Jeff nodded finally. "I'll believe it if you will."

"Believe what? It wasn't your fault?"

"Believe it wasn't your fault, either."

Collin looked at her hands. Jeff said strongly, "Nothing you said or did made Mitch go after you. His choice, his fault. Not yours." Jeff made sure to catch Collin's gaze.

Collin nodded. The corners of her mouth twitched. "His mistake."

Jeff laughed. "Yes, it was." He smiled. "You are one special lady, Collin. Why wouldn't I try to save you?" Jeff recounted his part of the story, saying only he and Bo continued the search after the others went home. How Jeff heard Collin's singing, how it led them to where they found her and Mitch. How the Mountain Rescue teams helicoptered in, carried Mitch and Collin to town and the clinic, how Mitch tried to paint a different picture of the events for Bo, but no one bought it.

Collin waited until Jeff finished. She looked him full in the eyes and said, "Thank you."

Jeff smiled. "You're welcome."

Collin motioned to the windows. "Can we walk outdoors? Not far. Just out to the patio. Please?"

Jeff stood, carried the now-empty plates into the kitchen, returned, and offered his arm to Collin. It frustrated her that she leaned on him to get up, but once standing, motored more under her own strength.

Except her own strength proved insufficient for the trip. Three-quarters of the way there, she found herself leaning more and more on Jeff. He did not comment but supported her all the way out to the patio, to a bench where Collin could sit with her back supported against a stone retaining wall. Jeff sat beside her, waiting for her to speak.

Collin looked out over the steep passages to the river below, knowing it rolled on and on, not caring a whit about her. She leaned back against the stone, closed her eyes. "Can I tell you a story? It's about a girl I know."

"A friend?"

"I'm never quite sure."

Jeff nodded. "Sure. I like stories."

"You might not like this one. It's not a very happy story."

"Even bad stories can have happy endings, Collin."

Collin opened her eyes to stare out over the river. "Once upon a time, there lived a man whose parents were quite wealthy. As the eldest of the three sons, he looked to inherit control of the vast empire his father possessed. Sadly, the father died before the eldest son reached twenty-one. Their mother became concerned about the wanton and shameful behavior of her sons and feared for the family legacy. She devised a plan to leave control of the estate to the first-born grandchild. There would be money aplenty for the young men themselves, but the lion's share of the estate would go to the first grandchild.

"The eldest son decided he would supply the first child and

secure the fortune for himself. He found a woman, got her pregnant, and presented his mother with a grandson. His mother was delighted to have a child to love and spoil but informed her son the—to him—insignificant detail of not having a marriage license disqualified the child from being the heir. Only a legitimate offspring would suffice.

"Having paid off and sent away the little boy's mother, the man looked for another wife. One who would give him the son he wanted."

Collin looked at Jeff. "Son, mind you. Not child. Son. Females were useless. Girls marry, and the family fortune passes into a stranger's hand. No, no girls. A son. He wanted another son."

Collin turned back to face the river. She felt a lump growing in her throat. Jeff moved closer to her side. Collin cleared her throat and continued. "The first two pregnancies ended in miscarriages after four months. The man secretly celebrated, for both had been girls. But he had to keep trying. His next younger brother graduated from high school and looked to be giving him competition."

Jeff closed his eyes. "Collin…"

"You want me to stop?"

Jeff reached out and put his arms around her. "No. Keep going. If your friend endured the living, I can endure the telling."

Collin ducked her head and continued. "Finally, the woman had a pregnancy go into the third trimester. They watched and monitored and cared for her with all the finest medical treatment available twenty-plus some years ago. At eight months, the woman went into labor and delivered two three-pound twins."

"It must have made the man happy."

"He could have been. But no, he became furious. You see, the twins were a boy and a girl. But because the little girl could never stand to be late for anything, she came out first."

Collin closed her eyes. A tear trickled down her cheek. "The babies needed medical attention, of course. The man demanded the best care money could buy for the tiny little boy, but tried to refuse anything beyond the minimum legal requirements for the hated girl. Fortunately for her, good doctors and nurses, who cared nothing for money, kept her alive and made sure she and her brother both thrived.

"In the end, they both came home. The doctors refused a bribe to alter the birth order. The twins' grandmother recognized the little girl as the family heir and life went on."

Collin swung her foot back and forth, kicking the stone bench lightly. "The man never got over the girl beating her brother out of his 'rightful inheritance.' The children's father vowed she would never beat her twin at anything again. Mysteriously her arm broke so she couldn't crawl first. Her ankle broke about the time she started walking."

Collin stared out over the valley. "He never allowed her to win any games, play sports, or do anything which would outshine her brother."

Jeff pulled Collin even closer. His face reflected the pain Collin remembered too well. She leaned against his arms. "I told you it's not a happy story. My friend doesn't like to tell people about it. People don't like sad stories."

Jeff cleared his throat. "Don't stop. I want to know how it ends."

"It hasn't. Not yet."

"Maybe we can write our own ending."

Collin ducked her head slightly. "Maybe." She fell silent and took a deep breath. "When the twins were about five, the father announced they would go on a picnic. He took his wife, the twins, a blanket, a ball, and a basket of lunch down to the park by the river. The water ran high and fast from all the rain that fell during the spring. Signs posted with warnings about the danger lined the banks.

"The weather was fine, the day fair. The children kicked the ball, or threw it, or ran races around their parents. The father played with the twins for several hours until they grew tired. They all ate lunch, and the children lay down on the blanket for a nap. Even the mother fell asleep.

"Once everyone's eyes closed, the father jostled the little girl awake and told her he wanted to show her something special, something he hadn't shown her brother. It made the little girl very excited. Her father wanted to spend time with her. She skipped and danced beside her father—"

Jeff's voice strangled. "Don't, Collin. Don't call him a father. No father would ever treat his child like that. Call him a man, nothing more."

Collin eyed him a long moment. "Okay. The man swung her along, laughing and teasing. He swung her high in the air, let her drop, then caught her at the last moment. She squealed with delight. Her fath…the man took her down by the river. He made sure no one could see them and continued to swing the girl high in the air. She laughed and shrieked…"

Collin's eyes closed, and she felt the blood drain from her face. Her voice became hollow. "…and the man swung her out one last time, high over the river, out where she could do nothing but scream in terror until she plunged into the racing waters."

Jeff groaned, "Collin…"

Tears flowed. His or hers, it didn't matter. One size fits all.

Collin continued, unable to stop short of conclusion. "Some fishermen around the bend in the river saw the little girl struggling in the torrent. Someone shouted, and two of them jumped in to try to rescue her. Their yelling alerted the man, and he feared discovery. He ran down the banks, screaming in despair for someone to save his baby. She swept past her would-be rescuers and finally washed into the shallows, where they rescued her from the bottom of the river. Someone did CPR. She revived at about the time the man arrived."

Collin hiccuped. "The man grabbed the little girl from her benefactors, refused their offer of transport to the nearest hospital, and took her back to where her mother and brother waited. He proceeded to punish her for sneaking off and playing by the river, telling her falling in had been God's punishment for being a wicked and disobedient little girl."

Jeff closed his eyes and began rocking Collin back and forth. And still, the story went on. "The girl developed pneumonia, but the man wouldn't take her to the doctor until the man's mother paid a visit. Grandmother informed him of a new clause in the family will. If the firstborn should die before inheriting, then the heir would be the firstborn of the second son to produce a child. Meaning if the little girl died, the firstborn of either of his brothers would get the money.

"In plain words, the man's son would never, ever, inherit the family fortune. And if anything did happen to the little girl, the man could be sure his mother would be first in line to accuse him of foul play."

Collin let out a long, slow breath. "Attempts on the girl's life stopped. The hatred and the abuse didn't. Her life became little more than misery. Her brother tried to shield her, but even he couldn't stop all the mistreatment. Then he died when they were fourteen, and she was...relocated to Oakton. For two years she lived on the streets, surviving on her own.

"But the Lord had plans for her. She ran into a street preacher with a mission for the homeless. He took her in, introduced her to the Lord, helped her finish high school, and made sure she went on to college."

Collin sat up straight. "The girl graduated and has done okay since then. She has a good job working with kids, volunteers at the street missions, and is diligently waiting for God to bring one good man into her life. But she can't handle running rivers."

Collin turned and looked Jeff in the eyes. "Until last night. Out there on the water, God took the fear." She ducked her head to the side. "I still want to ride with my crew"—she held up a hand to ward off his objections—"but I'll let them vote me off instead."

Collin sat back against the wall, drained from the telling. "So now you know my deep dark secret. I'm not brave, I'm not strong, I'm not in control of anything. That's more truth than most men can handle."

Jeff kissed Collin gently. "I'm not most men."

Collin looked down and shook her head. "No, you certainly aren't."

Jeff stood. "You up for a short walk across the yard?"

Collin stared at him. "Where?"

"Admin building. It's time you met the owner."

Collin looked at him sideways. "It's nearly nine o'clock. He's not still working, is he? And I'm not exactly dressed for a formal introduction."

Jeff nodded. "Yes, he's still working this late. And you look fine. You can never look anything but beautiful. Come on."

Collin's eyes widened as Jeff pulled her to her feet and led her away from the patio. "Jeff, I can't barge in on the man at the end of the day. What will he think?"

"Someone wants to meet him. He appreciates interruptions. Makes his day go faster or something. I'm not sure. But it will be fine, I know."

Collin felt bewildered and lost. Why now? What prompted this sudden need to go now? *What did I say? What did he say? We were talking about my past. How does that make sense?*

Jeff half-carried Collin to the front of the office building. He stopped and made sure Collin could stand on her own, then unlocked the outer door. He smiled. "Janitors have keys to everything."

Even my heart. It sounded too...too...something. She left the thought unspoken. Jeff led her down a short hall and stopped in front of a solid wood door. He kissed Collin again, very lightly. "Wait five minutes. Then knock. Go in after you do. McFa'ell will be waiting for you."

Collin's eyes widened. "Where are you going? You've got to stay and introduce us. You can't drop me off and leave me. Jeff, this is crazy."

Jeff's eyes pleaded with her. "Collin, please. Do this my way. Please? You'll understand it all after you meet McFa'ell. Please?"

Collin studied his face, his eyes...his eyes...

She nodded. "Fine. We'll do this your way. Five minutes, I knock, he answers, I go in. Right?"

Jeff nodded, the relief palpable on his face. "Thanks. I'll be back after the two of you are done." He reached down, kissed her one last time, then disappeared around the corner.

Collin looked around the area. The corridors stood empty but well-lit for this late in the evening. *Would McFa'ell keep his secretary working this late as well?*

I don't think I ever met a secretary for him. Or any assistant at all.

Collin stared at the door. "Camp Grace" was emblazoned on the door. Underneath, in letters she almost couldn't see, was printed the name, "Geoffrey McFa'ell, President."

Collin circled her foot around on the floor. Her eyes narrowed. "Geoffrey. Jeffrey?" She took in a sharp breath. "McFa'ell. Mc is son of...son of Fa'ell." But what kind of name... *"Fa'ell residence."* Collin sagged against the wall. "No. No. No, I couldn't be that blind. Please tell me I'm not." All the things Jeff said about the camp echoed back in her head. *"I couldn't love it more if I owned it... God owns it and has a silent partner... I wouldn't call him old..."* Collin banged her head against the wall. "How stupid can one person be?"

Why? Who are you, Jeff? Rich man, poor man? Janitor or owner? And why the charade?

Answers are behind the door if you're brave enough to open it.

Collin straightened her shirt, took in a deep breath, and knocked on the door sharply.

"Come in."

Collin stepped into an office that looked like it spent most of its time unoccupied. *I'll bet.* A large table with chairs for eight sat in the center. Along the wall sat two bookcases filled with what looked like treasures received from campers: painted pinecones, clay bears (maybe), pictures of boats on the lake. A hand-lettered "We Love Camp Grace" poster adorned the back wall.

Also on the back wall sat a single desk with a high-back chair. The chair faced away from Collin, but she could tell it was occupied. She cleared her throat. "Mr. McFa'ell? I'm Collin Walker, and I want to thank you for this wonderful camp you own." She smiled slightly. "I know, you don't own it, God does. But He's used you to bring His vision to life." Collin's throat caught slightly. She cleared it. "I have some things I want to say, so please, let me get them out before you say anything, okay?"

McFa'ell shifted in his chair. Uncomfortable already? Collin's eyes narrowed in mischief. "First, I want to tell you how much I appreciate what you're doing for these kids." Mischief subsided, replaced by honesty. "I never dreamed a place like this would make the changes I've seen in my kids, in just one week. They're working together. Southside, Eastside, North...all the gangs are being broken down. My kids are being kids again. They see they can make it, can be something more than street rats. They know someone believes in them. And they're believing in themselves, too. A little. So thank you."

Collin took a moment to pull her emotions back under control. "You also provided a place where I faced my worst nightmare and learned God would walk me through it like He walks me through everything else. One step at a time."

McFa'ell started to stand. Collin said quickly, "No, wait. Please. One more thing. I came here thinking this place couldn't be real. Instead, I met real people who love God, love kids, and are living out their faith. And the most special one of all is your maintenance man, Jeff Farrell."

The chair shifted. Collin pushed ahead. "He's warm. He's caring. He's a genuine friend who will lay his life down for you. Whatever you're paying him, it isn't enough."

Jeff stood and faced Collin, guilt all over his face. Collin continued talking, ignoring him. "He'll do anything to keep this place going, almost as if he owned it himself. And if I hadn't been so bound up in my own fears, I would have recognized him sooner." She rolled her eyes. "It's not like he didn't give me plenty of hints."

Jeff walked to Collin's side, his head down. Like he needed her forgiveness. Collin reached out and took his hand. She pulled him close and kissed him. "Why? Why the charade?"

Jeff leaned back against the table. "McFa'ell is for political and government entities who want to know their regulations are being observed. He goes to meetings and dinners and conferences. Janitors get to stay in the background, can watch and see what is really going on in the camp. Is it doing what it's supposed to? Are we reaching the kids? The adults? What problems are there? What can we change? What should we change?" His face darkened. "Like our hiring procedures."

Collin bumped him. "Stop. You couldn't know about Mitch. The sheriff interviewed him and dismissed him. How could you know? So stop. Mitch was not your fault. Okay? Leave it." Jeff ducked his head side to side but finally nodded. Collin leaned beside him. "So who does own Camp Grace?"

"I do. I bought it with sweat equity several years ago when the original owners decided to sell out. My family would come up here in the summers and camp and fish and have great times. I dreamed of providing something like this for all the kids that never got to come here. God made the way, and here it is."

"Are you a paramedic, then, too?"

"Yes, and I work for my dad like I said I did. And I'm in grad school. And I've got too many irons in the fire, and I know it."

Collin smiled. "I think you need to ask McFa'ell for some time off. I need time to really get to know his janitor." She looked into Jeff's eyes, and for once, did not look away.

A long, warm, sweet kiss followed. Jeff broke first. He backed up, a foot or so from Collin. "Um...we should get back to the patio. Or the hall. Someplace other than here." He shuddered. "A monastery. That would work."

"Or nunnery." Collin nodded. Her hands trembled. A little. Matched the trembling in her heart.

Jeff walked Collin out of McFa'ell's office, then out of the administration building, turning lights off as they passed through each room. At the entrance, he closed and locked the door. Jeff leaned in for one final kiss. Collin met him halfway. A quick one.

Jeff chuckled. "I should report myself for being alone with a camper of the opposite gender."

"To who? McFa'ell?"

"No, Steve. But I think he'll understand." Jeff shrugged. "I'll probably get off with a warning not to do it again." He smiled at Collin. "Which will never be a problem, ever again."

Jeff supported her back to the main hall. He angled toward one of the benches along the windows. Collin's heart hammered. *What is he doing? Why are we going to sit out here?*

Maybe he's got more to say.

I'm not ready for more. More would be dangerous. Scary. Threatening.

Listen to him.

Jeff set her down so she could be comfortable. Instead of sitting beside her, he knelt down on one knee. "Collin Walker—"

"Don't!" Collin felt panic rising. She saw the look of hurt in his eyes. "Not yet. Not until you know me better. You don't—"

Jeff interrupted her. "I don't need to know. You answered everything I ever dreamed of in a wife. A woman who loves the Lord, is passionate about following Him, and isn't ashamed to shake hands with the janitor, stained hands and all." He continued to kneel in front of her.

Colin couldn't meet his eyes. Her voice trembled. "You don't know my history. The girl who 'relocated' to Oakton? She..." Collin closed her eyes. "She lived on the streets. She—"

Jeff interrupted her. "She met the Lord. He forgave her everything. Paid it all. The same as he did for me. I said it before, and I meant it. What happened before you met the Lord, or before I met the Lord, doesn't make any difference."

Collin bit the corner of her mouth to still the trembling. "Easy to say."

Jeff nodded. Collin heard a small groan. She patted the bench beside her. "Sit down, or you'll get stuck down there."

Jeff got up with an exaggerated moan and sat beside her. He took her hand. "Collin, I love you. I want to marry you. Can you believe me?"

No. No. No. No. "It's hard, Jeff. I don't... I can't... I..." Collin looked at her hands. "I want to. I want to believe you." She looked up. "I want to believe I can love you. I don't know if I can."

Jeff smiled, reached out, and touched her mouth. "You've got a little blood there. You really need to stop hurting yourself, milady." He pulled her head close to his. "Collin, my love, I'm going to be here, by your side, until you make up your mind." He looked at the floor, then at her. "That makes me sound like a stalker. Not what I meant." He grimaced. "Um...let me try again."

Collin laughed and bumped him with her shoulder. "I know what you meant. And I want you by my side." She studied him a long moment. "Six months."

"Six months what?"

"Six months, and then you can ask me."

Jeff nodded. "I can do a six-month engagement."

"No! Not an engagement. Just six months for you, me, and the Lord to work out if this is real. And what He wants."

Jeff lowered his head but gazed at her. "I've already asked Him. He said yes."

Collin held her palms up. "I don't know yet. I need to know it's His will."

Jeff nodded. "Okay, do it this way. Flip a coin. If it lands on the floor, the answer is yes. If it suspends halfway between, then the answer is no. But you might want to try two out of three to be absolutely sure."

Collin lifted her head, leaned back against the window, and banged it lightly on the glass. "You."

"Five months?"

Collin closed her eyes, ducked her head, and rocked back and forth. "Jeff..." She looked at him sideways. "I love you."

He smiled. "Made you say it, didn't I?"

"Yes."

"And the world didn't end." Jeff's tone became gentle.

"Someone told you it would. Bad things would happen if you ever said those words to a person. And now you've said them, and the world is still turning." He stood, lifted Collin to her feet, and escorted her to the women's hall door. "Tomorrow when you wake up, the sun will shine." He held her gaze. "And I'll still be here. Always."

Collin smiled. She touched his cheek with her hand. "I'll see you in the morning, Jeff."

"Good night, milady."

Collin turned, went through the door, made her way down the corridor to her room. She went in, closed the door. She leaned against the wall and whispered, "Only Your voice, Father. Only Yours."

I give you peace. Not like the world gives, expecting something in return. My peace is free. My love is free. I freed you so you could share My love with others. Be free, My child.

Collin pushed off from the wall, made her way to her bed. She changed into pajamas, turned the light off, slipped under the covers. She lay her head on the pillow. She listened to the silence. All the voices were quiet. No one condemned. No one accused. No one questioned her purpose or decision. Quiet.

Collin let out a deep sigh, closed her eyes, and slept.

SATURDAY

Jeff called it right. Collin woke in the morning. The sun still came up. The world still turned. Nothing came crashing in. But her feet weren't on the floor yet. *Your voice, Lord. Only Yours.*

No voice, but a sense of peace and well-being came over her. She rose, dressed, and went out to meet the day.

Breakfast became a raucous affair as awards and achievements were lauded, certificates passed out, goodbyes sobbed, numbers exchanged. Thirty-four campers and their still-odder counselors climbed on the bus, waved, and started the five-hour trip home.

Collin and her crew waved them off in return. Collin sensed the brewing excitement in her kids waiting to explode. The bus pulled out of the parking lot. Ta'waan stood and waved and waved, but asked Niles, "When can I stop, dude? My arm hurts!"

Collin chuckled. "You can stop anytime."

In unison, the crew turned and began jumping up and down. "We get to fly home! We get to fly home!" Chonnell and Pardner did little victory dances around Nyla. The male contingent high-fived, low-fived, fist-bumped, and generally expressed their happiness in the body language of the day. Collin laughed. "You are bad, all of you. Rotten."

Nyla spoke to the defense. "We ain't never flown before. And now we get a ride in a private jet? Ain't no one gonna believe it, even if we did take pictures. We gotta enjoy it while we can."

The group began the walk to the dock. Chonnell and Pardner ran ahead, the boys followed, and Collin and Nyla brought up the rear.

Collin ducked her head. "Okay, I get it. Truth? I did not want to get on the bus, either."

Nyla's eyes twinkled with mischief. "Oh, no. You want to spend more time here with some maintenance man."

Collin looked at her sideways. "What are you talking about?"

Nyla lifted her head. "I ain't telling. But I ain't blind, either. You and Jeff been cozy since the kidnapping. I seen it."

Collin stopped walking. Her eyes widened, then narrowed. "Seen what?"

Nyla laughed. "Seen you two after dinner last night. Out sitting on the patio. 'Course, wasn't hard to figure after that."

A cold knot formed in her gut. What else did Nyla see? Did she think they'd gone into the admin building to be alone? She looked at the girl. "Nyla, Jeff took me to meet the owner last night. That's all that happened in the offices. I swear it."

Nyla giggled. "I believe you. I jus' wanted to see your face! Everyone knows Jeff wouldn't be doing anything wrong. He too straight a guy."

Collin breathed a silent prayer of thanks. "Yes, he is."

The group reached the dock. The yellow raft waited along with the two rafting instructors. Collin stepped between the boat and her crew, making them face her. "I got something to say."

Rob interrupted her. "You ain't going."

Collin frowned at him. "Let me talk, okay, bro?" She looked at her crew again. "I owe you guys everything. The six of you brought me through this week in a way I never imagined. You saved my life. You did. That's something I can't ever repay." Her voice tightened up. "I love all of you."

She gathered the teens into her arms for a group hug. Everyone joined in. The moment would be forever precious in Collin's memory.

As they broke, Rob quipped, "But you still ain't going."

Collin grabbed him and hugged him. "Rob! What am I going to do with you?"

Rob grinned. "You gonna let me get in the boat, that what you gonna do." He grabbed her around the middle, careful not to harm her ribs, hugged her tight. He spoke barely above a whisper for Collin's ears only. "You gonna teach me how to be a man like Jeff. How to follow the Lord and be straight in everything. That's what you gonna do."

Rob looked up in her face, and Collin saw the tears in his eyes. Must have matched her own. She kissed the top of his head, then shoved him. "Go. Have fun. Stay in the boat. And I'll see you at the bottom of the run."

The crew grabbed their gear, slipped into their positions. They pushed off from the dock, began synchronized paddling, and pulled away. Collin stood and watched until the boat cleared the channel and made the turn down the river proper. When she could no longer see them, she turned and made her way back up the hill.

Jeff waited for her. "Thought you'd want time with just the crew and you."

"You thought right." Collin took Jeff's outstretched hand. "I really wanted to go, you know."

Jeff nodded. "I know, milady. Maybe on our honeymoon, we'll come up here and ride the river together."

Collin rolled her eyes. "You're impossible."

Jeff nodded. "Mostly. Thing is, if we wait four months, it'll be December, and we can't raft in the winter."

Collin stopped in her tracks. Her mouth fell open. "Four months? Four?"

Jeff nodded. "I'm good with four."

Collin lowered her head and waved it side to side. "We are not getting married in four months."

Jeff smiled. "Okay. We'll talk about it later. I need to drive the flatbed down to bring the raft back when they're done." He studied her. "It's not going to give you flashbacks, is it?"

Collin thought about it a moment. "No. I'll be fine. How does the crew get back?"

"Camp van. Which, if you'd rather ride in it, I'd understand. My feelings would be hurt, but I'd understand." Jeff pulled a long pout on his face.

Collin covered his face with one hand. "I'll spare your feelings and ride with you."

"Good." Jeff bounced out of the pout. "Because I've got a list of things we can compare to see what we prefer. You know, thin-crust or thick, vanilla or chocolate, paper or plastic. The important stuff. Stuff like that makes or breaks a marriage, you know."

Collin continued to shake her head. "No, I don't."

Jeff's voice took on a more sober tenor. "They do. When one

party won't compromise and insists their way, and only their way, is right, it creates problems. We have to communicate, Collin." He turned her to face him. "I'm in this for the long haul, milady. No 'try it awhile' and see if it works. I love you, and I will be with you for life."

Collin cupped Jeff's face in her hand. "When I say I'm in, I will be in for life as well. No half measures."

Jeff's eyes glowed. "I expect no less." A quick kiss, then they started walking again.

* * *

Three hours later, they reached the rendezvous spot, where the raft would put in, everyone would disembark safely, and the trip back to camp would commence. The camp passenger van, with three able-bodied helpers, arrived slightly before Jeff and Collin. Both vehicles parked on the dirt road opposite the flats where the raft would be beached.

Collin got out, shielded her eyes with her hands, and looked as far up the river as she could. Sycamore trees lined the river creating a shaded tunnel for tired boaters after a long day on the water. The riverbed curved wide and washed up on the shoals before sweeping back to continue its interminable path to the Atlantic.

No raft. She turned to Jeff. "I thought they would be waiting on you."

Jeff shrugged. "Sometimes. The current might slow down in spots and delay their timing."

Collin kicked small holes in the dirt while she waited for the raft. *I should have been with them, Lord. I could have done it.*

Peace, child. Who is Sovereign?

You are.

Collin muttered under her breath, "But I still could have done it."

Jeff looked at her. "What?"

Collin looked up quickly. "Nothing. Nothing at all." She glanced up the river again. "Shouldn't they be coming around the curl by now?"

Jeff smiled. "Patience, grasshopper. They'll be here when they finish the run. We don't keep a stopwatch on these classes."

Collin glared at him. "You should. You promised a handful of parents and guardians you would get their children back tonight. They're not going to take kindly having to wait for hours at the parking lot."

"They won't. Mr. McFa'ell promised to deliver the children directly to their homes." Jeff shoved his hands in his pockets, looking pleased with himself.

Collin's eyes widened, and her jaw went slack. "You did what?"

"Promised to take them home. Is that a problem?"

Collin threw her hands in the air. "Jeff! Yes, it's a problem. It will be after dark, and there's not a taxi service in Oakton that will go anywhere near the places these kids live. How do you expect to get them home?"

Jeff closed one eye, his chin crinkled. "We'll rent a limo."

"If a taxi won't go there, what makes you think a limo will?" Collin shook her head, her shoulders, her whole body. "Jeff, I love you, but you have no clue sometimes."

Jeff smiled. Collin looked at him and asked in frustration, "Why are you smiling?"

"You said you loved me. I like how that sounds."

Collin dropped her head back and groaned at the sky. "Lord! What am I going to do with him?" She looked back at Jeff. "This is not a joke. We've got kids—"

"—we need to get home to the inner city of Oakton. I know, Collin. Remember, I'm a firefighter, too. Which means I have some contacts in diverse parts of the city. Including the downtown. Kids may get to arrive home on a firetruck, but they will get home."

Collin closed her eyes and dropped her head. "Only you."

The van driver yelled, "I see something."

Collin and Jeff looked where he pointed. The raft made the bend and would soon be sweeping into the washout designed to hold her. Collin's eyes went wide, and she stopped breathing. The raft...the raft sailed upside down. It crashed happily on the rocks, bounced off a tree stump, then let the current carry it into the shoals.

Jeff, the van driver, and the three workers jumped into the

shallows to flip the raft. Empty. Collin breathed out only enough to draw a deeper breath for prayer. *Lord, please. Bring them back safely. All of them. Please. Please.*

Jeff ordered, "Vince, go up to the bend, be lookout for anyone coming down." He turned, put both hands on Collin's shoulders, stared her dead in the eyes. "Do not think of diving in after anyone, you hear me? I can't concentrate on saving one of them if I have to think about you, too. And you can't help anyone in the shape you're in. Stay on the bank."

Collin nodded, more from numbness than from comprehension. She strained her eyes back up the river, trying to see anything that looked like a lifejacket, a paddle, a body...anything that might have come from the raft.

From his vantage point up the river, Vince yelled, "I see jackets."

Please let there be bodies in them. Live bodies. Please, Father.

Jeff and two of the landing crew waded out halfway into the river to catch and drag to shore anyone coming past. Collin watched as they caught one...two...three...life jackets with sputtering humans and dragged them to the shallows. From there, Collin grabbed the initial survivors and shoved them higher onto the bank, where they coughed and spat and choked water out of their lungs. Chonnell, Nyla, and one of the guides collapsed onto the gravel.

Three. Where are the others? Please please please...

Another shout. Two more bodies came around the bend, both upright and fighting the current to get to the shore: Ta'waan and the second guide.

Please please please. All of them. Please.

A minute passed. Collin dug towels out of the van to wrap the campers and their guides.

Two minutes. Collin rubbed Chonnell's arms sharply to pump warmth into the girl. The youngster's lips looked purple. Collin hugged her tightly.

Three minutes. Nyla coughed the last of the river out. "Where Niles? Where my brother?"

Four minutes. The pitch in Nyla's voice went higher. "Where is he? Where Niles?"

"There's another one coming."

Collin stayed beside Chonnell, trying to keep the child from hypothermia. But every thought became a prayer. *Lord. Father. Lord God. Please. Please. Help them. Please.*

She heard the shout, "It's Pardner." *Thank you. Thank you. Two more, please. Please.* Jeff scooped the girl from the water, cradled her in his arms, then handed her off to the man on the shore. He handed her to Collin; she wrapped the shivering child and sat her beside Chonnell.

Nyla stood to her feet, dropped her towel, and stared up the river. "Niles!" The sound of her screams tore through Collin's heart to the memories of her own screams for the brother she would never see again.

A second scream brought her back to now. "There they is! I see them!"

Collin looked to where Nyla pointed. Two figures came down the river, true. But neither flailed around in panic; neither moved at all. Both sailed face-up. Vince jumped in the water to help with retrieval. Four men carried the last two members of the crew onto the shore. Jeff put his head to the first boy's chest, rolled him up on his side, and pounded his back. The boy began choking and spluttering and coughing out water. Jeff whirled and put his head to the second boy's chest. Instead of rolling the boy on his side, he began the short, sharp compressions of CPR.

The men bunched so tightly around the boys Collin couldn't tell who breathed and who didn't. Nyla tried to force her way between them to see, but Collin pulled her back. "Let them work, Nyla. They know what to do. Don't get in their way."

She hugged the girl tight, feeling Nyla's body wracking with sobs. Colin prayed, "God, Father, Abba Daddy, please. Help them. Help him. Bring him back to us. Please. Please."

Nyla sagged against Collin's arms. "God. Please. Please don't let it be..." The girl stopped. Her eyes flew open wide. Her jaw went slack. She began sobbing in earnest. "I'm sorry! I'm sorry!"

Collin held Nyla close. "It's okay, Nyla. It's okay. I know."

Nyla cried harder. "No, it ain't okay. It ain't." The girl bowed her head. "God, I'm sorry. I...I want Niles to live. But I want Rob to live, too. Please. Help them both."

Collin echoed. "God, please. We want Your will, but we want them alive. Mercy, God. Please."

She saw Jeff sit back from the boy he worked on. *He wouldn't give up. You never stop until the paramedics show up. Except... He's checking for a pulse, right? Oh, please, let there be a pulse.*

The men moved apart. Collin saw two young men, both sitting up, both still coughing out river water, but both alive. Collin threw her head back and shouted, "Thank You!"

Nyla looked. Her eyes widened, and she screamed, "Niles! You alive!" She shoved the men apart and dropped on the ground beside her brother, hugging and holding him, kissing his head. She repeated, "You alive. You alive. You alive."

Collin made her way to Rob's side. Jeff supported the young man, who continued to spit water. Collin looked in Jeff's eyes. He caught hers, then ducked his head a fraction of an inch. Collin sat on the rocks beside Rob, waiting for Jeff to finish his work. Jeff held up fingers for Rob to count. Made him count backward. Say the month. Day. Year. Asked him to identify the people around him.

Rob looked at Jeff. "You Jeff, the janitor. When you ain't being cool and helping everyone do everything." He looked at his crewmates. "That Nyla. Niles. Chonnell. Pardner. Ta'waan." He looked at Collin, and she saw the hint of a sparkle of life in his eyes. "She... she the one make my life so miserable I gotta ask God to save me. An' He did." Rob leaned back against Jeff, obviously exhausted. "Twice now, I guess."

Collin reached over and hugged the boy. "Don't do that to me, Rob. Ever again. You promised me you'd stay in the boat."

Rob gave a half-chuckle and shrugged his shoulders. "Yeah, about that..." He looked at the rest of the crew and the guides, all huddled together, but all watching him. He lifted one fist in salute. "We made it!"

The tension broke. Fear and dread exhaled; joy inhaled. Laughter, shouts of triumph, sounds of backs being pounded, and feet jumping washed over the group. Collin leaned her head on Rob's, still holding him close. "I love you, bro. I love you."

Collin reached out and caught Jeff's arm, pulling him into the embrace. "Thank you, Jeff. I love you."

Jeff wrapped his arms around Collin and Rob both. "I know."

Collin slugged him. Rob did the same. Jeff looked surprised. "What'd I say?" Then he smiled.

* * *

The flight home proved almost as exciting as the river ride. No one fell out, the plane didn't crash, no turbulence. But the plush seats, the open refrigerator, the cabinet stocked full of snacks...yeah, it ranked up there with the rafting.

Collin did call them together shortly before they landed to ask the crucial question, "What did you learn? What are you taking away from this week?"

Pardner chewed her lower lip. "Guess it's like the man said at the start. Learned I can. Put my mind to it, work hard, work long and hard"—she drew it out for emphasis— "loooong and haaard..."

Chonnell threw a peanut at her. "You ain't worked no harder than the rest of us, you know."

Pardner didn't back down. "I's the littlest, so I worked hardest. Thing is, I did." She looked around and corrected herself. "We did. All of us."

Niles chimed in. "I know what you mean. If someone told me I'd be working together with a Southsider and a white lady"—he looked at Collin and grinned— "and a little kid—" Chonnell stuck her tongue out at him. Niles returned the gesture. "I'd a probably killed 'em. Ain't no way. But now...now it don't seem like it should ever been a big deal."

Nyla's eyes softened. "Maybe I learned I'm not in control of my own life like I been thinking. Like maybe things happen we ain't planned on. Then it's what we do that counts. People can say anything, but don't make 'em real. What they do, 'specially when it's hard, makes 'em real."

Collin smiled. "You know, I bet the owner would love to get a note telling him how much the camp meant to you. I can get you his name and address..."

She trailed off as looks and expressions of derision met her statement. "What? What'd I say?"

Nyla mimicked Collin's words. "'I can get you his name...' Like we don't know who he is. Get real, girlfriend."

Ta'waan pounded the armrest of his chair. "You ain't for real gonna sit there and think we don't know who he is? Everybody knew it the first night we got there."

Collin felt her face burn. "I'm a little slow..."

Niles hooted. "A little? You only one didn't figure it out, then.

He couldn't been more obvious."

Collin felt a suspicion come over her. What did she miss, besides everything? "How did you know?"

Nyla laughed. "Way he dressed. Way he acted. Too obvious."

Collin looked to Rob. "Did you know about this, too?"

Rob caught Collin's eyes. The sudden shift spoke loud. "Sure. We all be knowing it."

Collin cocked her head. "Well, explain it to me, because I still don't get it."

Nyla looked at the floor of the compartment. "Oh, you so blind. First night we there. When they introduce all the staff? We knew the owner'd to be there to see who he's invited. Mr. Parks, he looks like a director. Slacks, button-up shirt. Got director written all over him. Mr. Ted, well, he got on the warm-up suit and whistle. He the coach. No problem. Ms. LeeAnn, she got on her secretary stuff, so she right like she should be. Only one not right? 'Dr. Wallace.'"

Nyla said his name with total sarcasm. "You ever seen a doctor in cowboy boots? With a ponytail? Dude didn't even stand up when they called his name. Jus' lounged on the desk. Someone that lazy gotta be the one what owns the place. And no one ever saw him do any doctor stuff all week. I hear Jeff even put the stitches in your hand. What kind of doctor does that, huh?"

Collin looked around the aircraft. "You all agree with that?"

Niles spoke up. "Only thing what makes sense. Never saw anyone in a suit, never saw anyone driving around looking important. Could only be Dr. Wallace. Or whatever his name be in real life."

Collin dipped her head. "Well, then, I guess it makes sense. Nice bit of detective work. I still say you should write to him and tell him what you learned."

General mutters seemed to indicate assent, if not with enthusiasm. Collin sat back in the leather reclining seat and closed her eyes. She sensed a body sliding in next to her. Rob touched her arm. "Caseworker lady." He kept his voice low.

Collin matched her volume to his. "Yeah."

Rob ducked his head. "Jeff told me before we left. He wants me to come up next spring, during spring break, and then next summer. Says he can put me to work for him. I'd get a summer away from Oakton and could build some skills for a job if I wanted it."

Collin caught Rob's hand in hers. "I think that would be a wonderful idea, bro."

"Yeah. I want to spend all the time I can with him. I got a lot to learn 'bout being a real man that follows the Lord."

"He'll be a good teacher."

"Yeah, but one thing he said don't make sense to me. He said he got to come see me in three months and ask me for your hand." Rob looked confused. "What he talking about?"

Collin closed her eyes, dropped her head, and whispered, "Jeff."

ABOUT THE AUTHOR

Colleen K. Snyder has always had a passion for writing. She authored two previously published books: *Journey to Amanah: The Beginning* and *Return to Tebel-Ayr: The Journey Continues* (B&H Publishing). She lives on a "ranchette" in California and is training as the (very) junior ranch hand. She serves on her church prayer team and exercises a ministry of encouragement. Colleen has worked as a factory line worker, pharmacy technician, USAF missile systems analyst, janitor, nanny, teacher, and whatever else the Lord required. Her story is for His glory, always.

Made in the USA
Monee, IL
12 July 2024

61714251R00149